FALSE GOD OF ROME
VESPASIAN III

Robert Fabbri read Drama and Theatre at London University and has worked in film and TV for 25 years. He is an assistant director and has worked on productions such as *Hornblower, Hellraiser, Patriot Games* and *Billy Elliot*. His life-long passion for ancient history inspired him to write the VESPASIAN series. He lives in London and Berlin.

Also by Robert Fabbri

THE VESPASIAN SERIES

TRIBUNE OF ROME
THE CROSSROADS BROTHERHOOD (novella)
ROME'S EXECUTIONER

Coming soon…

ROME'S FALLEN EAGLE

FALSE GOD OF ROME
VESPASIAN III

ROBERT
FABBRI

CORVUS

Published in hardback in Great Britain in 2013 by Corvus,
an imprint of Atlantic Books Ltd.

10 9 8 7 6 5 4 3 2 1

A CIP catalogue record for this book is available from the British Library.

Hardback ISBN: 978 0 85789 741 1
Trade paperback ISBN: 978 0 85789 742 8
E-book ISBN: 978 0 85789 976 7

Printed in Great Britain by the MPG Books Group.

Corvus
An imprint of Atlantic Books Ltd
Ormond House
26–27 Boswell Street
London
WC1N 3JZ

www.corvus-books.co.uk

For Anja Müller, without whom this would not have happened.
Will you marry me, my love?

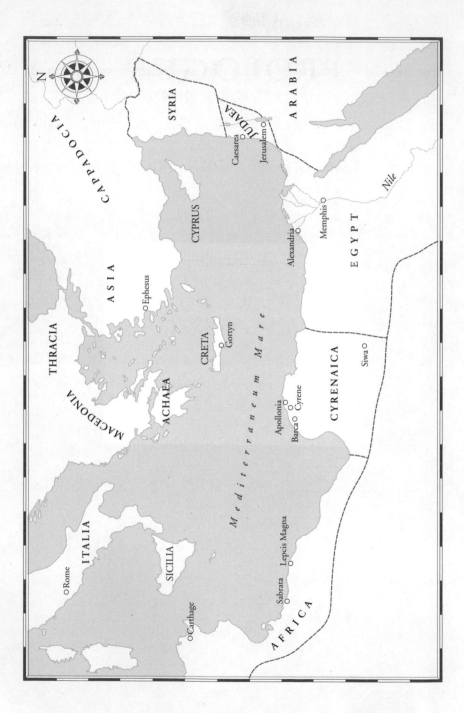

PROLOGUE

JERUSALEM, APRIL AD 33

AN ABRUPT KNOCK on the door woke Titus Flavius Sabinus with a start; his eyes flicked open. Momentarily unsure of his whereabouts, he jerked his head up off the desk and looked around the room. The muted light of the fading sun seeping in through a narrow open window was enough for him to be able to make out the unfamiliar surroundings: his study in the tower of the Antonia Fortress. Outside the window the Temple soared to the sky, dominating the view. Its high, white marble-clad walls glowed an evening red and the gold leaf that adorned its roof glistered with sunset. Such was the scale of the Jews' most holy building that it dwarfed the huge columns supporting the expansive quadrangle that surrounded it; they in turn made the multitude of figures, scuttling between them and back and forth across the vast courtyard that the colonnade encompassed, seem no larger than ants.

The tang of blood from thousands of lambs being slaughtered within the Temple complex for the Passover meal that evening infused the room's chill air. Sabinus shivered; he had become cold during his brief sleep.

The knock was repeated more insistently.

'Quaestor, are you in there?' a voice shouted from the other side of the door.

'Yes, enter,' Sabinus called back, quickly arranging the scrolls on the desk to suggest that he had been immersed in diligent work rather than taking a late afternoon nap to recover from his two-day journey to Jerusalem from Caesarea, the provincial capital of Judaea.

The door opened; an auxiliary centurion marched in and snapped to attention before the desk, his traverse-plumed helmet held stiffly under his left arm. 'Centurion Longinus of the Cohors Prima Augusta reporting, sir,' he barked. His face was tanned and wrinkled as old leather from years of service in the East.

'What is it, centurion?'

'Two Jews are requesting an audience with the prefect, sir.'

'Then take them to him.'

'He's dining with a Jewish prince from Iudemaea and some Parthians who've just arrived in the city; he's drunk as a legionary on leave. He said that you should deal with them.'

Sabinus grunted; since being sent to Judaea ten days previously, to audit its tax revenues at the behest of his superior – the Governor of Syria, who held ultimate authority over Judaea – he had already had enough dealings with Prefect Pontius Pilatus to realise the truth of the statement. 'Tell them to come back in the morning when the prefect is more approachable,' he said dismissively.

'I have, sir, but one of them is a *malchus*, or captain, of the Temple Guard sent by the High Priest Caiaphas; he was most insistent that the information that he has concerns something due to happen this evening, after the Passover meal.'

Sabinus sighed; although new to the province he had gleaned enough knowledge of the complex political infighting between Rome's turbulent subjects to know that Caiaphas owed his position to Roman favour and was therefore the closest thing to an ally that he could expect to find among the mainly hostile Jewish population of this combustible city. With the city bursting with pilgrims it would be bad politics to upset an ally during the Passover that he and the prefect had both come to Jerusalem to oversee.

'Very well then, centurion, show them up.'

'Best you come down, sir, where we can keep them at a distance from you.' Longinus pulled two short, curved knives from his belt. 'We found these hidden in the clothes of the other man.'

Sabinus took the knives and examined the razor-sharp blades. 'What are they?'

'*Sicae*, sir; which would mean that he's a member of the Sicarii.'

Sabinus looked blankly at the centurion.

'They're religious assassins, sir,' Longinus continued by way of explanation, 'they believe that they're doing their god's work by eliminating those they consider to be impure and blasphemers; that covers just about everybody who's not a member of their sect. He'd think nothing of trying to kill you even if he died in the attempt. They believe that if they're killed doing holy work then, when this Messiah who they've been awaiting for ages finally shows up, they'll be resurrected along with all the other righteous dead, on what they call the End of Days, to live in an earthly paradise under their god's laws forever.'

'They make the Zealots seem like reasonable people,' Sabinus observed, alluding to the Jewish sect that had hitherto been the most unreasonable bunch of religious extremists he had heard of.

'There's no such thing as reason in this arsehole of the Empire.'

Sabinus paused to reflect upon the truth of that statement. 'Very well, centurion, I'll come down; go and announce me.'

'Sir!' Longinus saluted and marched briskly out of the room.

Sabinus shook his head; he rolled up the scrolls containing the audit of Jerusalem's tax revenues for the past year – the cause of his earlier slumber – adjusted his toga and then followed. Although it offended his *dignitas* to go down to meet the Jews rather than have them shown into his presence he knew enough of their nature to take the advice of this seasoned centurion; he did not want to become the victim of some suicidal religious fanatic.

'My name is Gaius Julius Paulus,' the shorter of the two Jews announced in an impatient tone as Sabinus entered the Fortress's great hall. 'I am a Roman citizen and a captain in the Temple Guard and I demanded to see the prefect, not his underling.'

'The prefect is indisposed so you will talk to me,' Sabinus snapped, taking an instant dislike to this self-important, bow-legged little Jew, 'and show me the respect due to my rank as quaestor to the Governor of Syria, the prefect of Judaea's direct superior, or otherwise, citizen or not, I'll have you flogged out of the Fortress.'

Paulus swallowed and ran a hand through his thinning hair. 'Forgive me, quaestor, I meant no offence,' he said with a voice suddenly oozing obsequiousness. 'I come with a request from the High Priest concerning the agitator and blasphemer Yeshua bar Yosef.'

'Never heard of him,' Sabinus said flatly, 'what's he done?'

'He's another one of those Messiah claimants, sir,' Longinus informed him. 'We've been trying to apprehend him for sedition since he caused a riot when he arrived in the city four days ago. He threatened the authority of Caesar by claiming that he was a king; quite a few people were killed, including three of my auxiliaries. Then he pissed off the High Priest by going to the Temple and offending just about everyone he could before turning over all the money changers' tables.'

'What are money changers doing in the Temple?' Sabinus asked, genuinely curious.

'The Jews think that our money is idolatrous as it has Caesar's head on it, so they're allowed their own Temple currency to buy sheep for sacrifice and such like. The changers make a tidy profit on the exchange rate, as you might imagine.'

Sabinus raised his eyebrows; he was ceasing to find anything surprising about these people. He turned back to the two Jews; the second man, tall, full-bearded with oiled, black hair flowing from beneath a headdress wound about his head, remained motionless staring at Sabinus with hate-filled eyes. His hands had been bound in front of him. He was no rough, country peasant. His long-sleeved, light blue robe fell to his ankles; it was clean and seamless, expensively woven as one piece of material, the sign of a wealthy man. The fine quality of the black and white mantle that he wore draped over his shoulders added to that impression.

'What has this man to do with Yeshua?' Sabinus asked Paulus.

'He is one of his followers,' Paulus replied with ill-concealed dislike. 'He was with him for the two years that Yeshua spent causing trouble up in Galilee. He claims that after the Passover meal Yeshua will declare that the End of Days is at hand; he'll proclaim himself the long awaited Messiah and lead a revolt against Rome and the Temple priests. Caiaphas is asking for the prefect's permission to arrest him for blasphemy and to try him before the Sanhedrin, the religious court; this man has said that he will lead us to him tonight.'

Sabinus turned back to the other man. 'What's your name, Jew?'

The man carried on staring at him for a few more moments before deigning to answer. 'Yehudah,' he said, drawing himself up.

'I'm told that you are a Sicarius.'

'It is an honour to serve God,' Yehudah replied evenly in near perfect Greek.

'So, Yehudah the Sicarius, what do you ask for in return for betraying the man whom you've followed for two years?'

'It's for reasons of my own that I do it, not for reward.'

Sabinus scoffed. 'A man of principle, eh? Tell me why you do it so that I can believe that it's not a trap.'

Yehudah stared blankly at Sabinus and then slowly looked away.

'I could have it tortured out of you, Jew,' Sabinus threatened, losing his patience with the man's lack of deference for Roman authority.

'You can't, quaestor,' Paulus said quickly, 'you'll offend Caiaphas and the priests, who've asked you for help in apprehending a renegade. With more than a hundred thousand pilgrims here for the Passover, Rome needs the priests' support to keep order; there has already been one riot in the past few days.'

Sabinus glared at the squat little Temple Guard, outraged. 'How dare you tell me, a Roman quaestor, what I can or cannot do?'

'He's right though, sir,' Longinus assured him, 'and it won't do to refuse a request for help from the priests; it ain't how things are done here, especially as we owe them a favour.'

'What for?'

'Straight after the riot that Yeshua caused they handed over the murderers of the three auxiliaries to us; one of them, another Yeshua, Yeshua bar Abbas, is almost as popular with the people as his namesake. The prefect condemned all three upon his arrival yesterday; they're due to be executed tomorrow.'

Sabinus realised that Longinus probably was correct: he had no choice but to acquiesce to Caiaphas' request. He cursed Pilatus for having put him in this position by neglecting his duties through drink; but then reflected that it was probably the intolerable situation in the province that had driven him to it.

'Very well then,' he growled, 'tell Caiaphas you may proceed with the arrest.'

'He requests a Roman officer to accompany us,' Paulus replied. 'Without one we will be lacking in authority.'

Sabinus glanced at Longinus who nodded his agreement to that assessment. 'Very well, I'll come with you. Where should we meet?'

Paulus looked at Yehudah. 'Tell him.'

The Sicarius raised his head and looked disdainfully at Sabinus. 'We will be eating the Passover meal in the upper city, there is only one staircase up to the room so it would be easy to defend and was purposely chosen as such; but later we will be meeting new initiates outside the city walls. Meet me by the Sheep Gate at the start of the second watch; I will lead you to him.'

'Why not grab him in the street as he leaves the room?'

'It will be quieter at Gethsemane.'

'You let the Temple Guards take this rabble-rouser,' Prefect Pilatus roared at Sabinus, slurring his words, 'to be tried by his fellow Jews. Then you let his armed followers wander off to cause whatever mayhem they feel like at a time when this filthy city is

13

crammed full of the most militant religious bigots that anyone has ever had the misfortune to conquer.'

'The Temple Guards let them go once they'd secured Yeshua; their captain had had half of his right ear cut off and they didn't have the stomach for a fight. I didn't have any other troops with me.'

'Why not?' Pilatus' bloodshot eyes bulged with fury, his bulbous drinker's nose glowed red like a branding iron; droplets of sweat rolled down his saggy cheeks. Sabinus' report on Yeshua's arrest had, to say the least, disappointed him. His three dinner guests sipped their wine in silence as he slumped down on his dining couch and rubbed his temples. He reached for his cup, drained it in one, slammed it back down onto the table, staring at Sabinus malevolently, and then turned to an elegant, middle-aged man reclining on the couch to his left.

'Herod Agrippa, I need your advice. The quaestor has let this rebel outmanoeuvre us.'

Herod Agrippa shook his head, swaying his hair that hung in oiled ringlets to just below his close-clipped beard, framing a thin, firm-jawed face that would have been handsome had it not been for the large, hooked nose that protruded, like a hawk's beak, from between his dark eyes. 'You're right, prefect,' he said holding out his cup unsteadily to be filled by the slave waiting on him, 'the priests walked into Yeshua's trap without...' He stopped as the slave poured wine over his shaking hand. 'Eutyches! You're almost as useless as this quaestor. Get out!'

Sabinus stood, staring straight ahead, scowling and making no attempt to conceal his dislike for Herod.

'In our country a man would lose his eyes for the quaestor's incompetence,' the elder of the two men reclining on Pilatus' right observed, stroking his long, curled beard.

Herod threw his cup at the retreating slave. 'Unfortunately, Sinnaces, they don't have the same freedom here to mete out deserved punishment to idiots as you do in Parthia.'

Sabinus shot Herod a venomous look. 'I would remind you, Jew, that I am a senator, watch your tongue.' He turned back to

Pilatus. 'The priests offered us the opportunity to have this man arrested so I acted on my own initiative as you didn't wish to deal with it, being... otherwise engaged.'

'I was not "otherwise engaged", I was drunk and now I'm even drunker; but even in this condition I would have known to bring that madman back here into Roman custody and not let the Jews have him, no matter how many fucking priests I upset. Fuck 'em all, quaestor; do you hear me? Fuck 'em all.'

'But the priests will try him and find him guilty; it's in their interests to do so,' Sabinus argued.

'They're already trying him and are keen to pass a death sentence on him; in fact, they're so keen to condemn him that they've even broken their Passover Sabbath to try him overnight. Caiaphas sent me a message asking me to come to the palace first thing in the morning to confirm their sentence before they stone him.'

Sabinus looked at his superior uncomprehendingly. 'So what's the problem, then?'

Pilatus sighed, exasperated; he closed his eyes and ran both hands through his hair, pulling his head back. 'You're new to this dump so I'll try and explain it in simple terms,' he said with more than a degree of condescension. 'By your own admission, in your report, Yeshua organised his own arrest; he sent Yehudah to deliver him up to the priests because he wanted *them* to find him guilty, not *us*. Because of his popularity with the ordinary people he's gambling that they will rise up against the priests and all the Temple hierarchy for condemning him to death as well as against Rome for confirming the sentence. In one massively naive blunder you've enabled Yeshua to drive a wedge between the people and the only power they respect: the priests, who owe their position to Rome and therefore have nothing to gain from a revolt.'

Sabinus suddenly saw the depth of his error of judgement. 'Whereas if *we* condemned him the priests would be able to appeal for calm and expect to be listened to; and that, along with a show of force by us, should be enough to stop an uprising.'

'Exactly,' Pilatus said mockingly, 'you've finally got there. So, Herod, I've got to defuse this quickly before Yeshua's followers start rousing the people. What should I do?'

'You must go to the palace first thing tomorrow.'

'To overturn the sentence?'

'No, you can't let this man live now that you've finally got him. You've got to reunite the priests with the people so that they can control them.'

'Yes, but how?'

'By turning a Jewish stoning into a Roman crucifixion.'

'This man must die,' the High Priest Caiaphas hissed at Pilatus through his long, full grey beard. Regaled in his sumptuous robes and topped with a curious, bejewelled domed hat made of silk, he looked, to Sabinus, much more like an eastern client king than a priest; but then, to judge by the size and splendour of the Jews' Temple, Judaism was a very wealthy religion and its priests could afford to be extravagant with the money that the poor, in the hope of being seen by their god as righteous, pumped their way.

'And he will, priest,' Pilatus replied; never normally in the best of moods for the first couple of hours after dawn, he was striving to keep his fragile temper. 'But he will die the Roman way, not the Jewish.'

Sabinus stood with Herod Agrippa watching the struggle between the two most powerful men in the province with interest. It had been an acrimonious meeting, especially after Pilatus had, with great relish, pointed out the trap that Yeshua had set for Caiaphas and how he had been politically maladroit enough to fall into it.

'To avoid an uprising,' Pilatus continued, 'which, judging from the reports I've had, Yeshua's followers are already initiating, you must do as I've ordered immediately.'

'And how can I trust you to do what you've promised?'

'Are you being deliberately obtuse?' Pilatus snapped, his temper no longer able to take the strain of dealing with this self-serving priest. 'Because in this instance we are both on the same side. The preparations have been made and the orders given. Now go!'

Caiaphas turned and walked, with as much dignity as he could muster after being summarily dismissed, out of the magnificent, high-ceilinged audience chamber, the centrepiece of the late Herod the Great's palace on the west side of the upper city.

'What do you think, Herod?' Pilatus asked.

'I think that he'll play his part. Are the troops ready?'

'Yes.' Pilatus turned his bloodshot eyes to Sabinus. 'Now's your chance to redeem yourself, quaestor; just do as Herod has told you.'

The noise of a raucous mob grew as Sabinus and Herod approached the main entrance to the palace. Stepping out of the high, polished cedar-wood doors, they were confronted by a huge crowd filling the whole of the agora before the palace and overflowing into the wide avenue at its far end that led up to the Temple and the Antonia Fortress.

The shadows were long and the air chill, it being only the first hour of the day. Glancing up to his left Sabinus could see, on the hill of Golgotha beyond the Old Gate in the city walls, a cross that was always left standing between executions as a reminder to the populace of the fate that awaited them should they seek to oppose the power of Rome.

Caiaphas stood on the top of the palace steps with his arms raised in an attempt to quieten the crowd. He was surrounded by a dozen fellow priests; behind them, guarded by Paulus and a group of Temple Guards, stood Yeshua with his hands bound and with a blood-stained bandage around his head.

Gradually the noise subsided and Caiaphas began his address.

'What's he saying?' Sabinus asked Herod.

'He's appealed for calm and now he's telling them that, because of his popularity with the common people, Yeshua is to be pardoned and released from Jewish custody in a gesture of mercy at this time of Passover.'

A loud cheer went up from the crowd as Caiaphas stopped speaking. After a few moments the High Priest raised his arms, again asking for quiet before continuing.

'He's now asking them to return to their homes,' Herod translated, 'and he says that Yeshua will be freed immediately.'

Sabinus watched, knowing that his moment to act was imminent; Caiaphas turned and nodded at Paulus who reluctantly began to untie his prisoner's hands.

'Now!' Herod hissed. 'And try not to say anything stupid.'

'That man is now a prisoner of the Senate of Rome,' Sabinus bellowed, walking forward; behind him Longinus led a half-century of auxiliaries out of the palace, quickly surrounding the Temple Guards and their erstwhile prisoner. From the direction of the Antonia Fortress a cohort of auxiliaries marched down the avenue and formed up behind the crowd, blocking the road and any chance of escape.

'What is the meaning of this?' Caiaphas shouted at Sabinus, playing his part rather too theatrically.

'The Senate requires that this man, Yeshua, be tried before Caesar's representative, Prefect Pilatus,' Sabinus replied in a high, loud voice that carried over the agora. Angry shouts started to emanate from the crowd as those who could speak Greek translated Sabinus' words for their fellows. As the noise of the crowd grew, the cohort behind it drew their swords and began to beat them rhythmically on their shields.

Pilatus stepped out of the palace accompanied by a bedraggled and bruised Jew. He walked past Sabinus and, standing next to Caiaphas, signalled for silence; the shouting and the clashing of weapons died down.

'My hands are tied,' he declaimed, crossing his wrists above his head. 'Quaestor Titus Flavius Sabinus has demanded, on behalf of the Senate, that I try Yeshua for claiming to be a king and inciting rebellion against Caesar; as a servant of Rome I cannot refuse such a demand. If he is found guilty it will be Rome that is sentencing him, not me, your prefect. I wash my hands of his blood for this is not of my doing, it is the will of the

Senate.' He paused and brought the Jew who accompanied him forward. 'However, in a spirit of goodwill and to show the clemency of Rome I will, in honour of your Passover festival, release to you another Yeshua whom you hold dear: this man, Yeshua bar Abbas.'

To roars of approval Pilatus ushered the freed man down the palace steps to disappear into the joyous crowd.

'They've had their sop, priest, now use your authority over them and get them to disperse before I have to massacre the lot,' Pilatus hissed at Caiaphas as he turned to go. 'Herod, come with me.'

'I think that I will absent myself now, with your permission, prefect. It would not be good for a Jewish prince to be associated with this man's death, and besides I should be entertaining my Parthian guests.'

'As you wish. Longinus, bring the prisoner to me once you've softened him up a bit.'

'So you're the man who calls himself the King of the Jews?' Pilatus asserted, looking down at the broken man kneeling on the audience chamber floor before his curule chair.

'They are your words, not mine,' Yeshua replied, lifting his head painfully to meet his accuser's eyes; blood, from the wounds inflicted by a thorn crown, rammed mockingly on his head, matted his hair and dripped down his face. Sabinus could see that his back bore the livid marks of a severe whipping.

'Yet you don't deny them.'

'My kingdom is not of the physical world.' Yeshua raised his bound hands to touch his head. 'It is, like all men's, in here.'

'Is that what you preach, Jew?' Sabinus asked, earning an angry glance from Pilatus for interrupting his questioning.

Yeshua turned his attention to Sabinus and he felt the intensity of the man's look pierce him; his pulse quickened.

'All men keep the Kingdom of God inside them, Roman, even Gentile dogs such as you. I preach that we should purify ourselves by baptism to wash away our sins; then by following the Torah and by showing compassion for fellow believers, doing unto them as we would be done by, we will be judged righteous and worthy to join our Father at the End of Days, which is fast approaching.'

'Enough of this nonsense,' Pilatus snapped. 'Do you deny that you and your followers have been actively encouraging people to rebel against their Roman masters?'

'No man is master of another,' Yeshua replied simply.

'That's where you're wrong, Jew, I am your master; your fate is in my hands.'

'The fate of *my* body is, but not *my* fate, Roman.'

Pilatus stood and slapped Yeshua hard around the face; with a vicious leer, Yeshua ostentatiously proffered the other cheek; blood trickled from a split lip down through his beard. Pilatus obliged with another resounding blow.

Yeshua spat a gobbet of blood onto the floor. 'You may cause me physical pain, Roman, but you cannot harm what I have inside.'

Sabinus found himself mesmerised by the strength of will of the man; a will, he sensed, that could never be broken.

'I've had enough of this,' Pilatus fumed. 'Quaestor, have him crucified with the other two prisoners immediately.'

'What's he been found guilty of, sir?'

'I don't know; anything. Sedition, rebellion or perhaps just that I don't like him; whatever you like. Now take him away and make sure that he's dead and in a tomb before the Sabbath begins at nightfall, so as not to offend Jewish law. He caused enough trouble while alive and I don't want him causing more when he's dead.'

The sky had turned grey; droplets of rain had started to fall, diluting the blood that ran from the wounds of the three cruci-fied men. It was now the ninth hour of the day; Sabinus and Longinus walked back down the hill of Golgotha. Thunder rumbled in the distance.

Sabinus looked back at Yeshua hanging on his cross; his head slumped forward and blood oozed from a spear wound in his side that Longinus had administered to hasten the end of his suffering before the commencement of the Sabbath. Six hours earlier he had been whipped up the hill dragging his cross, aided by a man from the crowd. Then he had endured, in silence, the nails being hammered through his wrists; he had seemed barely to notice the nails being pounded home through his feet, fixing them to the wood. The savage jolting as the cross was hauled upright, which had caused the screaming of the other two crucified men to intensify to inhuman proportions, had brought no more than a shallow groan from his lips. He looked now, to Sabinus, to be at peace.

Sabinus passed through the cordon of auxiliaries who were keeping the small, mournful crowd of onlookers away from the executed men and saw Paulus, standing with a couple of Temple Guards, gazing up at Yeshua; a bandage around his head was spotted with blood from the wound to his ear. 'What are you doing here?' Sabinus asked.

Paulus seemed lost in his own thoughts and did not hear him for a moment, then blinked repeatedly as he registered the question. 'I came to check that he was dead and take his body for burial in an unmarked tomb so that it doesn't become a place of pilgrimage for his heretical followers. Caiaphas has ordered it.'

'Why were you all so afraid of him?' Sabinus enquired.

Paulus stared at him as if looking at an idiot. 'Because he would bring change.'

Sabinus shook his head scornfully and pushed past the malchus of the Guard. As he did so a group of two men and two women, the younger one heavily pregnant and carrying an infant, approached him.

The elder man, a wealthy-looking Jew in his early thirties with a dense black beard, bowed. 'Quaestor, we wish to claim Yeshua's body for burial.'

'The Temple Guards are here to claim it. What claim do you have on his body?'

'My name is Yosef, I am Yeshua's kinsman,' the man replied, putting his arm around the shoulder of the older of the two women, 'and this woman is Miriam, his mother.'

Miriam looked pleadingly at Sabinus, tears rolling down her cheeks. 'Please don't let them have him, quaestor, give me my son so that I can take him back to Galilee and bury him there.'

'My orders are that he is to be buried before nightfall.'

'I have a family tomb, just close by,' Yosef said, 'we will put the body there for now, then move it the day after the Sabbath.'

Sabinus looked back at Paulus with a malicious smile. 'Paulus, these people have the claim of kin over the body.'

Paulus looked outraged. 'You can't do that; Caiaphas demands his body.'

'Caiaphas is Rome's subject! Longinus, have that hideous little man escorted away from here.'

As Paulus was manhandled away, protesting, Sabinus turned back to Yosef. 'You can take the body; Rome has finished with it.' He turned to go.

Yosef bowed his head. 'That was a kindness that I won't forget, quaestor.'

'Quaestor,' the younger man called, stopping Sabinus, 'Rome may be our master now, but be warned, the final age is approaching and Yeshua's teachings are part of it; a new kingdom will rise, new men with new ideas will rule and the old order will start to fade.'

Recollecting the Emperor Tiberius' astrologer, Thrasyllus, two years previously predicting the coming of a new age, Sabinus stared at the young man; he recognised him as the man who had helped Yeshua with his cross that morning. 'What makes you so sure of that, Jew?'

'I come from Cyrenaica, Roman, which was once a province of the Kingdom of Egypt; there they await the rebirth of the fire-bird. Its five-hundred-year cycle is coming to an end; next year the Phoenix will be reborn in Egypt for the last time and all things will begin to change in preparation for the End of Days.'

PART I

❧ ❧

CYRENAICA, NOVEMBER AD 34

CHAPTER I

'HAVE YOU GOT it?' Vespasian asked as Magnus walked down the gangplank of a large merchant ship newly arrived in the port of Appolonia.

'No, sir, I'm afraid not,' Magnus replied, shouldering his bag, 'the Emperor is refusing all entry permits to Egypt at the moment.'

'Why?'

Magnus took his friend's proffered forearm. 'According to Caligula it's on the advice of Tiberius' astrologer, Thrasyllus; not even Antonia could get him to change his mind.'

'Why did you bother coming, then?'

'Now that ain't a very nice way to greet a friend who's travelled fuck knows how many hundreds of miles in that rotting tub at a time of year when most sailors are tucked up in bed with each other.'

'I'm sorry, Magnus. I was counting on Antonia getting me the permit; it's been four years since Ataphanes died and we promised to get his gold back to his family in Parthia.'

'Well then, another couple of years or so ain't going to make much difference, are they?'

'That's not the point. Egypt is the neighbouring province; I could have made a short diversion to Alexandria on my way home in March, found the Alabarch, given him Ataphanes' box and made the arrangements for the money to be transferred to his family in Ctesiphon and still be back in Rome before next May.'

'You'll just have to do it some other time.'

'Yes, but it'll take much longer going from Rome. I may not have the time; I've got the estate to run and I plan to get elected as an aedile the year after next.'

'Then you shouldn't go making promises that you can't keep.'

'He served my family loyally for many years; I owe it to him.'

'Then don't begrudge him your time.'

Vespasian grunted and turned to make his way back along the bustling quayside through the mass of dock-workers unloading the newly docked trading fleet. His senatorial toga acted as an intimidating display of his rank, ensuring that a path was cleared for him through the crowd, making the hundred-pace journey along the quay to his waiting, one-man litter an easy affair.

Magnus followed in his wake enjoying the deference shown to his young friend by the local populace. 'I didn't think quaestors were normally treated with this much respect in the provinces,' he observed as one of the four litter-bearers unnecessarily helped Vespasian onto his seat.

'It's because the Governors always hate it here and rightly so, it's like living in a baker's oven but without the nice smell. They tend to spend all their time in the provincial capital, Gortyn over in Creta, and send their quaestors here to administer Cyrenaica in their name.'

Magnus chuckled. 'Ah, that'll always help people to respect you, the power of life and death.'

'Not really, as a quaestor I don't have Imperium, no power of my own. I have to have all my decisions ratified by the Governor, which takes forever,' Vespasian said gloomily, 'but I do have the power to procure horses,' he added with a grin as a dusky young slave boy led a saddled horse up to Magnus.

Magnus took the animal gratefully and threw his bag over its rump before mounting. 'How did you know that I'd be arriving today?'

'I didn't, I just hoped that you would be,' Vespasian replied as his litter moved forward, passing a theatre looking out over the sea. 'When the fleet was sighted this morning I decided to come down on the off-chance, as it's probably the last one of the season to arrive from Rome. Anyway, it's not as if I had anything else worthwhile to do.'

'It's as bad as that here, is it?' Magnus raised a wry eyebrow as the slave boy began fanning Vespasian with a broad, woven palm-frond fan on a long stick.

'It's terrible: the indigenous Libu spend all their time robbing the wealthy Greek farmers; the Greeks amuse themselves by levelling false accusations of fraud or theft against the Jewish merchants; the Jews never stop protesting about sacrilegious statues or some perceived religious outrage involving a pig, and then the Roman merchants passing through do nothing but complain about being swindled by the Jews, Greeks and Libu, in that order. On top of that everyone lives in fear of slave-gathering raids by either the Garamantes from the south or the nomadic Marmaridae to the east, between here and Egypt. It's a boiling pot of ethnic hatred and the only thing that they hate more than each other is us, but that doesn't stop individuals throwing money at me to rule in their favour in court cases.'

'And you take it, I hope?'

'I didn't at first but I do now. I remember being shocked when my uncle told me that he took bribes while he was Governor of Aquitania, but now I understand the system better and realise that it's expected of me. And anyway, most of the wealthy locals are so unpleasant it's a pleasure to take their money.'

'Sounds much like Judaea judging by Sabinus' descriptions of it,' Magnus mused as they passed into a crowded agora surrounded by dilapidated ancient temples dedicated to the Greek gods and overlooked by civic buildings cut into the hill above.

'It's worse, believe me,' Vespasian replied, recalling his conversations with his brother upon his return from the East, concerning the utter ungovernability of the Jews. They had over-lapped for two days in Rome before he had sailed for Creta at the end of March. 'There you only had to deal with the Jews; they could be kept in line by their priests and by offering them small concessions. But here if you were to offer a concession to one group, then every bastard would want one until you'd find your-self giving the whole province away and hauled up in front of the

Senate, or worse, on your return to Rome. That's why I give nothing away to any of them unless I'm well paid for it; that way the other factions can't complain that I've showed any favouritism because they know that I was bribed. Surprisingly, that seems to make it all right for them.'

'I'll bet that you wish you were back in Thracia,' Magnus said, admiring the exertions of the slave boy who was managing to keep a constant flow of air moving around his master and maintain his footing despite the bad state of repair of the paving stones; the city had seen better days.

'At least we had some decent troops to threaten the locals with. Here all we've got is one cohort of local auxiliary infantry, made up of men who are too stupid to earn their living by thieving; then there's the city militia, which comprises men too stupid to be an auxiliary; and finally an *ala* of local auxiliary cavalry, who are meant to protect us from the nomads, which is a joke because most of them have camels.'

'What's a camel?'

'It's like a big, brown goat with a long neck and a hump on its back; horses hate the smell of them.'

'Oh, I saw some of them at the circus once; they made people laugh but they didn't put up much of a fight.'

'They don't need to – according to the cavalry prefect, Corvinus, they can run all day across the desert; our cavalry hardly ever get near them.'

They passed through the city's gates, guarded by marble lions to either side, and started the gentle eight-mile ascent to the city of Cyrene, set on the limestone plateau above. Vespasian sank back into a maudlin silence, contemplating the futility of his position in this part of the combined province of Creta and Cyrenaica. During the seven months he had been there he had achieved nothing, mainly because there was hardly any money to achieve anything with. For centuries the wealth of Cyrenaica had been in silphium, a bulbous-headed plant with a long stalk, whose resin was much prized as a rich seasoning and as a cure for throat maladies and fever; the meat from animals that grazed on it was also sold at a premium. It grew along the dry coastal plain – the Cyrenian plateau being more conducive to the cultivation of orchards and vegetables. However, in recent years the crop had mysteriously begun to fail to the point where it was no longer fed to livestock, thus killing off the meat industry; and over the last couple of years the quality of each crop had deteriorated no matter how intensively it was farmed.

Vespasian had tried to persuade the local farmers to produce other crops, but the thin nature of the soil and the paucity of rain on the plain, combined with the farmers' fervent belief that if enough gods were sacrificed to on a regular basis the silphium would return to health, had thwarted him. Consequently the tax revenues were drying up as those with money hid it away and spent very little buying goods from those with even less. With very little money in circulation, grain, imported from the more fertile neighbouring provinces of Egypt and Africa, had reached sky-high prices as a consequence of greedy speculation by the merchants who controlled the trade. They had all denied it, when he had called them into his presence to explain themselves, and had put the blame squarely on the reduced amount of grain being received from Egypt in the past year; yet there had been no mention of a failure of the Egyptian harvest. The result was that the poor, whether Greek, Jewish or Libu, were always on the verge of starving and civil unrest was a constant threat.

Without sufficient troops to quash an uprising among the almost half a million population of Cyrenaica's seven major cities, and without the authority to act in his own name, Vespasian had felt impotent and frustrated throughout his tenure of office. This feeling was now compounded by the Emperor Tiberius' refusal to grant him an entry permit to the imperial province of Egypt, a province so rich that senators were allowed to visit it only with express permission from the Emperor himself; to do so without would be a capital offence.

Chiding himself for falling into a self-pitying reverie, he turned back to his companion trotting along beside him. 'Did Sabinus finally manage to get himself elected as an aedile?'

'Yes, just,' Magnus replied. 'But as your brother always says: just is good enough. Although he was relieved that he wasn't contesting the praetor elections until next year – all those positions were filled by the sons of Macro's cronies.'

'So we're back to having a Praetorian prefect who interferes with politics, are we? You would have thought Macro would have learnt a lesson from his predecessor's untimely demise. I can't imagine that's endeared him much to Antonia: she believes that meddling in politics is the prerogative of the imperial family and, specifically, herself.'

Magnus indicated to the litter-bearers.

'Don't worry about them, they don't speak Latin,' Vespasian informed him, 'and the boy's a deaf mute.'

'Fair enough. Well, since you left in March some strange things have been happening; Antonia's getting quite concerned.'

'I thought that she didn't tell you anything other than what to do.'

'No, I get most of the inside gossip from your uncle, Senator Pollo; although she does occasionally let things slip, afterwards, if you take my meaning?'

'You old goat!' Vespasian smiled for what felt like the first time since he had arrived in Cyrenaica, enjoying the unlikely and unequal sexual relationship between his old friend and the most formidable woman in Rome, his patron Antonia, sister-in-law to the Emperor Tiberius.

'Yeah, well, that doesn't happen so much these days, I'm pleased to say; she's getting on a bit, you know, sagging somewhat. Anyway, she's concerned about Caligula's relationship with Macro, or more precisely Caligula's new relationship with Macro's wife, Ennia, which Macro seems to be encouraging.'

Vespasian smiled and waved a hand dismissively. 'Caligula's had his eye on her for some time; he'll no doubt tire of her, he's notoriously insatiable. Macro's just being sensible about it; he's well aware that if he makes a fuss about it now he'll be in a very precarious position if and when Caligula becomes emperor.'

'Perhaps, but your uncle thinks that there's more to Macro's behaviour than just being polite, he reckons that he's trying to ingratiate himself with Caligula because he wants something from him if he does become emperor.'

'As Praetorian prefect he's the most powerful person in Rome outside the imperial family; what more can he want short of becoming his heir? Caligula may be a lot of things but he's not stupid.'

'That's what's worrying Antonia, she doesn't understand what he's aiming for; and what she doesn't understand, she can't control, which pisses her off considerably.'

'I can imagine, but I wouldn't call that very strange.'

'No, the strange bit is the other person who Macro's cultivating,' Magnus said with a conspiratorial look in his eye. 'Herod Agrippa. He used to be a friend of Antonia's and used to borrow money off her but he never paid her back, thinking that because he was a favourite of Tiberius and a good friend of his son Drusus – they were educated together – he was owed a living. However, when Drusus died he fled Rome and his debts and went back to his homeland, Iudemaea.'

'Where's that?'

'Fuck knows, but close to Judaea, I should think, as he's Jewish. Anyway, he soon had to leave there, debts again, and then spent his time pissing off every petty king and tetrarch in the East demanding a position of power or a loan just because he's the grandson of Herod the Great. A couple of months ago he returned to Rome and managed to wheedle his way back into Tiberius' favour. According to your uncle he's organised an embassy of Parthian rebel noblemen to come to Rome next year; they want Tiberius to help them depose their king. As a reward Tiberius has made Herod Agrippa tutor to his grandson Tiberius Gemmelus.'

'So what makes it strange that Macro and he should be friends?'

'Because while Macro is trying to ingratiate himself with Caligula, he's at the same time snuggling up to Herod, the person who has the most influence over another possible heir, Gemmelus.'

'So he's backing both chariots?'

Magnus grinned and shook his head. 'No, sir, it would seem that he's backing all three. Herod Agrippa has another contact, a very good childhood friend of his who was educated alongside him and Drusus: the third possible heir from the imperial family, Antonia's son Claudius.'

The sun was beginning to dip in the west and the sea sparkled bronze below as Vespasian and Magnus passed under Cyrene's principal gate into the lower city. The litter-bearers had to force their way through scores of beggars – refugees from the failed silphium farms hoping to receive alms from newly arrived merchants before they tired of being importuned by the count-less destitute now obliged to rely on charity.

'I'm getting to really hate this place,' Vespasian commented as he pushed away supplicating hands. 'It just rubs my face in the fact that my family's standing in the Senate is very low; only the most insignificant quaestors get sent here.'

'You drew it by lot.'

'Yes, but only the insignificant quaestors go to the ballot; the ones from the great families get the plum jobs in Rome. Sabinus was lucky to draw Syria last year.'

Magnus kicked away an overly persistent old crone. 'I've got a letter from Caenis in my bag, hopefully that'll cheer you up; you certainly seem to need it.'

'It'll help,' Vespasian shouted back over the torrent of abuse that Magnus was receiving from the floored crone, 'but I don't think that I'll feel cheerful until after the sailing season starts again in March and my replacement arrives. I need to get back to Rome, I need to feel that I'm making progress rather than festering in this arsehole of the Empire.'

'Well, we've got four months to kill, I'll keep you company. To tell you the truth, when Antonia failed to get your Egypt travel warrant I told her that I'd still come anyway to bring the bad

31

news. Things are a little too hot for me at the moment in Rome; your uncle is going to smooth it all over while I'm away.'

'What did you do?'

'Nothing, just a bit of business looking after the interests of my Crossroads Brotherhood; I've left my second, Servius, in command, he'll look after things.'

Vespasian knew not to pry into Magnus' underworld life as the leader of the South Quirinal Crossroads Brotherhood; protection and extortion were the primary business of all the Brotherhoods. 'You're welcome to stay but there isn't much to do.'

'What about the hunting; what's that like here?'

'It's not up to much close to the city, but apparently if you go south for a couple of days you might find some lions in the foothills of the plateau.'

'It's your birthday in a few days; we'll kill a lion to celebrate,' Magnus suggested.

Vespasian looked at his friend apologetically. 'You go and celebrate by yourself, I'm afraid that I can't. I'm not supposed to leave the city unless it's on official business.'

Magnus shook his head. 'I can see that this is going to be a very dull few months.'

'Welcome to my world.'

'What are the whores like?'

'I'm told they're nice and old, just as you like them, but rather sweaty.'

'Now come on, sir, don't mock, it's not out of choice; I just do as the good lady tells me. And, as I said, it doesn't happen much nowadays.'

Vespasian smiled again. 'I'm sure that Quintillius, my clerk, can procure something suitable to make up for that.'

The street opened out into the busy main agora of the lower city.

'What's going on there?' Magnus pointed at a large crowd of mainly Jewish men jeering at a tall, broad-shouldered young man standing on a plinth attempting to address them. Next to him stood a young woman carrying a one-year-old girl-child; a three-year-old boy squatted at her feet looking fearfully at the crowd.

'Another Jewish proselytiser, I expect,' Vespasian replied with a sigh. 'There seems to have been an influx of them recently, preaching some new sort of Jewish cult. I'm told that the elders don't like it, but as long as they don't cause any trouble I leave them alone. The one thing that I've learnt here is that it's best to keep out of Jewish affairs, they're impossible to understand.'

Unimpeded now by beggars, the litter-bearers made good progress along the lower city's wide main thoroughfare, lined with the old and tatty, but still imposing, two-storey houses of the richer merchants, and they soon started the short ascent to the upper city.

Heartened somewhat by the prospect of reading Caenis' letter, Vespasian turned his thoughts to his lover whom he had not seen for over seven months. Still a slave in the Lady Antonia's household, she would be thirty in three years' time and he lived in hope of her being freed upon attaining that age, the youngest allowed by law for the manumission of slaves. Although it was against the law for a man of senatorial rank to marry a freed-woman, he hoped to take her as his mistress as soon as she was able to make decisions in her own right. He planned to set her up in a small house in Rome with the money that he was quite quickly accruing from the bribes and gifts that naturally came his way from provincials anxious to have the favour of the highest ranking Roman official in the area. Now that he had put his scruples to one side and was taking the bribes he hoped that by the time he got back to Rome he would have enough not only for a house for Caenis but also for himself and the wife he must soon take to fulfil his duties to his family. A series of letters from his parents, now living in Aventicum, in Germania Superior, where his father had purchased a banking business, had impressed upon him the need to produce an heir for the security of the family.

They soon reached the street of King Battus in the upper city; at its eastern end was the Roman Forum, beyond which stood the Governor's Residence – a much more modern building that had been purpose-built by the Romans one hundred years previously after Cyrenaica had become a Roman province.

Vespasian's litter was set down in front of the Residence and, brushing off his bearers' attempts to help him, Vespasian stepped down, adjusted his toga and mounted the steps.

Magnus followed, grimacing at the quality of the four auxiliary guards beneath the portico as they brought themselves haphazardly to attention. 'I see what you mean,' he commented as they passed through the doors and into a large atrium with clerical staff working at desks down one side, 'they're a fucking shambles; not even their mothers could be proud of them.'

'And they're among the best from the first century,' Vespasian replied. 'There're a couple of centuries who can't even dress themselves off into a straight line; the centurions are getting through vine-sticks at an incredible rate.'

Before Magnus could express his opinions on the effectiveness or otherwise of beating discipline into sub-standard soldiery, a well-groomed, togate quaestor's clerk approached them.

'What is it, Quintillius?' Vespasian asked.

'There's been a woman waiting to see you for three hours now; I tried to get her to make an appointment to come back at a more suitable time but she refused. She said that as a Roman citizen it's her right to see you as soon as you return. And also that it's your duty to see her as her father was your uncle's clerk when he was a quaestor in Africa.'

Vespasian sighed. 'Very well, have her shown to my study. What's her name?'

'That's the odd thing, quaestor, she claims to be a kinswoman of yours; her name's Flavia Domitilla.'

'And it's now a month and a half since he went southeast and he promised me that he wouldn't be gone more than forty days.' Flavia Domitilla sobbed into a silk handkerchief, then dabbed her eyes carefully so as not to smudge the thick line of kohl that outlined them.

Whether she was genuinely upset or just using her feminine wiles to the full, Vespasian could not tell, nor did he very much care; he was transfixed by this elegant and immaculately presented young woman. Tall with curved hips, a thin waist and high, rounded breasts, her body was sumptuous. Her intelligent, sparkling, dark eyes, a slender nose and a full mouth were framed by a mound of high-piled black hair with braids falling to her shoulders on either side. Apart from a few slave girls he had not had a proper woman since he last saw Caenis; and Flavia Domitilla was undoubtedly a proper woman. Her clothes and jewellery spoke of wealth and her coiffure and make-up told of the time that she had to enjoy it; she was exquisite. Vespasian stared at her, inhaling her feminine scent, heightened by the heat and augmented by a delicate perfume, as she whimpered softly into her handkerchief. He felt the blood pulsing in his groin and, to cover any embarrassment, adjusted the folds of his toga, grateful, for the first time since arriving in the province, to be wearing the garment. In an effort to tear his mind away from carnal thoughts, he raised his eyes to study her features. Other than a slight roundness of the face he could make out nothing that would suggest a close kinship; however, her name was irrefutably the feminine form of Flavius.

Suddenly realising that he had been too busy admiring her to take in what she had been saying, he cleared his throat. 'What was his name?'

Flavia looked up from her handkerchief. 'I told you; Statilius Capella.'

'Oh yes, of course; and he's your husband?'

'No, I'm his mistress; haven't you listened to anything?' Flavia frowned. 'His wife is back in Sabratha in the province of Africa; he never takes her on his business trips, he finds that my charms work much better on his clients.'

Vespasian could well believe it; they had certainly worked on him and, dizzy with desire inflamed by her sensual scent and ripe body, it was as much as he could do to keep his hands clamped on the arms of his chair and concentrate on what she was saying. 'And what was his business again?'

Flavia looked at him exasperated. 'You've just been sitting there staring at my breasts, haven't you, because you've evidently not heard a word I've said.'

Vespasian opened his mouth to deny the accusation – he had been staring at more than just her breasts – but thought better of it. 'I'm sorry if you think that I've been inattentive, I'm a busy man,' he blustered, his eyes involuntarily resting again for a moment on the magnificent swell of that part of Flavia's anatomy.

'Not too busy to sit and stare at a woman's body rather than listen to what she has to say. He's a wild-beast master; he procures animals for the circuses in Sabratha and Lepcis Magna. He was making a trip out into the desert to try and get some camels; they don't put up much of a fight but they look funny and make people laugh. We don't have them in the province of Africa but there's a tribe here that does.'

'The Marmaridae.'

'Yes, that sounds right, the Marmaridae,' Flavia agreed, pleased to have his full attention finally.

'So your er… man has gone to try and buy camels off a tribe that doesn't acknowledge Rome's hegemony in the area because we've never been able to defeat them in battle as they're nomadic and almost impossible to find?'

'Yes, and he should have been back five days ago,' Flavia added, quivering her bottom lip.

Vespasian bit his, trying to banish thoughts of where that lip might go. 'You should hope that he hasn't made contact with them.'

Flavia looked at him in alarm. 'What do you mean by that?'

'Because they're notorious slavers; they take whomever they can find and sell them, hundreds of miles away in the south, to the Garamantes, who apparently have massive irrigation works that enable them to grow crops down there; it's very labour intensive.'

Flavia burst into fresh tears.

Vespasian fought to resist the urge to comfort her, knowing that once he touched that body he would be lost. 'I'm sorry, Flavia, but it's the truth. He was absolutely mad to go out there. How many men did he have with him?'

'I don't know for sure, at least ten, I think.'

'Ten? That's preposterous; there are thousands of Marmaridae. Let's pray that he hasn't found them and that his water hasn't run out yet; how much did he take?'

'I don't know.'

'Well, if he doesn't turn up in a couple of days then I'm afraid you'll have to fear the worst. If he's gone southeast then the first place that he can get water – if he hasn't taken a local guide to show him where the wells are hidden – is the oasis at Siwa just before the Egyptian border; that's over three hundred miles away and can take between ten and twenty days to get to, depending on the conditions.'

'Then you'll have to go and find him.'

'Find him? Do you have any idea how big an area we're talking about and how many men I'd have to take just to ensure that we'd get back?'

'I don't care,' Flavia snapped. 'He's a freeborn Roman citizen and it's your duty to protect him from slavery.'

'Then he should have asked me for an escort before he went off on that idiotic trip,' Vespasian retorted, aroused even further by the spirit that she was showing. 'For a reasonable price I could have provided him with some cavalry.'

'Then provide him with the cavalry now instead,' Flavia insisted, rising to her feet. 'I'm sure that he will prove generous when you find him.'

'And what if I refuse?'

'Then, Titus Flavius Vespasianus, kinsman or not, I will go to Rome and let it be known that you sat by and did nothing as a member of the equestrian order was abducted and sold into slavery. And I will furthermore allege that the reason that you did nothing was because you wanted to bed his woman.' With that she turned on her heel and stormed out of the room.

Vespasian watched her go appreciatively, drew a deep breath and exhaled, shaking his head; she was certainly right about one thing: he did want to bed her. But she could give him more than just pleasure and, as his heart continued to send the blood racing around his body, he knew that he would risk anything to possess her.

Reacting out of instinct, Vespasian punched his left arm up, catching the lightning-swift downward cut of a *gladius* on the guard of his *pugio*. Twisting the dagger left, he forced the sword aside and down as he thrust his gladius forward at belly height to feel it parried to the right by firmly held iron.

'So we may get some lion hunting in after all,' Magnus said, pulling away from the embrace that the move had ended in. He was looking pleased for the first time since arriving in Cyrenaica; sweat glistened on his scarred torso.

'I haven't decided whether or not to go yet,' Vespasian replied, taking the on-guard position: standing crouched, almost square-on, gladius low and forward with his pugio to one side and slightly withdrawn.

They were exercising next to a pomegranate tree in the court-yard garden at the heart of the Governor's Residence, taking advantage of the cool of twilight. A couple of slaves worked their way around the colonnade lighting torches; the smoke that billowed off the freshly lit pitch-soaked rags contrasted sharply with the clean, fresh smell of the recently watered garden.

Magnus feinted to the right and then brought his gladius back-handed slicing towards Vespasian's neck; parrying it with his pugio, Vespasian launched a series of criss-crossing strokes, forcing Magnus ever back as he struggled to counter them. Sensing victory he lunged for Magnus' throat; Magnus ducked under the stroke and, thrusting his sword down onto Vespasian's dagger, blocking it, he pushed his right shoulder up under Vespasian's extended sword arm, knocking him off-balance while curling his right leg behind his opponent's left, sending him crashing to the ground.

'You were too anxious to win there, sir,' Magnus said, pressing the blunted tip of his practice sword against Vespasian's throat.

'My mind was on other things,' he responded as he pushed away the weapon.

Magnus leant down to help him up. 'Well, she spoilt your concentration. Anyway, if you don't go she could make trouble for you back in Rome.'

Vespasian scoffed and brushed some dirt from his arm. 'No, she couldn't; everyone would understand why I did nothing. Who's going to sympathise with an idiot who goes off into the desert with hardly any escort in search of a tribe of slavers?'

Magnus looked disappointed. 'So you ain't going to go?'

Vespasian walked over to the pomegranate tree and sat down on the bench beneath it. 'I didn't say that; I just said that I wouldn't go just because Flavia was threatening me. If I go it'll be for different reasons.'

'Because it might be fun?'

'Did you see her?' Vespasian asked, ignoring the question. He picked a jug up from the table and poured two cups of wine.

Magnus joined him on the bench taking a proffered cup. 'Yes, briefly; she looked expensive.'

'That's true, but it was a good look: pure woman. And she showed spirit and loyalty; imagine what sort of sons a feisty woman like that would bear.'

Magnus looked at his friend, astonished. 'You're not serious, are you? What about Caenis?'

The words of love in Caenis' letter flashed though Vespasian's mind and he shook his head regretfully. 'As much as I'd want to, I could no more have children with Caenis than I could do with you. You because, no matter how hard and often I tried, you'd be barren; and Caenis because the children wouldn't be recognised as citizens, being the product of an illegal union between a senator and a freedwoman.'

'Yes, I suppose so; I'd never really thought about it like that before,' Magnus said nodding and quaffing his drink. 'So you'll have to look elsewhere for your brood-mare?'

'And Flavia seems to be perfect and to cap it all she's a Flavian.'

'What difference does that make?'

'It means that her dowry will be staying within the clan and therefore her father is likely to make a larger settlement on her.'

'Well, you'll need it if you're going to keep her in all that finery; she ain't going to be cheap. So I suppose it's pointless going to try and rescue her lover; much better to let him disappear out of the way.'

'On the contrary, I'm going to take four *turmae* of cavalry and go and find him; if I don't, then Flavia will never consider marrying me because she's a loyal woman.'

'If you don't find him that will be fine, but if you bring him back then she'll stay with him.'

'Not necessarily.' Vespasian grinned slyly at his friend. 'If I do find him, I'll give him the option of staying out in the desert and not having to pay the costs for his own rescue or returning with us to civilisation and a large invoice.'

'What? The cost of keeping the cavalry supplied for however long it takes us to find him?'

'Yes. Plus, of course, my own private expenses.'

'Which will be how much?'

'Oh, no more than Capella can afford to pay; say, one woman?'

CHAPTER II

'HOW MUCH FURTHER, Aghilas?' Marcus Valerius Messala Corvinus, the young, patrician prefect of the province's Libu light cavalry snapped, wiping away the sweat that flowed freely from beneath his broad-brimmed straw hat.

The dark-skinned Libu scout pointed towards a small, rocky outcrop shimmering in the heat haze, some two miles distant. 'Not far, master; it's in among those rocks.'

'And not a moment too soon,' Magnus muttered, easing his hot and sore behind in the saddle. 'It's only three days since we came down off the plateau and I've already had enough of the desert.'

'You didn't have to come,' Vespasian reminded his friend. 'You could have stayed in the foothills and gone hunting; I'm sure Corvinus would have left you a couple of guides.'

Corvinus glanced at Vespasian in a way that assured him that he was completely mistaken on that point.

Magnus looked ruefully at the stout hunting-spear jiggling upright in a long, hardened-leather holster attached to his saddle and shook his head. 'No, I wouldn't have wanted to miss the fun; I just didn't realise that there was so much desert.'

There was indeed a lot of desert.

Since descending from Cyrene's plateau, two days after leaving the city, they had headed southeast, over a hard, dun-brown, rock-strewn wilderness that stretched to beyond the province's vague southern border and then as far as the imagination; it provided a natural defence against whomever or whatever lived beyond this wasted land. Despite it being November the sun burned down during the day with a ferocity that belied the

41

season; winter, however, caught up at night when the temperature plummeted and ice would form in the necks of their water-skins.

The hundred and twenty men of the four turmae detachment of Libu light cavalry, armed with light javelins, a cavalry *spatha* – a sword slightly longer than the infantry gladius – and curved knives and protected by small, round, leather-clad shields, took the conditions in their stride. Wide-brimmed straw hats shaded their faces and long, thick, undyed lambswool cloaks, worn over similar woollen tunics, protected them from the sun's intense rays during the day and kept them warm in the freezing night air – fires were impossible as there was nothing to burn. Their Roman decurions had followed their men's example for this expedition, since metal cuirasses and helmets were impractical in the scorching heat.

Each man carried a water-skin that held just enough for him and his mount to last for two days; that, together with the extra water, as well as grain for the horses and spare rations for the troopers, carried by the trail of pack-mules following the column, meant they could last for three days without resupplying. Navigation through the almost featureless landscape was therefore crucial as they were obliged to travel via two wells, part of a network of ancient wells dug throughout the desert by the Marmaridae, generations ago, to enable them to make the crossing from their grazing lands in the north, near the coast over a hundred miles east of Cyrene, to the oasis at Siwa and beyond.

'How the fuck does Aghilas find his way out here?' Magnus asked Corvinus as they approached the outcrop where, their guide had assured them, they would find the first well of their journey. 'There's nothing to navigate by.'

Corvinus looked haughtily at Magnus before deigning to reply. 'He was taken as a slave by the Marmaridae when he was a boy and lived with them for ten years before escaping. He's made countless trips across the desert; I've used him before and he's never let me down.'

'When was the last time you were out here?' Vespasian enquired, trying to be friendly to this aloof patrician; he had not had much contact with Corvinus, who spent most of his time at Barca, southwest of Cyrene, where the auxiliary cavalry were based.

'Just before you arrived, quaestor.' There was almost a tone of mockery in his voice as he used Vespasian's official title. 'We chased a raiding party for a couple of days; didn't catch them, though. Their camels aren't as fast as horses in a gallop but they can do eighty or ninety miles in ten hours without stopping for water; at that speed and in this heat our horses just collapse.'

'Have you ever caught any?'

'No, not once in the seven months that I've had the misfortune to be stationed here. And I don't know what makes you think that it'll be any different this time; you'd have to surprise—'

A sharp cry from Aghilas as he fell from his horse cut Corvinus short; an instant later his own mount reared up, tipping him onto the ground. Vespasian heard the hiss of an arrow passing just over his head followed immediately by the cry of a trooper behind him.

'Form line by turma,' Corvinus shouted, jumping to his feet as his horse crashed, screeching, to the ground next to him; a blood-soaked arrow protruded from its chest.

The four thirty-man turmae fanned out across the desert; the whinnying of wounded horses and the shrill blare of the *lituus*, a cavalry horn, filled the air.

A hundred paces away among the rocks Vespasian could see their attackers breaking cover and sprinting towards a dozen or so similar-coloured, smaller, more rounded rocks. A few moments later these rocks seemed to spring to life as the fleeing men jumped on them and they rose from the ground, as if they had suddenly grown first back legs then front; they turned and galloped away southwards.

'Decurion, take your turma and get those camel-fucking Marmaridae bastards; we're close enough to catch them. I want one alive,' Corvinus bellowed at the nearest Latin-looking face.

As the turma peeled away Vespasian shot Magnus a questioning glance.

'I don't hold with fighting mounted but I suppose it'll make up for not hunting lions,' Magnus said, kicking his horse forward.

With a grin Vespasian followed, urging his mount into a gallop. The wind immediately tore his hat from his head and it fluttered behind him attached by the loose, leather strap around his throat.

They quickly cleared the outcrop and Vespasian felt that they were gaining on the slower but more durable camels, less than two hundred paces ahead; he could count about twenty of them. The turma had spread out into dispersed order, the troopers expertly guiding their horses around the larger stones that littered the baked, cracked ground. The occasional wild shot passed overhead or to one side but there were no hits – accurate archery from a moving camel at an enemy behind you would prove difficult, Vespasian surmised from the ungainly gait of the strange beasts.

After a half-mile, the Marmaridae were less than a hundred paces away; sensing that they would certainly catch their attackers, the troopers urged their horses to greater efforts. Sweat foamed from under their saddles and saliva flecked from their mouths as they responded to their riders' wishes.

Vespasian reached behind him and pulled one of the ten light javelins, which each man carried, from the carry-case strapped to his saddle and slipped his forefinger through the leather thong halfway down the shaft. Their target was now little more than seventy paces ahead and Vespasian felt the familiar thrill and tension of imminent battle; he had not been in combat since the attack on his parents' estate at Aquae Cutillae over four years previously and his desire for it was heightened by the ennui of the last few months.

With only sixty paces separating the two groups, the Marmaridae, realising that they had no chance of escape, suddenly turned their camels and charged the turma, releasing a volley of arrows. To Vespasian's right a trooper was punched out of the saddle with a scream; his horse raced on, taken up by the excitement of the charge.

'Release,' the decurion yelled with fifty paces to go.

More than thirty javelins hurtled towards the oncoming camelry, quickly followed by a second volley as the troopers endeavoured to cause as much damage as possible with their primary weapons. Scores of iron-tipped shafts slammed into the Marmaridae punching through the chests and heads of men with bursts of blood or burying themselves deep into their mounts, crashing them to the ground in a cacophony of guttural, animal bellowing.

Whipping long, straight swords from their scabbards and screaming death from behind their cloth face masks, the seven survivors of the onslaught, black cloaks billowing out behind them, thundered into the turma as they drew their spathae.

The strong, unfamiliar smell of the camels caused the rider-less horse next to Vespasian to shy abruptly to the left; it crunched into his mount's withers as a shimmer of burnished iron flashed down towards him. Agonised by the pain of the blow, his horse raised its head, whinnying madly, and took the vicious sword cut, aimed at Vespasian's neck, in the throat. Blood sprayed over Vespasian's face as he brought his spatha down, severing the sword arm of his adversary who howled as his camel crashed into the now side-on riderless horse. Both beasts and the one-armed tribesman, blood spewing from his freshly hewn stump, plunged to the ground with a cracking of bones and bestial roars of anguish.

With the severed hand still gripping the sword embedded in its throat, Vespasian's horse galloped on for five paces and then crashed onto the desert floor. Vespasian hurled himself forward so as not to be crushed beneath the dead weight of his erstwhile mount and tumbled across the rough ground. Jarring to a halt he looked back and immediately leapt to his left, narrowly avoiding being trampled under the galloping hoofs of a rolling-eyed horse whose blood-spurting, decapitated rider sat firm in the saddle, the muscles in his thighs still gripping his directionless mount.

'Are you all right, sir?' Magnus shouted, pulling his horse up next to Vespasian.

'I think so,' he replied watching, with a morbid curiosity, the progress of the headless rider; within a few dozen paces the thigh muscles gave out and the body slithered from the saddle, leaving the horse charging off towards the deep-blue horizon.

Looking around, Vespasian counted another couple of riderless horses as the turma pulled up and rallied. The ground was littered with dead camels and their riders but fifty paces away, back towards the outcrop, one camel remained standing; the Marmarides pulled it around to face them, brandished his sword above his head and then charged.

'He's got balls, I'll give him that,' Magnus commented, jumping from his horse and grabbing his hunting spear. 'He's mine, all right, pull back,' he shouted at the troopers who did as they were ordered, grinning in anticipation of the interesting contest.

Magnus stood four-square to the charging camel, holding his eight-foot-long oaken-shafted spear across his body; the leaf-shaped iron head glinted in the sun. The troopers shouted encouragement at him as the rider closed, screaming the ululating war cry of his people and slapping the flat of his blood-stained sword against his camel's side to urge it into more speed.

Magnus remained motionless.

An instant before the camel hit him, Magnus dodged to the left, ducking under the wild swipe of the Marmarides' fearsome sword, and jammed his spear, point first, sideways between the animal's forelegs. Its right shinbone snapped as it cracked against the solid shaft; its forward motion twisted the spear around and, as Magnus let go, forced it up into the belly of the beast. With a terrified bellow the camel sank onto the spear as its right leg buckled unnaturally beneath it, catapulting its rider from his saddle; its momentum pushed the weapon up through its juddering body, shredding its innards, until it burst through the beast's back in a shower of gore just above the pelvis. Screeching and snorting violently, the camel thrashed its back legs in a vain attempt to lift itself off the cause of its torment. Magnus grabbed the unconscious Marmarides' discarded sword and raised it two-handed into the air; with a monumental growl of exertion he sliced the blade down onto the writhing creature's neck, cleaving through its vertebrae and almost severing its head.

The body convulsed with a violent series of spasms and then went still.

A mass of cheers and whoops went up from the watching troopers.

Vespasian walked over to his friend, shaking his head in mute admiration.

'I saw a *bestiarius* deal with a camel like that in the circus,' Magnus admitted, 'so I thought that it'd be fun to have a go myself, seeing as they don't put up much of a fight.'

'Paetus would have appreciated that,' Vespasian replied, thinking of his long dead friend, 'he loved a good wild-beast hunt.'

'I think I've lost my spear, though. I'll never pull it out of that.'

A moan from behind distracted them and they turned to see the Marmarides stirring.

Vespasian turned the man over. His headdress had fallen off; he was young, no more than twenty, short and wiry, curly-haired with a thin nose and mouth and three strange curved lines tattooed on each of his brown-skinned cheeks. 'We'd better get him back for questioning; he might have seen Statilius Capella's party.'

'If you're thinking about torturing him, forget it,' Magnus said, standing over the prostrate man, 'see if there's another one alive.'

'What do you mean?'

'I mean you're not going to hurt my property. He's now mine, I'm going to keep him; I think I won him fairly.'

'You're in luck,' Vespasian said, kicking the recumbent form of Magnus awake as the sun glowed red on the eastern horizon the following morning. 'I've just been to see Corvinus; Aghilas the guide is going to pull through, the arrow was removed from his shoulder without too much loss of blood and he seems to be fine this morning.'

'Why does that make me lucky?' Magnus asked groggily, unwilling to come out from under his blanket.

'Because it means that we won't have to force your new little friend to show us where the next well is,' Vespasian replied, looking at the young Marmarides sitting against a rock with his hands bound behind his back. 'If you want any breakfast you'd better hurry, the turmae are saddling up. We need to get a move on; it's five more days to Siwa.'

Refilling the water-skins of one hundred and twenty men at the well had taken most of the rest of the day after the skirmish, so they had camped at the outcrop. One of the tribesmen had been found sufficiently alive to be able to confirm through a translator – with the help of the skilled use of one of the trooper's curved knives – that Capella and a couple of his men had been captured by the Marmaridae; they had been taken to Siwa to await the departure of the next slave caravan bound for the distant city of Garama, seven hundred miles to the southwest.

Grumbling, Magnus roused himself and rummaged in his bag for a strip of dried pork and some semi-stale bread; his new slave looked greedily at the food.

'I think he's hungry,' Vespasian observed, 'you'd better feed him otherwise you'll find yourself owning a dead playmate.'

Magnus grunted. 'Keep your sword handy while I untie him, then.' He moved over to the Marmarides and manhandled him round to get at the knot. 'You'd better behave yourself, savvy?' he hissed in the man's ear as the rope came loose. Understanding the tone of voice the captive nodded.

Magnus cut a hunk of bread and a slice of pork and handed them to him; taking them gratefully in one hand he touched the other to his forehead while saying something in his own language.

'I think he's thanking you,' Vespasian commented.

'So he ought to, he owes me his life.'

After quickly swallowing a couple of mouthfuls, the young man looked up at them and pointed to himself. 'Ziri,' he said nodding, 'Ziri.'

Vespasian laughed. 'Oh dear, you know his name now, you'll have to take him home.'

'Ziri,' he said again and then pointed at Magnus.

'Master,' Magnus said, pointing to himself, 'master.' He then pointed to Vespasian. 'Sir. Sir.'

Ziri nodded vigorously, looking pleased. 'Master. Sir,' he repeated.

'Well, that's got that sorted out,' Magnus said, biting into a lump of bread.

Aghilas, much weakened by his wound, guided them without mishap to the second well, just two days from Siwa. Here the landscape changed; the hard-baked ground gave way to sand. At first it was just a thin coating on the desert floor but as they journeyed further from the well it became thicker until by late afternoon they were travelling over sand dunes as tall as a man. Their horses started to struggle in the soft footing and eventually they were forced to dismount and walk. The scalding hot sand on their sandalled feet was a torment to them all.

'I'm beginning to think that this is much too much effort to go to just so that you can get yourself a good breeding wench,' Magnus grumbled as they crested yet another mound of loose and treacherous sand with Corvinus and Aghilas; behind them the four turmae trailed into the shimmering distance.

'We're also rescuing a Roman citizen from a life of misery as an agricultural slave in the middle of nowhere,' Vespasian reminded his friend.

Magnus grunted and battled with his unwilling horse, trying to encourage it to make the descent down the other side of the dune.

'Horse, go!' Ziri shouted, whacking the recalcitrant beast on the rump; it jumped forward and skidded down the dune, sitting on its back legs, taking Magnus with it in a flurry of sand, much to Vespasian's and Ziri's amusement.

'I'm going to stop teaching you Latin, you fuzzy-haired little camel-botherer, if that's the use you put it to,' Magnus spluttered, trying to pull himself out from under his struggling horse.

Vespasian laughed as he led his horse down the dune. 'I thought that was a perfect use of the language; he chose exactly the right two words from his vocabulary of at least twenty to make the horse go.'

Ziri grinned broadly, displaying his ivory teeth as he came down to Magnus. 'Ziri master help?'

'I don't need your fucking help, desert-dweller,' Magnus replied as he managed to extract himself. He brushed the sand from his tunic and began to lead his horse towards the next dune; with another grin Ziri followed.

'Why's Ziri so cheerful?' Vespasian asked Aghilas as they struggled up the loose sand. 'If I'd just been enslaved I think I'd be pretty upset.'

'It's the way of the Marmaridae. Because they're slavers they would rather die than become a slave, that's why they were so suicidal at the well. Their honour required them to exact a blood price for our taking their water but then, when it was obvious that we would catch them, they chose to fight and die. As far as Ziri's concerned he died as a Marmarides in that battle; the fact that Magnus beat him in single combat, yet let him live and made him his slave, means that he can never go back to his people. He now has a completely new life and accepts his fate.'

'So he's happy to be a slave and never see his family again?'

'Yes, it's the only thing he can do. If he was married and had children he is dead to them; to go back to them would mean a slow and painful death at the hands of his own family. All he has left is a new life serving Magnus.'

'So Magnus can trust him?'

'With his life, yes.'

'Even against the Marmaridae?'

'Especially against the Marmaridae.'

Vespasian looked at the young Marmarides following Magnus up the dune like a faithful hound and wondered what he was going to make of Rome. His musing was brought to an abrupt end by a cry of alarm from Ziri who stopped suddenly and pointed to the south. Vespasian squinted into the sun, shading his eyes with his hand. The horizon, normally a straight, sharp divide between light brown and blue, appeared smudged and indistinct.

'Gods help us,' Aghilas muttered.

'What is it?' Corvinus demanded.

'Sandstorm, and it looks like it's coming this way; if it is, it'll be here before dark.'

'What can we do?' Vespasian asked.

'I've never been caught in one so I don't know, but nothing, I think; it'll catch us out in the open, there're no rocks to shelter behind for miles. We must just keep going as fast as possible and pray that it misses us, because if it doesn't and if it's a big one it'll bury us alive.'

For the next couple of hours they pressed on over the unforgiving terrain with all possible haste; the sun had sunk onto the western horizon. News of the impending maelstrom had filtered down the column and the men glanced nervously south at the ever enlarging threat, now no more than ten miles away in the half-light. It had turned from a smudge on the horizon into a massive dark brown, land-based cloud and was increasing in size at an alarming speed.

'Make your peace with your gods,' Aghilas said, 'there's no avoiding it now; we're dead men.'

Ziri ran up to Aghilas and said something in his own language; a brief conversation ensued.

'He says the only way to have a chance of survival in a sandstorm,' Aghilas announced, 'is to make your camel lie down on the top of a dune and shelter behind it; he doesn't know if horses are big or heavy enough but it may work.'

'Pass the word down the column,' Corvinus shouted, 'shelter behind the horses or mules on top of the dunes.'

Vespasian pulled his horse down next to Magnus and Ziri. Sensing an imminent change for the worse in the weather conditions all the animals were skittish and needed to be firmly held in place. He peered over his horse's back and felt the wind start to stir on his face.

'Vulcan's boiling piss, look at the size of it,' Magnus exclaimed, 'that's got to be three or four hundred feet high.'

Vespasian stared at the rolling brown cloud in amazement; it was as least as tall as Magnus' estimate but that was not as awe-inspiring as its speed. Now only a couple of miles away it rolled across the desert at a pace that not even the fastest chariot horse in the circus could outrun. As he watched wide-eyed it raced towards them, like a massive moving mountain eating up the ground before it.

Suddenly it went dark.

Then it hit them.

Within an instant the wind had accelerated from a moderate breeze into a howling gale that strained the ears. The temperature rose and visibility plummeted, so that he could only just make out Magnus sheltering behind his horse two paces away, as the air filled with tiny, sharp particles of sand moving at colossal speeds; they cannoned into the horses' sides, stinging them sorely even through their coats. Vespasian jerked down his mount's bridle as it attempted to stand and flee from the all-encompassing rage that surrounded them; despite the horse's struggling he held it down with every fibre of strength until it acquiesced and lay still. Breathing became increasingly difficult. He pulled his tunic up over his nose, curled into the foetus position and squeezed his eyes tight shut, offering up prayers to every god he could think of, as the wind ripped around him, tearing the hat from his head and dragging relentlessly at his cloak, which cracked like a whip with the unremitting pressure.

The sun went down and darkness became complete.

Vespasian lost all sense of time.

'Pull, you curly-haired little bugger!' Magnus shouted, startling Vespasian back to consciousness.

He felt strong hands grasping his ankles, stretching his legs and then he started to slide downhill. Suddenly he could see stars, thousands of them.

Magnus loomed over him. 'Are you all right, sir?'

Spitting out a mouthful of sand, Vespasian raised his head. 'I seem to be,' he replied with difficulty; his mouth was desert-dry.

Ziri held a water-skin to his lips. 'Sir, trink.'

Vespasian drank and felt the lukewarm liquid course into his body.

Ziri pulled the skin away from him. 'Sir, stop.'

'He's right, I'm afraid,' Magnus said, holding out his hand to help Vespasian up. 'It's the only water we've got unless we can dig some more out.'

Vespasian got unsteadily to his feet and looked around. It was peaceful, there was no wind. The three-quarter moon splashed the rippling sand dunes with silver; to the north the monstrous shape of the sandstorm could just be discerned, ravaging its way towards the coast. Here and there Vespasian could see a few figures, no more than twenty, singly or in pairs, digging in the sand. 'Where's Corvinus?' he asked, looking back to where he last saw the cavalry prefect and his mount.

'He's fine,' Magnus replied, 'he's organising the search parties, although I don't know how fruitful they'll prove to be. Most of the horses bolted, only the lads that kept theirs down have survived. I'm afraid that Aghilas didn't have the strength to hold onto his.'

'Shit, we're lost then.'

'Not quite,' Magnus said with a grin, patting Ziri's frizzy hair like a favoured pet, 'Ziri knows how to get to Siwa.'

The Marmarides nodded. 'Master, sir, Ziri, Siwa, yes.'

'He's becoming quite talkative,' Vespasian observed.

'He is,' Magnus agreed, 'and so are we when we should be digging to see what we can salvage.'

The first rays of direct sunlight hit Vespasian's face and it felt so good to be alive as he scrabbled in the sand searching for his precious water-skin. He had despaired during that timeless oblivion that he had spent curled up in the lee of his now dead horse.

At first he had been able to push away the sand as it piled up near his face but as the storm had intensified great swathes of it had been deposited all around and over him; keeping above it had meant that he was slowly rising and would eventually be higher than his protective mount. Giving up the unequal struggle he had managed to pull his cloak over his head and concentrated instead on keeping a small air pocket in front of his face, which, with the help of his long cavalry spatha acting as a tent-pole, he had maintained until he had lost consciousness in the stifling conditions.

How he had survived he did not know. He could only surmise that the goddess Fortuna had held her hands over him and that she really was safeguarding him for whatever destiny the gods had decreed for him, as he had, at the age of fifteen, overheard his mother profess. That day he had heard his parents speak of the omens surrounding his birth and what they proph-esied. Since then no one had been willing to tell him of their content, bound as they were by an oath administered by his mother to all those present on the day of his naming ceremony, nine days after his birth.

At first this had irked him but gradually his curiosity had waned out of necessity and he had put it to the back of his mind. His curiosity had been briefly reawakened, four years previously, after he and his brother, Sabinus, had been read a deliberately obscure prophecy at the Oracle of Amphiaraos in Greece. This had alluded to a brother telling the truth to the King of the East. Whether it had meant anything to Sabinus he did not know as his brother had been unforthcoming, claiming to be still bound by their mother's original oath.

In the two years between completing his time as one of the *triumviri capitales* and being elected quaestor, time mainly spent running the estate at Cosa left to him by his grandmother, he had thought little about it; until now. Now he was convinced that he had been preserved by some unseen hand; how the others had survived he did not know but he knew that he should have suffocated last night, buried in the sand on the twenty-fifth anniversary of his birth.

'It's not looking too good,' Corvinus said, tight-lipped, walking up behind Vespasian with Magnus as he finally managed to find his water-skin, 'there are twenty-six survivors, plus us four, and only eight water-skins, all of which are half-empty.'

'Nine now, prefect,' Vespasian replied, pulling the skin from the deep hole in the sand. 'Surely we can work out where the horses were and dig down to them?'

'We've been trying to but most of the horses and all but one of the mules bolted taking the provisions with them. They're all lost out there somewhere,' Corvinus snapped, waving his arm around, 'we'll never find them. All we've been digging up is dead auxiliaries; I've lost three of my four decurions. They didn't deserve to die like that, it's a fucking shambles.'

'Well, if there's no hope of any more survivors then we should get going quickly before the sun gets too hot.'

'Go where?' Corvinus shouted.

'To Siwa as planned, prefect; it shouldn't be more than a day away.'

'And what are we going to do when we get there? We've got hardly any men left; you've managed to lose most of them on this mad scheme of yours.'

'Let me remind you who you're talking to, prefect,' Vespasian retorted, pointing a finger at the young cavalry prefect's face.

'I don't need to be reminded that I'm talking to an upstart of a New Man with no breeding and a Sabine accent.'

'Whatever your patrician prejudices might make of me, Corvinus, I am the Governor's, and therefore the Senate's, representative in Cyrenaica and you will do as I order without question. And if you think that saving citizens from slavery is a mad scheme then I pray that should that fate befall you there is someone like me around willing to come after you. Now get the men ready to—'

A distant, mournful, wailing cry from high overhead cut him off.

Vespasian looked east towards its source. 'What the fuck was that?'

'Another poor sod who's had the misfortune to follow you into the desert,' Corvinus spat. He turned on his heel and stormed away, barking orders at the surviving auxiliaries who were looking nervously at the sky.

'I think that you should have made it clear,' Magnus said, watching Corvinus go, 'that you'd only come after him if he has an attractive woman in tow, if you take my meaning?'

Vespasian shot his friend a venomous look. 'Very funny!'

'I thought so; and not so far from the truth either.'

Vespasian grunted; he could not deny it to Magnus: if it had not been for his desire for Flavia, they would not be here and a hundred or so men would still be alive. But then, if a man's destiny was pre-ordained, those men must have been destined to die here; Fortuna had only held her hands over a few of them to be spared for other tasks and deaths. What, he wondered, was the task for which he had been spared?

CHAPTER III

'SIWA, SIWA!' ZIRI shouted, sending his arms and legs flying out at all angles in a wild, capering, silhouetted dance on top of a sand dune.

Vespasian looked up at him wearily through eyes squinting against the sun's midday ferocity; his lips were cracked and his head throbbed from the heat beating down directly onto it in the absence of his hat.

It was the second day after the sandstorm and they were all in a weakened state having only had three cups each of their precious water on the previous day and one cup each at midmorning today. Only Ziri seemed to be unaffected by the conditions and he carried on his exuberant jig as his companions struggled up the dune.

'Not a moment too soon,' Magnus croaked, working his feet hard to get purchase in the soft sand. 'I've been dreaming all morning about drinking my piss.'

'That's a coincidence,' Vespasian replied with as much of a grin as his parched lips would allow him, 'I've been dreaming all morning about drinking your piss too.'

'You'd have had to fight me for it.'

Vespasian's reply stuck in his dry throat as he crested the dune. Two miles in front of him, stretching away beyond the horizon, was nothing but green; an oasis of life in an otherwise barren and hostile terrain. Fifty miles long and over ten wide it covered the desert floor like a lush, verdant carpet.

Corvinus stopped next to Vespasian. 'Thank the gods, we've made it.'

'Yes, but how do we get back?' Magnus muttered.

As they stood marvelling at such an expanse of fertility after days of nothing but brown, wasted land and intense blue sky, the distant sound of rhythmic drums, sonorous horns and clashing cymbals drifted up through the air.

'What's that?' Vespasian asked.

'Dunno,' Magnus replied, 'but it sounds as if someone's having a party.'

Having drunk the last of their water, the final couple of miles felt easier and within an hour they passed under the first date palms. The sound of the music grew steadily but there were no other signs of human habitation. The temperature started to drop considerably until it felt like no more than a scalding hot summer's day in Rome.

Working their way forward for another mile through the gradually thickening trees, enjoying the ever growing shade, they came suddenly, and unbelievably, to a lake. Without hesitation all of them rushed forward and plunged into the cool, life-giving water and drank their fill while submerging their overheating bodies in its fresh depths, diffusing, at last, the sun's relentless intensity.

Refreshed, they made their way deeper into the oasis in the direction of the music. Coming upon a well-used track they followed it; the sound of chanting could now be heard under the drums, horns and cymbals. After a few hundred paces they passed a couple of low, flat-roofed, mud-brick houses. Vespasian and Magnus looked through the open windows; they were deserted.

'I suppose everybody's at the party,' Vespasian observed as they carried on towards another larger collection of similar dwellings.

The music was now very close. The road turned sharply to the right and passed between two more houses, then opened up into a huge, crowded, square agora surrounded by mud houses seemingly piled one upon the other. The music and the chanting came to a crashing crescendo; everyone in the agora jumped into the air raising their arms above their heads.

'Amun! Amun! Amun!' they shouted to the crash of cymbals and the beating of drums.

Then silence.

At the far end of the agora a priestly-looking man, dressed in a leather kilt with a broad, golden belt, stood on the steps of a small temple; on his head he wore a tall, brimless, black leather hat with golden images of the sun fastened to it. He lifted a crook into the air; his congregation prostrated themselves.

He began to incant a prayer and then stopped abruptly as he noticed Vespasian and his comrades still standing. Pointing his crook at them with a shout he indicated that they too should get down onto their bellies. Over a thousand heads turned to stare at them.

'However bad this will feel I think we'd better do as he says,' Vespasian said, getting down onto the ground. Magnus, Corvinus and the troopers followed his lead.

Grovelling in the dust was not a natural thing for a Roman to do: more used to mastering others, they were accustomed to looking down rather than up, and Vespasian, Magnus and Corvinus prostrated themselves reluctantly. Ziri and the Libu troopers followed their lead without humiliation.

Once satisfied that the whole congregation was showing due deference the priest carried on his incantation for what seemed like an age.

'Amun!' he called to the sky finally.

'Amun!' the crowd repeated.

With the prayer session evidently at an end the people got back onto their feet.

Vespasian rose and tried to wipe the dirt off his wet tunic with little success.

The priest strolled through the crowd towards them and stopped in front of Vespasian.

'What are you doing here, stranger?' he asked in Greek.

'I'm no stranger,' Vespasian replied with as much dignity as was possible covered in wet dirt, 'I am Titus Flavius Vespasianus, quaestor of the province of Creta and Cyrenaica of which this is a part.'

The priest bowed. 'Quaestor, you and your men are welcome.'

Vespasian could feel the release of tension among the troopers behind him.

'My name is Ahmose,' the priest continued, 'priest of Amun, He who is hidden, He who came first. You will find us loyal subjects to Rome here and I will assist you in any way I can. I think that first you need to eat and then you can tell me how you managed to appear out of the western desert on foot.'

Sitting rather uncomfortably on the carpeted floor, Vespasian, Magnus and Corvinus joined Ahmose in his surprisingly richly decorated house for a meal of bread, olives, dates and a roasted meat that none of them had tasted before; although slightly tough they were all hungry enough to eat it without worrying too much about its provenance.

'So you're looking for the Marmaridae's slave caravan,' Ahmose said, having listened to the tale of their journey. 'They will still be here; a party of them arrived only four days ago, that's why the camel tastes so fresh.'

'This is camel?' Magnus exclaimed, looking at the cut of meat in his hand.

'Most certainly. The Marmaridae always pay for the right to use our water with camels each time they pass through; we also give them bread, dates and olives as part of the exchange.'

'Well, they don't taste as bad as they smell,' Magnus commented before taking another bite.

'Yes, it's quite flavoursome; their milk is good to drink too.'

Magnus screwed up his nose. 'Now that is disgusting.'

'Don't you have trouble with the Marmaridae taking your people as slaves?' Vespasian asked, trying to get the image of drinking camel's milk out of his mind.

'No, they need us for water and supplies before they set off to Garama; if we denied them that then the journey would be even more hazardous than it already is.'

'They could just take it,' Corvinus pointed out, taking a bite of a large green olive.

'There are over ten thousand people living in the oasis, we could fight them off; and if we were having trouble we could appeal to Caesar as we used to appeal to the Pharaohs when we were a part of the Kingdom of Egypt.'

Vespasian doubted very much that any sort of an army would be sent to defend this outpost of the Empire, but he kept his thoughts to himself. 'How do we find the Marmaridae's caravan?'

'They'll be at the last lake in the southwestern corner of the oasis, about six miles from here.'

'We'll need horses.'

'I'm sure you would requisition them if we didn't give them freely.'

'I'm afraid we would; as the quaestor I have that power.'

'As the quaestor you also have the power to make those horses part of the tax that we pay each year.'

Vespasian smiled at the old priest. 'If you include javelins and enough supplies to take us back to Cyrene, then I'm sure that that could be arranged.'

'Done, quaestor.' Ahmose spat into his hand and proffered it; Vespasian took it rather gingerly. 'But that is all the help that I can give you; if I give you men it might upset the delicate balance that we have with the Marmaridae.'

'I could requisition them as well.'

'You could but I think you would have a problem: we are celebrating a festival of Amun at the moment, it runs from today for three days, in memory of Alexander coming here three hundred and sixty-seven years ago to receive the wisdom of Amun. There will be a feast tonight in honour of him; you are welcome to join us. I will have the horses and weapons ready by dawn; you can leave then.'

Vespasian opened his eyes; it was thick night. His head spun slightly from the effects of the date wine that had been served in copious quantities during the feast. Magnus had been able to consume cup after cup without too many ill-effects but Corvinus and all of the troopers had drunk themselves, very quickly, unconscious. Vespasian had not been surprised, it was heady stuff and he had limited himself, very early, to just a cup every so often; even so he was still less than sober. Ziri had not touched a drop all evening as he waited upon Magnus' every need; he now lay curled up, sleeping at his master's feet.

A metallic clink from outside the window caught Vespasian's attention; he was sure that it was the same noise that had just woken him. He listened intently trying to filter out Corvinus' snores and Magnus' heavy breathing. There it was again; there was someone or some people just outside the window, he was sure of it.

He reached with his left hand for his spatha on the floor next to his mattress and eased it onto his chest; his right hand gripped the hilt as he listened again.

Nothing; he started to relax.

A distant, sudden crack of wood breaking followed by shouts jerked him upright; he unsheathed his spatha.

'Magnus!' he shouted but got no further.

The door crashed to the floor; moonlight and dark figures spilled in.

With a roar he leapt to his feet and hurled himself at them, spatha in the air. Briefly aware of Magnus drawing his sword and Ziri jumping up, he slashed wildly in the dark, felt his blade make contact and was rewarded with a shrill scream and a jet of blood in his face. He kept his forward momentum going and with a backhand cut felled another of his shadowy assailants; Magnus hurtled into the man next to him, flooring him with a body-check and a jab to the belly. Ziri threw himself at another of them, crunching his forehead into the man's nose, taking him down. Driving his left foot forwards, Vespasian brought his right knee up, squelching into the groin of the next figure who dropped like a dead man to the ground with a guttural roar that was stifled as he started to hyperventilate with pain. Strangulated gurgles came from the floor as Ziri despatched his opponent with his bare hands. Magnus' straight thrust into the right eye of his next opponent was enough to convince their attackers to withdraw at speed.

'What the fuck was that all about?' Magnus asked, breathing heavily.

'Don't know, but we certainly should get out of here; help me with Corvinus,' Vespasian replied, thrusting the tip of his spatha into the throat of the man clutching his crushed testicles.

Finding Corvinus in the dark from the direction of his snoring proved easy enough; what was not easy was waking him.

'Shit, we'll have to carry the bugger; Ziri, here,' Magnus said after a third sharp slap had proven fruitless.

Magnus and Ziri quickly slung an arm over each shoulder and dragged Corvinus to the open door.

Peering outside into the moonlit agora, Vespasian could see no one close by, but their attackers were running over to the other side of the square where a group of figures surrounded the storeroom to which the comatose troopers had earlier been dragged to sleep off the date wine.

'There's nothing that we can do about them,' Vespasian hissed, turning away and grabbing Corvinus' ankles, 'they'll have butchered them by now. Let's get out before those bastards get their reinforcements.'

Running as fast as possible with the dead weight of Corvinus between them, they skirted around the edge of the agora; coming to an alley leading away, they turned up it as an almighty shout came from over by the storeroom.

'Shit! That's them after us,' Magnus said as they raced up the dark alley. Corvinus started to moan; his head lolled from side to side. 'I fucking wish old matey-boy here could hold his drink.'

Suddenly the alley opened onto a main street; they paused and looked each way, it was deserted. Darting across the road they found another alley and sprinted up it. Behind them they could hear the shouts of their pursuers growing closer.

Almost a hundred pounding heartbeats later the mean houses on either side of the alley abruptly ended and they came out into a date palm forest.

'Straight ahead!' Vespasian puffed. 'And keep an eye out for somewhere to hide; we'll never outrun them with him dragging us down. Let's pray that they didn't see which alley we went up.'

'Why don't we just leave him?'

'If it comes to a choice between all four of us getting killed or just him, we will.'

'I think we've just reached that point, sir,' Magnus observed as a horde of silhouetted figures flooded out of the alley, just over a hundred paces behind them.

With a quick glance between them they dropped Corvinus and sprinted away.

Weaving through the moonlit palms they managed to put on a good turn of speed but their pursuers, more used to the terrain, were gaining on them.

'Split up,' Vespasian shouted, veering left, 'we'll meet up back at that lake soon after dawn.'

With a grunt of acknowledgement Magnus ran off to the right, taking Ziri with him, leaving Vespasian pelting through the night on his own; his legs were beginning to ache with the exertion. His chest started to tighten and his heartbeat thumped in his inner ears. The shouts of the pursuers told him that they were following him and catching up.

He burst out into a clearing, cursed himself for breaking cover and sprinted towards the far side.

Ten paces before gaining the comparative safety of the palms an ear-splitting cry stopped him in his tracks; he fell to the ground, hands over his ears. The cry then turned into a wailing note, mid-range and wavering at first, like a beautiful, mourning hymn of the gods; it worked its way ever higher until it reached peaks of such a piercing intensity and clarity that all other senses retreated as Vespasian listened to the sublime sound. Gradually it started to slow and ease down in pitch, as if the singer, tired by the emotion of the song, had decided to bring the piece to a close with a series of exquisite notes, ever lowering, ever softening, until, after one final gentle breath, there was silence.

Vespasian got to his knees, stunned by the aural experience that he had just been subjected to. He looked back; his pursuers were all grovelling on the ground on the far side of the clearing.

A sudden, golden flash caused him to shut his eyes tight and lower his head; he felt a warmth on his skin that began to grow gradually. He opened his eyes; the clearing was awash with light, gaining in intensity as if it were imitating visually the song just sung.

'Bennu! Bennu!' the grovelling men cried.

Vespasian looked up and, shielding his eyes, saw that the source of the light was a beacon perched implausibly on top of a tall date palm close to him on the edge of the clearing. Golden sparks fell from it, turning orange and then red as they floated to the ground to collect in an ever growing pile of glowing embers at the base of the tree.

Burning with increasing ferocity the flame became pure white at its peak; heat from it scorched Vespasian's face and hands as it bathed him, kneeling on the ground, in a pool of light.

Cries of 'Bennu! Bennu!' filled the air.

With a sharp crack, like a Titan crashing two boulders together, the fire was suddenly extinguished as if it had unexpectedly consumed all its fuel, leaving no morsels with which it could die down gradually.

The last of the sparks fell to the ground and the light died.

In the dark the mound of embers glowed softly, like an untended campfire in the cold hours before dawn.

Vespasian turned to see his pursuers on their feet, still chanting 'Bennu', halfway across the clearing, walking towards him.

As he turned to run a cloud of hot ashes exploded over him from behind; a cry rose to the sky. He swivelled to see the mound of embers gone and replaced by a mist of glimmering red dust.

The cry ceased and the red mist started to swirl as if it were being wafted from above by a giant fan. Vespasian felt a wind beating towards him; it grew stronger with every pulse as if a great bird were swooping down on him from the dark. He ducked away from the unseen threat as a colossal gust caught him off-balance and threw him to the ground.

The air went still.

After a few moments Vespasian opened his eyes to see a pair of feet in front of him; he looked up.

'You will not be harmed,' Ahmose said, holding out his hand to help Vespasian up. His men surrounded him, looking at Vespasian with a mixture of fear and wonder. Ahmose's eyes, wide with religious fervour, sparkled down at him in the moon-light. 'You are blessed of Amun; you are safe.'

'What about my comrades?' Vespasian asked, getting to his feet.

'They are still alive; we will sell them as slaves to the Marmaridae.'

'Fuck your blessings,' Vespasian spat, jabbing the priest with his right fist in the solar plexus. 'We had a deal, you little shit.'

Ahmose doubled over as a half a dozen restraining hands grabbed hold of Vespasian.

After struggling a few moments for breath Ahmose looked up at him. 'Do you really think that we could stop the Marmaridae picking off our people and sending them as slaves to Garama? We're not warlike as they are, we are farmers; we have to sell them some slaves every year to keep them happy. Your friends will do nicely, but you won't go; as a priest of Amun, it's my duty to take you to His Oracle in the heart of Siwa where, if you are truly blessed by Him, you will, like Alexander himself and a few other chosen ones through the ages, hear His wisdom.'

Vespasian looked at the treacherous old priest with loathing. 'Why is it your duty?'

'You have been touched by the Wind of the Bennu and have bathed in the light of its fire. Amun knows that I have witnessed it.'

'What is the Bennu?'

'The sacred bird of Egypt whose death and rebirth marks the end of one age and the start of a new. A man who has bathed in its light and has felt the wind of its beating wings as it flies to the holy city of Heliopolis to lay its nest on the altar of Ra is destined to play a part in the new age. You know this bird in your language as the Phoenix.'

Vespasian was led east for the remainder of the night and all of the following morning. His sword had been taken from him but his hands were not bound; however, he made no attempt to escape, surrounded as he was by a dozen armed men. Even had he just been accompanied by the double-crossing Ahmose he would have followed willingly, saving his vengeance for another time, curious to hear what the Oracle of Amun would tell him; curious whether it would throw light upon the prophecy of the Oracle of Amphiaraos.

As they travelled deeper into the oasis they passed more bodies of water, much larger than the lake that he had bathed in only the day before. Irrigation channels had been dug to siphon the precious liquid to the smallholdings cultivating olive groves, chickpeas and vegetable gardens that clustered near them; sheep and goats grazed on rough pasture around the shores. People grew more numerous. Men in headdresses worked in the fields, tilling, picking fruit or loading their produce onto carts; women washed clothes and children at the lakes' shores, fetched water in earthenware pots that they carried on their heads, or cooked over open fires outside their mud huts. It looked far more prosperous to Vespasian than the tax receipts from Siwa had led him to believe; evidently a quaestor had never visited to make a proper tax assessment. Making a mental note to review the demand on his return to Cyrene as part of his revenge on the people for so barbarously abusing the laws of hospitality, he calculated that the wealth of the oasis would go far to improving the province's struggling finances.

Shortly before midday they came to a mud-brick wall and passed through a wide gate into a town brimming with life. His escort was forced to push its way through the crowded streets lined with farmers selling their produce on blankets or palm-frond mats laid out on the ground. The smell of exotic spices and human sweat filled the air.

On a hill at the town's centre stood a temple, built of sandstone, with a tapered tower protruding from its northern end. As they approached it Vespasian could see that rows and rows of tiny figures were carved into the stone walls.

'What are they?' Vespasian asked Ahmose, his curiosity outweighing his antipathy.

'They are hymns to Amun, lists of priests and records of kings who have visited since the temple was built over seven hundred years ago.'

'That's writing?' Vespasian was amazed that these strange depictions of animals and curious signs could be strung together to form coherent sentences.

Ahmose nodded as they mounted the steps leading to the temple's door together, leaving their escort at the bottom.

The temperature drop was considerable as they entered the building. Symmetrical rows of columns, three paces apart, supported the lofty ceiling, giving the impression of an ordered stone forest. From a few windows, cut high in the south wall, shafts of light, with motes of dust playing within them, sliced down at a sharp angle through the gloom of this interior, petrified grove. The musky residue of incense and the cloying smell of ancient, dry stone replaced the fresh scents of woodland in bloom. The clatter of Vespasian's hobnailed sandals resounded off the flagstone floor.

A raised, disembodied voice in a language that Vespasian did not understand stopped them by the first row of columns.

'Ahmose, your fellow priest of Amun,' Ahmose replied in Greek so that Vespasian could understand.

'And who accompanies you?' the voice continued, switching to the same language.

'The Bennu flew last night.'

'We do not understand the reason for its coming here.We heard it pass over the temple and have checked the records; it is exactly five hundred years to the day since it was last seen in Egypt but it is five times that number since it was seen so far in the west here in Siwa.'

'This man felt the heat of its fire and the downdraught of its wings.'

There was silence.

Vespasian looked around; there was no sign of the source of the voice.

Presently he heard the soft patter of unshod feet on smooth stone and two priests appeared in different directions from the depths of the forest of columns. Both were dressed similarly to Ahmose except that they each had two long feathers stuck into the tops of their tall hats.

Walking side by side down a straight, columned path they stopped in front of Vespasian and examined him closely with wide-eyed wonder. He felt very uneasy under the close scrutiny of the priests, one of whom was, now that he could make out their features in the gloom, very old indeed; yet he had the bearing of a young and healthy man. The second priest was in his twenties.

The old priest who had spoken spread his hands, palms up and called to the air. 'Thou wilt find him who transgresses against Thee. Woe to him that assails Thee. Thy city endures, but he who assails Thee falls. Amun.'

'Amun,' intoned the second priest and Ahmose.

'The hall of him who assails Thee is in darkness, but the whole world is in light. Whosoever puts Thee in his heart, lo, his sun dawns. Amun.'

'Amun.'

'If this man did not indeed feel the Wind of the Bennu and bathe in the light of its fire, Amun, the inapparent and apparent, the omniform, will not speak to him and he will be banished from His sun and see no more the dawn. And you, Ahmose, will share his fate.'

'I saw it with these eyes, may they be taken from me if what I say is not true. He knelt in the light of the Bennu's fire and then was blown by a wind so strong as the Bennu passed over him that he was cast down into the sand. Amun, whose name is not known, will speak to him.'

'Very well,' the second priest said, 'we will prepare for the Oracle.'

CHAPTER IIII

'HAIL TO YOU, who brought Himself forth as one who created millions in their abundance. The one whose body is millions. Amun.'

Vespasian knelt before the surprisingly small statue of the god set upon an altar in a chamber, lit by two flaming sconces, at the heart of the temple; the three priests surrounded him chanting their hymn. The statue represented Amun seated; in his right hand he held a sceptre, in his left, an ankh; his face was that of a man, the mouth was open and hollow. Across his legs was laid a sword in a richly decorated scabbard of great antiquity. The smoke of pungent incense wafted through the room making Vespasian feel very light-headed and euphoric.

'No god came into being prior to Him. No other god was with Him who could say what He looked like. He had no mother who created His name. He had no father to beget Him or to say: "This belongs to me." Amun.'

Vespasian felt himself being lifted to his feet; oil was poured on his forehead and left to trickle down his face. He felt at ease and smiled.

'You who protect all travellers, when I call to You in my distress You come to rescue me. Give breath to him who is wretched and rescue me from bondage. For You are He who is merciful when one appeals to You; You are He who comes from afar. Come now at Your children's calling and speak. Amun.'

'Amun,' Vespasian found himself repeating.

The word echoed around the room.

Then silence.

70

Vespasian stood staring at the god; around him the priests were motionless.

The room became chill. The smoke hung, still, in the air. The flames in the sconces died down.

Vespasian felt his heartbeat slow.

He heard a soft breath emanate from the statue's mouth and in the dim light he could see the smoke begin to swirl around the god's face.

Another breath, more rasping this time, moved the smoke faster; the low flames flickered.

'You come too soon,' a voice whispered, billowing the smoke around the statue's mouth.

Vespasian's eyes widened in surprise; he leant forward slightly to assure himself that the voice came from the mouth.

'Too soon for what?' he asked, wondering if some elaborate trick was being played on him.

'Too soon to know your question.'

If the smoke had not moved again Vespasian would have sworn that the voice was in his head.

'When will I know?'

'When you can match this gift.'

'That gift?' He looked down at the sword placed across the statue's knees.

'Equal it.'

'With what?'

'A brother will understand.'

'When?'

'When you need him to.'

'How will I...' he began.

A whistling drawing of breath sucked the smoke into the statue's mouth in one continuous funnelling gulp; the flames sprang back to full strength.

The spell was broken.

Vespasian looked around; the three priests suddenly convulsed as if coming out of a trance. As one they recommenced their incantation.

'Everything that comes from His mouth the gods are bound by, according to what has been decreed. When a message is sent it is for the giving or taking of life; for life and death depend on Him for everyone. Nothing exists which He is not. Everything is Him. Amun.'

'Amun,' Vespasian repeated as the priests turned and walked away from the altar; with a brief, quizzical look at the statue, he followed.

'What did that mean?' Vespasian asked as they re-entered the forest of columns.

'We cannot tell you,' the first priest replied, 'we heard nothing. What He said was for you alone. All we know is that you were spoken to by the God and that you are blessed by Him. No one can harm you now in His sacred land of Siwa; you and those who travel with you are under His protection.'

'It's too late for that; this man has sold my travelling companions into slavery.'

'Then to atone he will have to buy them back,' the younger priest stated.

'Good, and while you're about it, Ahmose, you can buy back the man we came to rescue, a Roman by the name of Capella.'

'I will,' Ahmose said with a touch of nervousness. 'You should thank me for bringing you here.'

'I'll do no such thing,' Vespasian snapped, finding himself hating the man almost as much as his now dead enemy, the Thracian chief-priest Rhoteces, 'you said it was your duty.'

'And so it was,' the older priest confirmed, 'he would have been cursed by the God if he'd failed to bring one touched by the Bennu before Him.'

'He will take you back safely, Roman, and reunite you with your friends; he will also return your sword.'

'Who gave the god that sword?'

'That was a gift from the great Alexander, he left his sword in thanks for the counsel that he received here.'

Vespasian walked out of the temple wondering how he could ever match such a gift and, even if he could, what question would possibly make him want to make the arduous journey across so much sand to Siwa again to deliver it. Sand? He recalled the prophecy of Amphiaraos:

Two tyrants fall quickly, close trailed by another,
In the East the King hears the truth from a brother.
With his gift the lion's steps through sand he should follow,
So to gain from the fourth the West on the morrow.

Bearing a gift across sand in the lion's steps; a gift suggested by a brother to match that of Alexander, Alexander, the lion of Macedon. But if he was to be the bearer of that gift he would be the King of the East; how could that ever be?

Vespasian did not say a word on the journey back to Ahmose's town; his mind was at first busy with contemplating the prophecy and what he had just heard from the mouth of the god: tyrants, kings, brothers and gifts to gain the West; where did he fit in to all that and why would a question drive him to return to this place?

After rolling these thoughts around his head and getting nowhere he turned his mind to the rescue of his comrades and Capella and whether the duplicitous priest who walked ahead of him would keep his word. Ahmose had indeed given him his sword back with fawning apologies to a favoured one of Amun and had promised to purchase Capella's freedom as well as buying back his men for what he had been paid for them. Vespasian doubted that the Marmaridae would go for such a deal.

The following afternoon, as they approached Ahmose's town, a familiar voice shouting cheered Vespasian's heart.

'Hold it there, priest, or by Pluto's dark realm I'll skewer you and send you down to him.' Magnus appeared through the palms with Ziri, both with raised spears.

Ahmose's men drew their swords and turned to face the threat.

'It's all right, Magnus,' Vespasian called back, 'things have changed; it would seem that I'm blessed by Amun; none of us are in any danger here.'

'We just watched Corvinus and the lads being sold to the Marmaridae yesterday; I call that fucking dangerous.'

'And this little shit is going to get them back for us, aren't you?' Vespasian glared at Ahmose who nodded unhappily. 'Good; we'd better get going then.'

'But first I have to get what's needed to buy your men back.'

'You'll need far more money than they bought them for.'

'I won't be buying them with money; it'll be a straight swap.'

'Marmaridae, sir, master, there,' Ziri said pointing through the palms.

'How many of them are there?' Vespasian asked Magnus as they peered through the fading light at the Marmaridae's camp set by a large pool at the southwestern corner of the oasis.

'I counted at least a hundred yesterday but there seem to be more now.'

Thirty to forty four-man tents, supported by single, central poles, six feet tall, were clustered in two concentric rings around the pool. Fires were lit and camels were being led down to the water's edge to drink. It would have been a peaceful sight had it not been for the closely guarded corral, on the southern edge of the camp, in which at least two hundred men, women and children sat, miserably bound to posts hammered into the ground.

Vespasian looked back to Ahmose at the head of the thirty or so men he had brought from his town to escort the miserable lives that were to be the currency in this deal. 'Well, priest, off you go. We'll be watching from here.'

'I won't be long, this will be straightforward; Amun will watch over me as I'm doing his work.'

'I do loathe a religious fanatic,' Magnus commented as the priest led his party towards the Marmaridae's camp.

Vespasian nodded in agreement. 'I think that I despise anyone who makes his living by being a professional priest, selling religion to the fearful poor and then enjoying the comfort and the power that their money buys him. We do it much better at home where priesthoods are rewards for service to Rome and not a means to an easy life.'

'You've got a point there, sir; but in general those who have priesthoods conferred upon them are already rich, although I've never known that to be a reason for not wanting more.'

Vespasian smiled. 'Quite the opposite, normally.'

'Indeed,' Magnus agreed as they watched the Marmaridae gather around Ahmose and his men.

A brief conversation ensued after which Ahmose was led to a tent larger than the rest.

Vespasian, Magnus and Ziri waited in the twilight. Torches lit around the camp washed it with an orange glow. The temperature started to drop.

Eventually Ahmose reappeared from the tent with a grey-bearded man and gestured for his men to bring forward the goods to be bartered. Grey-beard inspected each one, checking teeth and feeling muscles in arms and legs as if he were looking at chariot horses that he was contemplating buying. Once each man had been checked Grey-beard turned back to Ahmose; it was clear by his demeanour that he was not happy.

'Looks like we may have to fight our way in somehow to get the lads,' Magnus observed as hand gestures became more frenetic.

The raised voices of the argument floated over the pool to where they lay hidden.

'It's not looking good,' Vespasian agreed.

Suddenly the Marmaridae drew their swords and surrounded Ahmose's men, disarming them. Five were then separated from the rest and were dragged struggling to Grey-beard for inspection; seemingly satisfied, he shouted an order and a party of Marmaridae headed off towards the slave corral.

'Looks like the price just went up,' Vespasian commented. 'That's not going to endear Ahmose to his men.'

Night had now fallen and torches burned all through the camp; in their flickering light Vespasian could see a group of men being led away from the corral. 'That's our lads, I can see Corvinus.'

Magnus squinted. 'I can't see anyone who could be Capella.'

'We'll have to come back for him; at least we now have the men to do that.'

The auxiliaries were brought to Grey-beard and Ahmose who both counted them off; once satisfied they nodded to each other and Ahmose led his men and the auxiliaries away from the camp while their unfortunate replacements were taken off to the corral.

'Where's Capella?' Vespasian asked Ahmose upon his return.

'They wouldn't exchange him.'

'Wouldn't or was the price too high?'

'I had to give him an extra five of my own men just to get back the ones I sold him yesterday,' the priest barked. 'I can't afford any more.'

'An extra five of your own men? You mean to say that none of those men you bartered were slaves?'

'We don't have slaves, it's pointless, the Marmaridae steal them. I had to give them free men from the town. They drew lots and those who lost were willing to go with the blessing of Amun upon their heads.'

Vespasian stared at the priest in disbelief. 'You sold your own people into slavery?'

'It was Amun's will; you heard the priests say so at the Oracle.'

'But why didn't you try and buy my men back with the silver that the Marmaridae paid for them?'

Ahmose frowned as if he could not understand the question. 'That silver is Amun's.'

'And Amun would put more value on it than the lives of those men?'

The priest shrugged.

'Of course he wouldn't, but *you* would; living in comfort while all those around you have to toil in the heat; you disgust me, priest. We'll go back to your town where you'll lend me all of your fighting men, because I'm not leaving here without Capella and freeing those poor bastards who you sacrificed to your greed.'

'You can't do that; the will of Amun must be obeyed.'

'His will or yours, priest?'

'Vespasian, you Sabine country bastard, you left me to the slavers,' Corvinus shouted storming up to him, 'I'll not forget that.'

'I had no choice, you were dead drunk and slowing us down. And I would remind you, prefect, that I came back for you and your men and you are now free because of me, which wouldn't have happened if we were all imprisoned in that corral together; so don't forget that part of it either.'

'And learn to hold your drink,' Magnus advised him, 'then perhaps you won't find yourself taken prisoner so easily.'

Corvinus lashed out with his right fist at Magnus, who ducked under it and delivered a solid punch into his belly.

'You picked the wrong man to box with,' Magnus said as Corvinus crumpled to the floor, 'I used to do it professionally.'

Vespasian came between them. 'That's enough! Get to your feet, Corvinus, and next time we rescue you I suggest that you say thank you rather than picking a fight and insulting me.'

The prefect looked up at Vespasian with hatred in his eyes. 'You'll regret this one day, quaestor, I promise you that.'

'We'll see; in the meantime we've got a citizen to rescue who's about to suffer the same fate that you've just been saved from. Now go and see if any of your lads speak the local language.'

Two hours later they arrived back at the town's agora. It was deserted; a few lamps burned behind shuttered windows.

'Rouse your people, Ahmose,' Vespasian ordered, 'you and I are going to address them.'

'Now?'

'Yes, now! And you will translate for me. And have my men's swords retrieved from wherever you've hidden them.'

The priest issued a command to his men and they fanned out through the town banging on doors and ordering the people to the agora.

Soon the square, now lit by flickering torches, was full of chattering people curious to know what was occurring. Vespasian, followed by Magnus and Ziri, mounted the temple steps with Ahmose and the auxiliary who Corvinus had found who spoke the local Siwi language.

'You're to make sure that he translates everything correctly,' Vespasian told the auxiliary, as Corvinus' men, now rearmed with their spathae, took up position at the foot of the steps, 'and when he refuses to, which he will, you will make the translation.'

'Yes, quaestor.'

'Ahmose, bring them to order.'

A horn sounded and the noise in the agora died down.

Vespasian stepped forward to address the crowd. 'Two nights ago the Bennu was reborn to begin its new five-hundred-year cycle,' he declaimed. He paused as Ahmose translated his words. After a quick glance at the auxiliary to confirm that the translation was true he continued. 'I was warmed by its fire and felt the wind of its wings and your priest took me to the temple of Amun where the god spoke to me.'

There were looks of awe on the faces of those listening as Ahmose repeated this line.

'I am blessed by Amun and I and all who travel with me are under His protection. Yet your priest sold my companions, Roman soldiers, to the Marmaridae.'

Ahmose shot Vespasian a nervous glance.

'Translate, priest,' he ordered.

After the priest had spoken Vespasian turned to the auxiliary who shook his head. 'He didn't translate the second sentence; he just made something up about the glory of Amun.'

'What a surprise. Do it for him, then.'

As the auxiliary translated the real version a look of surprise turning to panic washed over Ahmose's face as he realised that he was losing any control that he had over the situation.

'To buy them back he used thirty-two of your compatriots; free men now forced into slavery by your priest.'

'I did it for Amun,' Ahmose shouted at Vespasian.

'No, you do nothing for Amun, everything you do is for yourself, like so many of your kind. Now, are you going to translate or is he?'

With a howl Ahmose leapt at Vespasian only to find himself pinioned by the firm grips of Magnus and Ziri. Vespasian nodded at the auxiliary as the priest struggled helplessly to escape his captors.

Roars of indignation emanated from the crowd as the auxiliary translated; they began to surge forward only to be held back by Corvinus' men.

Vespasian held his arms aloft, appealing for calm. 'This priest of yours, who lives in luxury off the money you give him, has no concern for your wellbeing, only his.'

The crowd shouted their agreement as they heard the translation.

'He delivered Roman soldiers and your own people to the slavers and in doing so has brought the wrath of Rome and Amun down on you all. To redress his actions I will lead you tonight to the Marmaridae's camp and we shall destroy them together and free your people.'

A huge cheer greeted these words once they were translated.

'But first, I, who am favoured by your god, demand vengeance on this priest for his treatment of my men; his life is forfeit.' Ahmose's legs buckled; Magnus and Ziri held him upright. 'I could execute him now or, if you wish it, I will give you your priest, who thinks nothing of selling thirty-two of your number into a life of servitude, to punish as you see fit; you are free of him.'

As the auxiliary finished the translation the crowd's reaction was clear; Vespasian gestured to Magnus and Ziri. They forced the screaming Ahmose down the steps, through the cordon of auxiliaries, and threw him to the people who kept him in luxury yet whom he valued so little.

With animal ferocity they drew him into their midst, feet, fists and nails lashing at him, their cries of hatred drowning his shrieks as they battered and pummelled him mercilessly. Vespasian and his companions watched with grim satisfaction as the bloodied priest was hurled, wailing, into the air to be caught by many pairs of hands. Gripping his ankles and wrists strong men pulled Ahmose, eyes bulging with fear and agony, in opposing directions; others cut at his body with knives, concentrating on his joints. His shoulders and hips dislocated under the pressure, which grew until, to a savage roar from the crowd, his left arm, its sinews severed by multiple slashes, ripped from his shoulder, followed, a moment later, by his right. Ahmose's head crashed down onto the ground as the macabre trophies were waved in the air. The men holding his ankles then pulled his legs apart, heaving on them with all their might, rending the ligaments and muscles until the right leg parted at the knee in a welter of blood. Unable to tear any more off him the crowd then took it in turns to batter out of Ahmose what little remaining life was left in him with his own dismembered limbs.

'I think that's got their blood up,' Magnus said, nodding with approval at the manner of the priest's demise.

'Let's hope so,' Vespasian replied. 'We'd better get them to the Marmaridae's camp while they're still in the mood.'

It was past midnight and the moon had set. Vespasian crept through the gloom of a palm grove guided only by the light of the few torches and fires that still burned within the Marmaridae's camp. Behind him just over two hundred men from the town waited in the darkness along with Corvinus and his auxiliaries.

Upon reaching the edge of the grove he dropped to his knees behind a palm and peered around its trunk towards the slavers' camp; all was quiet. Having satisfied himself that, apart from a few sentries dozing by campfires, there was no one abroad, he slipped back through the dark to his waiting men.

'They're not expecting any company,' he whispered, crouching down next to Magnus and Corvinus. 'I could see about half a dozen guards, most of whom seem to be asleep, none of them were patrolling; everyone else is in their tents.'

'How can you be sure?' Corvinus asked, dubious about the wisdom of the attack.

'Because I couldn't see them anywhere else; but you're right, it is an assumption. However, that's no reason not to do this thing; we outnumber them by a good fifty men.'

'But most of ours are townspeople with improvised weapons; they'll be up against trained fighters.'

'Which makes the need for speed and surprise all the more essential, Corvinus, so let's stop talking about it and do it; unless you'd prefer that I cancel the whole thing and tell the Governor that I was obliged to let a Roman citizen be carried off into slavery because my cavalry prefect shied away from a fight?'

'You bastard.'

'That's better; now leave me the translator and take your men around to the south of the camp; Magnus and I will take the townspeople and cover this side and the east and west. Deal with the guards around the corral as quietly as possible; once they're dead secure the corral and signal to me here by waving one of the torches. We'll then move in on all sides setting fire to the tents and killing as many as we can before they wake up; after that it'll be a hard fight. If we hear any screams before your signal we'll charge in immediately.'

Corvinus grunted his assent.

'And try not to kill the camels,' Vespasian added.

'Why not?'

'Because we'll need them to get home.'

Corvinus got to his feet, brushed the sand from his knees and moved off to muster his men.

'What do you think?' Magnus asked.

'I think that he'll do as he's been ordered; he's a good officer, he just doesn't like me.'

'Let's hope that won't cloud his judgement.'

'Come on; let's get our rabble army in position.'

*

After Vespasian had briefed the townspeople, through the translator, with orders to do nothing until they saw him go forward, they had moved into position in silence over the loose sand. Vespasian and Magnus waited, with swords drawn, in the darkness looking out over the Marmaridae's camp that was now surrounded by a man at every five paces. Ziri lay next to Magnus clutching a spear. Apart from the occasional snort from one of the many hobbled camels scattered among the tents it was quiet. The sentries dozed peacefully by their dying fires.

Vespasian felt the tension of coming conflict rise within him, knotting his insides. He offered a silent prayer to Fortuna that she would preserve him from the desert's warriors as she had done from the desert's elements and felt confident that it would be so. However, others would not be so fortunate and, in the dark, in the privacy of his thoughts, he could not but help compare his actions and Ahmose's. They had both sacrificed men for their own desires; the priest for luxury and he, Vespasian, for lust. It had cost Ahmose his life and it had made Vespasian an enemy in Corvinus, a man whose high birth would ensure that he would one day be able to keep his promise of vengeance. Capella had better pay his dues and Flavia had better be worth the risk and effort.

As time dragged on the tension of the wait started to play on the men's nerves and Vespasian began to hear the odd rustle of clothing or the clink of a dagger as men changed their positions and fidgeted in the dark.

'Come on, Corvinus, what's keeping you?' he murmured.

'Perhaps he's just fucked off along with his men and left us to it,' Magnus whispered back.

Vespasian was just beginning to fear the worst when a muffled cry floated through the air from the direction of the corral.

'Shit!' he hissed, looking around at the sentries. A couple of them stirred and looked about but then, after a few snorts from a camel, wrote the cry off as an animal sound and settled back down to their snoozing.

Vespasian relaxed a fraction, knowing that Corvinus and his men were playing their part.

After a few more tense heartbeats a torch near the corral was raised from its holder and waved in the air.

'Let's go,' Vespasian said quietly, getting to his feet at a crouch.

The townsmen on either side followed his lead, sparking off a ripple effect around the perimeter of the camp as each man felt his neighbour rise in the darkness; soon, more than two hundred crouching men were converging from all angles in grim silence upon the unsuspecting Marmaridae.

Vespasian approached the outer ring of tents on the northern side of the pool; behind them was the first of the sentries' fires. Indicating to Ziri to retrieve a nearby torch and then for Magnus and the townsmen to stay covering the tents' entrances, Vespasian edged forward. The sentry was sitting, facing him, cross-legged on the ground with his head on his chest and drawn sword in his lap. Holding his breath, Vespasian gently approached the sleeping man, his spatha at the ready. An instant before he could strike, the sentry, sensing a presence close by, opened his eyes to see a pair of sandalled feet before him in the dim firelight. He jerked his head up, wide-eyed in alarm, to witness Vespasian's sword slamming towards him; it was the last thing that he ever saw. The tip of the spatha punched through his neck just beneath his bearded chin and crunched on up into the base of his skull; any cry that he attempted was drowned by the explosion of blood in his gorge, swamping the vocal cords and clogging his windpipe. He fell into the fire, face down, dead. Almost instantaneously his oily woollen robe and cloak caught alight, illuminating Vespasian.

'Now,' he hissed at Magnus.

Grabbing the torch from Ziri, Magnus thrust it at the bottom of the tent flaps. The flames caught immediately, eating their way up the dry, coarse linen until the opening of the tent was a rage of fire. Ziri stood at the entrance, spear in hand; the first Marmarides, dressed only in a loincloth, hurled himself through the blaze, straight onto its razor point. With a thrust and a twist Ziri gutted him, then kicked him back into the fire, his spilled, moist intestines hissing and steaming in the heat.

Screams rang out as Magnus and those townsmen who had managed to retrieve a torch moved around the ring, fire-raising as they went. The bolder townsmen, shouting encouragement to each other, as the attack was no longer a secret, surged forward to deal with the other sentries, battering them down under a hail of blows and jabs.

All around the outer ring tents were ablaze as the townsmen used the Marmaridae's torches against them. Urging his men forward, Vespasian moved into the inner ring; but here fewer tents were burning and the tribesmen, now fully alerted to the danger, had roused from their sleep and were now dashing to defend themselves. The terrified bellows of the hobbled camels unable to move away from the fires merged with the shrieks and howls of the wounded and the dying into a raucous dissonance.

Standing to the side of a burning tent's entrance, Vespasian brought his spatha slicing down as the flaps burst open, but he mistimed the blow and severed the escaping man's outstretched hands. Leaving him to roll away in blood-spurting agony, Vespasian swiped his sword back at the tent's opening, slashing it across the chest of the next man out as a Marmarides, burning like a beacon, hurtled past him to plunge with a scream and a hiss of steam into the pool at the camp's centre.

Vespasian despatched the last man to emerge from the tent and then swiftly looked about; Magnus and Ziri were meting out the same treatment to the occupants of a tent nearby. All around the camp similar scenes were being played out as the enraged townsmen, brandishing clubs, farming implements and daggers, fell on the unprepared slavers who had been so long a cause of fear to them and a threat to their peaceful way of life; now with thirty-two of their compatriots to save from a living death they took to their task with ferocity. Smoke billowed all around as the torched tents turned into fierce infernos; blazing men flung themselves from them to be impaled on pitchforks or mown down by scythes. The tang of their crisping skin blended with the acrid smell of burning natural fibre.

Through the chaos of the thickening fumes and flames Vespasian could see that a few knots of Marmaridae had managed to group together and were now mounting a vigorous defence; the ill-armed and inexperienced townsmen facing them were beginning to fall beneath the vicious slashes of their long swords and their taste for the fight against more organised defenders was leaving them.

'Magnus, with me,' he bellowed, leaping over the pile of corpses at his feet. Pulling his pugio from its sheath with his left hand, he sprinted towards a group of three Marmaridae advancing steadily, with swords flashing, upon a thin line of wavering townsmen. Crashing through a gap in the unsteady line, Vespasian ducked under a wild sword swipe, headbutting its perpetrator in the belly while plunging his spatha deep into the groin of the tribesman next to him. The three of them went down in a flurry of sand as the townsmen took advantage of the remaining slaver's momentary surprise at Vespasian's sudden arrival and set upon him with a renewed confidence. Rolling off his opponent as they landed, Vespasian thrust his dagger down into the man's ribcage, puncturing his lung.

'I thought you were calling for assistance,' Magnus said, hauling Vespasian to his feet by his sword arm as Ziri thrust his spear into the throats of the two stricken men.

'I was,' Vespasian panted; his heart was racing. 'Some of them are starting to form up; let's keep working our way round until we link up with Corvinus' lads.'

Passing two collapsed, flaming tents, whose trapped and screaming occupants were being mercilessly battered to death, they were faced with a mob of fleeing townsmen who brushed them aside, almost toppling them into a burning tent in their anxiety to escape the terror behind them: Grey-beard.

'Fuck!' Magnus swore as all three of them came to an abrupt halt; the heat of the burning tent singed the hair on their arms and legs.

Swinging an enormous two-handed sword, the Marmaridae chief, flanked by four of his followers, strode towards them, vengeance in his eyes. At the sight of the Romans Grey-beard snarled and ran forward with his sword raised above his head, bearing down upon Vespasian; his men followed, the two to his left spotted Ziri and hurled themselves screaming at him.

With a deft flick of his spear, Ziri heaved the burning tent into the air to land over the two men as Vespasian parried Grey-beard's crushing downward blow, which slid along his blade in a grating spray of sparks to come to a jarring halt on the oval guard. He was just aware of Magnus, next to him, throwing himself to the ground at the feet of the men to Grey-beard's right, tumbling them over, as the Marmaridae chief put ever more downward pressure on his spatha, forcing him to one knee; screams from the men struggling beneath the burning tent rang in his ears. In a swift double movement Grey-beard slammed his foot into Vespasian's chest, sending him crashing onto his back, and raised his sword, growling, his teeth bared, with the effort; as it reached its zenith the motion suddenly stopped and blood spewed from his mouth. Grey-beard stood immobile for a few moments, as if frozen in time, then his sword fell behind him and he turned his head to look at Ziri whose spear was embedded in the side of his chest. With a slow nod to his killer, which seemed to Vespasian to be a look of understanding, the Marmaridae chief collapsed to the ground.

The sound of fighting next to him forced Vespasian to take his eyes off the dying Grey-beard and look round. Magnus was astride a tribesman, each had their hands around the other's throat. Just beyond them a second tribesman, with blood gushing from an empty eye socket, raised his knife and aimed at Magnus' exposed back. Vespasian whipped his sword arm round, letting go of the spatha's hilt and sending the weapon spinning through the air to crack side-on into the man's midriff, winding him. He leapt to his feet and, hurdling Magnus, jumped on the one-eyed Marmarides, pummelling his face with his fists as the two of them fell to the blood-stained sand. Blow after blow he dealt in a frenzied attack that carried on after the man's nose was flattened and his jaw shattered, until a hand grabbed his hair and he felt a blade at his throat.

'Relax, quaestor,' Corvinus' voice shouted in his ear; Vespasian froze. 'Someone should warn you about losing control in combat.'

'I already have,' Magnus said, getting up off his freshly dead, bulging-eyed opponent. 'It seems that he's forgotten that that's how you end up dead.'

'Let go of me, prefect,' Vespasian ordered, coming back to his senses and shaking Corvinus off.

'I could have slit your throat, which I was very tempted to do,' Corvinus snarled as he dropped his sword, 'had it not been for him.'

Vespasian turned round to see Ziri holding his blood-drenched spear to Corvinus' neck. 'It's all right, Ziri,' he said, gesturing slowly for him to lower his weapon.

Ziri nodded and pulled away.

Vespasian got to his feet and looked around; tents still blazed, up-lighting the surrounding palms that stood motionless in the windless night with a soft amber hue, but the sound of fighting had died down. Groups of townsmen and auxiliaries walked through the carnage; every now and then one would raise a weapon and bring it down to despatch a wounded tribesman.

'Did any escape?' he asked no one in particular as he picked up his spatha.

'I don't know but I doubt it,' Corvinus replied. 'The slave corral is secured; some of my men are guarding it.'

'Good, let's go and have a look at them.'

'Time to see if Capella will give you his woman in grateful thanks for all your effort,' Magnus commented. He did not see Corvinus frown at his remark.

As Vespasian and Magnus turned to go they noticed Ziri looking down at the still burning bodies; he speared them both in the heart.

'Come on, Ziri,' Magnus said, tugging at his sleeve.

Ziri shook his head. 'They Ziri brothers,' he said matter-of-factly.

Vespasian looked aghast at the young Marmarides and, with a sense of foreboding, pointed down at Grey-beard. 'And him, the man you killed to save my life,' he asked, recalling Aghilas' words: *especially against the Marmaridae.*

Ziri looked at him with no emotion in his eyes. 'He Ziri father.'

CHAPTER V

'STATILIUS CAPELLA! STATILIUS Capella!' Magnus shouted over the wailing of the terrified female captives and the crying of their children as he, Vespasian and Corvinus wove their way through the tightly packed slave corral, carrying torches.

'Over here,' a voice eventually called out as they approached the centre.

'Corvinus, release the freeborn and freed,' Vespasian ordered, 'but keep bound all those who were slaves before the Marmaridae caught them. And get some of your men to round up the camels; I'm going to have a little chat with the idiot who dragged us all the way out here.'

'Does that mean you're going to talk to yourself for a while, then?' Magnus asked with a grin as Corvinus walked off.

'Very funny. If you want to do something useful, make sure the townspeople are burying the dead and getting the corpses out of the lake; we should leave no trace of this camp. And then go and search what's left of the chief's tent; I imagine that there will be quite a bit of money stashed away there, Capella's purse for a start.'

Magnus nodded to his slave standing a little way off in quiet thought; his face registered no emotion. 'I won't ask Ziri to help, considering the circumstances.'

'How is he?'

'He seems to be fine; as I'm sure we all would be having committed a double fratricide followed by a patricide.'

'Well, there's no doubting his loyalty to you and me after that.'

'Yes, that's true, but what a way to prove it. I don't know what gods the Marmaridae have but it's going to take a lot to appease them if he doesn't want to live the rest of his life under a curse.'

Vespasian glanced at Ziri, taking in his youth. 'Do you think that he'll know how to do that?'

'I don't know; but he'll have to find a way. What he did ain't natural and nothing good can come out of something that ain't natural.'

'Apart from saving our lives, you mean?'

Magnus grunted and stalked off.

Vespasian made his way towards Capella, wondering just what sort of death Ziri would have suffered at the hands of his father and brothers, had they captured him, for him to have been able to kill them so easily and apparently without feeling.

'I am Titus Flavius Vespasianus, quaestor of this province, and you, Statilius Capella, are an imbecile,' Vespasian informed Capella upon finding him.

'That's a very quick judgement to come to about someone whom you've only just met, young man,' Capella replied; he had his hands and neck bound to the post that he was sitting against. He was much older than Vespasian had expected, early- to mid-forties, but still with a good head of curly, black hair, a lined but handsome face and a trim physique. He was surrounded by a strong smell of faeces; he had been obliged to defecate where he sat.

'Who else but an imbecile would go off into the desert with a small escort in search of a tribe of slavers in order to buy camels off them?'

Capella smiled. 'Ah, you've been talking to Flavia. Well, release me then, seeing as she must have sent you all this way to rescue me; she's very persuasive, I know.'

'All in good time; first of all we have to discuss the terms of your release.'

'Meaning?'

'Meaning that over a hundred men, expensively trained Roman auxiliaries, have lost their lives in finding you; not to mention the loss of over a hundred and twenty horses and another thirty mules and all the equipment that they were carrying. That amounts to a good few thousand denarii, which, seeing as you are the cause of all that financial loss, it would seem only right that you should reimburse.'

'And you no doubt think that I'm also obliged to you personally?'

'Naturally.'

'And if I refuse?'

'Then the whole enterprise would be a tragic and colossal waste of time and money. We came all this way and couldn't find you.'

Capella burst into laughter despite the rope constricting his throat. 'You'd leave me here?'

'I wouldn't leave you tied to that post, no; but yes, I would leave you in Siwa to make your own way back and more than likely fall into the hands of the Marmaridae again. What would give you the right to enjoy my protection on the journey back to Cyrene if you refuse to pay Rome for the damage that your reckless actions have caused?'

'I see your point, quaestor, if you look at it that way and assume that my actions were reckless; which indeed they would have been had I really been trying to buy camels from slavers.'

'You weren't, then?'

'Young man, if I'd wanted to do that, do you really think that I would have come all the way out here when I could have sailed a hundred miles along the coast from Apollonia to the Marmaridae's grazing grounds and bought camels from them there, negotiating from the safety of a ship as I have done many times before? Of course not, that would be imbecilic.'

'Then why did you tell Flavia that?'

'Cut me loose and you may get an answer.'

Vespasian had little choice; feeling slightly stupid, he took his sword to the ropes. All around, the wails of the captives were turning to shouts of joy as Corvinus' auxiliaries moved through the corral cutting the bonds of the free and freed; only the slaves were left sitting glumly against their posts to await their fate.

'That's better,' Capella said, rubbing his sore wrists and walking back towards the corral's entrance. 'Now I'm going to wash my arse in the lake and then I would appreciate a clean tunic, a loincloth and something to eat.'

Vespasian followed him. 'You said that you'd answer my question.'

'I said that I might, but fair enough; I told Flavia that I was buying camels because I couldn't tell her what I was really doing. I told her that I would be back in forty days because I knew that if I wasn't she would persuade someone like you to come and find me. And I was right because here you are; she is very hard to refuse, as you've evidently found out.'

'I'm here because I was told that a Roman citizen had probably been taken as a slave,' Vespasian replied airily.

'Bollocks; you're here because you wanted to impress Flavia.'

'Don't be ridiculous, it was my duty,' Vespasian blustered.

Capella smiled at him. 'Don't feel ashamed about it, I don't blame you one bit and, who knows, if you impress her enough she might even leave me for you, and I wouldn't blame her either.'

'She struck me as being very loyal to you.'

'Oh she is, and will continue to be so until someone else can command her loyalty. She likes to make sure that her loyalty is well rewarded, shall we say. Anyway, she's done her job and saved me from a very unpleasant end to my life.'

'Which you must pay for; as well as recompensing me for my efforts.'

'Quaestor, I'm sure that my patron for this trip will be only too delighted to pay out a measly few thousand denarii, if you bring me back to Cyrene with what I'm carrying for him. As to what *you* want, you'll have to ask her yourself.'

Vespasian frowned and glanced at Capella, wondering if he really had made his desire for Flavia so obvious. 'You'd give Flavia to me; why?'

'Because I'm tiring of her; she's a big drain on my income and very demanding – although her charms go some way to making up for that. If you're rash enough to take on the expense then you're welcome to her, but I couldn't give her to you; it would have to be Flavia's decision. So let's take that as agreed, then, and get going once your men have retrieved my possessions.' Capella stopped by the corral's entrance and proffered his forearm, smiling genially.

Vespasian took it, stunned that Capella would so easily give up such a woman. 'You're very generous, Capella.'

'Am I?'

'Quaestor, you'd better come and look at this,' Corvinus called from over by the tents, interrupting them.

Vespasian turned and walked towards him. 'What is it?'

'Magnus has uncovered a chest buried beneath the chief's tent.'

'Ah good,' Capella exclaimed, following, 'that'll be mine.'

They found Corvinus watching Magnus and Ziri heaving a small wooden chest out of a shallow hole in the sand.

Vespasian pointed at Ziri. 'What's he doing helping?'

'He insisted; showed me where to look, as a matter of fact,' Magnus replied as they put the chest down next to a pile of valuables retrieved from the tent; two keys were tied to a handle.

'Yes, that is mine,' Capella confirmed.

'How can you prove it?' Corvinus asked him, as Vespasian bent down and untied the keys.

'That's simple. I could tell you what's in there and then let you open it, but I don't think you'll thank me if I did.'

Vespasian slipped the keys into the locks at either end of the chest. 'Why not?'

'Because the chest may be mine but the contents belong to my patron. I'd completed his business here in Siwa and was on my way back to Cyrene when the Marmaridae caught me. If my patron were to find out that you'd seen what I'm carrying for him, he would be obliged to kill you.'

Vespasian looked at Magnus. 'What do you think?'

'I think that it depends on who his patron is.'

Capella nodded his approval. 'Your man is very wise, Vespasian; it's always best to keep out of imperial politics, if you can avoid it. My patron is – how should I put it? – almost at the top of the imperial tree.'

Vespasian took the keys out of the locks.

Dawn was breaking and Vespasian surveyed the camp; the townsmen and released captives had worked hard overnight. All trace of the burned tents and dead bodies had been buried; areas of damper sand marked the positions of the pits, but they would soon dry out.

Everything salvageable had been loaded onto the camels and the hundred or so slaves had been roped into lines with their hands tied behind their backs. The freed captives and the towns-folk had formed up into a rough column; they were ready to move back to the town.

'Lead off, Corvinus,' Vespasian ordered.

With a sharp word of command from their prefect the auxil-iaries leading the column moved forward.

'Let's hope that the Marmaridae come to the conclusion that their caravan was buried by the sandstorm in the desert and not by those townspeople in this place,' Vespasian said to Magnus as they watched the column shamble forward, 'otherwise they'll be in the shit.'

Magnus shrugged. 'Perhaps that'll teach them to observe the laws of hospitality in future instead of getting their guests drunk and then selling them.'

'Well, they'll have all those slaves to sell next time the Marmaridae come calling; by rights I should try and reunite them with their owners but I think that would be virtually impos-sible, so I've given them to the townspeople in exchange for everything that we need to get back across the desert.'

'I take it that you had a successful little chat with Capella, seeing as he seems to be coming with us.'

'Yes, very successful, thank you.'

'And?'

'And he said that his patron would reimburse the loss to the province.'

'And?'

'And that he would let me have Flavia, if I asked her myself; and she so wished.'

'As simple as that?'

'Yes.'

Magnus started laughing.

'What's so funny?' Vespasian asked, annoyed.

'He's sharp, that one.'

'What makes you say that?'

'I'll bet he said: take her if she wants to go, she costs me a fortune and I'm getting bored with her.'

'Words along those lines, yes,' Vespasian admitted, taken aback by the accuracy of Magnus' guess.

'You've been had.'

'What do you mean?'

'You should have made him swear to repudiate her, then she wouldn't have had much choice but to go with you or find herself alone in a strange province without anyone to protect her. Whereas what he's done is say: go and ask her, I don't care.'

'And I will,' Vespasian asserted through gritted teeth.

'Come on, sir, don't you get it? She's going to take one look at you, a quaestor in one of the least prestigious provinces in the whole Empire, who'll be lucky to finish his term with enough cash to keep a woman like her in jewellery and perfume for the next couple of years; and then she'll look at her rich man who has the contract to supply wild animals to the circuses in Africa, probably owns his own ship and has contacts in high places. What is she going to decide?'

'I am wealthy, I've got my estates.'

'Yes, but that money is tied up in land, mules and slaves. She's not going to want to go to the jewellers with you dragging a braying mule behind you to pay with, is she? Nor is she going to want to live on the estates surrounded by bumpkins; she'll want a fine house on the Esquiline.'

'I've got cash,' Vespasian almost shouted; his voice had gone up in tone.

'Not as much as Capella.'

Vespasian opened his mouth and then realised that it was futile to argue; Magnus was right. He put a hand to his forehead, massaging it for a few moments. 'He's offered me the chance to have her, knowing that she'll say no; his obligation to me is then discharged without costing him a copper coin. Brilliant!'

'I'd say so.'

'The clever bastard; and I can't now go back on the agreement we made.' Trying but failing to hide the embarrassment that he felt for being so duped, he strode off, leaving Magnus with an amused look on his face.

Walking briskly up the column as it entered the palm forest, Vespasian reflected upon his naïvety. He had been carried away by his own self-importance in everything that he had done since meeting Flavia, thinking that he was acting in his own interests; whereas he now realised that it had been Capella, a man older and cannier than he, who had played him all along. Now Capella was to deny him the prize that he had used to tempt him: Flavia.

Capella had been right: he was here solely to impress her.

He remembered his last conversations with his grandmother, Tertulla, and knew that she would be horrified at his recent behaviour. He had not been following an instinct in his heart that he deemed to be right but had been acting upon a base desire, using his power in an immature and rash way solely for his own ends, and all those men had died because of his arrogance. He had forgotten the ideals that he had espoused when he had beheld Rome for the first time – back when he had felt it wrong even to take a bribe – and he was heartily ashamed.

'Quaestor!' a voice from the heart of the column called, bringing Vespasian out of his damning introspection.

Vespasian turned to see a man in his early thirties push his way towards him through the ex-captives. 'What is it?' he asked, pleased to turn his mind to other things.

'Firstly I must thank you for saving us from a living death in the desert,' the man said as he fell into step beside him.

'You should thank the men who died in doing so; not me,' Vespasian responded, looking side-on at the man; judging from his features and headdress Vespasian supposed him to be Jewish.

'It is the mark of a compassionate man to give such an answer,' the Jew replied. 'However, you led them to our rescue when you could have just remained in Cyrene and left us to our fate.'

'If only you knew the truth of the matter,' Vespasian said, almost to himself.

'Whatever the truth may be it cannot change the fact that you are responsible for our freedom, so all the people here are in your debt; I for one will never forget that.'

Vespasian grunted his acknowledgement. 'And secondly?'

The Jew looked at him quizzically. 'What?'

'You said "firstly", so I assume that there'll be a "secondly".'

The Jew carried on staring at him for a few paces as they walked along. 'Forgive me for asking, quaestor, but you look very much like a man I met in Judaea, a good man: Titus Flavius Sabinus.'

'He's my elder brother,' Vespasian confirmed, wiping the sweat from his brow as the sun and the temperature both rose higher.

'Then I am doubly in your debt because he hastened the death of a kinsman of mine on the cross; he had his centurion finish him cleanly with a spear rather than break his legs and let him die in agony. He then returned the body to us.'

'Why was this kinsman crucified?'

'That is something that no one has ever really understood.'

'He must have been found guilty of some crime.'

'The priests wanted him stoned for blasphemy because he preached that we Jews should put aside our ten commandments and follow just one new one: love your neighbour as you love yourself.'

'But if he was crucified he must have been judged according to Roman law.'

'Yes, and yet no reason for the sentence was ever read out. But what is done cannot be undone. His teachings live on among my people, beyond his death, through those who were closest to him and admired his compassion, although we are now persecuted for doing so.'

'We?'

'Yes, I am one of those who preach his words.'

'Then why aren't you back in Judaea doing so?'

'Because there's no place in his vision of Judaism for the priests and they wish to hold onto their power, so they hound us relentlessly.'

'And so you ran away.'

'No, quaestor, I'm a merchant, I trade in tin; I have to earn a living as well as preach and so I preach to the Jewish communities in the ports that I pass through. I was on my way to the tin mines in southern Britannia, outside of the Empire, when the Marmaridae captured me and two companions as we filled our water caskets between Alexandria and Apollonia; which brings me to the "secondly".'

'Which is?'

'After I was captured my ship must have sailed on to Apollonia to take on fresh supplies and to drop off a friend of mine who was returning to Cyrene; but after that I don't know whether it carried on west or whether it turned back to Judaea because the crew were afraid of going on without me, as only I among them have made the voyage to Britannia before.'

'So what do you want me to do about it?'

'I need a small favour from you, quaestor, although I'm aware that I'm already heavily in your debt.'

Vespasian looked at the man; there was no guile in his eyes. 'Name it.'

'To know which way they went, so that I can follow them, I need you to look at the port aedile's records; I assume that he sends you a copy every day.'

'He does; come and see me when we get back to Cyrene.'

'Thank you, quaestor,' the man said, visibly pleased. 'My name is Yosef; I'll ask for you at the Governor's Residence.'

'I'll make sure that you are expected, Yosef.'

*

The column arrived at the town shortly after midday and Vespasian slept for the remainder of the day and right through the night. It was his first decent period of sleep since arriving in Siwa and not even the constant hammering and sawing of carpenters constructing the sixty sleds that he had ordered could disturb his slumber.

'You should wake up now, sir,' Magnus said, shaking Vespasian's shoulder. 'It's almost dawn and the column is forming up.'

Vespasian roused himself, feeling much rejuvenated and as ready as he would ever be to face the arduous three-hundred-mile return journey to Cyrene.

He tied on his army sandals, belted his tunic and then followed Magnus out into the torch-lit agora. The camels stood in three rows of twenty; each had a sled attached to it, piled high with full water-skins. These, Vespasian hoped, together with the skins loaded onto the camels' backs, would provide them with sufficient water to make the crossing without having to rely on the Marmaridae's wells. He planned to give these a wide berth, if at all possible, for fear of his ill-protected column falling prey to the slavers. The sleds would also carry the weak, whose numbers would grow during the long trek as the skins were emptied and discarded. Forty or so of the freed captives of Egyptian origin had elected to stay in Siwa to await the next caravan to Alexandria; the rest, just over eighty, were bound for Cyrene, knowing only too well the hazards of the journey.

With a harsh word to the headman of the town reminding him that those staying behind were his companions and therefore under Amun's protection, Vespasian mounted one of the twelve horses that they had been able to exchange, in addition to the water-skins, food and sleds, for all the slaves and a few camels, and gave the order to move out. The first rays of the sun, now cresting the eastern horizon, cast long shadows before them as Vespasian led the slow-moving column from the town and ventured out once more into the unforgiving desert.

CHAPTER VI

THE PLATEAU OF Cyrene had been growing larger for the past three days. Vespasian estimated that the foothills were now less than ten miles away and they would be camping among the sparse vegetation that clung to their lower reaches that evening.

It was the morning of the sixteenth day since leaving Siwa and he knew now that they would make it back. There had been many times on the painfully slow journey across the baking, featureless wilderness that he had doubted it. The auxiliaries without horses, and those few of the ex-captives who were able to, had ridden on camels but the rest had been obliged to walk. Starting before dawn and carrying on until well after sundown, with a halt for a few hours during the day in order to avoid the worst ravages of the midday heat, they had managed to average about twenty miles a day. As the water was used up, more space had become available on the sleds for the women and children and the weaker of the men; they spent the journey being dragged over the rough ground, semi-delirious in the scalding heat. The first death from sunstroke had been on the fourth day and not a day had passed since without at least one more body being abandoned on the desert floor to mark the progress of the column.

Vespasian had noticed Yosef tending to the sick as they lay on the sleds, trying to keep their heads covered and helping them to cups of water during the few instances in the day when he, Vespasian, allowed the precious skins to be broached.

Sitting at ease upon a camel, Ziri had guided them; keeping to the south of the Marmaridae's wells and then veering back to the northwest, he had avoided the routes frequented by the slavers at the cost of extending the journey by a couple of days. Seemingly impervious to the heat, swathed in his woollen robe and head-dress, he had maintained Vespasian's, Magnus' and Capella's morale by his attempts to speak Latin – his proficiency was growing by the day – and his throaty renditions of Marmaridae songs. On a few occasions, as a more poignant ballad came to an end, Vespasian caught him looking mournfully towards his people's grazing lands to the north as if saying farewell to the life that he could never know again.

As the day wore on and the foothills got ever closer, the speed of the column seemed to increase as the desire for relief from the torment that they had endured put energy into the legs of all those still obliged to walk. Before long they started the ascent to the plateau, weaving through the huge boulders and wiry scrub that littered the ground. A pair of jackals – the first signs of life that they had seen since leaving Siwa – darted across their path, startling Vespasian's horse.

'How do you get the slaves to Garama, Ziri?' Vespasian wondered, having calmed his mount. He looked back and pointed at the bedraggled column as it trailed up the gentle incline. 'They're almost dead after three hundred miles; Garama's seven hundred.'

'Garama, very slow, two moons full,' Ziri replied, flashing his white teeth. 'One well three days, slaves live. One well four days, slaves die.'

'It's worth the effort, though,' Capella said, 'the Garamantes pay handsomely for slaves and can afford to; it's a surprisingly rich kingdom.'

'Have you been there?' Vespasian asked as he kicked his horse forward again.

'Once, to trade slaves for wild beasts; I can get a lion there for just two slaves. It's an amazing place; there are six or seven towns built upon a range of hills that just rise up out of the desert. The Garamantes have dug wells and found a seemingly endless supply of water, which they channel through irrigation canals.'

'Much water,' Ziri agreed, nodding his head.

'They have fountains and running water in the streets, in the middle of the desert – it's incredible. They grow wheat and barley and figs as well as vegetables; they even grow grass and graze cattle on it. They're completely self-sufficient apart from wine and olive oil and of course the one commodity that they need most: slaves to work the land. There are thousands of them, more slaves, in fact, than Garamantes.'

'When the slaves realise that, the Garamantes will be in for a nasty shock,' Magnus put in.

'Oh, they're well guarded, in fact—' Capella was cut short as his horse shied as a couple more jackals raced across its path. As he got it back under control a gazelle sprinted past following the jackals. 'Shit, I've never seen that before: jackals chased by a gazelle.'

Vespasian laughed and turned to Capella; the laughter froze on his face as he realised the true cause of the animals' flight. A massive shape leapt up onto a boulder and, without pausing, descended, with a bellowing, guttural roar, upon the wild-beast master.

'Lion!' Vespasian yelled, pulling on his mount's reins as the lion crashed onto Capella, sinking its razor-like claws into his shoulders and hurling him, screaming, to the ground.

The roar of the beast mauling its prey drowned out the neighing of the horses as they bucked and reared, throwing their riders; Ziri's camel bolted. Vespasian landed with a bone-jarring thud next to Magnus, three paces away from the now limp Capella. They froze rigid, staring at the huge male lion; it raised its mane-crowned head and snarled at them, baring its bloodied teeth while pawing Capella's chest, shredding his tunic and ripping his flesh.

'Where's my fucking hunting spear when I need it?' Magnus muttered, slowly drawing his spatha.

'Propping up a camel,' Vespasian replied, reaching carefully for his sword.

'We're going to have to kill this bastard, sir; if we run it'll have us as sure as a vestal plays with herself.'

The lion gave another heart-stopping roar as Corvinus came running up with a dozen auxiliaries.

'Stay back, Corvinus,' Vespasian ordered while keeping his eyes fixed firmly on the lion. 'Any sudden movement and it will have one of us.'

The lion's tail flicked menacingly from side to side.

'One of us is going to have to face its charge,' Magnus said out of the corner of his mouth, 'while the other takes it from the side.'

'Well, you were the one who was so keen to go lion hunting; I'll take it from the side.'

'I was hoping that you would've forgotten about that.'

Vespasian started to edge to his left. The lion tossed its head and gave out another mighty roar as it spotted the movement; Vespasian froze.

'Here puss, here puss,' Magnus called out.

With a low growl, the lion turned its attention back to Magnus, and Vespasian carried on moving cautiously a couple more paces to the left.

'Ready, sir?'

'As I'll ever be.'

Magnus tensed himself; the lion crouched on Capella's chest, sensing a threat. With a yell Magnus leapt forward, sword arm extended; the lion pounced straight at his head. Vespasian sprang to his feet and ran, aiming the tip of his spatha at the beast's muscular neck as Magnus ducked under the outstretched paws, punching his sword blindly up at the mass of fur flying over him. The lion twisted around, swiping a paw at Magnus' back as Vespasian jumped at it, thrusting his spatha into its mane; with an agonised roar the beast thrashed round at his new assailant in a blur of fleet motion, snapping his teeth at him, catching his tunic sleeve and bringing its hindleg up to claw its way bloodily down Vespasian's left thigh. Magnus propelled himself upright, punching his shoulder into the beast's soft underbelly to send its hindquarters up into the air and pushing its head forward and down. It crashed to the ground, dragging Vespasian with it by his sleeve; he landed on its right shoulder blade, his spatha still lodged in the neck. The lion twisted onto its back, throwing Vespasian off it as Magnus dived between the claw-tipped legs scrabbling in the air and thrust his sword into the midriff, rotating it as it sliced through muscle and gut and pushed it on up under the ribcage. With the unnatural strength of a desperate animal, the lion flashed a giant paw at Magnus' chest; claws sliced through his skin. The blow knocked him away, leaving his sword still buried within the creature. Vespasian grabbed the sword, heaved his body up and fell on its hilt as the lion sank a claw into his shoulder. Screaming with agony, he pushed down with all his might and forced the point into the beating heart of the beast. He felt the lion's claw in his shoulder tense as its heart exploded inside it; its thrashing hindlegs suddenly stiffened then went limp, and it fell back pulling Vespasian with it, the claw still lodged in his flesh.

Magnus got painfully to his feet and stumbled over to him. 'Hold still, sir,' he said, and grasping the huge paw he prised it off Vespasian's shoulder, tearing the claw out of the puncture.

Vespasian felt dizzy with pain. 'Fuck me, that was one savage beast,' he said through gritted teeth.

'But what a fight, eh?' Magnus grinned, breathing heavily; blood oozed from four slashes running diagonally across his chest.

'Worthy of the circus back home,' Corvinus agreed, walking up to them. 'You two have got balls of iron taking on that thing, I'll give you that much.'

'It didn't give us much of a choice in the matter,' Magnus muttered while helping Vespasian to his feet.

'It didn't give poor Capella any choice,' Vespasian said, limping over to the twisted and bloodied form of the wild-beast master. 'Get the column formed up again, Corvinus.'

He knelt next to Capella and gently turned his head. His eyes slowly opened and focused on Vespasian; his breathing was light and irregular and his chest was shredded.

'A delicious irony, wouldn't you say?' Capella wheezed; he essayed a thin smile as blood spilled from both corners of his mouth. 'The beast master killed by the beast.'

'You're not dead yet,' Vespasian replied as Magnus joined them.

'I will be soon, I can't feel my body. Now listen, Vespasian, I'm forced to trust you; you must ensure that my chest gets to my patron. He's a freedman in the household of Claudius, the son of Antonia; his name is Narcissus.'

Vespasian kept his face neutral. 'I know of him,' he said, not quite truthfully.

'Then you may know that he's a ruthless man and not to be crossed.'

That had not been Vespasian's experience of Narcissus but he could well imagine that Capella's assessment of him was correct. 'Most people who move in those circles are.'

'It's imperative that you get the chest to him without it coming to the notice of anyone else in the imperial family. That's why I met his agent in Siwa, so as to smuggle it out of Egypt. Had it been put on a ship in Alexandria it would have been inspected by the customs officials, impounded and no doubt given to the prefect, Aulus Avilius Flaccus. He's completely loyal to Tiberius and would have sent the chest to him, which is something that my patron would wish to avoid at all costs.'

'Then what you're asking of me is treason, isn't it? What makes you think that I will agree?'

'Money. Take the keys; they were around my neck so they should be close by. In the chest there's some gold, not much, fifty aurei or so, what's left of my travelling expenses.'

'That's not enough.'

'My business isn't done with cash. There's also a bankers' draft, payable to the bearer, for a quarter of a million denarii, drawn from Thales of Alexandria; it's redeemable either with him for a five per cent fee or with the Cloelius brothers in the Forum Romanum for twenty per cent.'

Magnus sucked in a breath through his teeth. 'Either way that's a lot of money, sir.'

'Narcissus will consider it well spent if you make sure the other contents end up with him.'

'And these other contents are?' Vespasian asked, wondering what could be so valuable.

'Land deeds. Over the last three years Narcissus has been buying up huge tracts of land in Egypt on behalf of Claudius.'

'What's wrong with that? His mother, Antonia, owns masses of land in Egypt.'

'Yes, but she's not a potential heir to the Purple.' Capella's voice was getting fainter; he was fading. 'In a year with a good harvest the income from this land is enormous; Narcissus has made fortunes for his master.'

'Fortunes with which he hopes to make him emperor?'

Capella nodded weakly, his eyes closed. 'Exactly, by buying the loyalty of the Praetorian Guard; Claudius must be the next Emperor.'

'What about Caligula?'

'Caligula will be the ruin of Rome.'

'Caligula is my friend.'

Capella's eyes half opened in weak alarm. 'Gods below, what have I done?' he croaked; his breathing became more erratic. 'Narcissus will have my family killed for this.'

Capella took another faint breath, then, with a choke, died.

'What are you going to do, sir?' Magnus asked as Vespasian closed Capella's eyes.

'Find the keys to that chest.' Vespasian got up with difficulty and started looking around; the gashes on his thigh stung and his shoulder throbbed.

Magnus made no attempt to help him. 'I mean with that chest.'

'Take it to Antonia, of course, and let her decide what to do with it.'

'I've got a much better idea. Why not just take the gold and the draft and then burn the rest of it? That way you'll keep well clear of imperial politics. Last time you got involved I seem to remember nearly being thrown off a cliff.'

'Found them,' Vespasian said, bending down and picking up the missing keys. 'I'm afraid it's too late for that; I'm already involved. When Capella doesn't show up in Rome with the land deeds, Narcissus will do some investigation; it won't take long for his agents to find out that I rescued him from the Marmaridae but he died on the return journey. He will assume, rightly, that I have the deeds and, even though he's in my debt, he'll come after me to get them. If I've burned them, he won't believe me and I'll have nothing to use against him. So I've only got two options: give them to him immediately and incur Antonia's wrath or give them to Antonia and incur Narcissus' wrath.'

'Antonia needn't find out.'

Vespasian looked at his friend with raised eyebrows. 'You really think that would be possible?'

'Well no, I suppose not; she'll have a spy in Claudius' household. In which case you're right, Antonia's your best bet.'

'I think so, she'll be able to protect me from Narcissus much better than he'd be able to protect me from her; and besides, if I went against her I would lose all contact with Caenis.'

'That may not be such a bad thing, if you don't mind me saying.'

'Why?'

'Well, with Capella dead who's going to have the job of looking after Flavia? You struck me as being rather keen to fill that particular vacancy, if you take my meaning?'

Vespasian smiled. 'Oh I do, but this is a rare stroke of luck; the money in that chest will help me to set up both of them.'

Vespasian was becoming increasingly concerned as they approached Cyrene's southern gate in the evening two days later; what had seemed from a distance to be just the normal discharge of fumes from the city's bakeries, forges and cooking fires was now quite obviously thicker over the northeastern part of the city.

'It looks like there's a fire in the Jewish Quarter in the lower city,' he said to Magnus, who was riding between him and Ziri.

'Well, as long as it doesn't spread to the bath house in the Governor's Residence, I couldn't give a fuck,' Magnus replied, scratching his heavily bandaged chest, 'I've got a whole desert to scrape off me.'

Vespasian felt his injured shoulder; it still throbbed incessantly and had started to ooze yellow pus. 'You're right, I'm not going to do anything either until I've had this cleaned and cauterised. I'll send for Marcius Festus, the prefect of the auxiliary cohort, when I get back; whatever it is that's burning I'm sure he's got his men dealing with it.'

They clattered through the gate, strangely devoid of beggars, and headed towards the Governor's Residence at the heart of the city. Behind them the column dissolved as the exhausted people went their separate ways knowing that they could expect no more help from Rome. The lucky few had homes within the city but the rest would have to rely on the charity of kin, friends or strangers to take them to their final destinations.

As the last of the ex-captives disappeared down side streets the lack of anyone else abroad became apparent to Vespasian. 'Corvinus,' he called back to the cavalry prefect behind him, 'does this look normal to you?'

'No, and look at the windows, most of them are shuttered.'

'Perhaps there're some games going on,' Magnus suggested. 'There is an amphitheatre here, isn't there?'

'Yes, but even then there would be a few people around, those who couldn't get in or the squeamish.'

'I hate the squeamish.'

Upon reaching the Forum they found it deserted too. Vespasian eased himself down from his horse in front of the Governor's Residence and looked at Corvinus and the small body of surviving auxiliaries. 'Prefect, you and your men are dismissed, thank them for me.'

'What's left of them,' Corvinus replied sourly, 'and I doubt that your thanks will recompense them for their lost comrades or the hardships that they have faced on this ill-considered mission that you led them on.'

'Take the camels and sell them and use the money to raise replacements,' Vespasian offered, ignoring the jibe.

'Very well.'

'You are welcome to spend the night here and dine with me before you return to Barca.'

'Thank you, quaestor, but I prefer to choose my own dinner companions.' Corvinus turned his mount. 'You'll be hearing from me one day, Vespasian,' he said menacingly as he kicked his horse and cantered away; his men followed with the camels.

'You were right,' Magnus observed, 'he really doesn't like you.'

'Sod him,' Vespasian said, mounting the steps. 'I held out the olive branch to him and he didn't take it. If he wants to be my enemy let him.'

'Let's hope that you don't come to regret that.'

'Quaestor, thank the gods that you're back,' Quintillius, the quaestor's clerk, said rushing over to Vespasian as he entered the atrium.

'What's going on, Quintillius?'

'The Jews have been fighting among themselves for the last three days; there have been hundreds of deaths all over the city.'

'Where are Marcius Festus and his auxiliaries?'

'He's managed to contain the fighting now, just to the Jewish Quarter.'

'Have him come here to report to me and get the doctor to attend to my wounds.'

'We've managed to put most of the fires out but there are a couple still burning in the area controlled by the rioters,' Festus reported, holding an oil lamp for the doctor to see better in the fading light. 'There're a couple of thousand of them but we've bottled them up into eight streets in the Jewish Quarter; they've built barricades, which I plan to storm at dawn tomorrow.'

'So you've no idea what started the violence?' Vespasian asked Festus through gritted teeth as the doctor swabbed out his shoulder wound with vinegar.

Festus shook his head; in his late thirties he was a career soldier who had worked his way up from the ranks. 'No,

109

quaestor, not for certain but it seemed to start in the lower city's agora. There's been a young man preaching there regularly and more and more people have been coming to hear him. I've watched him a few times but he never says anything against Caesar or Rome so I've ignored it as you ordered.'

'What does he preach?'

'I don't know; stuff about their Jewish god. I've heard him say "redemption at the End of Days" a few times but I don't really pay much attention; he always has a young woman with two children with him but she never says anything.'

'Ah yes, I remember seeing him a couple of days before I left for Siwa; do you know who he is?' Vespasian grimaced as the doctor began applying stitches to his shoulder.

'All I know is that he arrived on a Judaean trading ship just over a month ago.'

'What sort of trader?'

'Tin, according to the port aedile's records.'

'Tin? Is the ship still here?'

'No, the records show that it left the day after the violence started.'

'Right, we'd better crush this outrage tomorrow and then find that preacher. If he's the cause of all this, I'll send him to the Governor to have him nailed up. Quintillius!'

'Yes, quaestor?' the clerk said, bustling in through the door.

'A Jew by the name of Yosef will be asking for an interview; I need to see him as soon as he arrives.'

'Yes, quaestor.'

'And find out where that woman who came to see me, Flavia Domitilla, is staying; I would like her to come to dinner tomorrow, once this Jewish problem has been resolved.'

'Yes, quaestor. Will that be all?'

Vespasian flinched as the doctor began cleaning the gashes on his thigh; he waved a hand, the clerk bowed and retreated.

'Thank you, Festus, you've done well, return to your men; I'll come down at first light to assess the situation before you storm the barricades. Have the Jewish elders arrested and brought there to explain their people's behaviour; I want to know if there's any reason to show these rioters mercy.'

Vespasian strode through the atrium in uniform before dawn the following morning eager to quash the riot, as he was keen to turn a clear mind to the seduction of Flavia Domitilla that evening.

Magnus was waiting for him, sitting on the edge of one of the clerks' vacant desks. 'Good morning, sir, how are you feeling?'

'Much the same as you, I expect: stiff,' he replied, rubbing his heavily strapped thigh. 'But at least my shoulder's stopped throbbing. What are you doing up? You don't have to come.'

'And miss out on a nice bit of street fighting? Bollocks; I was in the Urban Cohorts, if you remember? We used to love it when the racing factions rucked with each other after the races. They were the only fights we'd get; great fun they were, unless we had to lay into the Greens, in which case I'd ease off a bit, if you take my meaning?'

'Well, there won't be any Greens among this lot.'

'Right, I'll imagine that they're all Reds then, the bastards.'

'Quaestor,' Quintillius said, coming through the main door, 'that man Yosef is among the petitioners waiting outside.'

'Good. Did you find Flavia Domitilla?'

'No, quaestor, there wasn't enough time last night but I'll send some more men out as soon as it's light.'

'Do that.' Vespasian stepped out into the cool pre-dawn air.

The crowd of petitioners immediately started waving scrolls in his face and calling out the requests and boons that they desired of him.

'Wait here until I return,' he shouted, brushing away the supplicating hands, 'I'll deal with you then.' He spotted Yosef at the back of the crowd and pointed at him. 'Yosef, walk with me.'

'Yes, quaestor.' Yosef broke off from the crowd and fell in next to Vespasian as he descended the steps to the Forum. Magnus shoved away the last couple of persistent supplicants.

'Did this man to whom you were giving passage to Apollonia have a young woman with two children accompanying him?'

'There was a woman with two children on the ship but she wasn't accompanying Shimon; she was making her own journey to southern Gaul to escape the persecution she faced in Judaea at the hands of the priests.'

'Well, she seems to be accompanying this Shimon now; she's been with him while he preaches his insurrection.'

'Shimon wouldn't preach insurrection.'

'No? Then explain to me why the Jewish Quarter of this city is in uproar.'

'That's not Shimon's doing; he preaches peace, as do I. We follow the true teachings of my kinsman, Yeshua.'

'Was he the man who you said was crucified?'

'Yes, quaestor. He was a good man who believed that we Jews should have love and compassion for one another because the End of Days is close at hand and only the righteous will be saved on that Day of Judgement.'

'Saved from what?' Vespasian asked as they left the Forum; debris from the last three days of fighting littered the ground.

'Eternal death; they will live forever, along with the resurrected righteous, in the earthly paradise under God's law that will follow the End of Days.'

'And this just applies to the Jews?'

'Any man can convert, provided he follows God's law as set down in the five books of the Torah and accepts circumcision.'

'What's that?' Magnus asked as he stepped over a smashed market stall.

'It's the removal of the foreskin.'

Vespasian looked at Yosef in disbelief. 'I'll never understand you Jews; do you seriously expect me to believe that to become righteous a man has to slice off his foreskin?'

Yosef shrugged. 'It's God's law.'

'Well, you're welcome to it if it makes you happy but stop trying to force it upon other people.'

'We don't, we only preach to our fellow Jews who've lapsed.

112

Yeshua was quite clear upon that subject: we shouldn't take the word of God to the Gentiles or even to the Samaritans who follow a heretical form of the Torah.'

Vespasian grunted and walked on in silence, down towards the lower city, wondering why these people thought that they had an exclusive insight into the will of God to the extent that they could accept no one else's point of view.

Turning right, off the lower city's riot-damaged main street, as the first rays of the sun hit the high-altitude clouds with an orange glow, Vespasian saw the centuries of auxiliaries forming up to the bawling of their centurions and optiones.

'What a fucking shambles,' Magnus declared as they passed by the ranks of the chain-mailed soldiers struggling to form a line in the semi-darkness, cursing one another as their oval shields became entangled with their neighbours' javelins and enduring the savage swipes of their centurions' vine-sticks.

'This'll be the first action that most of them have seen,' Vespasian informed him, wondering whether they would have the discipline to work methodically through the quarter, rooting out the rioters.

'And if they form a line like that it'll be their last as well.'

'Good morning, quaestor,' Festus said as they came to the head of the first century. 'The Jewish elders are waiting for you.'

'Thank you, prefect, have them brought here.' Vespasian peered down the street; in the dim light he could make out a substantial barricade about a hundred paces away.

Three old men with bushy grey beards and wearing long white robes and black and white mantles shuffled forward. Vespasian looked them up and down hoping that he might get some sense out of at least one of them.

'Who speaks for you?' he asked.

'I do, quaestor,' the middle of the three replied, 'my name is Menahem.'

'So tell me, Menahem, what caused all this?'

'A man preaching a heresy, quaestor.'

'Shimon?'

'You know him?'

'I know of him. What could he have said that could justify all this destruction and killing?'

'He has converted hundreds of our people to his way; they no longer follow our teaching.'

'Ah, so that's the problem, is it: you're all scared of losing your influence?'

'What he preaches is blasphemous.'

'I thought that the teaching of Yeshua is for Jews to love each other and follow the Torah – what's blasphemous about that?'

Menahem's eyes widened in surprise. 'You are knowledgeable for a Gentile, quaestor. You're right, there is nothing blasphemous about that; however, Shimon claims that Yeshua was the Messiah and the son of God. We cannot accept that.'

'So you told your people to kill him and his followers.'

'We didn't tell them to do anything. There was an agitator in the crowd, someone we'd never seen before; he started it when Shimon made another even more blasphemous claim.'

'Well?'

'That after Yeshua was executed he came back to life three days later as proof of the resurrection of the righteous.'

'What nonsense. And you did nothing to try and restrain your people?'

'After this claim the agitator addressed the crowd. He got them so worked up that they wouldn't listen to us; he said that the shortage of grain and failure of the silphium was God's judgement on us for listening to Yeshua's lies.'

'But that's been failing for years.'

Menahem shrugged. 'They're poor people made poorer by the failure of the crop and now can't afford the high grain prices so they're happy to blame any scapegoat. They threw themselves at Shimon's supporters while the agitator urged them on, shouting that they should get the woman and her children who are always with Shimon. She escaped with the children while Shimon's supporters held back our people, and since then there have been running battles in the streets as this agitator looks for them.'

'And so now they've barricaded themselves into the Jewish Quarter until they find them, I suppose?'

'I'm afraid so,' Menahem agreed sadly, looking towards the auxiliary centuries that had now managed to form up. 'This man is a fanatic; he's caused the deaths of a lot of our people already and a good few more will die before the day is out.'

'What does he look like?'

'He's quite short with bow legs and has half an ear missing.'

'Well, we should be able to recognise him from that. But tell me, Menahem, what has this man got against the woman and her children?'

'He said that in order to purify God's chosen people in Cyrene, so that He would make the silphium grow again, Yeshua's bloodline must be wiped out; he claimed that they were Yeshua's children.'

CHAPTER VII

T HE SUN HAD burst over the horizon and there was now enough light to be able to see any ambushes that may be lurking up the narrow alleys to the left and the right of the barricaded road. Looking ahead to the barricade of overturned carts, barrels and broken-up furniture, Vespasian could see a mass of men behind it; a few heads peered over, back towards the Romans. The houses beyond them were more dilapidated than in the rest of the city, attesting to the poverty of the Jewish Quarter.

'Order the advance, Festus,' he called to the auxiliary prefect standing next to him at the head of the first century, formed up eight abreast.

Magnus handed him an oval auxiliary shield. 'I can't believe that they're going to be stupid enough to resist us.'

'They're desperate – since the silphium started to fail they've been getting poorer and poorer. Now they believe this liar who tells them that if they kill two children then all their woes will disappear as their god will restore the crop.'

A *cornu* blared out four, deep, rumbling notes, and the *signiferi* of each century dipped their standards; the attack began.

'Shields up!' Festus shouted.

Fifty paces from the barricade Vespasian heard the tell-tale hiss of a volley of arrows.

Vespasian tightened his grip on his shield and hunched down behind it so that he could just see over its curved rim; he felt the auxiliary behind him raise his shield over his head and prayed that the man was experienced enough to hold it firm. An instant later came the staccato hammering of many iron-tipped arrows thumping into the leather-covered wooden roof above the century's heads. A few screams from within the ranks confirmed the lesser effectiveness of the oval shields in forming a perfect cover and the inexperience of some of the auxiliaries holding them.

The pounding of the soldiers' hobnailed sandals striking the paving stones in step reverberated off the brick walls to either side and around the makeshift wooden box encasing them.

'The fucking racing factions never shot arrows at us,' Magnus grumbled loudly beside him as two barbs from a second volley slammed into his shield with a sudden, double, vibrating report.

Vespasian felt the wind of a shot passing between the curved rims of his and Magnus' shields; with a gurgled cry the auxiliary behind him collapsed to the ground, his shield striking Vespasian's helmet with a ringing blow as he fell. He shook his head to clear it; a moment later he sensed another shield being thrust over him as the file behind closed up to seal the gap.

With twenty paces to go a third volley buffeted the century.

'Javelins ready; aim over the barricade,' Festus shouted as the last shots pounded into them. 'Shields down!'

The auxiliaries hefted their javelins overarm, ready to throw.

'Release!'

Seventy or so sleek missiles soared away from the advancing century, most clearing the top of the barricade, to rain down upon the unshielded defenders as they reloaded. Although not as heavy as a legionary *pilum*, the auxiliaries' javelins crunched through unprotected chests and skulls and skewered arms and legs, hurling men to the ground with bursts of blood and howls of pain.

A ragged volley of arrows followed without doing any damage to the advancing Romans.

'Charge!' Festus yelled over the screams of the wounded.

Drawing their swords, the auxiliaries broke into a trot, hunched behind their shields held firm before them.

Vespasian closed his eyes with the shock of impact as his shield crashed into the barricade; the auxiliary behind thrust his shield into his back pushing him forward as the weight of successive men down the file was added to the momentum. With a rasping of wood grating roughly over stone, the barricade shifted back a few feet, and then suddenly splintered apart as the century behind added their impetus to the heaving scrum. Gasping for breath, Vespasian was hurled forward among the flying debris of the disintegrating obstacle; his feet became entangled with a plank, sending him sprawling forward. He just managed to duck under the wild sword thrust of a bellowing defender and rammed the raised plume of his helmet into the man's groin. Clattering to the ground, Vespasian felt the auxiliary behind him thrust his sword into the exposed chest of his screaming adversary as he stepped past to fill the gap that his fall had created.

All around him Roman legs surged forward as he tried to regain his feet in among the chaos of the breakthrough. The yelling auxiliaries did not notice him in their eagerness to close with the poorly armed defenders, and his arms and legs suffered kicks and stampings before he was finally able to heave himself up and then move on to rejoin the surge.

Clearing the shattered barricade, he kept moving forward and realised that the enemy must have fled under the onslaught. His thought was confirmed a moment later by the low boom of a cornu sounding 'halt'.

He pushed through the panting auxiliaries, up to the front of the first century where he found Festus looking at a dozen or so prisoners kneeling fearfully on the ground amid the bloody litter of their dead comrades.

'Ah, quaestor, there you are,' the prefect said, looking relieved to see him, 'what do you want me to do with these? I was just about to have them executed.'

'No, leave them alive, prefect; if the Jews see that we're taking prisoners they might think it sensible to give up this ridiculous affair. Detail one of the less steady centuries to guard them and then let's fan the other ones out through the quarter and get this over with. Let all the centurions know that from now on I want as little killing as possible, and no women or children are to be harmed under any circumstances.'

As the first century moved deeper into the Jewish Quarter the scale of the killing became increasingly apparent; bodies lay everywhere either in groups marking the position of a fight or singly as if cut down in an attempt to escape. Most of them were male of varying ages but Vespasian saw a few women and children; however, none looked to him like the ones who had accompanied Shimon.

Working their way methodically down the main street, with the other centuries taking parallel routes, they had managed to break up a few skirmishes and relieve some houses under siege, sending the beleaguered occupants to safety, taking scores of prisoners and killing the more persistent rioters of either side. As the morning wore on the combined efforts of the cohort were forcing the violence into a smaller and smaller area.

'These Jews must fucking hate this new cult,' Magnus said, kicking a hairy, severed forearm towards the body that had evidently once owned it. 'I can't understand it. Just think of the chaos we'd have if we spent our time fighting among ourselves about whether Mars should have a black bull sacrificed to him and Jupiter should have a white one or the other way round; we'd never get anything done.'

Vespasian stepped to his left to avoid treading in the spilled intestines of a gutted youth. 'And there would be a lot fewer of us. No one can take offence because they feel that their favoured god receives less respect than someone else's when we give every god equal credence. And thank the gods, in equal measure, of course, that we do.'

'Which leaves us free to conquer the world,' Magnus chuckled as raucous shouting started to emanate from somewhere close by.

'We've had our own share of civil wars, don't forget; but they at least were political and I would suppose that it's far easier to bridge a political divide than a religious one. According to Sabinus the Jews spend all their time squabbling with each other about religious doctrine, which is probably one reason why they never had an empire, thank the gods; imagine living in a world with this sort of religious intolerance? It would be...'

'Intolerable?'

'Precisely,' Vespasian agreed, grinning as the main street turned a sharp corner and then opened out into the small agora that was at the heart of the Jewish Quarter.

'Shit!' Festus spat as the source of the shouting became obvious. 'Centurion Regulus, have the century form line here and send a couple of runners to get the nearest two centuries to come and support us at the double.'

'Sir!' the primus pilus of the cohort barked, saluting smartly before turning to carry out his orders.

Before them, just fifty paces away, was a crowd of at least four hundred rioters concentrating their attention on three houses at the far end of the agora, one of which had already started to burn. Black smoke swirled around the mob.

The first century streamed in from the main street and formed up, with a clatter of hobnails, two deep across its entrance as the first of the rioters became aware of their presence. With a roar the rear elements of the crowd began to peel off and move towards the thin auxiliary line, brandishing swords, clubs and bows.

Loud shouts from either side of him drew Vespasian's attention; a century emerged from each of the two parallel streets and quickly formed up on either flank of the first century.

The lead rioters stopped in their tracks, not wanting to engage with over two hundred armed and shielded soldiers, while those at the back pressed on, compacting the crowd as more and more of the men at the front refused to move forward.

At a shouted order from Festus, a cornu sounded; with a resounding clash of swords on shields, the auxiliaries of the three centuries stamped their left legs forward, thrust their shields in front of them and pulled their blades back, to their right hips, angled slightly up, ready to do their deadly work.

'They seem to be getting the hang of it,' Magnus commented from behind his shield, surprised by the near unison of the manoeuvre.

'Their blood's up,' Vespasian said, watching a short man push his way out of the crowd. 'That looks like the agitator that Menahem described; he's got a nerve showing himself.'

'Who commands here?' the man shouted at the Romans.

'I do,' Vespasian called back, stepping forward from the line but keeping his guard up.

'Meet me in the centre,' the man ordered, moving forward on his bow legs.

'Why should I parley with you, Jew?' Vespasian asked, disliking intensely the presumption of the man. 'Tell your men to put down their weapons and then we'll talk.'

'Are you Titus Flavius Vespasianus, quaestor of this province?'

'I am,' Vespasian replied in surprise.

'Well, quaestor, I suggest you talk to me,' the man said flatly, stopping midway between the two sides.

With the choice between meeting the Jew or fighting immediately, Vespasian walked forward, wondering what this little man with his imperious attitude could possibly have to say to quell the riots. 'My name is Gaius Julius Paulus, a citizen of Rome,' Paulus said. He pulled a scroll out of a bag hanging from his belt, with a self-important sneer. 'I hold a commission from the High Priest in Jerusalem, ratified in the name of the Emperor by Pilatus, the prefect of Judaea, and Flaccus, prefect of Egypt. It was also countersigned by your direct superior, Severus Severianus, the Governor of this province, when I visited him in Gortyna last month to ask permission to do my work in this province. Now will you parley?'

Vespasian looked at the odiously smug little man; half his right ear was missing, confirming that he had been the agitator who had started the riot. 'I don't give a fuck who's signed your little piece of papyrus, Jew,' he snarled back, unable to control his aversion to him, 'you've started three days of rioting and caused many deaths; I can't imagine that anyone has given you authority to do that.'

'I am charged to do everything necessary to stamp out the heresy promoted by Yeshua, which his followers call "The Way". I am further charged with ensuring that all large communities of Jews understand that this new cult is unacceptable and will be the cause of misery for God's people.'

'Like the rubbish that you spread about it being responsible for the silphium failing?'

Paulus looked at him slyly. 'A lie becomes the truth if it gets the result that God wants.'

'Show me that warrant.'

Paulus thrust the scroll at Vespasian, who sheathed his sword and took it.

'"I, Caiaphas, High Priest of the Jews,"' Vespasian read aloud, '"loyal subject of the Emperor Tiberius, do authorise Gaius Julius Paulus to use whatever means necessary to eradicate the teachings of Yeshua bar Yosef which threaten the Emperor's peace, both here in Judaea and in the Jewish communities around his dominions."' He glanced at the seals and signatures: Caiaphas, Pilatus, Flaccus and Severianus. He handed the scroll back.

Paulus smiled complacently. 'So you see, quaestor, I'm a very important man with powerful patrons. I've been successful in Caesarea and Alexandria and now I'm nearly done in Cyrene; when I've finished here I shall go back East.'

'This does not give you the right to commit murder.'

'This is not murder, it's execution,' Paulus replied, 'and it's a purely internal Jewish matter. I've already put the preacher, Shimon of Cyrene, to death and now in one of those houses behind me are Yeshua's wife and his children; while they live they will carry on spreading his lies. So, quaestor, allow me to finish God's will and then I'll not trouble you any more, for I have work to do in Damascus where this abhorrent sect has also taken root.'

'I have seen children executed before because they bore their father's name and I will not see it done again.'

'You haven't got the power to stop me.'

Vespasian grabbed Paulus by the arm and twisted him around; slamming his shield arm across his throat, he drew his pugio and stuck the point next to his kidneys. 'I may not have the power, but I do have the will. One false move, you nasty little shit, and it'll be your last. Festus! Eight men here to arrest this agitator.'

A roar of protest went up from the crowd, but they did not move to intervene; the threat of the auxiliaries held them back.

'You can't arrest me,' Paulus shrieked, 'I have a warrant.'

Vespasian pushed his pugio into Paulus' skin, drawing blood. 'Then you had better tear it up because if I can't arrest you my dagger might just slip.' He pulled his blade across Paulus' flesh, slicing it.

Paulus cried out in pain, squirming unsuccessfully to release himself. He took the scroll and slowly ripped it down the middle, then across and dropped the pieces. 'You are as arrogant as your brother whom I had the misfortune to meet in Judaea,' he declared contemptuously.

'Your opinion means nothing to me, you're irrelevant now.'

'I am a man of great potential, quaestor, held back by the petty ambitions of people like you; I will be very relevant to you one day, I assure you.'

Vespasian shoved Paulus into the arms of the waiting auxiliaries. 'Take him down to the port and have him put aboard the next ship heading for Judaea.'

Paulus glared at him with loathing and spat at his feet.

Vespasian turned his back on him and addressed the crowd. 'Your leader has torn up his authority and is on his way back to Judaea. All those who throw down their weapons now will live; those who don't will die. Those already in custody will be sent to the Governor for trial with the recommendation of death and I will not negotiate on that point. My soldiers stand ready; what's it to be?'

Almost instantaneously the rioters started throwing their weapons to the ground.

'Prefect, round them up and put them all to work dousing the fires and clearing up the damage; if anyone refuses they can join the prisoners being sent to Creta. And bring the woman and her children to me at the Governor's Residence, and Yosef as well.'

'How can I thank you, quaestor?' Yeshua's woman sobbed with relief as Quintillius showed her and Yosef into Vespasian's study. She fell to her knees and kissed his feet; her two children stood shyly behind her next to Yosef.

'What's your name?' he asked, bending down from his chair and lifting her chin.

'Mariam, quaestor.'

'Well, Mariam, what would you have me do with you?'

'Allow me to take my children to safety.'

'To Gaul?'

'To Carthage first then in the spring I'll make the crossing to Gaul.'

'Why Gaul?'

'There are very few Jews there, I won't be recognised.'

'Why do the Jewish priests want you dead?'

'I can answer that, quaestor,' Yosef offered. 'On the third day after Yeshua died she and some of his disciples went to his tomb in order to take his body back to Galilee; they found it empty.'

'Someone else took the body?'

'We don't know. Caiaphas the High Priest wanted it buried in an unmarked grave so perhaps the Temple Guards took it secretly after we had placed it in the tomb. They were waiting for it but your brother gave it to me. But perhaps he still lives. There have been a number of people who claim to have seen and spoken with him; some say that he has gone into the East.'

'But that's ridiculous, the man was crucified; even if he did survive somehow he would be a cripple.'

'I know.' Yosef spread his hands, hunching his shoulders. 'But nevertheless his body wasn't in the tomb and he has been seen. Perhaps he didn't die, perhaps he was resurrected as those who have seen him claim, or perhaps it's just someone impersonating him. It doesn't matter, the priests are hunting down everyone who can bear witness to the empty tomb or to Yeshua still being alive.'

'Believe whatever nonsense you like.' Vespasian's mind started to turn to thoughts of Flavia. 'You are both free to go but how and where is up to you; your ship turned back eastwards a couple of days ago according to the port aedile's records.'

'God will provide,' Mariam said as she got to her feet.

'I am again in your debt; God be with you, quaestor,' Yosef said, walking towards the door.

'I prefer to have more than one god looking after me.'

Quintillius opened the door and let them out.

'Quaestor,' the clerk said once they were alone, 'we found the house where Flavia Domitilla was staying.'

'Excellent. Did she accept the invitation to dinner?'

'She wasn't there.'

'Then go and wait until she comes back.'

'I'm afraid that would prove fruitless. The landlord told us that the day after the fighting started Flavia Domitilla boarded a Judaean trading ship heading east.'

PART II

❧ ❧

ROME, JULY AD 35

CHAPTER VIII

'WHAT IN THE name of Mars are they doing?' Vespasian asked Magnus in alarm as a group of seemingly demented women came rushing towards them, across the Forum Boarium, beating themselves with branches.

'Nothing in Mars' name, sir,' Magnus replied, restraining Ziri who had dropped the hand-cart containing their belongings and Capella's chest in order to defend them from the oncoming screaming women. 'They're slaves and they do that in Juno's name. It's the Caprotinia; all the female slaves in the city get the day off and run around hitting themselves with fig-tree branches.'

'Whatever for?'

'No one's really quite sure.' Magnus helped a very confused Ziri pick up the hand-cart as the women rushed past. 'I've heard that it was something to do with a woman prisoner in the Gallic camp during their invasion of Italia. She gave a signal from a fig tree for our lads to storm out of the city and take the hairy buggers by surprise. Anyway, who gives a fuck why they do it, the important thing is that they do and it's always a great night; by the time they've finished running about beating themselves they're extremely excited and very amenable, if you take my meaning?'

'I'm sure I do,' Vespasian said, wondering if Caenis was out whipping herself up into a frenzy and found himself quite interested by the idea.

Another band of women, some of them baring their breasts, came howling into the Forum, scattering passers-by who laughed good-naturedly at their antics.

Magnus licked his lips appreciatively. 'We're back just in time; not only do we get very enthusiastic, half-naked women, but we also get a nice few days at the circus to recover from any excesses that we might have indulged in, as the Caprotinia falls during the eight days of the Apollo Games. I love July.'

'I can imagine,' Vespasian agreed, unhappy to be reminded that it was already over halfway through the year and he was only now arriving back in Rome.

His disappointment at the disappearance of Flavia Domitilla had been compounded by his enforced extended stay in Cyrenaica; he had then been obliged to wait until June for his replacement, a sour-faced young man, who had evidently felt the posting far beneath him and had shown little desire to arrive promptly in the province. Once he had eventually been relieved, unseasonal gales had delayed his return for another two frustrating market intervals.

Apart from a longing to see Caenis again and to forget about Flavia in her arms, his main reason for wanting to get back to Rome as soon as possible had been to hand over Capella's chest – minus the gold and the bankers' draft – to Antonia. Narcissus would soon become concerned enough by its non-arrival to instigate an investigation, which would in all likelihood lead to Vespasian, and he did not like the idea of being waylaid and relieved of his newfound wealth by hired thugs in the pay of Claudius' ambitious freedman.

Passing out of the Forum Boarium with the huge facade of the Circus Maximus to their right they turned left onto Vicus Tuscus, heading to the Forum Romanum. Ziri's face, already slack-jawed with amazement since entering the city, became a picture of disbelief as he looked up at the monumental House of Augustus with its high marble walls, dominating the summit of the Palatine.

Magnus clapped his slave on the shoulder. 'A bit different to the arse-end of a camel, eh, Ziri?'

'Fucking right, master; I never fucking seen such a fucking thing, fucked if I has.'

Vespasian frowned. 'You've got to stop him from swearing all the time, Magnus; it'll get him into trouble.'

'He's all right; you should be impressed by how quickly he picked up Latin.'

'Yes, I am; the trouble is that he's picked up your sort of Latin.'

'Who are you to talk with your country-bumpkin Sabine burr, if you don't mind me saying, sir? At least he sounds like a Roman.'

'Yes, I sound like a Roman, sir,' Ziri said with pride, 'I no sound like a cunt.'

'Ziri!' Magnus snapped, clouting him around the ear.

'Sorry, master.'

Having made their slow way through the festival crowds up the Quirinal Hill they eventually arrived at the familiar door of Vespasian's uncle, Senator Gaius Vespasius Pollo. Magnus knocked and, after a brief delay, it was opened by a young and very attractive dark-skinned youth.

'My uncle's broadening his tastes, it would seem,' Vespasian observed to Magnus once he had given the lad instructions to show Ziri around to the slaves' entrance with their belongings, Magnus having first relieved him of Capella's chest.

'Change pleases,' Magnus quoted as they walked through the vestibule and into the atrium.

'Dear boy,' boomed Gaius, walking out of his study, 'and Magnus, my friend! I heard someone at the door and was praying that it would be you; I've been worried sick for the last few days.' He came waddling at great speed across the mosaic floor, the ample flesh on his plump body wobbling frantically under his tunic. He enveloped Vespasian in a smothering embrace while planting a moist, rubbery kiss on his cheeks. 'When I heard of the foul weather out at sea I was worried that you may have shared the fate of the first grain fleet of the season heading from Egypt.' He grasped Magnus' forearm and gave him a hearty slap on the shoulder.

'What happened to it, Uncle?' Vespasian asked, putting his hand to his face, as if in concern, in order to surreptitiously wipe off the excess saliva from each cheek.

'Only two out of the thirty transports made it through, the rest were shipwrecked off Kithria; that's why I was so concerned for you two. The humorists are saying that the only reason the storms stopped is because Neptune's now too busy baking bread. Sabinus is having a terrible time of it: he's the aedile in charge of the grain supply in the city and the granaries are getting low and the mob are getting angry. Thankfully, for Sabinus and the Senate, most of their anger is directed towards Tiberius for staying on Capreae and – as they see it – deserting them. But come and sit down.' Gaius led Vespasian through the atrium towards the *peristylium*. 'Aenor, bring wine, and take Magnus to the kitchen for some refreshments,' he called to the young, blond-haired, blue-eyed German slave boy who had been hovering in the background, waiting to be of service, while his master greeted his guests. 'And cakes, we must have honeyed cakes.'

'It would seem, my dear boy, that you're in a tricky position,' Gaius mused, looking at the contents of Capella's chest. 'Your instinct to take it to Antonia for her to decide what to do about it is correct, but that could also be seen as an act of treason.'

'What do you mean, Uncle? I'm not aiding Narcissus; he's the one who's committing treason by buying up land for Claudius in Egypt without the Emperor's permission.'

'No, you're not aiding him, I grant you that; but neither are you exposing him as a traitor, and if you cash his bankers' draft that could be seen as a bribe. Since the restarting of the treason trials that might be considered to be a little foolhardy.'

Vespasian went to protest but Gaius held up his hand. 'Hear me out, dear boy. You must remember that you are no longer a mere thin-stripe military tribune or a lowly member of the *vigin-tiviri*; you are now a senator. Your duty is to the Senate and to the Emperor, not to Antonia, who is purely a private citizen and a female one at that. Yes, she is very powerful in her own way but

she is not the government or even an official part of the State.'
Gaius paused to take a sip of his wine and reach for the last
remaining cake.

The air in the courtyard garden was pleasingly cool and the
wine delicate and refreshing; had his uncle not just given him
cause for concern Vespasian might have found himself relaxing
for the first time since Capella's chest had come into his possession.

'You're recommending that I take the chest to the Senate or
directly to the Emperor then, Uncle?'

'I didn't say that, I was just pointing out where your duty lies.
Your obligation, however, is an entirely different matter and
that's why you're in a tricky situation. If you were to go to the
Senate with this thing, Antonia would never forgive you for
putting her son, however much she dislikes him, in danger; she
considers that to be her prerogative.'

'And then I'd have her, as well as Narcissus, as an enemy,'
Vespasian groaned. He put down his cup and held his head in his
hands, cursing the day that he met Flavia and his arrogance that
had led him into this situation. 'I could take it directly to one of
the Consuls in private,' he suggested after a few moments'
thought.

'Good thinking but it won't work with the Suffect Consuls
that we have this half of the year. Decimus Valerius Asiaticus is
Antonia's man, he used to look after her interests in Narbonese
Gaul. He owes everything to her, not least his being the first
Consul of Gallic origin. Antonia would hear of it within the hour.
His junior, Aulus Gabinius Secundus, is a talentless, vicious man
who would use the information to cause as much trouble as he
could for everyone involved. I'm afraid that I can see only one
course of action for you to take and that is to steer the middle
ground.'

'How do you mean?'

'You can't do your duty to the Senate until it next meets in
three days' time, after the close of the festival of Apollo, so in
the meantime I suggest that you fulfil your obligation to

132

Antonia. Show her the land deeds and explain the predicament that you find yourself in, emphasising of course that your loyalty to her was the reason why you brought it to her first, and ask her if you should take it to the Senate. You never know, she might surprise you.'

'What if she doesn't?'

'Then, my dear boy, at least you would have some sort of defence if the worst should come to the worst; you could truthfully say in court that Antonia told you not to take it to the Senate.'

'But how could I prove that?'

'Ask Antonia for a formal meeting; then you'll get a copy of the minutes.'

'But she could still deny it.'

'Not if you take a witness. Unfortunately I won't do and nor would Sabinus; a court won't believe that we're not just supporting your case through family loyalty.'

'Who, then?'

'I would have thought that that's quite obvious: your old comrade from the Fourth Scythica, Corbulo. I know that he's in Rome at the moment as he's trying to get elected as a praetor for next year; he's desperate to come above Sabinus in the poll. His father told me a long time ago that he feels that his family is obliged to us for you saving his son's life in Thracia; I'll call in the favour immediately.'

'I can't say that I'm too happy to be doing this, Vespasian,' Gnaeus Domitius Corbulo told Vespasian as they approached Antonia's house on the Palatine. 'Especially if you won't tell me what it's about.' He pointed over his shoulder vaguely at Magnus who was flanked by two of his crossroads brothers, Marius and Sextus; Ziri brought up the rear. 'I can only assume that it's something to do with what's in the chest that your man's carrying.'

'That'll be Magnus, Corbulo,' Magnus said lightly, 'remember? You sat in my shit and I sat in yours in that cart all the way across Thracia, nine years ago, after we'd been captured by some very nasty tribesmen.'

Corbulo wrinkled his nose at the memory of the journey and subsequent near escape from the Thracians, but refused to acknowledge that he could recollect the name of someone so beneath him after such a long time.

'Pompous arsehole,' Magnus muttered, but not entirely to himself.

Corbulo held his chin in the air disdaining to hear the comment. Vespasian shot Magnus a withering look over his shoulder; Magnus shrugged and smiled innocently.

'Believe me, Corbulo, it's best if you don't know what it's about unless you have to,' Vespasian said, trying to get back onto the subject. 'You're right that it's to do with what's in the chest. I plan to show the contents to the Lady Antonia and then we'll discuss what to do about them in your presence. That way you won't be put in any danger because you won't know what we're talking about; I just need you to witness what she asks me to do about it so that you could back me up in court if it came to it.'

Corbulo looked down his long nose at him. 'You're way out of your league, Vespasian. However, I'll do this to repay the debt that my father insists that I owe you, but that's it – the slate is clean afterwards.'

'Let us both pray that there *is* an afterwards,' Vespasian muttered as they approached the tall, single-storey villa that belonged to the most formidable woman in Rome.

Vespasian mounted the steps as the sun slipped behind the Aventine Hill throwing Rome into shadow. He rapped on the door; the viewing slot snapped back and two eyes appeared. 'Titus Flavius Vespasianus and Gnaeus Domitius Corbulo request an interview with the Lady Antonia.'

The slot closed and the door opened immediately; the doorman let Vespasian and Corbulo into the vestibule, leaving Magnus, Ziri and the brothers outside with the chest. As they walked through into the imposing and exquisitely furnished atrium a familiar voice came from across its vast length.

'Masters Vespasian and Corbulo, how good to see you again,' Pallas, Antonia's Greek steward, said in his faultless Latin. 'I trust that the natives of Creta and Cyrenaica weren't too tiresome.'

'They were as belligerent as one would expect, Pallas; and it's very good to see you again too,' Vespasian replied with a smile.

Corbulo grunted his acknowledgement.

'You are too kind, masters; I am honoured that you should be pleased to see me, a mere freedman.'

'There's nothing mere about…freedman, did you say?'

Pallas pulled his right hand from behind his back and placed a *pileus*, the conical felt cap that marked a freedman, on his head. 'Indeed, sir. My mistress was good enough to give me my freedom soon after you left for your province; I am now Marcus Antonius Pallas, a freed citizen of Rome.'

'My congratulations, Pallas.' Vespasian proffered his forearm to the Greek for the first time in their acquaintance.

Pallas clasped it in a firm grip. 'Thank you, Vespasian. I will always remember with gratitude the respect, far beyond that due to my servile rank, that you, your brother and uncle have showed me in the past.'

Corbulo muttered a perfunctory felicitation to which Pallas responded with a slight inclination of his head.

'Now, gentlemen, I will see if the Lady Antonia is able to receive you.'

'We would like a formal meeting, if that would be convenient, Pallas?' Vespasian requested, somewhat nervously. 'What I have to discuss with her is of a very delicate nature for all concerned. Magnus and some of his brothers are outside with an item that I must bring to the Lady's attention.'

Pallas raised an eyebrow but otherwise his face remained neutral. 'I see.' He clapped his hands twice. 'Felix!'

A Greek appeared from the far end of the room and walked with self-assured poise towards them. Vespasian looked at him curiously; apart from a deep suntan he was the exact image of Pallas when he had first met him nine years previously.

'Felix, there are some men outside, see them round to the stable yard and get them some refreshment. They should wait there until they are summoned.'

'Yes, Pallas,' Felix replied, heading to the front door.

'Follow me, gentlemen.' Pallas walked off towards Antonia's formal reception room.

'Is he your brother, Pallas?' Vespasian enquired.

'I cannot deny it.'

'How long has he been in Antonia's household?'

'He arrived here just recently, but the Lady Antonia has owned him for most of his life. He was the steward of her household in Egypt and she's brought him here to take over my position, once I've trained him up in the etiquette of Rome.'

'What are you going to be doing, then?'

'I'm afraid that that's between the Lady and me, Vespasian,' Pallas said as they entered the beautiful high-ceilinged reception room, littered with expensive but tasteful furniture and sculptures from all over the Empire. He gestured to Vespasian and Corbulo to sit. 'Wait here, gentlemen, I will send you some wine while I relay your request to my Lady.'

Night had fallen and the room was now ablaze with scores of oil lamps; their fumes hung in the air veiling the ceiling, depriving it of their light.

Vespasian and Corbulo had waited for more than an hour, the wine jug and two cups on the low table between them stood empty. However, the time had passed reasonably quickly as Corbulo brought him up to date with the machinations of the various factions in Rome, slanted, of course, from his own conservative, aristocratic perspective.

'I find the presence of that oily little New Man, Poppaeus Sabinus, back in Rome an affront to my honour,' Corbulo was saying. 'It was bad enough that Antonia wouldn't let me implicate him in Sejanus' plot and thereby have my revenge on him for trying to get me killed in Thracia...'

136

'And get me killed as well, Corbulo,' Vespasian reminded him.

'Yes, indeed, and you, but now he's back here it's intolerable; he seems to be working with Macro, bringing charges against anyone to whom he bears a grudge, even if they're from families of the highest order. There have been over twenty of them. Pomponius Labeo was arraigned just after you left last year on a charge of maladministration of his province during the three years that he took over Moesia from Poppaeus.'

'The slippery little shit.'

'Indeed. Now you can say what you like about Pomponius' personal habits but I found him to be an honourable man and a decent legate of the Fourth Scythica.'

'So what happened with his case?'

'You mean you don't know?'

'I only just got back to Rome today, I don't know any of the news, other than what you've just been telling me while we've been waiting.'

'Ah yes, of course.' Corbulo paused and drew breath. 'Well then, I'm sorry to have to tell you,' he carried on with a look as close to concern on his rigid face as he could muster, 'that Poppaeus hounded him and his wife Paxaea to suicide last year.'

Vespasian was visibly shocked. 'The little bastard. How? Why? The charge against him was just maladministration, that doesn't carry a death sentence.'

'It was at first but then Poppaeus discovered that Pomponius had been speculating in grain. He told Macro who informed the Emperor and Tiberius took up the charge himself; he doesn't take kindly to grain speculators. After that Pomponius had no choice but to take his life in order to ensure that his property wasn't confiscated. As to why, that's easy: because of Pomponius reporting to the Senate that Poppaeus allowed his army to acclaim him "imperator" and did nothing to stop them. Poppaeus has been living in fear of Tiberius' vengeance ever since, which, unfortunately, has never been forthcoming.'

'Quite the reverse, in fact – he was reinstated as Governor of both Moesia and Macedonia in my last year in Thracia.'

'Quite so, quite so, but that was at Sejanus' suggestion; he kept Poppaeus safe from Tiberius while he was still alive, but since his downfall no one can understand why Poppaeus led such a charmed life – until he returned to Rome in the summer of last year…'

'When it turned out that he was working with Macro,' Vespasian said, finishing Corbulo's sentence.

'Oh, you heard?'

'Yes, you just told me.'

'So I did.'

'Gentlemen, I am so sorry to have kept you waiting.' Antonia appeared in the doorway causing them both to jump to their feet.

'Domina,' they said in unison, bowing their heads.

'I hope that I haven't inconvenienced you?'

'Not at all, domina,' Vespasian replied as she walked towards them with Pallas following, 'it is I that am inconveniencing you.'

'With a rather strange request from somebody whom I consider to be a friend.'

'I'm sorry to ask this, domina, but I hope that you will understand when I explain what brings me here.'

Antonia stopped in front of him, her piercing green eyes bored into his; he felt the potential menace that lurked behind them and quailed. The nervous look on his face caused her to raise her eyebrows and then smile. 'The land deeds of the properties that Narcissus has been buying up in Egypt on behalf of my son, Claudius?'

Vespasian's mouth dropped open.

'And you are worried that not reporting this act of treason to the proper authorities would be construed as treason on your own part?'

Vespasian nodded.

'And so you brought my dear friend Corbulo as a witness of the most unimpeachable character and requested a formal meeting so that you could keep a copy of the minutes?'

'Yes, domina,' Vespasian managed to mumble. 'How did you know?'

'It's what I would have done, had I been in your position.'

'I mean, how did you know about the land deeds?'

'Because since I discovered that there may be more to my idiot son than meets the eye I've made it my business to know everything that goes on in his household. How I know is something that I may divulge later.' She turned to Pallas. 'Is the Consul here yet, Pallas?'

'Yes, domina, he and dinner await you in your private room.'

'Excellent. Have Magnus bring the chest there. Gentlemen, we should eat.' Antonia turned and walked towards the door.

Glancing at Corbulo, who shook his head slowly and tutted, Vespasian followed her, feeling totally out of control of the situation.

'Decimus Valerius Asiaticus, may I present Titus Flavius Vespasianus; Gnaeus Domitius Corbulo I believe you already know,' Antonia said as they entered her private domain where the Senior Consul for the final six months of the year stood waiting, admiring the intricately glazed bay window that dominated the room.

Asiaticus turned and nodded a brief greeting to Vespasian and Corbulo before addressing Antonia. 'Lady Antonia, may I ask what is so urgent that I am summoned from my dining table?'

'Consul, I do apologise; I hope that my cook has created some dishes that will make up for your spoilt supper. Gentlemen, shall we recline? Consul, please take the couch to my right; the two younger gentlemen to my left.' She settled onto the middle one of the three couches set around the low walnut-wood table, leaving the men in no doubt that it was an order, not an invitation.

Pallas clapped his hands and three slave girls, each carrying a pair of slippers, appeared from the serving room next door; they took the men's togas and swapped their sandals for the slippers and then retreated as two more went around the diners washing their hands and spreading napkins out on the couches before them.

Vespasian hoped that he had managed to hide his disappointment at Caenis not being present to attend to her mistress.

139

Once they were all settled with full cups of wine and the *gustatio* had been set out on the table Antonia dismissed the slaves and Pallas took up his customary position by the door.

Antonia spooned a small portion of anchovies onto her plate. 'Gentlemen, we shall fend for ourselves without anyone to wait upon us. Consul, I owe you an explanation.' She paused to make sure that the three men were following her lead and helping themselves. 'When Vespasian arrived here late this afternoon asking for a formal meeting and bringing the esteemed Corbulo along as a witness I made an educated guess as to what it was concerning. Pallas, ask Magnus to bring in the chest.' The steward stuck his head around the door to pass on the order to an underling outside as Antonia continued. 'I immediately understood his fears and so sent for you.'

Vespasian now realised the cause of the long wait.

The door opened and Magnus entered with Capella's chest.

'Put it on the table, Magnus, and then go and find some supper for you and your companions.'

Magnus mumbled something incomprehensible and left the room, leaving the four diners staring at the chest.

'Vespasian, I know that this is not a formal meeting – that would be impossible to grant in the circumstances – but as you are now reporting your discovery to the Senior Consul as well as myself I believe that it should cover you from any charge of treason.'

'Yes, domina,' Vespasian replied, in awe, as ever, of Antonia's ability to read his mind.

'Treason, Lady?' Asiaticus was alarmed.

'Yes, Consul, treason,' Antonia confirmed, taking a sip of her wine. 'Treason committed by my useless and idiotic son whom you, for some reason that eludes me, consider to be a friend. But no matter. Vespasian, open the chest.'

Vespasian got to his feet and slid the keys from around his neck and, placing them into the locks, lifted the lid.

Asiaticus and Corbulo both strained their necks to see what was inside.

'Those, Consul,' Antonia said without bothering to look, 'are the deeds to seven very large grain-producing estates in Egypt. They were purchased secretly, over the last three years, on behalf of Claudius by an agent of his freedman, Narcissus.'

'But that's...'

'Treason, Consul, I know. No one, not even I, may buy property on that scale in Egypt without the permission of my brother-in-law, the Emperor.'

Asiaticus looked at her aghast and drained his cup; his appetite had disappeared in an instant. 'But what do you intend to do about it, Lady?'

'That, Consul, is what you are here to discuss. Pallas, would you pour some more wine for my guests? Meanwhile, Vespasian can tell the Consul how he came into possession of this thing.'

When he had finished his short account of the events, Antonia gave Vespasian an appraising look, nodded her head and ordered the next course to be served. He had not left out any of the details concerning either Capella or Flavia – apart from his personal motives – as he had realised that Antonia already knew the story, though how, he could not guess.

Once the slaves had left them with two roast suckling kids in a honey and cumin sauce, Antonia turned to Asiaticus. 'So the question is: why has Narcissus gone to all that trouble to get the deeds to Rome when he could quite happily have kept them in a secure underground safe in any of his patron's new properties in Egypt?' She asked in a manner that suggested to Vespasian that she already knew the answer.

'It does seem a lot of effort to go to, not to mention the risk of them being discovered by Tiberius' agents or even lost.'

'Which they were.'

'Yes indeed, Lady, which they were. I can only assume that they are worth more to Claudius here than they would be in Egypt, but why, I don't know.'

'Nor did I, until recently.' She paused to carve off a few slices of tender meat from one of the kids and waited for her guests to do the same. Finally content that everyone around the table had sufficient and were at least picking at the succulent dish, she continued. 'You may not be aware, Consul, that my grandson Gaius Caligula is conducting an affair with Macro's wife, Ennia?'

The look on Asiaticus' face confirmed his ignorance. 'But I thought that he was getting married in Antium; the Emperor will be arriving there for the ceremony at the close of the festival of Apollo.'

'That's true, but my Gaius is a very busy little boy and, despite his coming wedding, has found the time to become infatuated with this harlot. It started when Macro moved her to Capraea last year; a strange thing to do, to say the least, unless he was deliberately pandering her to Gaius. I couldn't understand what Macro stood to gain by this so I watched and waited, saying nothing to Gaius about it in my letters as he's become increasingly dismissive of my advice and now tends to take the opposite course of action to that which I recommend. I was rewarded for my patience a couple of months ago when I received this. Pallas, if you please?'

Pallas walked over to the desk at the far end of the room and retrieved a scroll that he handed to his mistress.

'This was sent to me by Clemens, the captain of Gaius' guard. His loyalty to my grandson is matched by his distrust of Macro. It is a copy of a document, signed by Gaius, in which he swears to make Ennia empress when he inherits the Purple. In return for Macro's loss and also as a reward for ensuring that he does become emperor he promises to make him prefect of Egypt.'

Corbulo could not contain his outrage. 'He's sold his wife to gain a position of power! That's unthinkable.'

'No, Corbulo, that is modern day politics,' Antonia responded, 'wouldn't you agree, Consul?'

'Indeed I would. It seems that our Praetorian prefect has learnt from his predecessor's mistakes.'

Vespasian smiled; he suddenly understood the beauty of Macro's strategy. 'He knows that he can never become emperor, as attempting to do that cost Sejanus his life, so he's going for a smaller prize.'

'Smaller yes,' Antonia agreed, 'but in terms of wealth and power, huge; enough for him to use as a stepping-stone for what I believe to be his ultimate ambition: to imitate my father, Marcus Antonius, and divide the Empire in two by seizing the eastern provinces.'

There was a stunned silence; all thought of eating had now evaporated as Antonia's three guests contemplated how this could be achieved and what consequences it would have for the stability of the world as they knew it.

'I believe that some more wine would be in order at this point, Pallas,' Antonia requested.

With their cups refilled Antonia continued her analysis to her spellbound audience.

'Let us assume for a moment that Gaius does give Macro what he wants and it is not an idle assumption; my little Gaius may have many faults but lack of generosity is not one of them, he desires to be loved and is naïve enough to think that he can buy that love. Macro would then be in control of the wealthiest province in the Empire, a province that is defended by two legions and is, to all intents and purposes, a peninsula. An army cannot cross the desert to its west, as you now well know, Vespasian; the southern border is the edge of the Empire and to the north and east is sea. So other than a highly risky seaborne invasion the only way to attack Egypt is from the northeast, through Judaea and the collection of petty kingdoms and tetrarchies that surround it, using the only other four legions in the region, based in Syria. So to secure Egypt, Macro would only have to ensure that the Syrian legions were busy elsewhere; which he did last month with a move of far-thinking political dexterity.'

Asiaticus' eyes widened. 'The Parthian embassy,' he said slowly, 'brilliant.'

'Yes, it was admirable,' Antonia agreed, visibly pleased that the Consul had the political acumen to keep up with her reasoning.

'But they were a group of rebel nobles who wanted to replace King Artabanus on the Parthian throne with Phraates who was hostage here in Rome,' Corbulo said. 'What are they to do with Egypt or Macro?'

Vespasian vaguely recollected Magnus mentioning something about rebel Parthians on his arrival in Cyrenaica.

'Everything,' Antonia answered, 'if you look at the timing and who organised the embassy.'

'Herod Agrippa,' Vespasian stated, his memory clearing. He rewarded himself with a gulp of wine.

Antonia looked at him quizzically, wondering how he knew. 'Correct. Herod's been trying to persuade Tiberius for ages to reinstate Judaea as a client kingdom with him on the throne but Tiberius has always denied him. Macro must have offered Herod what he wanted in return for him using his considerable influence with the disaffected nobles in Parthia to persuade them that now was the time for a change of king. Herod's friend Phraates is the only survivor of the ancient Arsacid dynasty and therefore the rightful heir to the Parthian throne; he would have been only too happy to be of service.'

Asiaticus grinned. 'That is elegant. Tiberius went for it because since Artabanus put his son Arsaces on the throne of Armenia, the balance of power in the East has shifted towards Parthia.'

'Exactly, Consul; I know that Tiberius has made Phraates promise to return Armenia to Rome's sphere of influence in return for his throne. Tiberius thinks that he has done a good deal for Roman diplomacy and so sends Lucius Vitellius, the new Governor of Syria, off to Parthia with his legions for a war that will last at least two, perhaps even three, years; longer than Tiberius is expected to live. Once Macro and Herod had put the Parthian embassy in motion all they had to do was sit back and watch Tiberius fall for it.'

Comprehension spread over Corbulo's face. 'Ah, I see, Macro's expecting Tiberius to die, either naturally or with a little help, before the war is concluded; he'll then make sure Caligula becomes emperor and will be rewarded with Egypt. With the Syrian legions busy he'll be able to create a buffer state

144

by uniting Judaea with Galilee, Iudemaea, and all the other smaller Jewish tetrarchies with Herod as the King of a Greater Judaea.'

Antonia nodded. 'And Herod is already preparing the ground for that. On his way back to Rome last year he stopped off in Alexandria where his wife persuaded the Alabarch to lend them a lot of money, which Herod, rather than repaying his debts to me, has used to buy grain secretly from Claudius and Narcissus.'

'But that would have come to the attention of imperial agents, however secret the deal, and he would have been prosecuted,' Asiaticus pointed out correctly.

'Only if the grain had been diverted from Rome itself; but it wasn't. The estates that he bought it off had all fulfilled their quota to Rome; Herod bought grain destined for lesser provinces.'

'That explains why we had a severe shortage in Cyrenaica,' Vespasian observed, 'it was one of the causes of the Jewish unrest there.'

'I doubt that Herod cares about the Jews of Cyrenaica, he wanted that grain stockpiled ready to take with him to help him secure his new kingdom. An independent, united Jewish state would have a huge amount of manpower to call upon to form a considerable army, which would need to be fed. Herod will be a very powerful man, powerful enough perhaps to prevent Gaius sending an army through Judaea to invade Egypt.'

'And Caligula will be powerless to do anything else about Macro because he would hold a large percentage of Rome's grain supply in his hands, and would threaten to withhold it.'

'Precisely,' Antonia agreed. 'But before he can secure Egypt, Macro needs money and a lot of it to buy the loyalty of legions and the auxiliary cohorts stationed there. Money is the one thing that he's short of.'

'So that's why he's recently allied himself with Poppaeus,' Vespasian said, refilling his cup. 'His family's silver mines in Hispania would surely provide enough if they managed to finance the Thracian rebellion.'

'More than enough,' Antonia agreed while signalling to Pallas to refill her cup. 'And in return for Macro giving him a free hand in Rome to prosecute the many enemies he's made during his career, Poppaeus has agreed to lend him the money that he needs to become a wealthy landowner in Egypt by…?'

'Buying Claudius' estates,' all three men said simultaneously.

'The produce of which has just shot up in value due to the destruction of the last grain fleet.'

'But then surely the price of the estates has gone up?' Vespasian pointed out, pleased to be on a subject that he really understood: money.

'Indeed, but that's good for all four parties. Poppaeus will be delighted because Macro will have to borrow more money, so he'll make a fortune on the extra interest. Macro will immediately have a huge income from his new purchases with which to buy the loyalty that he needs. He doesn't care how much he pays now because it's not his money and once he's secured Egypt he'll be able to pay off the loan with the millions that he'll be receiving in taxes. Claudius will make even more of a profit on the investment he's already put out; and Herod is happy because he's not only already bought a massive amount of grain off Claudius but he's also been buying more since he's been in Rome with money borrowed from Poppaeus; part of which he can now sell at an inflated price to ease his cash-flow problems.'

'What a happy cabal they must be,' Asiaticus commented ruefully.

'There are two things that I don't understand, domina,' Vespasian said.

'I hope that I can answer them, although I only put it all together at the beginning of this year after I'd found out about Narcissus trying to get the deeds to Rome and Herod's grain purchases.'

'Yes, how did you know about that, Lady?' Asiaticus cut in.

Antonia smiled benignly. 'I suppose it won't do any harm telling you now. Once I'd found out about Claudius' and Narcissus' interest in Egypt I had my steward in Alexandria,

Felix, look into it for me; it wasn't long before he found out what they were doing. Since then he has been monitoring their land purchases. When Felix found out that Claudius had sold some of his harvest to Herod and then Narcissus' agent had taken the deeds of seven of the estates to Siwa, he realised that something very strange was going on and so immediately took ship to report it personally to me rather than risk a letter falling into the wrong hands.'

'But then how did you know that I had them, domina?'

'I didn't for sure until today. All I knew was that you met a man called Capella in Siwa who subsequently died, leaving you a chest. I couldn't be sure what it contained because my agent couldn't hear your final conversation with Capella; you'd ordered him to go and form up the column.'

'Corvinus!' Vespasian exclaimed in surprise. 'He was spying on me?'

'Not spying on you personally, Vespasian, he just works for me. Much like you, he has an obligation to me. When he heard Capella tell you, in Siwa, that the contents of his chest belonged to someone near the top of the imperial tree he thought that it would be of interest to me, so he wrote to me upon his return to Barca. He comes from a very ambitious family and is anxious to do well in Rome's service; his letter was most informative about the reasons that you went chasing off into the desert.'

Vespasian reddened, and wondered if there was anything that Antonia did not know.

'But don't worry,' Antonia said with a smile, 'it was fortuitous that you did, whatever your real motives. Now what were your questions?'

'Oh, yes,' he said, shaking his head and trying to get back his train of thought. 'I don't understand why Claudius is selling Macro all his estates when they will give him the means to wrest control of Egypt from the Empire that he may one day control.'

'Now that puzzled me for a while until I realised the simple truth: he doesn't know Macro's plans, nor does Narcissus; they might not even know that Macro is the purchaser. The deal has

147

been brokered by Poppaeus, who, as we know, is close to Claudius. All Claudius and Narcissus want is to pay off the huge loan that they took to buy the estates in the first place; but they're not selling all the estates, they bought twice as many. The profit they make from selling these seven will ensure that they own the others outright.'

'And I suppose there are no prizes for guessing who lent them the money in the first place,' Vespasian said with a wry smile.

'That's the beauty of it; Claudius gives the deeds to Poppaeus, he wipes out Claudius' debt and simply transfers it and the deeds onto Macro. No money changes hands and there is no record of the transaction and the three parties never meet.'

'So what's in it for Poppaeus apart from making money from all sides? It's not as if he needs any more.'

'This took me the longest to work out,' Antonia admitted, 'then it came to me in a flash. What has Poppaeus to gain by Macro taking Egypt and holding Rome to ransom? Nothing, unless he's part of it. Think about it: Macro is safe from attack from the west because of the desert, the Syrian legions are tied up in Parthia and Armenia and a sea assault is a very risky option; how would you attack Egypt in those circumstances?'

'That's easy,' Corbulo said, 'I'd march with six legions, along the Via Egnatia through Macedonia and Thracia, cross over to Asia and then all the way down the coast, overwhelming Herod on my way.'

'Exactly. But who is the Governor of Moesia, Macedonia and Achaea? Poppaeus. All he need do is withdraw his two legions and his ten auxiliary cohorts from the Danubius, cross the Hellespont and hold it against any army that comes. The eastern provinces would be completely in Macro's and Poppaeus' hands. The lower Danubius would be undefended and the northern tribes would take full advantage of that and swarm into Moesia, which would probably encourage the Thracians into another uprising. So any army that was sent east would have to deal with that before it could even think about trying to cross into Asia; that could take a couple of years. Anyway, where are these legions going to come from? The Rhenus frontier and leave Gaul open to the Germans? The upper Danubius and risk losing Pannonia? Or perhaps Hispania or Illyria where it's only their presence that keep the local tribes in order? Since Varus managed to lose three legions in the Teutoburg forest there are only twenty-five left in the Empire.'

'What about Lucius Vitellius?' Asiaticus asked.

'He would have a nasty choice once he'd concluded the Parthian war: either fight a civil war on two fronts, Poppaeus to the north and Herod and Macro in the south, and with the new King of Parthia – who would have much to gain by a divided and weakened Roman Empire – to his rear; not a pleasant prospect, as I'm sure you would all agree. So he would probably take the only other option and that is to declare his loyalty to the new regime and carry on guarding the eastern frontier.'

'Or commit suicide,' Corbulo suggested.

'It comes to the same thing: the legions won't want to fight. They've been stationed out there for so long it's now their home, what do they care who's in command?'

'We have to prevent this at all costs, Lady,' Asiaticus said as the truth of the matter sank in.

'We will,' Antonia affirmed, 'but I think for all our sakes we should not discuss what to do until we have had a pause to collect our thoughts; I for one need to leave the room for comfort's sake.'

CHAPTER VIIII

MAGNUS STARED STRAIGHT ahead, concentration etched on his face. 'So, because you went following your cock out into the desert,' he said through clenched teeth, 'Antonia has drawn you right back into her world and we're going to end up doing her dirty work.' With a relieved sigh his features relaxed.

Vespasian turned to his friend sitting next to him. 'Better?'

'Much.'

'It's not for certain that she wants me to do anything; she hasn't even decided herself what to do about Macro.'

'Bollocks, of course she has,' Magnus said, taking the strain again. 'Do you really believe that you and Corbulo would be sitting there with Antonia and the Senior Consul receiving the benefit of her views on a political problem if she didn't think that you were part of the solution?' He paused for a grunt of contentment. 'Of course you wouldn't; she's got something nasty planned for us, take my word for it, otherwise she would've just told you to leave Capella's chest on the table, thanked you sweetly and sent you back home for your supper.'

Corbulo walked in and with a brief glance at Magnus moved past him, removed his loincloth, hung it on a peg and perched on the hole to the other side of Vespasian. His relief was loud and almost instantaneous.

'This is more than I bargained for, Vespasian,' Corbulo asserted once he felt eased. 'I came here to witness a conversation, not to get involved in high politics.'

'No, Corbulo, you came here to repay a debt. If anything you should be thanking me because with the praetor elections only a few days away you're now involved with the Senior Consul whose opinion will count for a lot in the Senate. Perhaps you'll get in this year; you might even beat my brother in the poll.'

'I've worked that out for myself; and of course someone from my family should always beat a New Man like Sabinus,' Corbulo replied tersely. 'What concerns me, though, is that if Antonia puts a stop to this, five important people are going to be seriously upset.'

'What do you mean?'

'Well, Macro and Herod will lose the chance of real power, Claudius will lose a lot of money, Poppaeus will lose a lot of money and the chance of some power, and Caligula will lose face for being stupid enough to let this come about in the first place.'

Vespasian thought for a moment and realised that he was right.

'And if they all find out that you brought this to Antonia's attention,' Corbulo continued, 'and that I assisted you, then I really would have some enemies.'

'What did I tell you, sir?' Magnus said smugly. 'Keep clear of imperial politics.'

'Oh shut up and pass me the bucket.'

Vespasian pulled a stick, with a sponge attached, out of the bucket full of clear water; flicking away the excess liquid he squatted and began to sponge himself clean. 'Caligula won't hold it against us, surely? We're helping to save him from a terrible mistake.'

'Yes, I know,' Corbulo agreed as Vespasian dunked the sponge back in the bucket and swirled it round, cleaning it. 'And for Rome's sake it needs to be done, we can all see that; but will Caligula?'

'Of course he will.' Vespasian tied on his loincloth while Magnus took his turn with the sponge.

'Or will he see it as an interference with his plans for when he becomes emperor? Emperors can't be seen to make mistakes, so do you think that we would stand a chance of preferment during his reign if he knows that we've helped bring to light one of the biggest he's ever likely to make?'

'He's got a very good point there, sir,' Magnus said, giving himself a final scrub. 'Even if you consider Caligula to be a friend now, when he's the Emperor you might find yourself being an unwelcome reminder of past errors of judgement.'

'There, Vespasian, even your man has the wit to see that.'

Magnus picked up the bucket and banged it down at Corbulo's feet so that the now murky water slopped onto his slippers. 'Sponge, Corbulo?' he asked politely, handing him the unwashed implement.

'All of us are agreed that we must put a stop to Macro's scheme,' Antonia announced once they were all assembled again in her room. 'The question facing us is how to do it with the least damage to my interests.'

The three men stared at her. Only Asiaticus had the courage to ask what they were all thinking. 'Surely you mean Rome's interests, Lady?'

'That is the same thing, Consul. I'll be blunt with you; for the past few years I have been the only person who has stood between a reasonably stable government and a return to civil war. With Tiberius away and out of touch in his own world on Capraea it has fallen to me to play the various factions in the Senate off against each other, ensuring that none ever gets too powerful. It fell to me to deal with Sejanus because Tiberius was blind to his machinations and the Senate was too scared to face up to him.'

Asiaticus went to protest.

'Spare me your arguments, Consul; you were there in the Temple of Apollo when the Senate met believing that they were going to be asked to vote tribunician power to Sejanus. Tell me, if Tiberius' letter had asked for that then what would have been the result of the vote?'

Asiaticus pursed his lips. 'It would have been unanimous,' he admitted.

'Yes, because every senator there would have been too frightened to be seen to vote against it. Only those who had 'accidentally' forgotten about the vote and gone instead to their country estates or those who'd had the misfortune to eat a bad prawn the evening before would have been spared having to make such a tricky decision.'

Corbulo bridled at the remark, much to Vespasian's amusement; it had been the excuse that he had used to absent himself from that meeting.

'I take your point, Lady,' Asiaticus conceded.

'I mean no disrespect to you personally, Consul, I am just stating the facts as they are and this being the case it is vital that I can still play a leading part in the politics of Rome once my brother-in-law is dead; either through one of my grandsons, Gaius or Gemellus, or through my son Claudius – an option that I am now coming to consider.' She paused, enjoying the astounded look on her guests' faces. 'But I shall come to that. First let us consider the way to put a halt immediately to Macro's plans without him suspecting that I'm behind it, because if he does then he will act like a cornered beast and both Tiberius and I would be dead before the month is out. If I interfere with Claudius' and Narcissus' plans to sell the deeds, he'll be suspicious; likewise if I get Gaius to withdraw his promise, Macro is bound to see my hand behind it. So what to do?'

'Remove him, as you did Sejanus, Lady,' Asiaticus suggested.

'I have already taken my first steps along that path. Unfortunately it will be a long journey unless I have him assassinated, which I dare not do for fear of an uprising by the Praetorian Guard who are, as you know, very loyal to him and would see it as an attack on the position that they hold in Rome.'

'Remove Poppaeus, domina,' Corbulo said with a vengeful glint in his eye, 'without him there is no money.'

'Yes, but how? If I have treason charges brought against him I will alert Macro to the fact that I know what he's planning.'

'Then have him murdered,' Vespasian said, hardly believing that he was suggesting such a thing; how long had it taken him to go from taking bribes to suggesting murder?

'That would have the same effect as the previous suggestion,' Antonia said dismissively.

'Not if it were made to look like he died of natural causes, domina.'

Antonia looked at him; a smile slowly spread across her lips. 'Well done, Vespasian; that would work. If he just drops down dead Macro will simply have to accept it as bad luck and will have to start looking for another rich and treacherous sponsor, which could take months, even years. That is very clever.'

'But how could we achieve that and who would do it?' Asiaticus asked, evidently unconvinced. 'It's not as if we could get someone into his house and smother him in his bed, there'd be too many people in his household to get past.'

'I'll do it,' Corbulo offered in a low voice. 'I know that it's not an honourable way to kill a fellow senator but the way he tried to have me killed was even less honourable, so if this is my only chance for revenge, I'll take it.'

Vespasian knew that he would never feel comfortable looking Corbulo in the eye again if, having suggested such an unworthy way of killing their mutual enemy, he did not share in the deed. 'And I'll help you, Corbulo,' he said with a sinking heart. It grieved him that all the high ideals that he had felt when first entering Rome, almost ten years previously, should have come down to this. He realised, in that moment, that there was nothing that he would not do to keep his vision of Rome alight – a Rome ruled with honour, free from the civil wars that brought an end to the Republic. And yet here he was offering to protect that vision with murder; how his grandmother, Tertulla, would laugh if she could see him now, he mused.

'Thank you, gentlemen,' Antonia said with sincerity. 'I know how much this goes against everything that you have been brought up to believe in but I would not ask this of you if I could see any other way.'

Vespasian and Corbulo looked at each other and gave mirthless smiles; they both knew that they had volunteered to do something that they would never be able to forgive themselves for.

Asiaticus cleared his throat; uncomfortable with what had just been decided, but nevertheless understanding that it was the only possible course of action, he brought the conversation back to the practicalities of the matter. 'So how do we achieve this if we assume that to do it in his own house would be nigh on impossible?'

'Poison wouldn't work,' Antonia stated, 'it would take too long to administer small quantities to make it look like he was dying of a wasting disease, and anyway how would you get access to his food on a regular basis?'

There was a silence as everyone around the table tried to work out how to murder somebody and make it look like a natural death if they were not in their own bed or sitting at their study table or similar.

The silence was eventually broken by Pallas from his position by the door. 'May I be of assistance, domina?'

Antonia looked up. 'No doubt you have some of your valuable observations to make, Pallas; they are always a pleasure to hear, so, please, come to our aid.'

The steward stepped forward into the light. 'You are kind, domina. I have only one observation to make and that is: to achieve this thing convincingly it has to be done in private but the body must be found in public. Now if we rule out killing Poppaeus in his own home we have to find another private place in which to do it. Where else in Rome does Poppaeus go? The Senate, the baths, the law courts, his friends' houses for dinner? None of these are private. He would never accept an invitation from you, domina, nor would it be seemly if this act were perpetrated in the house of the Senior Consul – that would be taking dishonour too far.'

Asiaticus nodded his agreement. 'We would be trying the gods' patience if we were to sully the office of the senior magistrate in Rome with low murder.'

'Indeed,' Pallas agreed. 'So the only time in the near future that I can envisage Poppaeus needing to be in private is when he's doing a secret deal.'

'Exchanging the deeds for the debt marker at Claudius' house,' Vespasian exclaimed. 'Of course! But that would mean that Claudius and Narcissus would both have to be party to the plan.'

'I don't think that'll be a problem,' Antonia said, 'it comes down to money. If we wait until after the exchange has been made, I'm sure that both my son and his oily freedman will be only too pleased either to help or at least turn a blind eye, as they will end up with not only a signed-off debt marker but they'll also still be in possession of the deeds to those seven estates. That should be inducement enough and it also furthers my purposes: it will give Claudius the extra income that he will need should I decide that it would be better for Rome for him to become the next Emperor.'

'And might you decide that, Lady?' Asiaticus enquired, raising his eyebrows.

'It depends on how my little Gaius behaves himself in the next few months; but if I were you, Asiaticus, I would keep up my friendship with that idiot son of mine.'

'Oh, I intend to,' the Consul replied with a conspiratorial smile.

Antonia turned her attention back to her steward. 'Thank you for that timely observation, Pallas. Now that you've enlightened us on where to do it, do you have an observation on how it might be done?'

'I'm afraid not, domina,' Pallas replied apologetically, 'but I have an idea who might be able to help us with that delicate matter, bearing in mind the mysterious demise of one of the aediles last year. Shall I ask Magnus to come in?'

Antonia raised her eyebrows. 'I think that that's an excellent idea.'

Magnus' eyes flicked nervously around the room. 'I ain't sure that I understand exactly what you mean, domina.' He shifted uncomfortably on the hard wooden stool placed at the open end of the dining table.

'Don't play coy with me, Magnus,' Antonia ordered, 'it's a simple question, and I'm sure that you know the answer.'

'Well, there is one way; not that I ever tried it, but I heard about it from an acquaintance,' he admitted. 'Who I don't know any more; never really did, if you take my meaning?' he added quickly, glancing uneasily at the Senior Consul.

'It's all right, Magnus,' Antonia reassured him, 'the Senior Consul is here to gain the benefit of your wisdom, not to judge you.'

'If you're the same Magnus who leads the South Quirinal Brotherhood,' Asiaticus added, 'and if you're worried about the, shall we say, "natural" death of the aedile for that district last year, then don't be. Senator Pollo has completely convinced the Urban Prefect that you had nothing to do with it and it's quite normal for a healthy young man to be found dead in the street with no wounds or bruising on him whatsoever. However, I would be interested to know how it was done, so please, enlighten us.'

Magnus looked relieved. 'Well, it's quite simple really: you drown the man by forcing his head into a barrel of water, taking care not to get any bruising around the throat or chest as you hold him under. It's best to strip him first so that his clothes don't get torn or wet. Then you hang him upside down – put a blanket around his ankles so that the rope doesn't mark the skin – and pump his chest until all the water is out – but you must wait a little while before you do that as they can come back to life. Then take him down, rub his hair dry and dress him and there you go, one unmarked dead person. Oh, and when you hang him up it's best to do it in front of a large fire so as to keep him warm, if you want the body to be found quickly, that is.'

'Thank you, Magnus,' Antonia said, looking at him with a glint in her eye that Vespasian knew was more than just an appreciation of his knowledge.

'There is another way,' Magnus offered, warming to the theme, 'but that involves sticking a funnel up his—'

'That will do, Magnus; I think we have a workable solution. That'll be all – for now.'

'Yes, domina,' Magnus mumbled, leaving the room. Vespasian guessed that he would be unable to take advantage of the frenzied female slaves celebrating the Caprotinia that evening.

'Now, gentlemen,' Antonia said as the door closed, 'Poppaeus is dead, so how and where do we have this unfortunate occurrence discovered?'

'If I may, domina?' Pallas offered.

'I was hoping you would, Pallas,' Antonia said with a smile.

'Poppaeus generally walks with a stick and considers it beneath his dignitas to go anywhere in Rome unless he is carried in a litter, in which he will undoubtedly arrive at Claudius' house. We will need to get the body back in there and have the litter-bearers take him to the Forum where, I would suggest, the Senior Consul could waylay him and, pulling back the curtains, discover to his consternation that the good man has sadly passed away.'

Asiaticus laughed. 'A more public discovery would be hard to engineer. That's very good and I will be only too happy to play my part.'

'But how do we get the body back in the litter so it seems to the bearers that their master is alive and it's him that gives them the order to go to the Forum?' Vespasian asked.

'We will create the illusion that he is still alive.'

'But how?'

'Leave that to me, Vespasian; it won't be as hard as you might think,' Pallas assured him. 'But I will need you to leave the chest here.'

'Well, gentlemen, I think our business is concluded,' Antonia said with an air of finality. 'I thank you for your time. Consul, would you mind a private word?'

'Of course, domina.'

'Thank you. Vespasian and Corbulo, tomorrow morning Pallas and I will visit my drooling son and his odious freedman to make the arrangements and to inform them of the consequences of not complying with my wishes; you will join us there at the second hour.'

'With pleasure, domina,' Vespasian replied, less than truthfully.

Leaving the room, followed by Corbulo, and stepping out into the walkway surrounding the torch-lit peristylium, Vespasian was disappointed that he had not even seen Caenis, who was almost always at her mistress's side. Contemplating this as they walked in silence around the colonnade, he had the sudden unpleasant realisation that, as Antonia's secretary, Caenis would have made a copy of Corvinus' letter. She knew about Flavia before he had had a chance to explain it to her.

'What did I tell you, sir?' Magnus said, appearing out of the shadows. 'She did have something fucking nasty planned for us: cold-blooded murder by the sounds of it. Who's the target – Poppaeus?'

'Yes,' Vespasian replied, more tersely than he had meant to.

'Well, that makes it more palatable, I suppose, the revolting little shit.'

'But you were wrong; she hadn't already planned it. In fact, she was at a loss as to what to do. It was me who suggested murdering him.'

Magnus laughed. 'Of course you did, sir, but only after she'd dismissed all other options as being unworkable or taking too long, I'll warrant.'

'It was the only possible course of action, man,' Corbulo snapped. 'I volunteered to do it and Vespasian said he'd help; she didn't ask us to.'

'Of course she didn't, because it was the only possible course of action that she couldn't suggest.'

'What makes you think that?' Vespasian asked.

'Well, it stands to reason, don't it?' Magnus said, exasperated. 'Antonia has never been at a loss as to what to do about a situation in her life; the trouble was that she couldn't just say in front of the Senior Consul: "I want Poppaeus murdered in a way that it looks like death from natural causes; and by the way, Vespasian and Corbulo, would you set your honour aside and act like an eastern king's eunuch chamberlain or some vengeful woman?" You would have both rightly refused and she couldn't have blamed you for doing so.'

Vespasian and Corbulo looked at each other and realised that this was probably not far from the truth.

Vespasian groaned. 'But the fact that we suggested the idea made it possible for us to offer to do it and Antonia got what she wanted without being seen to ask two senators to murder another.'

'She does play well,' Magnus observed cheerily.

'You should know. Off you go and play with her and give her some bruises from me.'

'She likes that, it's what she wants; the rougher the better.'

'Well, they don't come much rougher than you. I'll see you tomorrow, we've got a visit to make; come over to Gaius' house at dawn.'

'Yes, I suppose I'll be finished here by then. Missing the fucking Caprotinia, though. Goodnight, sir. Ziri's staying with me but the lads will see you back.'

'How do you tolerate him, Vespasian?' Corbulo asked as Magnus went back to await Antonia's pleasure.

'The same way that I tolerate you, Corbulo: I like him.'

Outside the night air was cool, clear and still. A three-quarter moon hung low over the city; its watery light reflected off the marble walls and columns of the larger temples and public buildings, picking them out from the darker brickwork and terracotta roofs of the older or more humble constructions. Here and there columns of smoke from bakeries or forges rose vertically towards the heavens, paling and thinning as they gradually diffused into the atmosphere. The peaceful sight contrasted sharply with the noise of the relentless drunken hubbub, rising from the Subura, of the urban poor enjoying the last hours of the slave women's festival. The grating of iron-shod wheels and the sharp clatter of the horses' hoofs of the trade wagons, making their nightly deliveries to the city's factories and shops, added to their din.

With Marius and Sextus leading, Vespasian and Corbulo walked quickly down from the Palatine, saying little to one another and never meeting the other's eye. If there was ever a case of the ends justifying the means this was it, Vespasian mused, as Corbulo said a sombre goodnight at the foot of the Caelian and quickly headed up the hill, refusing the offer of company.

As they skirted the western end of the Subura the chaos of the festivities became increasingly apparent. Drunken gangs singing bawdy songs at the tops of their voices roamed the streets, fighting and whoring. The comatose bodies of the more excessive drinkers lay in pools of their own vomit and urine where they had fallen and public copulation and other lesser sexual acts were rife in every doorway and up each alley.

'The city's really enjoying itself tonight,' Marius commented regretfully as they passed a slave girl being attended to at either end by two rough-looking freedmen swigging from wineskins as they took their pleasure.

'Yeah, but we deserve it,' Sextus replied, 'what with all the new hardships and such at the moment.'

'What new hardships?' Vespasian asked.

'Well, the grain shortage of course, sir, don't you know?'

'Yeah,' Marius confirmed. 'The grain dole was cut in half a month ago and a lot of people are finding it hard to get by.'

'But that's only because the first grain fleet went down. As soon as the next one comes in things will get back to normal,' Vespasian reassured them.

'I wouldn't be so sure, sir,' Marius replied, as they started to climb up the Quirinal. 'The shortages started long before we heard about the grain fleet. My cousin works down at the granaries and he's never seen them so low. He said that it started getting bad at the end of last summer, when there seemed to be a little less grain arriving with each fleet. They've been keeping it secret, but he's heard talk about speculators.'

Sextus spat on the ground. 'It's always the fucking same, isn't it? The poor suffer while a few rich bastards make more money out of their misery. Fucking senators, begging your pardon that is, sir.'

'It's hardly likely to be senators,' Vespasian said, thinking uneasily about what Corbulo had told him about Pomponius. 'By law they can't involve themselves with trade.'

'Yeah, but that doesn't stop them,' Marius pointed out.

'I'm sure you're right in some cases, Marius.'

'I know I am. My cousin told me that one of the two surviving ships from the grain fleet had its cargo unloaded into a private warehouse and the grain aedile can't find out where it is or who it belongs to so that it can be impounded.'

'My brother's the grain aedile; I'll ask him why he can't find it.'

'Because it's well hidden, that's why; only a senator would want to keep that a secret.'

'But a senator would be foolish to involve himself in grain speculation; the Emperor would have his head and property if he so much as suspected it.'

'The Emperor? What's he to us? He hasn't been seen in Rome for nearly ten years. Stuck out there on his island he might just as well have been thrown into the Tiber; and it's not just me who says that.'

'I'd be careful who you repeat that to; that's treason.'

'Well, I don't know about that, sir, but what is for sure is there ain't enough grain to last the city another month and nobody's meant to know about it and, while the Emperor's doing fuck all about the situation, someone is trying to make a huge profit from it.'

They had arrived at Gaius' house and Vespasian dismissed the two crossroads brothers with a denarius apiece for their trouble. The attractive new, dark-skinned door-youth let him in with a sleepy countenance and then snuggled back down into his bedding-roll in the vestibule.

Vespasian walked through the silent house, contemplating his first day back in Rome; it had not gone as he had wished. He had not seen Caenis and had a good suspicion that he knew why. And, just as worrying for him, he was now involved again

162

with Antonia's schemes and was once more being drawn into a world where political necessity was the sole arbiter of men's actions. But what heightened his sense of unease, as he entered his room and slipped off his toga and tunic, was the issue of the grain shortage. He had seen the same thing happen while he had been in Cyrenaica, but he now knew that was due to Herod Agrippa buying the grain destined for that province for his own ends. Now it seemed that the same thing had been happening here in Rome.

He got into bed and stared at the whitewashed ceiling of his small room. Perhaps it was just down to no more than the sinking of the grain fleet or a few men's selfishness; but one thing that he did know for sure was that if someone wanted to destabilise the regime in Rome for their own ends, the way to do it was through the bellies of the poor.

CHAPTER X

VESPASIAN ROSE JUST before dawn the following morning. Walking through to the atrium he was surprised to find his brother Sabinus sitting with Gaius, by a small fire in the hearth, sharing a breakfast of bread, olives, garlic and well-watered wine, waited on by Aenor.

'So the young quaestor returns from his province,' Sabinus drawled, 'and manages to bring with him a chest full of trouble.'

'Piss off, Sabinus,' Vespasian snapped, handing his folded toga to Aenor and sitting while his uncle filled a cup for him.

'And it's lovely to see you again too, brother. Did you enjoy the camels?'

'I've just been explaining to Sabinus the predicament that you find yourself in,' Gaius said quickly and unnecessarily, but in an attempt to head off an argument. The siblings had never got on; although in recent years Sabinus had started to show more respect for his younger brother, he nevertheless still enjoyed goading him, especially after a long period of absence. 'Come and have some breakfast and tell us what Antonia said.'

'Murder?' Gaius exclaimed, having heard Vespasian's detailed account of his meeting with Antonia. 'That is not a pretty word.'

'It's a woman's weapon, I know, Uncle,' Vespasian said shamefacedly, 'but we could see no other way.'

'I think that you were right to suggest it,' Sabinus said, surprising Vespasian, 'it's the quickest and cleanest way to solve the problem, however effeminate.'

Vespasian ignored the jibe. 'And Corbulo and I get our revenge on Poppaeus.'

'Which is also satisfying,' Sabinus agreed, 'because it means that we keep a promise that I made on both our behalves to Pomponius Labeo.'

'What promise?'

'He sent for me on the day he opened his veins knowing that we owed him a large debt for sheltering our parents from Sejanus on his estate in Aventicum. To repay it, he made me promise that we would take vengeance on Poppaeus.'

'Well, I'm glad that I can be of service,' Vespasian said with more than a hint of sarcasm.

'Oh, you are. In fact, you've provided two services – you've just shown me how I can get even with Herod.'

'What have you got against him?'

'He humiliated me publicly in Judaea in an intolerable manner. I can't let it pass. Now, I'm the aedile supervising the grain distribution in the city this year and I can tell you in confidence that the price is rising because we're down to the emergency level at the granaries.'

'Yes, I heard.'

'What?' Sabinus was shocked. 'That's meant to be a secret.'

'It is: only you, me, Magnus' crossroads brothers and their friends and relations know about it.'

'Very funny,' Sabinus snorted.

'What about the grain from the second ship, why can't you find that to distribute?'

'How did you know about that?'

'It's another well-kept secret.'

'And what other confidences have the brethren been sharing with you? That I've been bribed not to find it, I suppose.'

'I should hope not, dear boy, that would be a capital offence,' Gaius exclaimed, taking a calming slug of wine.

'I'm not that stupid, Uncle. Anyway, the first African grain fleet is due any day and then things should start slowly getting back to normal. However, due to the shortages the price we have to pay is almost a fifth up on last year and is still rising and won't stabilise for a while yet. So anyone caught hoarding grain like our friend

Herod is doing will suffer harsh consequences. I'm going to write anonymously to the Alabarch and tell him how Herod has used the money he lent him in illegal grain speculation. I'll advise him to inform the prefect, Flaccus, before I do, implicating him in the deal as well. Flaccus is completely loyal to Tiberius so is bound to investigate the allegations. He'll find the stockpiled grain, report it and who owns it to Tiberius, and down goes Herod.'

'You should be very careful, dear boy,' Gaius advised, as a knock came from the front door. 'Herod bought that grain off Claudius; if that comes to light he'll also be in a lot of trouble. Antonia doesn't take kindly to people causing problems for members of her family; she reserves that right for herself.'

'That's the beauty of writing anonymously, she'll never find out that it was me and nor will Herod,' Sabinus replied as Magnus was let in looking less than refreshed.

Vespasian got to his feet and signalled Aenor to start draping on his toga. 'Antonia has a remarkable way of knowing about everything, Sabinus; one word from her and you'll have no chance in the praetor elections. If I were you I'd take Uncle's advice and think of another way to satisfy myself with Herod.'

Sabinus scowled. 'I'll think about it.'

'Good morning, gentlemen,' Magnus said once it became apparent that the conversation was at an end.

'Good morning, Magnus, we should go,' Vespasian replied as Aenor tucked in the last fold of his toga.

'Ziri's waiting outside, sir.'

'And I should be greeting my clients,' Gaius said, heaving himself to his feet. 'I wish you well in this unpleasant business, dear boy. Aenor, my toga.'

With a brief nod to his brother, Vespasian turned and followed Magnus out of the door and through the forty or so clients clustered around it waiting to pay their morning respects to their patron.

Finding Ziri at the back of the crowd they headed off down the Quirinal. It was a beautiful, fresh summer's morning with already a hint of warmth in the air. A light breeze blew from inland and Vespasian imagined that he could detect a trace of fresh mown hay and meadow flowers on it above the smells of the city; he thought of his estates at Cosa and Aquae Cutillae and realised that, at this moment, he would give anything to be at either one rather than on his way to plan a murder.

Claudius' house was not what Vespasian would have expected for a member of the imperial family, however out of favour. Set almost up against the city walls on a quiet side street on the Esquiline Hill, it looked more like the home of a merchant who had just suffered from a series of ill-advised business ventures. Peeling whitewash clung to cracked and crumbling plaster that all too often exposed the brickwork underneath. It was, however, substantial and what it lacked in glamour it made up for in privacy; a perfect place to live an unnoticed life, Vespasian mused as he waited nearby for Antonia and Corbulo.

Shortly before the second hour Corbulo came striding around the corner, accompanied by two slaves, looking very pleased with himself. 'Good morning, Vespasian,' he said, ignoring Magnus and Ziri's presence. 'Something good has come out of this sorry affair: Asiaticus wrote me a note this morning promising to endorse my bid for a praetorship. With his support in the Senate I stand a good chance of coming towards the top of the poll and would therefore be in line for the governorship of a propraetorial province after my year.'

'I'm very pleased for you, Corbulo,' Vespasian said with sincerity, 'and for myself.'

'Why, has Asiaticus promised you something too?'

'No, but seeing as it was down to me that you became involved with him I would say that puts you back into my debt; not such a clean slate after all, eh?'

Corbulo frowned, but before he could respond Antonia's litter turned into the street with Pallas walking next to it carrying Capella's chest.

The twelve taut-muscled Nubian bearers set the litter down next to the steps leading up to the front door. Antonia pulled aside the curtain and stepped down. Vespasian's heart jumped as Caenis followed her mistress out. She glanced up at him and gave a shy smile; her normally crystal-clear blue eyes were shaded with sorrow but still lingered on him, taking his breath away. He opened his mouth to try to explain everything to her but, suddenly remembering that they were surrounded by people, closed it immediately and essayed instead a nervous smile. Caenis gave a slight nod as if understanding that they needed to talk and then turned to collect her writing materials from inside the litter.

'Good morning, gentlemen,' Antonia said, bringing Vespasian out of his private world. The faint look of amusement on her face gave Vespasian the distinct impression that his and Caenis' tacit conversation had been a lot more public than they had intended. 'I will do the talking; you should remain silent unless I ask you to speak. Remember that you are here solely to work out the logistics of our...er...enterprise.'

Pallas mounted the steps and rapped on the door.

'I was t-totally unaware, M-M-Mother,' Claudius affirmed, dabbing with a handkerchief at a trail of saliva that leaked from the corner of his downturned mouth, 'of what would happen to the estates.' His alert grey eyes darted across to his freedman, Narcissus, seated next to him on a bench underneath a fruit-laden pear tree in the well-kept courtyard garden. 'As I'm sure was N-N-Narcissus.'

Vespasian and Corbulo sat either side of Antonia watching with interest as she interrogated her son. Claudius had twitched and stammered almost uncontrollably when she had showed him the deeds and he had admitted to knowing that Narcissus had been buying land illegally for him in Egypt. Narcissus had remained unruffled throughout the interview as if it were a matter of little import and consequently beneath his dignity to acknowledge. Vespasian glanced over to Caenis but she kept her head down, concentrating on recording the conversation on wax tablets on her lap. Pallas stood, expressionless, behind her.

'I'm supposed to believe that you were going to sell seven of the biggest wheat-growing estates in Egypt,' Antonia said, indicating to Capella's chest placed, open, on the table between them, 'to an unknown buyer without being remotely interested in who it was?'

'But we thought that we did know, good Lady, we thought it was Poppaeus,' Narcissus replied, stroking his oiled beard with a chubby hand; the ostentatiously bejewelled rings on each stubby digit glinted in the strengthening sun.

'I did not address that question to you, freedman,' Antonia snapped. 'You've already committed an outrage by sitting in my presence without invitation, do not make matters worse by talking out of turn; and I am "domina" to you.'

'Indeed, domina,' Narcissus replied, slowly inclining his head and spreading his hands in acquiescence.

'So you didn't know the end purchaser was Macro?'

'M-M-Macro!' Claudius looked horrified. Narcissus' full lips twitched. 'No, M-M-M-Mother. P-Poppaeus said that he would wipe off the debt for all the estates if I sold seven to h-him.'

'And he didn't tell you what he was going to do with them?'

'No, M-M-M-Mother.'

'Stop m-m-mothering me, Claudius. If you have such trouble saying the word then don't attempt it and this conversation might go a lot more swiftly.'

'Yes, M-M- – yes. We er … I, that is, assumed that he was going to keep them for h-himself.' Claudius glanced again at Narcissus who was studying his manicured fingernails; with an almost imperceptible nod of the head the freedman indicated that he had given the right answer.

'Well, he's not; he's going to sell them on to Macro. Luckily for you I believe your story. I know that even *you* aren't stupid enough to hand such potential wealth to a ruthless man set upon dismembering the Empire that you may one day rule.'

'M-m-me!' Claudius exclaimed in exaggerated surprise. Vespasian noticed a faint smile briefly tweak the corners of Narcissus' mouth.

'Yes, you, Claudius. Don't try to play the innocent with me; it's insulting to both of us. Now, if you want me to seriously consider you as a potential heir then you have to help me put an end to this deal without Macro suspecting that it was me who moved against him. And you must not tell anyone; not even your money-grabbing little friend Herod Agrippa.'

Narcissus placed a silk handkerchief to his mouth and delicately cleared his throat, raising both eyebrows and looking at Antonia.

'What is it?' she asked impatiently.

'My thanks, domina,' Narcissus purred, his voice oozing obsequious sincerity. 'We, that is, my master and I, will naturally do everything that you ask and you can rely on our discretion. I would suggest, if I may, that just stopping the deal or, indeed, eliminating Poppaeus would not be subtle enough to fool Macro.'

'Do you think that I haven't thought of that?'

Narcissus held his hands up and humped his shoulders, tilting back his head and half closing his eyes. 'No, domina, no, of course not. But might I suggest an accidental death?'

'No, you may not, you impertinent little man. We are going to stage a natural death and we're going to stage it in this house.'

Narcissus' eyes widened as he understood the implications. 'And this would be staged after we have done the deal, domina?'

'Yes, Claudius will end up with both the signed-off debt marker as well as the deeds.'

'May I compliment you on such finesse?'

'No, you may not; it was Vespasian's idea.'

Whether that was true or not, Vespasian did not know any more. He felt Narcissus' gaze and looked over at him; the freedman's eyes betrayed a mixture of admiration and appreciation; he gave a half-smile and inclined his head fractionally. Vespasian's mind turned to the bankers' draft; he would cash it with the Cloelius brothers as repayment of that debt once the deed was done.

'I will leave you to discuss the details,' Antonia said, rising and giving her son a stern look. 'Get this right, Claudius, and I might think better of you. Come, Caenis.'

The men all stood as Antonia left; Caenis followed with a hesitant look at Vespasian. He watched her walk out of the garden, wondering when he would get the chance to try to put things right with her.

'So to recap our plan then, masters,' Pallas said, putting down Capella's chest, as they entered the atrium having walked around the whole house and stable yard, where Magnus had joined them. 'On their arrival Poppaeus and his secretary, Kosmas, will be shown into the garden where the deal will take place. Once it is done Claudius will ask Poppaeus for a private word; Narcissus will take Kosmas to his study through the atrium where he will see us waiting for an interview with Claudius. Meanwhile, Poppaeus' litter will have been ordered around the back to the stable yard where it will be left as close as possible to the steps leading into the house. The litter-bearers will be offered food and drink in the kitchen and kept there until Magnus runs to tell them that their master is waiting at the front of the—'

A loud knock at the door interrupted his briefing. Before Narcissus could stop him, the doorkeeper opened it and in walked a tall, elegant, middle-aged man dressed in a jet black robe that fell to his ankles and a purple cloak edged with gold embroidery. A freedman accompanied him.

'H-H-Herod, my dear friend,' Claudius called, shambling over to greet the new arrival. His weak knees knocked together as his feet shuffled forward, making his walk more like a lurch that gave the impression that he would fall flat on his face if he lost his momentum.

Herod took Claudius' forearm in a firm grip. 'I'm sorry if I have intruded on anything,' he said, casting an interested look over Claudius' shoulder at the company. 'Come, Eutyches, Claudius is evidently busy; we should return later.'

The freedman turned and walked back out of the door.

'N-n-n-no, Herod, th-these g-g-g-gentlemen were j-just leaving.'

'Why are you stammering with me, old friend? That is most unlike you.'

Pallas glanced at Vespasian and indicated with his head to the door.

'We shall leave you with your new guest, noble Claudius,' Vespasian said, understanding the gesture and walking towards the exit.

'Not until you have introduced me, surely, Claudius?' Herod said, eyeing Pallas suspiciously. 'Pallas I know, he's your mother's steward; and Senator Corbulo, good day to you.' Corbulo nodded back. 'But I have not had the pleasure of this young gentleman's acquaintance.' He gave Vespasian an unctuous smile.

'B-but of course,' Claudius agreed, his long face reddening.

Vespasian stood in embarrassed silence as Claudius stammered his way through his full name, dribbling copious amounts of saliva from each corner of his mouth, which he tried to stem with a fold of his toga.

'You make your host very nervous, Vespasian,' Herod said, taking his forearm, 'now why would that be, I wonder?' He took another wary look in Pallas' direction and then looked back at Vespasian. 'I met your brother in Judaea and have had a couple of dealings with him here in Rome; please give him my regards.'

'I'll be sure to,' Vespasian replied, curious as to why Sabinus would have had dealings with a man who had insulted him.

'But please, do not let me detain you any further.'

'I look forward to enjoying a longer meeting with you, Herod,' Vespasian said politely if not quite truthfully.

'Indeed, and so do I,' Herod replied, equally politely. 'Eutyches, get back in here, you fool; you've business to attend to.'

'C-c-c-come, Herod, Narciss-ss-cissus will see them out, let us enjoy the g-g-garden. Good day, g-g-gentlemen.' Claudius grabbed Herod's elbow and led him from the room at a suspiciously fast speed as Herod's freedman came scuttling back into the house.

'My master thinks that he's adept at subterfuge, but unfortunately he's not,' Narcissus commented. 'I'll do my best to make Herod think that it was purely legal business or suchlike that brought you here. Unfortunately his eyes, ears and nose are trained to detect intrigue; he may well be a problem.'

'Then we should get this done as soon as possible,' Corbulo suggested.

'Your judgement is faultless, senator,' Narcissus crooned, 'and does you great credit. Poppaeus too is keen to seal the deal. I'm sure that he won't object to being here at the second hour tomorrow to do so; there is no meeting of the Senate owing to the festival of Apollo.'

'We shall be here at dawn unless we hear otherwise from you, Narcissus,' Pallas said, picking up the chest. 'I will let Asiaticus know to be in position in the Forum from the third hour onwards to waylay the litter.'

'Excellent, my friend; and I will have a rope and a barrel full of water ready. May the gods look kindly upon our venture.'

The doorman let them out into the street.

As the door closed behind them Pallas surprised them all. 'Fuck!'

They had left Corbulo at the foot of the Caelian Hill to make his way home and were now ascending the Palatine. Hundreds of people were making a slow progress up the hill singing paeans to Apollo while holding polished bronze discs in the air symbolising the sun. Unable to push their way through the densely packed crowd, they were obliged to walk at the steady slow pace of the three white oxen that led the procession.

'There's going to be a sacrifice to Apollo, Ziri,' Magnus explained to his slave.

'Apollo? What is?' Ziri asked looking around nervously at the crush of people.

'He's the god of lots of things: truth, shepherds, colonisation, archery, all sorts...' Magnus paused; Ziri's blank face showed that his Latin was not coping with his explanation. 'Never mind. After the sacrifice there're going to be gladiatorial games in the Taurus amphitheatre on the Campus Martius – we'll go along, there should be some good fights.' Magnus looked at Vespasian. 'You fancy it, sir?'

'No thanks; once I've spoken with Antonia I'm going to the baths,' Vespasian replied as they managed to leave the procession and turn onto Antonia's street. 'We haven't been since Creta,' he added, looking pointedly at Magnus.

'Yeah, well, one more day ain't going to make a difference then, is it? Besides, I'm looking forward to seeing how Ziri reacts to everyone having a good... well, you know.'

Vespasian frowned. 'Do you think he's ready for that?'

'I'm not sure that public masturbation every time a gladiator is killed is something that Romans should be overly proud of,' Pallas remarked.

Magnus grinned. 'Yeah, but it adds spice to it all, don't it? Especially if you've got a nice young whore to help you along, if you take my meaning?'

'Masturbation? What is?' Ziri asked.

'I'm afraid that you're just about to find out, Ziri,' Vespasian replied as they reached Antonia's door.

Dismissing Magnus and Ziri with orders to be at Gaius' house an hour before dawn, Vespasian followed Pallas indoors. After a brief wait Antonia appeared, accompanied by Caenis dressed in a hooded cloak.

'Is it set up?' Antonia asked Pallas.

'Yes, domina. But Herod Agrippa and his freedman, Eutyches, saw us there.'

Antonia's face froze. 'Herod! Of all people he'll see the coincidence in Poppaeus' death. I'll need some time to think about how to deal with this. Who's this freedman?'

'Herod was obliged to give him his freedom a couple of years ago so that he could sign for a loan on his behalf. I don't know much else about him, just that Herod has treated him as an idiot since he purchased him when he was a boy.'

'Is he loyal?'

'I doubt it. Who can be loyal to a man who has no loyalty to anyone but himself?'

'Perhaps we could try and talk to him; he might be willing to expose a few little secrets.'

In a moment of clarity a thought came to Vespasian as he remembered Sabinus' idea of how to expose a secret of Herod's. 'Domina, why not threaten to expose Herod as a grain speculator? You could do it without endangering Claudius for selling it to him in the first place.'

'How?'

'By using my brother. As the grain aedile he has the right to impound Herod's stockpile in Egypt in a time of shortage. I'm sure that Sabinus won't look too closely at where Herod bought it.'

She turned to Vespasian and smiled. 'Leaving Herod the choice between losing all that money or keeping quiet about any suspicions that he might have about Macro's property deal collapsing. Very good; you're learning, Vespasian. I shall start working on that immediately. Meanwhile, Caenis wants to go to the sacrifice at the Temple of Apollo; I know that it's very unusual to ask a member of the Senate to accompany one's slave but I thought that this once you might be willing to make an exception.'

Vespasian looked at Caenis who smiled shyly at him. 'It will be my pleasure, domina.'

'Good. Pallas, come with me. We have work to do; send a message to Sabinus to come here as soon as he's finished at the granaries.' With a reassuring squeeze of Caenis' arm she turned and left the room.

Vespasian took a step towards Caenis. 'Caenis, I...'

She moved away. 'Not here, my love, let's walk.'

'My mistress has explained,' Caenis said through gritted teeth, bringing both clenched fists down hard onto her thighs. 'I know now that we can never marry, but I'd never heard of that law until my mistress told me about it just before she gave me

Corvinus' letter to copy. I didn't understand why she was telling me that at the time, it just came from nowhere and hurt me deeply. I'd been dreaming of marrying you, my love; then I find out that I can't and moments later I understood why Antonia told me then: to prepare me for the news that you were after another woman.'

'It's my duty to have sons,' Vespasian replied rather lamely.

'Duty! I know it's your duty,' Caenis exploded, causing people all around them in the street to turn their heads. 'But what about me? Us? Where is our love in all this?'

'First and foremost, Caenis, as it will always be,' Vespasian replied, keeping his voice hushed, aware of the amusement that the perceived lovers' tiff was causing around them.

'So while you have a family with this other woman you just expect me to move aside, waiting for the odd morsel of comfort that you have time to cast my way on the rare occasions that you manage to free yourself from your duty to your family and to Rome? Meanwhile, I'm left to burn with jealousy knowing that my lover, my best friend, is being given something, by someone he claims not to love as much as me, that I am forbidden by law to give him, something that I so desperately want to give him: children.' Caenis stopped and squared up to him. 'How can I do that, my love? How can you expect so much from me?' she asked in a gentle, quavering voice.

'But Flavia has disappeared, I won't find her again.'

'You'll find another; it's only a matter of time.'

Vespasian looked into her pleading eyes, rimmed with tears, and felt a knot of raw emotion gnawing at his bowels. Caenis was right, that was exactly what he had expected of her; yet he had never thought of it in those terms. In all of his planning of his future domestic arrangements he had made the assumption that Caenis would make room for his future wife and that both women would submit to the arrangement; he could see now that he had been deluded. He had, whether consciously or not, considered Caenis' feelings only in relation to her social status – that of a slave soon to be freed. He saw her for the first time as his equal; now they were just a man and a woman deeply in love with one another.

'We're trapped, aren't we, my love?' he whispered, oblivious now to the crowds of people passing them on either side. Caenis was all he could see.

She took both his hands in hers. 'Yes, Vespasian, we are, unless I forgo the children that my body is screaming at me to give you, or you give up the position and career that your dignitas demands of you.'

'What do we do?'

She smiled weakly, lowering her eyes. 'For now all I can suggest is that we walk to the sacrifice.'

The crowd outside the Temple of Apollo was as large as it had been on that momentous day when Sejanus had fallen, almost four years previously. Vespasian and Caenis made their way to the front – his senatorial toga being sufficient to clear a path through the people – remembering the parts that they had played in that tumultuous event and its build-up. They talked as if they were simply on a pleasant outing together and managed to put to one side their emotional turmoil. Both were aware that it was merely a postponement of the decision they would soon have to take; until then, however, they were happy to seek refuge in easy companionship.

As they arrived at the steps to the temple Vespasian looked at Caenis: he had never loved her so much. She felt his gaze and surreptitiously grasped his hand, sending a shiver throughout his body.

'We are not unmindful of Apollo who shoots from afar.' The melodious voice of the presiding priest broke into their private world.

Behind the priest, in front of the closed temple doors, the three white bulls, adorned with golden ribbons, stood patiently under the portico, their halters held by youths with their faces painted gold. Two more priests stood either side of him with a fold of their togas over their heads. Arranged at regular intervals along the top step were three large copper basins. Musicians to either side flanked the sacrificial party.

'Father Apollo, I pray to you, all-seeing guardian god, be gracious to Rome and protect Her. Be ever vigilant and warn Her Emperor what subjects of his or strangers conspire against him; whatever treacherous plots there may be, keep him alert and prepared. Protect us and keep us safe always.'

With a clash of cymbals the temple doors opened, revealing the statue of the god garlanded with flowers and lit with a golden light by torches reflecting off highly polished bronze discs.

Caenis bowed her head at the sight and started to mutter a private prayer as the bulls were led forward to stand one in front of each basin. Three acolytes walked out of the temple; one carried a golden urn, another a flat golden plate, and the third a tray holding three sacrificial knives. A heavy mallet hung from each one's belt.

The presiding priest took three small flat salt cakes from the plate and crumbled one on each of the beasts' heads. A second priest followed behind him pouring a libation over the crumbs. The third priest retrieved the knives and distributed them to his fellows. The acolytes took up position, one next to each of the animals; they unhooked their mallets and held them ready.

'Turn to us now, Mighty Archer, we pray that finally now, Apollo, You will come to our aid. Father, hold Your hands over us and our Emperor. If You approve of what we do, then stir strength into us and into him who is of the utmost importance for the success of our city's venture. Father Apollo, deign to accept this gift.'

The three mallets cracked in unison onto the wide foreheads of the bulls, stunning them but not downing them. Three knives then flashed simultaneously up through the air, piercing the dazed animals' throats. With ever increasing surges of blood they sliced through the loose flesh severing arteries and windpipes. The beasts' hearts pumped on and the blood surges turned into constant streams, quickly filling the bowls beneath them before spilling over to flow in three separate rivulets down the steps. The two outside streams gradually converged into the central one as they followed the contour of the marble – more worn in the middle from long usage – down towards Vespasian and Caenis.

As the first of the great beasts crashed onto the stone floor the rivulet arrived at Vespasian and Caenis' feet. It split in two as it traced the groove around the irregular paving stone upon which they stood. They both watched as the two streams rejoined each other, surrounding the stone, leaving them standing on a little island in a river of blood.

Caenis looked up at Vespasian. 'I prayed that Apollo would give me a sign to guide my decision and he has,' she said, pointing to the ground. 'The blood of his sacrifice has encircled us showing me that we should always be together. I cannot argue with the will of Apollo. You must do what your duty requires of you. I will always be yours, whatever happens.'

Vespasian was desperate to kiss her but propriety forbade a senator to commit such an act in public. Caenis sensed his desire and whispered in his ear: 'My mistress told me to be back by dawn; take me to your bed, my love.'

CHAPTER XI

V ESPASIAN WAS WOKEN well before dawn the following morning by an insistent rapping on his bedroom door.

'Yes?' he called out dozily.

'It's time, master,' a young voice replied in a thick German accent.

Vespasian grunted and slipped an arm around Caenis' warm body. She stirred as he nuzzled the back of her neck.

'Is it morning, my love?' she asked, turning towards him.

'I'm afraid so.' He kissed her softly and held her close so that their bodies moulded into one another.

The relief that he felt at Caenis' decision was overwhelming; he had stared into the abyss of life without her and it had terrified him.

The sudden realisation that he could not just expect her to fit in with his plans had come as a shock; but what had been even more startling was the insight that he had had into his own priorities. Had it come to a decision between his love for Caenis and his duty to Rome, together with the advancement of his family – a duty that no man could in honour repudiate – he would have been obliged to let Caenis slip away, despite the misery to which he would have condemned them both. He lay, staring into the dark, holding her tight and thanked Apollo that he had not been forced to make that choice. He would offer a sacrifice in gratitude to the god once this day was done.

After a few more stolen moments they finally dragged themselves out of bed, dressed and walked into the atrium to find Magnus talking with Gaius. Ziri stood by the door gawping at Gaius' homoerotic artwork that dominated every angle of the room.

'Good morning, dear boy, and to you, Caenis,' Gaius said, 'I hope you both got some sleep, eventually.'

Vespasian grinned as Caenis blushed. 'Thank you, Uncle. Morning, Magnus.'

'Morning, sir; Caenis. We'd best be off if we've got to go to Antonia's first.'

A knock on the door interrupted them and Sabinus entered. 'Uncle, I need your help,' he said without any greetings. 'I'm going to see Antonia now and I'd like you to come with me.'

'Whatever for?'

'Because there is something that I didn't tell you.'

'Go on.'

Sabinus looked nervously at Caenis.

'I won't repeat anything that I hear in this house, Sabinus; you can trust me.'

Sabinus sat down and grabbed a cup of wine. 'Antonia called me to her house yesterday and asked me to meet with her and Herod Agrippa today to threaten him with impounding his grain in Egypt. Of course I couldn't refuse.'

'I thought that you would be pleased with a chance at revenge on Herod,' Vespasian said, unable to see why Sabinus was so agitated.

'You gave her the idea?'

'Yes, it seemed a safer way than writing to the Alabarch.'

'But I was going to write anonymously; Herod would never have known that it was me. If he does he'll expose me for what I've done and I'll be facing a capital charge.'

'What's he got on you, dear boy?' Gaius asked.

'The day I saw Pomponius he asked me to sell a stockpile of grain that he'd speculated in and give the money to his heirs. He told me that if anything was surer than his death it was that grain would be going up in price this year. He even told me who would risk buying it; but I didn't sell it.'

'Oh, you idiot!' Vespasian exclaimed. 'You went and speculated in grain as well, you bought it, didn't you?'

'Well, it sounded like an easy way to make money. I'd just come back from the East with a decent amount of cash, enough to buy the votes in last year's aedile elections and sponsor some games to raise my profile for the upcoming praetor elections, but then I would have been left with almost nothing.'

'So you poured the whole lot into Pomponius' grain.'

'His heirs got their money and I had the chance to make something out of the deal. It was just going to be for a year while the price rose. How the fuck did I know that I was going to be made the grain aedile? As soon as I was appointed I sold it as quickly as possible, but I still made a healthy profit on it.'

'A grain aedile profiting on a grain deal; that really is a capital offence,' Gaius agreed.

'Who did you sell it to?' Vespasian asked, dreading the answer. 'Or is that a stupid question?'

Sabinus' shoulders sagged. 'Herod Agrippa; how else would he know?'

Gaius' jowls wobbled in alarm. 'Why to him of all people?'

'Because Pomponius had suggested him and I knew him; he was the obvious choice despite what I felt about him.'

'Who else knows?'

'Just the Cloelius brothers in the Forum; they transferred the money to me and drew up the bill of sale, which I still have but they've got a copy and so has Herod. However, Herod's been using it to blackmail me; one of the two grain ships that survived the storm was in fact part of his Egyptian stockpile that he bought from Claudius. He's brought it over to sell on the black market at a huge profit. I know where it is in Ostia but if I impound it, as I should, he'll make the bill of sale from Pomponius' grain public.'

'But then he'll be just as implicated in grain speculation.'

'Yes, but he's not the grain aedile; I would certainly be executed.'

Gaius rubbed the back of his neck and inhaled through his teeth. 'I fear that assessment is unfortunately correct. So you want me to negotiate a way out of this for you with Antonia.'

Sabinus nodded unhappily.

'We'd better get going, then.'

'Yes,' Vespasian agreed, looking at his brother disapprovingly, 'let's get this day over with.'

Claudius was in a high state of agitation as Narcissus showed Vespasian, Corbulo and Pallas into his study. The fact that they were half an hour late, owing to Antonia detaining Pallas once she had been apprised of what Sabinus wanted to tell her, had not helped his nerves.

'H-H-Herod was very susp-p-picious. I don't think he b-b-believed me.'

'What did you tell him?' Pallas asked, placing Capella's chest down on the desk.

'That you were here on legal business of Antonia's,' Narcissus replied, saving them all a stammering explanation. 'He accepted the reason far too easily for my liking. I know he knew it was a lie; being an inveterate liar himself, he can spot them easily. I think that we should abort this.'

'We can't,' Vespasian insisted. 'Poppaeus will be here soon expecting to do the deal; if he goes away with nothing he'll become suspicious and if he leaves with the deeds we won't be able to stop him giving them to Macro.'

'I could just g-g-go out, as if I've forg-g-gotten,' Claudius suggested.

Vespasian, Corbulo and Pallas glanced at each other and then at Narcissus who lowered his eyes, embarrassed by his master's pathetic idea.

Claudius pressed on, unaware of what a fool he was making of himself. 'And then I could write t-to him to apologise, and sug-g-gest that we do it next month, when Herod has forg-gotten all about it.' He gave a triumphant look as if he had just solved the most difficult problem with a solution of stunning brilliance and finesse.

There was a brief, awkward silence.

'That is worthy of consideration, master,' Narcissus responded with such a degree of respect that Vespasian almost believed him.

'But unnecessary, noble Claudius,' Pallas assured him. 'Your mother is at the moment taking steps to, how should I put it? Isolate Herod for the foreseeable future.'

'How?'

'That is no concern of ours at the present, only Herod's. Now I suggest that we go about our business. Narcissus, my friend, you show Magnus and Ziri to the other room and we'll wait in the *triclinium* as planned while the noble Claudius greets his clients.'

An hour later they were sitting in silence in the spacious triclinium. The plates of bread, olives, ham and boiled eggs on the table in the middle of the dining room lay untouched.

'This is starting to play on my nerves,' Corbulo said, getting up to look through the wooden grille in the door that opened onto the garden. 'Claudius must have finished with his clients by now.'

Vespasian joined him and looked out to where two chairs had been set either side of a wooden table ready for the meeting with Poppaeus. A slave scuttled into the garden, placed a jug and two silver cups on the table and then disappeared off towards the gate that led to the stable yard at the back of the house.

As the slave closed the gate behind him Narcissus came into the garden with Capella's chest and placed it on the table. Claudius followed, clutching an armful of scrolls. He sat down and, unwinding a scroll, started to read. His constant twitching and the shaking of his hands added credence to Narcissus' earlier assertion that his master was less than adept at subterfuge.

'That idiot is going to ruin this,' Corbulo hissed as Narcissus went back into the house.

'Let's hope that Narcissus will do the talking,' Vespasian replied, thinking that Corbulo had a point. Then the blood drained from his face as he realised that they had all overlooked a possibility. 'Shit! What if Poppaeus doesn't bring his secretary?' He spun round and looked at Pallas.

'The illusion can still be maintained so long as everybody does exactly what I say.'

Vespasian's nerves were starting to fray but he steadied himself with the belief that Pallas and Narcissus knew what they were doing; all he had to do was to help Corbulo kill Poppaeus. He would keep his mind focused on that.

Footsteps coming from the atrium diverted his attention back through the grille.

'My master awaits you out here, proconsul.' Narcissus' voice oozed with deference as he led Poppaeus and a tall, wiry man with a sharp face and lank, greasy hair into the garden.

Vespasian had not seen Poppaeus up close for more than nine years and was amazed by how the little man had aged. His spine had rounded and he leant on his stick, making him even more diminutive. The skin on his face was thin and slack so that it hung in loose folds. His hair was gone. He was no longer the general who had shown such bravery on the wall in Thracia under a hail of arrows and slingshot; he was a frail old man.

'This is going to be disgusting murder,' Corbulo muttered.

Vespasian did not need to be told; he was feeling wretched. He turned back to the garden.

'My dear Pop-p-p-'

'Poppaeus, C-C-Claudius!' Poppaeus snapped, hobbling towards the table. 'Let's get this over quickly; I'd better do the talking.'

'Of c-c-course.' Claudius' eyes narrowed briefly and for the first time Vespasian caught a glimpse of the hatred that he harboured for people who mocked him.

'Kosmas, the marker,' Poppaeus ordered, sitting without invitation with his back to the grille, just five paces away.

The wiry secretary unslung a leather bag from his shoulder and gave it to his master as Narcissus produced the two keys to unlock Capella's chest.

'This is the debt marker for the fourteen and a half million denarii you borrowed from me,' Poppaeus said, pulling a scroll from the bag and handing it to Claudius. 'Show me the deeds.'

Narcissus pushed the chest towards him and Poppaeus began to examine each of the seven scrolls within, one by one.

Pallas joined Vespasian and Corbulo at the grille. 'As soon as the deal is signed we move into the atrium,' he whispered.

Poppaeus read the last scroll and then put it back in the chest. 'They're all in order.'

Narcissus handed the two keys to Kosmas who closed the lid and locked it. He placed the keys in his bag and took out a stylus and a pot of ink.

'Your signature, P-Poppaeus,' Claudius requested, handing the marker to Narcissus.

Vespasian's heart was thumping.

Narcissus spread the scroll on the table; Kosmas dipped the stylus in the ink and offered it to his master. Poppaeus signed with the diligence of a man whose eyesight was failing and then passed the scroll and stylus over to Claudius who signed it with a surprisingly steady hand. The two secretaries then witnessed the signatures making the document legal.

'Follow me,' Pallas said to Vespasian and Corbulo, leading them out into the atrium.

'That's our business concluded,' Vespasian heard Poppaeus say, 'I'll bid you good day.'

'There's another matter that I would like to discuss with you, concerning the upcoming elections,' Claudius replied with remarkable fluency. 'It'll take no longer than a cup of wine.'

There was a pause; Vespasian heard the sound of wine being poured and the jug set back down on the table.

'Alone,' Claudius insisted.

'Very well, but be quick. Kosmas, take the chest and wait for me outside.'

'A cup of wine in my study perhaps, my dear Kosmas?' Narcissus purred.

Pallas, Vespasian and Corbulo stood waiting by the far end of the *impluvium* as Narcissus ushered Kosmas, clutching the chest, in from the garden. 'Gentlemen,' he said, 'my master will not keep you long, he is with the proconsul Poppaeus.'

'It will be an honour to offer the proconsul our greetings as he leaves,' Pallas replied as Narcissus led Kosmas away with barely a glance towards the waiting group.

Pallas moved forward as the footsteps retreated. Vespasian followed with Corbulo; his mouth was dry and his stomach knotted. From the far end of the atrium they heard the door to Narcissus' study open and then shut.

'Whatever happens, don't let him cry out and don't bruise him,' Pallas whispered as they stepped into the garden.

Corbulo leapt forward and had one hand over Poppaeus' mouth and the other under his arm before the old man was aware of a threat from behind him. Vespasian stooped down to grab his ankles and they lifted him from his chair, knocking the table; Pallas caught the wine jug just before it toppled off.

'This way,' Claudius said, rising quickly to his unsteady feet and leading them to a door at the rear of the garden.

They manhandled their struggling captive into the room; Pallas closed the door behind them. Magnus and Ziri stood in one corner by a full barrel of water; a rope on a pulley hung from a hook in the ceiling in front of a blazing fire that provided the only light in the room. The air was fuggy and the windows shuttered. They immediately began to sweat.

'What is the meaning of this outrage, Claudius?' Poppaeus demanded as he was dumped unceremoniously onto the floor.

'This is what happens to people who try to make a fool out of me.'

'Then you have a long list to deal with,' Poppaeus spat contemptuously, rising to his feet and looking around. 'Corbulo!' he exclaimed as his weak eyes got used to the gloom; then his gaze rested on Vespasian. 'And you, I know you; you're Asinius' protégé who disappeared after that bloodbath in his tent. Vespasian, isn't it?'

'Yes, Poppaeus.'

'This is about more than just buying land deeds off an idiot—'

A sharp slap cracked across his face.

'Don't mark him, master,' Pallas shouted, grabbing Claudius' wrist to prevent the reverse swipe.

187

'I will not tolerate being called an idiot,' Claudius fumed, struggling to release his hand.

Poppaeus wiped a drop of blood from his lip, ignoring Claudius' outburst. 'What can I offer you, gentlemen? Or is this personal and beyond money?'

'It's way beyond money, Poppaeus,' Corbulo replied. 'You tried to have us killed along with two cohorts of your recruits in the most dishonourable manner.'

Poppaeus smiled; a drip of sweat rolled down his reddened cheek. 'So that has come back to haunt me, has it? I don't suppose telling you that it wasn't personal and that what we were doing was for the greater good would make any difference?'

'How can that have been for the greater good?' Vespasian exploded.

'Because, young man, Rome must have strong, clear government. If you accept that we can never go back to the pure Republic without risking civil war every generation then we must have an emperor. But just look at what we have now; Rome needs to rid herself of this remote, mad Emperor and his ridiculous family. Who's going to be emperor after Tiberius? Him?' Poppaeus asked, not even bothering to look at Claudius.

'You were supporting my claim at one time,' Claudius insisted.

'Only because you would have been the easiest heir to get rid of and replace with Sejanus.'

'But now he's dead you're supporting Caligula so that Macro can use his wife to buy Egypt, take over the East and split the Empire in two; how is that strong, clear government?' Vespasian demanded.

Poppaeus stared at him for a few moments. 'I can only imagine that an intellect far greater than yours has seen through what we had planned. I detect Antonia behind this; if that is so then I am dead, no matter how much I try to convince you that I was right. So if I am to be murdered I shall act with dignity, if only to shame you; although I'm curious to know how you plan to get my body away from here when there are so many witnesses.'

'Tell me first why splitting the Empire would be good for Rome.'

'Do you really think that it would remain divided? Of course not. Whoever holds Egypt holds Rome. Caligula and Ennia would have been dead within months and Macro would have been emperor with my daughter, Poppaea Sabina, as his empress at the cost to him of merely a wife.'

'And a new dynasty would have been founded,' Claudius pointed out with a sneer.

Poppaeus shook his head. 'No, that was the beauty of it. Had Sejanus succeeded then that would have become a problem, but with Macro it would have been different: he has no children and my daughter cannot have any more after the complications she had giving birth to the young Poppaea. There would be no male heir so Macro would have to choose the best man for the job and adopt him as his son, thereby creating a precedent that I hoped would last for the benefit of Rome. That's why I agreed to help him although he was my enemy. Yes, I admit that I wanted the honour for my family to be able to boast an empress, but more than that I wanted to free ourselves from this hereditary Kingship in all but name; we rid ourselves of the Kings five hundred years ago and now we have them again and it doesn't work. However, if Antonia is determined to keep her family in power despite its obvious unsuitability I want no part of it, so let's get this over with.' Poppaeus removed his toga and knelt on the floor. 'Give me the sword and I'll die like a Roman should.'

'It's not going to be done like that,' Vespasian said quietly, feeling a huge sympathy for his old enemy's views; if Rome was to be ruled in honour by an emperor, was it not best to select a suitable man rather than leave it to the vagaries of blood? He had expressed the same sentiments to Sabinus, Corbulo and Pallas in Tiberius' unfinished bedroom on Capreae as they had waited for the crazed old Emperor to read Antonia's letter damning Sejanus.

'How is it to be done, then?' Poppaeus asked, looking up.

'We are to drown you, sir,' Pallas informed him.

'I see, I wondered what that barrel was for. You're going to try and make it look like a natural death. Well, I suppose that suits Antonia's purposes better. So be it.' He got to his feet and walked over to the barrel. Magnus and Ziri moved away to give him room. 'I would appreciate it if you'd allow me the courtesy to do this myself; I think we would all feel a lot better that way. If I need help towards the end use one hand lightly; you won't need force, my strength is gone.' He plunged his head under the water and held the sides of the barrel firmly; the muscles under the loose, pale flesh on his forearms tautened with the strain of keeping his head submerged. A sudden reflex as his lungs filled with water caused his body to convulse and his head sprang back. Choking and spluttering, Poppaeus forced it back under. Corbulo cast a regretful look at Vespasian and walked over to the barrel. Another spasm from the dying man brought his head back out of the water again, his eyes bulged and his mouth was drawn back in a bare-toothed, silent scream; water spewed from his convulsing lungs. With a monumental effort of will he plunged back under; Corbulo rested his right hand on his head. Poppaeus' feet started to kick and his arms flailed but he remained submerged. His thrashing limbs gradually lost their force until, apart from the odd twitch as the nervous system shut down, they became still.

Poppaeus was dead.

There was silence in the room as they stared at the lifeless body slumped over the barrel. Corbulo withdrew his hand.

'Fuck me, that took some guts,' Magnus mumbled eventually, breaking the spell.

'He was a dis-dis-gusting traitor who planned to usurp power from its rightful place,' Claudius affirmed. 'He doesn't d-d-deserve respect.'

Vespasian, Corbulo and Pallas looked at the stuttering, slobbering potential heir to the Julio-Claudian line.

Claudius' eyes narrowed, perhaps reading their minds. 'G-get on with it,' he ordered, 'Narcissus can't keep Kosmas talking for too long.'

Magnus moved towards the body. 'Come on, Ziri, help me get his tunic off and string him up.'

Poppaeus' body swung upside down, naked on the rope in front of the blazing fire. Water was collecting in the roof of his mouth; it overflowed in trickles through his loose lips onto his face, filling his nostrils, and then dripped from his bald pate into a large puddle beneath him.

'Right, that should be enough time; you hold him firm, sir,' Magnus said to Vespasian.

Vespasian knelt and unwillingly placed his hands on Poppaeus' clammy, skinny back.

'Hold his mouth open, Ziri,' Magnus ordered as he placed his hands on either side of the ribcage. He began to pump with hard, regular squeezes. A gush of water suddenly erupted from Poppaeus' mouth, spraying over Magnus' face and tunic; he kept pumping as the flow lessened until it stopped completely. 'That should do it. Now we take him down and turn him onto his belly.'

Carefully they lowered the body face down on to the floor and undid the rope, removing the linen towels protecting his ankles. Magnus gave the back a few more squeezes to remove any residue still stuck in the windpipe.

'Now we dry him and dress him,' Pallas said once Magnus was satisfied that all the water was out.

Replacing the tunic and belt was easy but no one had foreseen the difficulty involved in draping a toga onto a dead body. Eventually, with Magnus and Ziri holding the lifeless mannequin upright, Vespasian and Corbulo managed to set the toga to Pallas' satisfaction as Claudius lurched to and fro reminding everyone, unnecessarily, that time was pressing.

'Get his arms over your shoulders and follow me,' Pallas ordered Magnus and Ziri as he opened the door.

'I never seen such madness,' Ziri told Magnus as he hefted the body up, 'not even at circus yesterday when you all started—'

'Yes, yes, all right, Ziri,' Magnus said, manoeuvring the body through the door.

Vespasian and Corbulo took a quick look around the room to make sure that none of Poppaeus' possessions remained and then followed out into the garden.

'I'll w-w-wait for you here,' Claudius said. 'It's the next bit that I'm looking f-forward to.'

'I think that the crippled bastard is enjoying this,' Corbulo complained as he and Vespasian slipped through the garden gate into a stable yard overshadowed by the huge bulk of the brick-built Servian wall of Rome at its far end.

Poppaeus' covered litter was next to the steps. Pallas pulled back the curtains and indicated to the mound of pillows at one end. 'Put him this way round with his head on the cushions.'

Magnus and Ziri heaved the body into the litter. Pallas then arranged it so that it appeared that Poppaeus was reclining on his right elbow. Vespasian and Corbulo helped him to stuff pillows around the torso, wedging it in position.

'Arrange his clothes,' Pallas said once satisfied with the pose, 'I won't be long.'

By the time Poppaeus' toga looked natural Pallas had returned carrying Capella's chest.

'How did you get that off Kosmas?' Vespasian asked, amazed.

Pallas gave a rare smile. 'I didn't, it's an exact copy that I had made when you left me the original; the same locks and seven fake land deeds inside.' He placed the chest next to Poppaeus and closed the curtains, tying them shut. 'Magnus, go and get the bearers from the kitchens; put the fear of the gods into them so that they rush, we don't want them looking inside the litter. Then follow them round to the front and stand in front of the only bearer who has a clear view of the steps, ready to open the litter curtains slightly when I give you the nod. Ziri, get the gate open.'

Magnus and Ziri hurried off; Pallas led Vespasian and Corbulo back into the garden where Claudius was waiting.

'Now to complete the deception as we discussed yesterday. Remember, we walk through the atrium talking loudly about the elections as if Poppaeus is in our midst,' Pallas reminded them as they walked through the garden. 'As we near the door Narcissus will bring Kosmas out of his study so that he will see us from the rear. The key to it is for each of us to say the name Poppaeus a few times and laugh a lot; but try to keep it sounding natural.'

As they passed the table Pallas picked up Poppaeus' walking stick and propped it up against the chair that he had sat in.

'B-but my dear Poppaeus,' Claudius almost shouted as they entered the atrium, 'I can see no reason for me to support young Lucianus, he's a b-b-buffoon.'

Pallas burst into laughter and Vespasian followed his lead. Corbulo's aristocratic reserve held rigid and he remained silent.

'Oh, well said, Poppaeus,' Pallas guffawed, 'you are so right.'

'Will you support my brother this year in the praetor elections, Poppaeus?' Vespasian asked, getting into the spirit of the ruse.

'His brother is another buffoon, don't you think, P-P-Poppaeus?'

They all gave another burst of laughter as they passed the impluvium.

'I would be honoured if you would support me this year, Poppaeus,' Corbulo blurted as Vespasian heard Narcissus' study door open.

'I missed that, Poppaeus,' Pallas said, 'what did you say?' He gave another burst of laughter to cover the missing reply. 'You are truly the wisest man in Rome, Poppaeus, it has been an honour to meet you.'

They passed through the vestibule and out through the open front door into the street with another round of laughter. Vespasian looked behind and saw Kosmas scurrying to catch up, clutching the real chest.

'P-P-Poppaeus, it's been a pleasure d-doing business,' Claudius said as they walked down the steps in a tight group towards the waiting litter; Magnus stood blocking the line of sight of the rear nearside bearer. 'I shall see you in the Forum presently.'

'Allow me to help you in, Poppaeus,' Pallas said, nodding at Magnus who pulled the curtain slightly open. Pallas took it with his left hand and passed his right hand up along the inside as if a head were rubbing against it as Kosmas came racing down the steps; Narcissus followed just behind him.

'Your stick, Poppaeus? Of course I'll send Kosmas back for it. Kosmas, your master has left his stick in the garden,' Pallas said, letting the curtain go and turning to the secretary. 'Here, let me help you while you go and fetch it.' He took the chest under one arm and opened the curtain again, exposing Poppaeus' legs for the secretary to see and placed the chest next to them as Narcissus walked around to the other side of the litter.

'Quickly, Kosmas,' Vespasian snapped, 'Poppaeus is in a hurry, he has an urgent appointment in the Forum.'

'I didn't know about that,' Kosmas said, looking confused.

Pallas stuck his head into the litter. 'Of course, Poppaeus, I'll tell him,' Pallas said, reappearing. 'The Forum Romanum, by the Rostra, as fast as possible,' he ordered the bearers before turning to Kosmas. 'He says to meet him there with his stick.'

Kosmas shrugged and hurried back inside as the litter was lifted and moved quickly off down the street exposing Narcissus, on the far side, standing with his back towards the house. Vespasian and Corbulo's eyes widened in astonishment as he turned to face them; he was holding Capella's chest.

'Quick, take this around the back,' Narcissus said as he handed the chest to Magnus, 'we wouldn't want our friend Kosmas to see it as he comes back out.'

Magnus had just enough time to clear around the corner as Kosmas came scuttling back out with Poppaeus' stick.

'Master,' Narcissus cried, putting his hand to his forehead, 'your book!'

'Of course, Narcissus, thank you; where would I be without you?' Claudius responded with equal melodrama. 'Kosmas, wait a few moments while I find the first four volumes of my History of the Etruscans that I'd promised to lend your master.'

The hapless secretary glanced down the empty street and then back at Claudius who was already walking back inside with Narcissus; his shoulders drooped and he trudged back up the steps.

Vespasian had to suppress an amused grin at the way he had been played. 'He won't be able to swear to anything other than Poppaeus left in a rush and had him running back and forth for everything that he'd forgotten,' he observed.

'That was the objective,' Pallas said, 'but his part's not over yet; Claudius and Narcissus will delay him a while longer and then we'll follow him down to the Forum and watch him react to Poppaeus being found dead.'

'Wouldn't the bearers have seen Narcissus take the chest from the other side of the litter?' Corbulo asked, still in a slight daze from the fast moving events.

'Only the man on the far side at the back could have seen it but Narcissus reached in as they bent to pick up the litter and always kept his back to that bearer. Anyway, no questions should be asked about the chest as the false one will be found along with the dead Poppaeus in the litter.'

Kosmas' arrival with Narcissus cut short their conversation.

'My dear Kosmas,' Narcissus crooned, placing a pudgy arm around the wiry secretary's shoulders, 'it has been a pleasure seeing you again. We secretaries should get together more often.'

'Yes, thank you, Narcissus, we should. I must hurry.'

'Of course you must. I shall see you soon.'

Kosmas bowed his head to Vespasian, Corbulo and Pallas and hurried off down the street with his master's stick and four cylindrical, leather book containers stuffed into his bag.

'We'll follow him, Narcissus,' Pallas said as the secretary disappeared around the corner, 'and make sure that Asiaticus does his bit.'

'We'll meet tomorrow, Pallas. Gentlemen, farewell.'

As Vespasian turned to go he felt Narcissus' hand touch his shoulder. 'By the way, Vespasian,' Narcissus whispered in his ear, 'if you're thinking of paying a visit to the Cloelius brothers while you're in the Forum you'd be wasting your time; I had that bankers' draft cancelled with them.'

Vespasian spun around and glared at him.

Narcissus grinned mirthlessly. 'Your expression tells me that I was right to do so. However, as I am in your debt on two accounts now, I have neglected to cancel it with Thales in Alexandria. If you ever manage to get permission to visit there, which I doubt, it's yours. I wouldn't want to make it too easy for you to misappropriate my master's money, would I?'

CHAPTER XII

VESPASIAN WAS SILENT as they tracked Kosmas down the Esquiline towards the Forum, keeping the secretary in view as he gradually gained on his master's litter. He contemplated the dignity with which Poppaeus had met his death and the motives that had caused him to become Antonia's enemy. He could not help but feel that Poppaeus had been right: the Julio-Claudian family was utterly unsuitable to rule. Denuded of its brightest talents through years of intrigue and poisonings, its male line was now reduced to a rump consisting of: Tiberius, a sexually depraved, mad old man; Claudius, a stuttering, power-hungry mediocrity; Vespasian's friend Caligula, an incestuous hedonist; and Gemellus, a young lad of no consequence whose only interesting feature was the speculation surrounding him as to which of his relatives would eventually murder him. And then there was Antonia, that brilliant political strategist; her ruthlessness in dealing with any threat to her family's position he had at one time, through the idealism of youth, mistaken for a high-principled defence of legitimate Roman government. But now, older and more jaded, he was beginning to see her for what she really was: a vicious gang-leader who would stop at nothing to maintain her power. He had made a choice as a callow youth and now he was stuck in Antonia's world as a very minor member of her gang. His grandmother had been so right all those years ago when she had warned him 'that the side that seems to serve Rome may not always be the most honourable'. But surely that must soon change; surely, with the murder of so many of the family, the bloodline of the Julio-Claudians must soon expire? Perhaps this, then, would be the new age that the Phoenix

197

heralded: an age where Rome was ruled with honour through merit and not through tainted blood. But then, he reflected, if he was destined to play a part in this new age of honour, how could he now, guilty as he was of despicable and dishonourable murder?

'Where's the litter?' Magnus asked, breathing heavily as he and Ziri caught up with them on the Via Sacra.

'About a hundred paces ahead,' Pallas replied, pointing through the crowd to where the roof of the litter could just be seen bobbing over the sea of heads. 'Kosmas is just in front of us but he's catching up with it; you and Ziri had better try and delay him until it gets to the Forum.'

'But he's seen me.'

'Barely, and he hasn't seen Ziri.'

'Fair enough.'

A huge roar from behind them caused Vespasian to turn his head towards the Circus Maximus.

'Missing the fucking racing,' Magnus moaned. 'Come on, Ziri, you're going to do some jostling.'

Ziri looked uncomprehendingly at his master.

'You'll get the hang of it, it's easy, you just have to use your elbows,' Magnus told him as he ploughed forward into the crowd.

They neared the Forum and the crowd got denser as the people of Rome who had not been lucky enough to get seats in the circus flocked to watch acrobats, jugglers and other entertainers performing in honour of Apollo.

Gradually they caught up with the litter until it was only ten paces ahead of them as it neared the Rostra. To his right Vespasian could see the tall figure of Kosmas battling to get past Magnus and Ziri. Suddenly the crowd shifted backwards and Vespasian could see, just ahead of him, the axe-heads on the tops of the fasces of twelve lictors making directly for the litter.

'Asiaticus is there,' he said as the lictors surrounded the litter.

'Good, we'll watch from here,' Pallas replied. Most of the crowd moved on past the official cordon, uninterested in the doings of the Senior Consul on a festival day.

'Proconsul Poppaeus,' Asiaticus shouted above the hubbub, 'how fortunate to have met you.' He stepped up to the litter and waited for a reply. 'Poppaeus?' he repeated after a few moments. Again receiving no reply he untied the curtains and looked in. 'Poppaeus?'

'Let me through, that's my master's litter,' Kosmas shouted, pushing through the lictors.

Asiaticus put his hand in and then withdrew it quickly. 'Jupiter! The proconsul is dead!' He pulled the flaps right back to expose Poppaeus' reclining form as they had left it; his head lolled down to one side, resting on the fake Capella's chest. There was a shocked intake of breath from the few people who stood watching the scene; more now joined them. The litter-bearers looked aghast at their dead master.

Kosmas rushed forward. 'Master? Master?'

'Your master appears to be dead,' Asiaticus informed him.

'Impossible, he was alive when I left him not half an hour ago.'

'Well, he's dead now; look.'

Kosmas lifted Poppaeus' chin and then let go in shock. 'But I swear that he was alive when we left Claudius' house, I saw him get into the litter; he sent me back for his stick.' He waved the stick at Asiaticus as if to prove the veracity of his story. 'He must have died on the way here.'

Vespasian and Corbulo glanced at Pallas, who allowed himself a brief smile of satisfaction.

'Who are you?' Asiaticus demanded.

'My name is Kosmas, I'm Poppaeus' secretary.'

'What's this?' Asiaticus asked, pointing at the chest.

'It contains some paperwork of my master's.'

'Let me see.'

Kosmas took the keys from around his neck and opened the chest.

Asiaticus took out a couple of the scrolls and gave them a cursory glance and sniffed them. 'There's nothing in there that could have killed him.'

Kosmas looked inside and nodded his agreement.

'You had better run back to his house and get his household to come and bear his body home in honour. It would be unseemly for such a great man to be carted home in a litter.'

Kosmas looked at the Consul then back to Poppaeus and then back at the Consul, unsure of what to do.

'Go on, man,' Asiaticus shouted, 'stop dithering, I'll stay here with the body.'

'Yes, Consul, thank you.'

'You'd better take this chest with you.'

'Yes, Consul.' Kosmas quickly closed the lid and locked it.

'Run!'

Vespasian grinned as the hapless secretary picked up the chest, balanced the stick on it and scampered off. 'He'll never believe his own eyes again.'

'Sadly for him he won't have much time to test them out,' Pallas said, nodding to someone at the far side of the crowd.

Vespasian followed his look and saw the younger version of Pallas nod back at his elder brother, patting the knife on his belt. Felix detached himself from the crowd and followed Kosmas out of the Forum.

'I think the Consul played his part admirably,' Pallas commented as they left the Forum, which was now buzzing with the news of Poppaeus' death. 'And there were enough people who heard Kosmas swear that Poppaeus was alive when he left Claudius' house. My mistress will be delighted.'

'I feel sorry for Kosmas, though,' Vespasian said, 'it's a shame that he had to die.'

Corbulo looked confused. 'Kosmas is dead? When?'

'About now, I should imagine,' Pallas informed him. 'My brother will ensure that the body disappears and then it will be assumed that a dishonest secretary took advantage of the situa-

tion and made off with the deeds to his master's property. Even if Macro suspected something was wrong, he wouldn't be able to prove otherwise without admitting that he knew about the Egyptian estates; which he could never afford to do.'

'So Claudius is now richer by fourteen and a half million denarii,' Vespasian said sourly.

'I'd rather it was him than Macro.'

'Would you, though, Pallas? Poppaeus made a good point about what would happen to the succession if Macro became emperor.'

'Yes,' Corbulo agreed, 'it reminded me of what you were saying on Capreae. The more I think about it the more it really makes sense. Rome cannot carry on with madmen in charge just because they are in some way descended from Julius Caesar.'

'It's idealism, I'm afraid,' Pallas told them. 'The aristocracy may hate the Julio-Claudian family with good reason, seeing as a lot of them have been killed as they came to power and more will die as they cling on to it; but the army and the people won't stop supporting them. They like stability and stability for them is one family ruling so that they know who's going to be doling out the largesse, the grain and putting on the shows in the arena. Not until there's been a succession of bad emperors and their living conditions are affected will they start to think about a better system.'

'That's a depressing view.'

'Not if you happen to be in the service of the ruling family.'

And that was just the problem, Vespasian thought, as they began to ascend the Palatine to the bellowing of the crowd in the Circus Maximus: there were so many people with a degree of power like Pallas, Asiaticus, Narcissus, the Praetorian Guard, his uncle, most of the Senate, whose fortunes where inextricably linked through patronage to the Julio-Claudians. The very thought of change frightened them because ultimately everyone was out for themselves and their families. All talk of high ideals about the governance of Rome came to naught if you feared that you had nothing to gain and everything to lose by a change of regime. It was human nature and there was nothing that he could do about it.

With that realisation Vespasian trudged up the hill to Antonia's house, contemplating the inevitable: an unprincipled life in which he would do as well as he could for himself by serving the people with real power. It was not what he had dreamed of when he first entered Rome. However, he reflected ruefully, he should be good at it; he had already stooped to murder.

Antonia had left a message asking them to wait until she had finished dealing with some business. Pallas showed Vespasian and Corbulo into the garden where, to Vespasian's surprise, Gaius and Sabinus were sitting at a table sipping wine; neither of them looked happy and both were sweating in the noonday sun. Four extra cups were placed on the table.

'I'll leave you gentlemen here while I attend my mistress,' Pallas said. 'I do believe that she is dealing with the one outstanding issue. Call if you need more wine.' He walked off towards the black lacquered door to Antonia's private room at the far end of the courtyard garden.

'Herod Agrippa?' Vespasian asked as he and Corbulo sat down.

'Yes,' Sabinus replied less than enthusiastically. 'He arrived just before you did.'

'Did Antonia agree to help you?' Vespasian asked, pouring wine into two of the cups and passing one to Corbulo.

'Yes, but she wasn't pleased. It meant that she'd have to find some other way to deal with Herod; she can't now threaten him with confiscation of his stockpile without him countering her by exposing me. He knows that I'm here, she deliberately let him see me as he came in.'

'What have you done?' Corbulo asked, taking a sip of wine.

'Nothing that concerns you, Corbulo,' Sabinus replied as two portly and bald, middle-aged equites were led into the garden by a slave. The colour drained out of Sabinus' face; he stood up. 'Primus and Tertius,' he spluttered, walking towards the new arrivals proffering his arm. 'What brings you here?'

'An inconvenient but impossible-to-refuse summons from the Lady Antonia, Senator Sabinus,' the slightly elder of the two replied, taking his forearm. 'And, judging by the documents she asked us to bring, you shouldn't be so surprised to see us.' He placed a leather bag on the table and gave a curt business-like nod to Gaius and Corbulo. 'Good day to you both, Senators Pollo and Corbulo.'

'Primus; Tertius,' they both replied, getting up as Sabinus greeted the younger man.

'Gentlemen, this is my brother, Vespasian,' Sabinus said as they all sat down again. 'Primus and Tertius Cloelius of the banking firm in the Forum.'

The conversation was sporadic and stilted as they waited in the strengthening sun for the black lacquered door to open. All attempts at small-talk were rebuffed by the bankers who spent the time perusing accounts on scrolls and checking them with the help of an abacus retrieved from Primus' bag. They had refused the offer of wine. Vespasian caught them a couple of times giving him surreptitious looks and wondered if Narcissus had mentioned his name to them when cancelling the bankers' draft. The rapid clicking of wooden balls on the abacus began to irritate him.

The door eventually opened. Antonia walked towards them with Herod, looking very pleased, by her side, followed by Pallas. 'Gentlemen, thank you for waiting. If you don't mind we will conclude our business here,' she said sitting and indicating that Herod should do likewise. 'I'm in need of some fresh air. Primus and Tertius, it's good of you to come. I hope that Secundus is well.'

'He's away on business, domina,' Primus replied.

'Good, he is well then. Did you bring everything that I asked for?'

Primus rummaged in his bag, brought out three scrolls and placed them on the table.

Antonia picked up a scroll and looked at it briefly. 'Herod, this is a bankers' draft for half a million denarii.'

Herod looked at it with relish.

'And this,' Antonia continued, picking up the second scroll and waving it at Herod to look at, 'is the Cloelius brothers' copy of the bill of sale for the grain that you bought off Sabinus as well as their copy of the certificate of ownership signed by you and Sabinus. The brothers are obviously anxious to hand them over to me knowing that it was highly illegal of them to take a percentage in a deal involving grain speculation.'

'A lack of judgement on our part,' Primus affirmed.

'Which I'm very happy to correct for you.' Putting the scroll back down on the table, Antonia turned to Sabinus. 'Your copies please, Sabinus.'

Sabinus obliged and handed her the documents.

Antonia smiled pleasantly at Herod. 'So, Herod, your copies are the last ones left that link this grain with Sabinus.' She gave the bankers' draft back to the Cloelius brothers, who each signed it; that done she offered it to Herod. 'The grain is worth a lot less than this draft. I suggest that it would be in your interests to swap.'

Corbulo's mouth dropped open in outrage; with a sharp motion of her left hand Antonia silenced him before he could express his opinion.

Herod took the bankers' draft. 'I will send over my freedman, Eutyches, with my copy of the bill of sale and the certificate of ownership as soon as I get home. The grain is now yours.'

'As is your loyalty, Herod, if you still wish to see Judaea reinstated as a client kingdom with you as king. That is within my gift, not Macro's.'

'I can see that now. On my way here I passed through the Forum; it seems that Poppaeus is dead on the day that he was due to do a certain deal with your son.' He looked around the table. 'I don't know how you did it but I assume that deal has not gone through and Macro is not in a position to offer me what I want.'

'I did nothing, Herod; any unfounded suspicions that you may have that I had a hand in this you will keep to yourself.'

Antonia picked up the third scroll. 'Macro is not in a position to cancel your debt to me, which, if I were to call it in, would send you fleeing back to the desert again; and believe me, this time you won't return.'

'As always, dear Lady, it's a pleasure negotiating with you.'

'It's a pleasure taking my money, you mean.'

Herod inclined his head and smiled. 'That I can't deny.'

'Now get out of my house.'

'With pleasure.' Herod got to his feet and bowed graciously. 'Good day to you, gentlemen.'

Antonia brandished the debt marker at him as he turned to leave. 'Never forget, Herod, I will always have this.'

'Dear Lady, my lips are sealed,' Herod said over his shoulder as he walked from the garden waving his bankers' draft in the air.

Antonia turned to the two bankers. 'Primus and Tertius, I know that I can rely on your discretion in this matter.'

'We deal in figures not tittle-tattle, domina,' Primus replied, rising while his brother collected up their scrolls and abacus.

'Very wise; a far more trustworthy commodity, especially when the tittle-tattle could involve your names. Now, as to that other matter?'

Primus took another scroll, the fourth, from the fold of his toga and handed it to Antonia. 'This is the final thing that you asked for, domina; our copy of the deceased gentleman's certificate of ownership from the other deal that interested you. You must understand that this is very irregular.'

'So is taking a ten per cent cut of an illegal grain deal, Primus, which, thanks to my discretion, shall now remain just between us.'

'Our humble thanks, domina. In the circumstances we will not be sending a note of our fees.'

Antonia unrolled the scroll and glanced at its contents with a satisfied smile. 'That would be appreciated, Primus, I know how adventurous you can be with arithmetic when it comes to calculating fees.'

'We have no sense of adventure, domina, we are bankers.'

With curt nods of their heads the Cloelius brothers departed.

'That was very expensive, thanks to you, Sabinus,' Antonia said as their footsteps disappeared, 'but by no means a disaster.'

Sabinus flushed and bowed his head in shame.

'Dealing in grain while being the grain aedile!' Corbulo finally exploded, his face puce with aristocratic ire. 'I should report this.'

'Of course you should but you won't, will you, my dear Corbulo?' Antonia said soothingly. 'That won't get us anywhere.'

'But he's trying get elected as a praetor; what he did goes against all the ancient principles that govern the behaviour of senators.'

'And what you did this morning doesn't?' Antonia snapped. 'Stop behaving as if you're one of the founding fathers of the Republic. Sabinus made a costly mistake but I have rectified it in a way that will protect us and do Herod a lot of damage; I don't trust him not to talk to Macro so I'm going to ensure that he can't. Pallas, bring Eutyches to us as soon as he arrives.'

'And you can swear to that?' Antonia asked Eutyches who stood before her. She laid the two scrolls that he had brought from his master on the table next to a pile of gold coins.

'Yes, domina,' Herod's freedman replied, 'my master said to your grandson Caligula: "I wish the old man would hurry up and die so that you can become emperor." I was driving them both in Herod's carriage; I heard it clearly.'

'And what did my grandson reply?'

Eutyches looked greedily at the pile of gold coins and then back at Antonia. 'What do you think he replied, domina?'

'I see that we understand each other, very good. I'm sure that he said: "Herod, that is treason; may Tiberius live forever. The next time you speak like that I shall report you."'

'That is exactly what he said, I'd swear to it.'

'My little grandson was always too forgiving.'

'A noble fault, domina,' Gaius agreed sadly.

'Let's hope that it doesn't get him into trouble some day,' Vespasian added, looking at his uncle and nodding in agreement.

'Thank you, Eutyches, you may have the money once this matter has been dealt with. You will remain here until then; Pallas, show him to where we keep our guests.'

Vespasian watched the unsuspecting freedman being led towards Antonia's private underground prison and wondered how long he would be kept incarcerated.

Antonia collected the money and slipped it back into a purse. 'I feel that it's my duty to correct my grandson's fault and report this. Macro's gone to join the Emperor at Antium for young Gaius' wedding so we should act now while he's away. Senator Pollo, I will have this written up and would be obliged if you would read it out at the next meeting of the Senate.'

'Of course, domina.'

A sudden burst of hysterical screaming from the atrium interrupted them.

'Get out of my way, I will see her; I know she's in there.'

A short, broad-hipped woman, in her late twenties, with ripped clothing and dishevelled hair came running into the garden brushing off Felix's attempts to restrain her. 'Antonia!' she screeched. 'I know what you've done!'

'My dear Poppaea Sabina,' Antonia said rising, 'calm yourself.'

'Calm myself? How can I be calm when I'm looking at my father's murderer?'

'I have only just heard about your father's death, these senators were just telling me about the tragedy.'

'Tragedy?' Poppaea screamed, looking intently at each of the men around the table. 'You killed him, and these men probably helped you. I know Senator Pollo and his nephews have always supported you against my father, he told me. You killed him, Antonia, because he was trying to remove your hated family from the throne. You killed him to protect yourself. I don't know how but if he died of natural causes then why was his lip swollen and cut? It wasn't this morning when I saw him. My family's reputation is impeccable and people will listen when I demand justice.' She spat on the ground, turned and, pushing past Felix, walked with dignity out of the garden.

'I'm sorry, domina, she...'

'That's all right, Felix, she was determined to see me. Did the other business go well?'

'Yes, domina, the body and the chest are in the Tiber; the head has been destroyed.'

'Good. Follow her out and see that she does no damage and send a message to Asiaticus to come here as soon as possible.' Antonia turned back to her guests around the table. 'It would seem that we now have two reputations to besmirch if we are to prevent Poppaea from gaining any sympathy in the Senate for her view. Gaius, save the report on Herod until after Asiaticus, Corbulo and Vespasian have done what I'm going to ask of them.' Antonia picked up the fourth scroll that Primus had given her and handed it to Sabinus. 'And then when your uncle has done that, Sabinus, please read out this, I think that it's safe for you to do so now that Herod is no longer in a position to blackmail you.' She patted Herod's copy of the bill of sale and the certificate of ownership of the grain that Eutyches had brought. 'I was going to save it for future use but I think in view of Poppaea's visit now would be a good time to make it public. I believe it might also help your cause in the praetor elections.'

Sabinus read it quickly and grinned. 'I'd be delighted to.'

'And so therefore, Conscript Fathers,' the Senior Consul, Asiaticus, concluded to a packed Senate House, 'I propose a vote of thanks from a grateful Senate to its servant, Gaius Poppaeus Sabinus, for the many years of selfless service he gave to us and our Emperor. I also propose that we vote him a bronze statue, paid for out of public funds, to be erected in the Forum.'

Asiaticus sat down to a chorus of approval from both sides of the House. Vespasian joined in thinking that Antonia would be pleased with the way the Consul had set up the debate exactly as she had asked.

'Senior Consul,' Corbulo bellowed over the din, rising to his feet, 'may I have the floor?'

'The Senate will hear Senator Corbulo,' Asiaticus cried, gesturing for silence.

Vespasian smiled to himself as Corbulo took the floor attempting to conceal a look of distaste for the first part of what he was about to say upon Antonia's orders.

'Conscript Fathers, I served with Poppaeus for three years in Moesia and Thracia, I would be honoured to second the Consul's proposal. I was, as were you all, shocked when Poppaeus was found dead in the Forum, but I consider it fitting that a man such as he should die at the very heart of our Empire. However, as we all know, Poppaeus allowed his troops to hail him as "imperator" so I think that a statue in the Forum, so close to those of our illustrious Emperor and his predecessor, would be an unpleasant reminder of that solitary error of judgement – some may call it an act of treason – made by this man whom we praise today.'

Corbulo sat down to mutterings of agreement.

Asiaticus took the floor again. 'Senator Corbulo has done well to remind the House of that unfortunate incident. We would not want the Emperor to think that his loyal Senate in any way condones Poppaeus' error, made, I am sure, in the heat of the joy of victory over Rome's enemies. The fact that the Emperor in his clemency has chosen to overlook this for so long should signal to us that, while a statue would be inappropriate, a vote of thanks would be acceptable for such a man who only made one mistake in his life.'

Vespasian got nervously to his feet for the first time in the Senate. 'Senior Consul, may I have the floor?'

'The House will hear the first speech of Senator Titus Flavius Vespasianus,' Asiaticus declared.

Vespasian felt the eyes of over five hundred senators upon him as he walked out to the middle of the floor. Putting his unease at speaking in public for the first time to the back of his mind, he cleared his throat. 'Conscript Fathers, many of you will be wondering what I, one of the most junior members of this ancient House, could add to this debate. I too was in Thracia with Poppaeus and out of loyalty to the Senate of Rome and our Emperor I cannot remain silent about what I saw. Senator Corbulo was right to bring to our attention the cries of "imperator" but he has not told the full story. He was not present at the victory celebration after the final battle, having been sent up the mountain with two cohorts to secure the defeated Thracians' stronghold and to mop up any survivors. He therefore did not see the way that Poppaeus basked in the cries of "imperator", encouraging them rather than trying to subdue them as any one of us would have done out of loyalty to the Emperor.'

Vespasian paused as the senators vied with each other to be the most vociferous in their loyalty to the Emperor. 'Shameful though it was to commit this offence against our Emperor, it was not the worst crime that Poppaeus committed that day.'

There was silence as the senators ceased their protestations of loyalty to hear what could be worse than a crime against the Emperor. 'I was present when your emissary, the proconsul Marcus Asinius Agrippa, brought Poppaeus the news of the honour that this House had voted him, and our Emperor had been pleased to confirm, Triumphal Ornaments. I witnessed Asinius order Poppaeus, in the name of the Senate and the Emperor, to immediately give up his command to Pomponius Labeo and return to Rome. Showing no gratitude for this extraordinary honour, Poppaeus refused, thereby committing a crime not only against the Emperor but also against this House. It was not until Asinius repeated the order in front of the whole army after the battle that Poppaeus felt obliged to lay down his command.'

Shouts of outrage forced Vespasian to pause again. Asiaticus sprang to his feet and bellowed for order.

'Senator Vespasian,' he shouted over the din, 'can you swear to this?'

'I can, but I can do better than that, Consul, I can get you proof. Senator Corbulo, where did you find Poppaeus on the night of the Thracian attack?'

Corbulo stood. 'In Asinius' tent.'

'Who else was there?'

'Asinius, you, King Rhoemetalces and Primus Pilus Faustus.'

'Unfortunately, Consul, Asinius is dead as is Faustus but King Rhoemetalces is not. Write to him and ask him for the details of the conversation that had taken place between Asinius and Poppaeus before Corbulo arrived; he will confirm everything I've said.'

Vespasian returned to his folding stool as the first of the many senators eager to express their disgust at such a disregard for senatorial authority jumped to his feet.

After a succession of speeches each railing at Poppaeus' behaviour and each one more damning and hypocritical than the last, Asiaticus brought the matter to a close.

'Conscript Fathers, I withdraw the motion that I proposed and recommend instead that we should mark Poppaeus' death with an acknowledgement that in his service to Rome he was merely up to the task and no more. We should write to the Emperor and ask him, in view of Poppaeus' behaviour, if he would wish us to strip him posthumously of his Triumphal Ornaments.' This was greeted with a unanimous shout of approval. 'I see no reason to divide the House on this issue.'

'Consul,' Gaius shouted, 'if we are to write to the Emperor, I have another matter to be brought to his attention.'

'Wishing the Emperor dead is a very serious accusation indeed,' Asiaticus told the Senate after Eutyches' statement had been read. 'We should have this freedman sent to the Emperor so that he can question him personally. Do you know where he is, Senator Pollo?'

'I do, Consul; the Lady Antonia has had him confined since he tried to blackmail her because her grandson merely reprimanded Herod for his views rather than reporting the treason.'

'Good, I shall ask her to keep him there until the Urban Prefect can arrange for his transfer. We should now discuss how to deal with Herod Agrippa.'

Sabinus got to his feet and waved the scroll that Antonia had given him. 'Consul, I have some information that relates to both the issues that have been discussed this morning.'

'You may have the floor.'

'I am pleased to report that the Lady Antonia has, out of her own purse, purchased a consignment of grain, which she has donated to the public granaries to help relieve the shortage.' Sabinus paused as the senators expressed their approval and gratitude for this selfless act of altruism. 'As I was processing the paperwork this came to my notice in amongst the newly arrived grain deliveries.' He unrolled the scroll with a melodramatic flurry. 'It is a certificate of ownership for a delivery of grain from Egypt, worth over a quarter of a million denarii; it was part of the consignment of the Egyptian grain fleet that went down in the storm. However, this grain was carried by one of the two transports that did make it to Rome, but I, as the grain aedile for this year, am unable to distribute it because it does not belong to Rome; it remains in a private warehouse in Ostia, all the time gaining in value as grain prices soar. This certificate shows that, once it had been offloaded in Ostia, the ownership of the grain transferred to Gaius Poppaeus Sabinus in payment of a loan he had made to Herod Agrippa.'

Uproar followed this revelation.

Asiaticus bellowed over the crowd in righteous indignation. 'Are you saying that Herod Agrippa has been using our city's current difficulties for his own profit so he can pay off debts?'

'It appears that way, Consul.'

'Show me that.'

Sabinus walked the length of the House and handed the scroll to Asiaticus.

After a cursory glance the Senior Consul rolled it up and placed it into the fold of his toga. 'Thank you, Senator Sabinus.' He looked up at the sea of expectant faces to find the Urban Prefect. 'Have Herod Agrippa brought before the Senate in chains.'

PART III

❧ ❧

ROME, MARCH AD 37

CHAPTER XIII

'HOW LONG IS it going to take to rebuild?' Vespasian asked Sabinus as they watched a work-gang of public slaves unload a delivery of bricks in front of the fire-blackened ruins of Sabinus' house on the Aventine Hill. All around them scores of other gangs were working among the charred ruins of the Aventine, resurrecting the once beautiful and prosperous hill overlooking the Circus Maximus. Heavy cloud and an incessant drizzle added a depressing sombreness to the scene of devastation; hardly a building remained untouched by the fire that had ripped through the area six months before, adding a sour note to Sabinus' year as a praetor. His denunciation of Herod Agrippa had resulted in the Jewish king being chained to the wall in a damp cell and Sabinus coming top of the poll in the election – beating Corbulo, much to his chagrin – and therefore eligible for the governorship of a senatorial province.

'It should be about three months, according to the foreman, but with almost every house on the Aventine being rebuilt he can't say for certain. It depends on the availability of building materials and slaves and also upon whether you, as the aedile in charge of roads, manage to do your job properly and keep the streets clear. Either way, now that the sea-lanes are opening up again, I've got to leave for my province in a few days so you'll have to oversee the work for me.'

'At least you don't have to worry about money, the Emperor's seen to that.'

Sabinus grimaced. 'Two hundred million sesterces might sound a lot, and there's no denying that it was very generous of Tiberius now that it's finally arrived, but that's not going to cover

214

the cost of every building on the hill. I'm going to have to find some money from somewhere if the house is going to be rebuilt to the standard that it was originally; Clementina won't accept anything less.' He shook his head regretfully. 'If only I hadn't bought it and just rented it, then it wouldn't be my problem.'

Vespasian glanced at his brother and judged that now was not the best of times to bring up the fact that he had advised Sabinus not to take the loan from Paetus with which he had bought the house.

Sabinus caught his look. 'I suppose you want to say "I told you so", you little shit. Well, you were right: if I'd lived within my means I wouldn't be in this trouble now. From now on, no more loans.'

'Have you paid it back yet?'

Sabinus looked embarrassed. 'No, I keep on meaning to then something happens like a new child, or this.'

'Well, you should; you promised to pay it back within two years.'

'Have you kept your promise to Paetus to keep an eye on his son, Lucius, for him?' Sabinus retorted.

It was Vespasian's turn to look embarrassed. 'No, I haven't. I must take more interest in him.'

'He must be seventeen now, starting out in life. We both seem to be at fault, brother, as far as Paetus is concerned, so don't lecture me. I'll pay it as soon as I've got the money.'

'And I'll look in on young Lucius. Anyway, you made some money as a praetor last year and should make a lot more from your province; Bithynia's very wealthy, it's not the worst place to be the Governor.'

'It's not the best either; but you're right, this time next year I'll be comfortable enough.'

'Sir! Sir!'

Vespasian and Sabinus turned to see Magnus running up the hill towards them.

'Have you heard the news?' Magnus puffed, pushing past a couple of slaves carrying a heavy wooden beam. 'It's all over the city.'

'Well, unless it's that my brother has temporarily lifted the ban on delivery carts in the city during the day for building materials for the Aventine,' Sabinus replied, 'it hasn't reached this burned-out quarter.'

'Your brother-in-law, Clemens, arrived an hour ago with a message from Capreae: Tiberius is dead.'

'Dead? When?' Vespasian asked.

'Yesterday. The Forums are all full of people demanding that his body is brought back to Rome so that it can be chucked into the Tiber.'

'Did he name Claudius as his successor?'

'The will hasn't been read yet, but apparently Caligula has the imperial ring on his hand and has proclaimed himself emperor. He's sent Macro to address the Senate and read Tiberius' will; according to Clemens he's a couple of hours behind him.'

Vespasian looked in alarm at his brother. 'Shit! Antonia isn't going to like that; we'd better go and present ourselves to her and see what she plans to do.'

'She can't do anything. If Caligula has the imperial ring and Macro throws the Praetorian Guard's support behind him, he's the Emperor and that's that. The best thing that we can do at the moment is to look out for ourselves and get to the Senate so that we don't stand out as being the only two senators not present to acclaim Caligula emperor.'

Clemens was standing at the foot of the Senate House steps as Vespasian, Sabinus and Magnus arrived. Scores of senators were arriving from all directions, pushing their way through the delirious mob, each as keen as the two brothers to have their loyalty to the new regime noted.

'I was hoping to find you here,' Clemens said, greeting the brothers with a grasp of their forearms and a nod to Magnus before leading them away from the crowd. His pinched, narrow face seemed more pasty than usual.

'You look worried, Clemens,' Sabinus observed.

'Of course I'm worried; everyone in their right mind should be worried. The Empire has just been stolen by a lunatic.'

'What do you mean "stolen"?'

'Caligula murdered Tiberius with Macro's help; they suffocated him, I'm sure of it. When I saw the body shortly after they came out of Tiberius' room to announce his death his face was discoloured and his tongue was swollen and sticking out of his mouth. Admittedly he was on death's door anyway but he had just changed his will.'

'In favour of whom? Claudius?'

'How would I know? It hasn't been read yet. All I know is Tiberius called me into his room and ordered me to send for his secretary to bring his will. Once the changes had been made the secretary came out with it and Macro seized it and read it with Caligula. Then they went into Tiberius' room and the next thing we knew Tiberius was dead, Caligula had his ring and the German Bodyguard were hailing him as Caesar. The secretary accused Macro and Caligula of murder so Caligula's first order as emperor was to have the man's tongue cut out and have him crucified.'

Sabinus shrugged. 'So Caligula's emperor; it was always going to happen if Tiberius let him survive, whatever Antonia may have tried to do about it. At least we know him and can claim an acquaintance, even if it was some time ago. It could work out quite well for us; and for you too, Clemens – you are the tribune of his personal guard, after all.'

'If he was sane then perhaps you'd be right; but he's not. Neither of you have seen him during the last six years but I've been with him all the time on that mad island. I've watched him become as sexually depraved as Tiberius but with the stamina that the old man didn't possess. He's never satisfied, no matter how many people he's fucked or who he's been fucked by. Tiberius encouraged him – I heard him joke that he was nursing a viper in Rome's bosom – by showing him how unbridled power can be used for limitless self-gratification, and Caligula has learnt well. But there was always one thing that restrained him and that was the knowledge that he was ultimately Tiberius' slave and could be executed on a whim as he'd seen happen to others so many times before; so there was never a better slave. Now with Tiberius gone he's the master and I promise you there will never be a worse master.'

'Then we'll just have to make sure that the master doesn't notice us,' Vespasian said. From what he knew of Caligula he feared Clemens was right.

'It's too late for that; he's looking forward to seeing you. He said to tell you that although he hasn't seen you for six years he still considers you both to be his friends and that now he's emperor and free to come back to Rome he's looking forward to the fun – as he put it – that he promised you would have together.'

'I'm not sure that I like Caligula's idea of fun, having witnessed it,' Sabinus commented, 'it seems to involve his sisters.'

'It doesn't always just involve his sisters; I'm more worried by the fact that he seems determined that it'll also involve *my* sister. I've already sent my wife, Julia, back to my estate at Pisaurum with the children to keep her from him. He's been telling me for the last few months that he can't bear the thought that someone as beautiful as Clementina should be deprived of the chance to sample his not inconsiderable manhood; and I'm her brother!'

Sabinus looked understandably concerned. 'I had better get her and the children out of Rome; I'll leave for Bithynia first thing tomorrow before Caligula arrives.'

'Leave now, my friend; if you go into the Senate your presence will be registered and Caligula will know that you left without waiting to greet him. I'll tell him that you left a couple of days ago before you heard the news; there is a chance that he'll believe that, now that the port of Brundisium has reopened again.'

Sabinus took his arm in a firm grip. 'That's good of you, Clemens.'

'Stay out there as long as possible, start a war or something. Caligula will only get worse, believe me.'

'I do.' Sabinus turned to Vespasian. 'If I don't see Uncle Gaius at the house say goodbye for me and thank him for his hospitality over the last six months since the fire.'

'I will and I'll send on everything that you need, Sabinus,' Vespasian said. 'Just go.'

'I'll have four of my lads escort you to Brundisium,' Magnus offered, 'they'll be at the house in an hour.'

'Thank you, Magnus, and you too, brother,' Sabinus said, turning quickly to go, 'and good luck with our friend.'

'I'll be fine,' Vespasian called to Sabinus' retreating back.

'You'll be fine,' Clemens agreed, 'so long as you bugger Caligula whenever he orders, like I have to; I'm worn out by it sometimes.'

'What? You, Clemens? You're joking.'

'Unfortunately I'm not and I can tell you that it's one of the least unpleasant duties that I'm forced to perform. But your problem is that Clementina isn't the only woman who Caligula's determined to bed; now that he's emperor I'm sure that he won't feel the need to take any notice of Antonia's injunction against having Caenis.'

The mob outside, in the Forum Romanum, was in full cry, celebrating the despised old Emperor's death and the accession of their new hope, Caligula; but there was near silence in the packed Senate House as Quintus Naevius Cordus Sutorius Macro entered, in military uniform, holding a scroll-case. He was flanked, outrageously, by four armed Praetorian Guardsmen also in uniform rather than wearing their customary togas, worn when on duty within the city. The looks on most senators' faces attested to what they felt about such an overt display of Praetorian power over the increasingly enfeebled Senate.

'He's making the point that this time the Guard has chosen the Emperor,' Gaius whispered to Vespasian over the muttering of their unhappy colleagues, 'and we have to ratify it or face their swords.'

219

Gnaeus Acerronius Proculus, the Senior Consul, remained seated on his curule chair as the small party clattered up the centre of the House. 'The Senate calls upon Quintus Naevius Cordus Sutorius Macro to brief it on the health of our beloved Emperor, Tiberius. Is the rumour true?' Proculus called, taking the initiative in an attempt to reassert senatorial authority.

'Of course it's true, as you well know, Consul,' Macro growled, 'and I'm here to tell—'

'Conscript Fathers,' Proculus cut in, 'the Praetorian prefect has brought us the most grievous news: confirmation that our Emperor is dead.' He began to wail theatrically.

The whole Senate followed his lead; cries of woe and anguish filled the House, drowning out Macro's attempts to make himself heard until, humiliated, he was forced to wait impotently to be allowed to speak.

Vespasian and Gaius joined in the protestations of grief, wholeheartedly enjoying the look on Macro's face. 'I don't know how wise a move that was,' Vespasian shouted in Gaius' ear, 'but it was well done and most amusing.'

'In as much as goading a lion is amusing,' Gaius replied. 'But if he was trying to wrest some authority back from the Guard to the Senate then it was certainly a good start.'

As the expressions of grief continued a pair of dark eyes locked with Vespasian's from the other side of the House; with a jolt he realised that Corvinus was back in Rome and had taken his seat in the Senate.

'I propose a ten-day period of mourning to start from this moment,' Proculus eventually called out above the din. 'All trials will be suspended, no sentences will be carried out and all public business, including that of this House, will cease. After that time we will ratify Tiberius' will and vote Gaius Caesar Germanicus all honours according to his station. The House will divide.'

'The House will listen to me!' Macro bellowed.

'The House will divide, prefect. You wouldn't want it said that you stopped the House voting a suitable period of mourning for an emperor, would you?'

'Fuck the period of mourning, Consul, I will be heard. The Emperor Gaius has sent me to give you Tiberius' will and tell you to nullify it.'

Proculus looked suddenly unsure. 'But surely it names him as Tiberius' heir?'

'It names him as the co-heir along with Tiberius Gemellus; it cannot be left like that, it's a recipe for civil war.'

'On what grounds can we change an emperor's will?'

'On the grounds that he was mentally incapable when he made it; and if that's not enough for you, do you hear that?' Macro gesticulated towards the noise coming through the door; there was now a violent ring to it. 'That is the sound of the people wanting to be ruled over by one man, not by one man and a boy. My men have been circulating among the crowd telling them the terms of the will and they don't like it; I can guarantee that none of you will get out of here alive until you change it. And while you're about it I suggest that you vote the Emperor all the titles and honours that you feel will please him; after that you can vote on what the fuck you like.' Macro threw the scroll-case at the Senior Consul, turned and marched smartly out with his escort.

Proculus' shoulders sagged; his attempt to reassert the Senate's authority as the legitimate power in Rome had come to a humiliating end. He knew that none of his colleagues would risk the wrath of the mob. He got wearily to his feet. 'I propose that this House nullifies Tiberius' will and votes Gaius Caesar Germanicus as his sole heir and therefore the only Emperor.'

Tears streamed down Caligula's face; his voice was high with emotion, straining with grief. 'In his modesty he refused the title of "Father of the Country"; he refused to be worshipped as a god, preferring instead to take his reward for his selfless service in the love that his people bore him for his just and benign rule.'

'I can't help but wonder if he is really talking about Tiberius,' Gaius muttered to Vespasian out of the corner of his mouth.

'If he is, it makes a nice change,' Vespasian replied, 'that's almost the first time that he's mentioned him.'

They had already stood through nearly two hours of Caligula praising his father Germanicus as well as his great-uncle Augustus and thereby reminding the people of Rome of the stock that he came from and securing in their minds his right to be emperor. Now it seemed that he had finally got on to the subject that he was meant to be eulogising, although, judging by the looks on the faces of the other senators standing with them on the steps of Pompey's Theatre in the Campus Martius, Vespasian could see that his uncle was not the only person having difficulty in trying to equate the new Emperor's words with the character of his predecessor.

Standing on a high dais, Caligula carried on his emotional eulogy, surrounded by actors wearing the funeral masks of Tiberius' ancestors. Next to the dais stood the unlit pyre upon which was set the bier that supported the corpse; it had been smuggled into the city under cover of night, partly to protect it from the mob but mainly so that nothing distracted attention from the political aim of the day: that the citizens of Rome accept Caligula as their Emperor.

The Campus Martius was heaving with people come not to hear the palpable nonsense that Caligula was spouting but to see the dazzling young Emperor himself, resplendent in purple laced with gold embroidery and crowned with a wreath of gilded laurels. When he had entered the city earlier that day they had hailed him as their saviour and shouted out affectionate greetings and called him their star, their pet and beloved son of the great Germanicus come to usher in the new golden age of Rome. The phrase had resonated in Vespasian's mind as he had looked on with a growing sense of dread mixed with a vague hope that perhaps this adulation would spur Caligula on to rule with temperance and prudence, keeping his vices private and his affability public.

After another quarter of an hour of unrestrained drivel about Tiberius' virtue, sobriety and sense of justice – with a brief foray into the truth by way of praise for his scholarship – Caligula finally drew to a close with a prayer of thanks to the gods for granting Tiberius such longevity, and regret – shared by no one else in the vast crowd – that his time had now come to meet the Ferryman. As his final words died away the pyre was lit and the professional mourners renewed their wailing and rending of garments with a fervour that amused the mob that had only a few days previously been calling for the hated Emperor's body to be cast without ceremony into the Tiber.

Flames quickly consumed the dry wood, coaxed on by bags of oil within the pyre, sending a heat shimmer and trails of smoke up into the crisp, early spring air. Priests and augurs scanned the sky for bird-signs, hoping to see an eagle do something auspicious that they would interpret, after careful consultation with the young Emperor, in a way that best suited the politics of the transition of power. But none came and nor could they fabricate one, since the event was being witnessed by such a large crowd, all of whom were also searching for omens.

As the bier caught light and the corpse began to sizzle, Caligula descended from the dais and, flanked by the Consuls and praetors and preceded by twelve lictors, made his way towards Pompey's Theatre, through the crowd who now cheered their new hero with an enthusiasm fuelled by the final consumption of the old Emperor's body. Caligula basked in their adoration, dispensing largesse and tickets for the funeral games to be held after the mourning period was ended.

'We'd better go in,' Gaius muttered, turning to follow the other senators into the theatre to wait to be addressed by their new Emperor.

'As to the titles and honours that you have voted me, I will allow them all except "Father of the Country", you can vote me that at a later date; and I shall postpone becoming Senior Consul until June. However, you will vote my grandmother Antonia the title of "Augusta" and my three sisters all the privileges of the Vestal Virgins.'

The senators, already almost hoarse from acclaiming Caligula as he had entered the theatre, cheered their assent to these orders.

'Do you think that last measure was meant to be ironic, Uncle?' Vespasian quipped out of the corner of his mouth. Gaius knew better than to smile at the joke.

As Caligula continued his address, Vespasian surreptitiously scanned the faces of the senators; most of them had screwed their faces into sombre expressions of acceptance as they listened to their new Emperor's demands, unable to find fault with any of them. As his gaze wandered to the end of a line those two dark eyes met his again and he felt the hatred that burned within them.

'Finally,' Caligula announced by way of conclusion, 'I will halt all treason trials; it is unimaginable that anyone would harbour a treasonous thought against an emperor so loved by his people. To this end I will burn all the papers containing evidence against members of this House that Tiberius had collected. I will do this in order that, no matter how strongly I may some day desire to harbour malice against any one of you for voting for my mother's and my brothers' deaths, I shall nevertheless be unable to punish him in the courts.'

This brought the loudest cheer of the meeting; the relieved senators felt themselves forgiven for their collusion, by way of opportunistic denunciations of members of Germanicus' family in an attempt to curry favour with Tiberius and Sejanus as, for separate reasons, the two men had pursued the destruction of so much of Caligula's family.

Caligula let them applaud his magnanimity for a good while before signalling for quiet and carrying on. 'But seeing as you have deprived me of a brother to share my consulship in June I shall have to look elsewhere for a colleague, and the most suitable one that I can think of is my uncle, Claudius.'

There was a stunned silence; the thought of Claudius stuttering and drooling his way through all the ancient rituals of the Senate was appalling to all those present.

'I understand your confusion, Conscript Fathers,' Caligula sympathised, with a barely concealed look of amusement on his face. 'Claudius is only an equestrian and not a member of the

Senate.' His eyes hardened. 'So I shall make him one immediately. The Consuls, praetors, aediles and quaestors may have the privilege of accompanying me to Augustus' House where I shall take up residence. That will be all.' He turned and walked quickly towards the exit with the senior magistrates scrambling in an undignified manner to catch up.

As the young Emperor drew close to where Vespasian stood, ready to take his place along with the other magistrates, his dark-rimmed sunken eyes fell on him; with a radiant smile Caligula beckoned him to join him at the head of the procession.

'My friend,' Caligula said as Vespasian fell into step next to him, 'I have been so looking forward to seeing you; what fun we shall have now.'

'I'm honoured, Princeps,' Vespasian replied, feeling the disapproving looks of the more senior magistrates upon him.

'I suppose you are. I shall have to get used to my friends being honoured by my favour.'

Having not seen Caligula close up for almost six years he was surprised to notice that the hair on the top of his head was thinning and wispy; he felt his eyes drawn to it. Caligula caught his look and the cheerful expression on his face disappeared in an instant.

'That is the last time you stare at my *full* head of hair,' he warned coldly. A warm grin suddenly replaced the icy glare. 'Tonight you dine with me; I've invited my grandmother, you can help me deal with her. I believe that she's going to try and give me advice and tell me what to do. I think that would be most unwise of her; don't you agree?'

'If you feel that it would be unwise then I would agree with you, Princeps,' Vespasian replied guardedly.

'Oh, stop that Princeps nonsense in private with me, Vespasian, we're friends. Now walk with me to the Palatine and tell me about the lovely Caenis.'

Vespasian swallowed hard.

*

'Over five hundred million denarii, can you believe it?' Caligula exclaimed as the imperial party reached the top of the Palatine, leaving the cheering masses below. 'Just lying there in the treasury, doing nothing. The old miser was just sitting on it.'

'It's always good to have a reserve,' Vespasian pointed out, still mightily relieved that Caligula's attention span was so short that he had tired of the subject of Caenis after no more than a couple of stumbling sentences. 'He was able to donate all that money for the rebuilding of the Aventine, for example.'

Caligula frowned. 'Yes, what a waste giving it to people who can well afford to have their houses burned down; I'll find a way to get it back off them, don't you worry about that. But just think what I could do with all the rest. We shall have games every day and I shall build, Vespasian, build.' He pointed to Augustus' grand house, towards which they were heading, and that of Tiberius next to it. 'I shall make these two feeble little dwellings into one huge palace fit for an emperor and his sisters, and I shall fill it with the best furniture, art and slaves from all over the Empire. And conquests, Vespasian, I shall make glorious conquests and celebrate Triumphs the like of which have never been seen. The Senate will be envious of my power and glory and will mutter and plot behind my back but will flatter me with titles to my face and I will mock them and humiliate them for their obsequiousness. They will hate me as they did Tiberius, but unlike him, I shall fill the city with the spoils of a hundred nations and fill the circus with thousands of captives to be slaughtered for the pleasure of the people, and they will love me and keep me safe.'

Vespasian glanced at Caligula as they mounted the steps to Augustus' House and saw that he was wide-eyed with enthusiasm and ambition. It was going to be an expensive time for Rome. What would he do, he wondered, when the money ran out?

'Gentlemen, thank you for accompanying me home,' Caligula said, addressing his following from the top of the steps. 'I shall rest now and gather my strength for the trials ahead of me. You may go.'

The senators vied with each other to be the loudest in shouting 'Hail Caesar' while Caligula lifted his right hand with the imperial ring, dazzling in the sun, on the forefinger and held his head back, lapping up the praise. Vespasian joined in with as much of a show of enthusiasm as the rest but with an unease brought about by Caligula's all too obvious enjoyment of being so hailed and his reluctance to bring it to an end. Was he already mocking the foremost men in Rome by seeing how long they would praise him for? Eventually he lowered his arm, turned smartly on his heel and entered the house. Vespasian stood rooted to the spot, watching Caligula leave, unsure as to whether or not he too had been dismissed or was still expected for dinner.

He was just about to leave when Caligula stuck his head back out of the door. 'Come on!' he shouted fiercely. 'You're my friend, you stay with me.'

Vespasian ran towards the door wondering what advantage there would be in being the Emperor's friend; if any.

CHAPTER XIIII

Vespasian found the scale of the interior of Augustus' House overwhelming; his family's whole house at Aquae Cutillae could have fitted into the atrium alone. Far greater in size than those of Antonia or her daughter Livilla, the two largest residences that he had visited on the Palatine, this had been built to overawe visiting dignitaries with the power of the man who had become the first among equals of the Roman ruling class. Yet there was no ostentation about it; it was an architectural study in power, not a bragging showcase of wealth. The columns supporting the high atrium ceiling were of the finest white marble and the intricate mosaics on the floor were beautifully executed scenes from the *Aeneid* in which the characters seemed almost to move, such was the realism with which they were depicted. However, the furnishings, ornaments and statuary were downplayed; each one a masterpiece in its own right but not gaudy or brash, their workmanship alone attested far better to their value than any extraneous gilding or augmentation with precious stones or lavish fabrics. It was a testament both to the taste and the political acumen of the man who had built it; he had not robbed Rome's coffers in order to live in outrageous eastern-style luxury while the large percentage of his people scrabbled for their living; he had built it to impress upon those who visited him to seek Rome's friendship and favour the enormous power of the combined force of all the citizens of Rome. He had built it in Rome's image: practical, strong, towering and, above all, without pretension.

'Miserable, isn't it?' Caligula complained as Vespasian caught up with him. 'Augustus had no idea of how to display his wealth; I'll be making a lot of changes to brighten the whole place up.'

'I think it's beautiful, Caligula, I wouldn't change it at all.'

'What would you know about beauty,' Caligula scoffed, 'you country boy with your Sabine accent? Anyway, you don't have any say in the matter, I'm the Emperor and you're just my subject.'

'Indeed, Princeps.'

'Gaius, my dearest,' Antonia said, appearing from the far side of the vast atrium, 'I have been waiting for you. Come here and let me look at my new Emperor whom I haven't seen for six years.'

Caligula stopped still. 'You come here, Grandmother; I do no one's bidding now, not even yours.'

Antonia approached with a fixed smile on her face and stood before her grandson, taking his face in her hands and gazing up into his sunken eyes. 'Juno be praised, you look well. I have prayed for this moment for a long time and now it's finally come; my little Gaius emperor.'

'I shall reward you for your prayers, Grandmother, although in truth they were unnecessary, I was destined for this. I have already ordered the Senate to vote you the title of "Augusta".'

'You are generous, Gaius, to have me so honoured.' She reached up automatically to ruffle his hair, as she had done so many times when he had been a child in her care, and withdrew her hand instantly as she saw how thin it had become.

'It's your constant ruffling that's to blame,' Caligula snapped. 'Have a care, woman, just because I've bestowed an honour on you one moment doesn't mean that I won't demand your death the next. I can treat people any way I want now.' He stormed off, leaving Antonia looking concerned at Vespasian.

'It's worse than I feared,' she said quietly, 'he'll be the death of us all.'

Caligula roared with uncontrolled, high-pitched laughter. 'Aren't they priceless?' he finally managed to get out. 'I had them sent from Alexandria four years ago, they cost me a fortune, but they're worth every denarius.'

Vespasian watched politely the antics of a group of naked dwarf acrobats as they performed what he hoped was their finale. The sixteen males had formed a tapering column, five dwarves high, around and up which four females were climbing, using the erect penises of their fellow performers as hand-holds and foot rests, to an accompaniment of frenzied percussion and ululations from a half-dozen wild-eyed female drummers who were hardly any taller than their instruments.

'Tiberius used to love them,' Caligula enthused, 'especially when they all start rutting. Sometimes they just can't stop themselves.'

'I can imagine,' Vespasian said as enthusiastically as possible, hoping that this evening they would find the necessary control. However, judging by the close attention that the females were giving to each one of their hand-holds he was prepared to be disappointed; as disappointed, in fact, as he had been in Caligula's behaviour towards Antonia all through dinner. He had not wasted a single opportunity to gainsay her or dismiss her opinions such that it was apparent that he was doing it out of bloody-mindedness rather than because he believed her to be wrong. Antonia had borne the insults with an external appearance of indifference even when, having advised him to keep away from his sisters, he had proceeded to describe, in loving detail, exactly what he intended to do with each one of them once they returned to Rome. Vespasian had tried to steer the difficult path between not annoying his power-drunk Emperor and not appearing to be too sycophantic towards him in Antonia's eyes, but had erred on the side of caution; a predicament that Antonia had, with a few sympathetic looks while Caligula's attention had been elsewhere, indicated she fully understood.

Caligula's juvenile enjoyment of the dwarves' performance for the past half-hour was proving a cringing embarrassment to both of them because he was so obviously revelling in Antonia's disgust.

'Gaius, I'm not sure that this is appropriate entertainment for after-dinner,' Antonia observed, unable to resist a comment any longer. She was peeling an apple while studiously ignoring the acrobats' gradual ascent.

'Oh come on, Grandmother, it's just a bit of fun. It's very tame compared to some of the acts that Tiberius had on Capreae.'

'This is not Capreae, Gaius dear, this is Rome, and certain standards need to be kept.'

'What standards? The standards of aristocrats? Hanging onto sweaty and bloodied boxers, after they've fought one another to a standstill, to get a good, rough going over after your guests have left? Those are your standards and I don't judge them if that's what you like. I like my dwarves, they make me laugh and I advise you not to criticise me for it because at least I'm honest about it. In fact, I'm probably the only honest man of senatorial or equestrian birth in this hypocritical, Janus-faced city.'

Antonia placed the half-peeled apple on her plate and got to her feet; the airing of her sexual preferences in front of Vespasian had evidently proved too much for her. 'I don't criticise you for it, Gaius, I just prefer not to share it. I'm now tired, as is the prerogative of an old and disappointed woman, so I shall bid you both goodnight. It's been an interesting evening, thank you.' She walked briskly away, not looking back.

'I'll have Vespasian send his man, Magnus, around to cheer you up, Grandmother,' Caligula shouted as she left the triclinium. With a triumphant laugh he turned back to Vespasian, who was trying not to show the shock and alarm that he felt at being involved in Caligula's worst jibe of the evening against his benefactress. 'I think that's made it perfectly clear as to where she stands with me, don't you?'

'I thought that you handled her expertly,' Vespasian replied, resorting to full-blown sycophancy now that the restraining presence of Antonia had gone and hating himself for it. 'And you are right: you are the only honest man in Rome.'

Caligula smiled knowingly at Vespasian. 'Because I'm the only one who can afford to be. The Senate have lived for so long with Augustus' conceit that they and the Princeps share power, whereas in reality they slavishly proposed and voted for what they deemed to be his and then Tiberius' will, in the hopes of gaining favour. They've forgotten what honesty is; you might just as well have a flock of sheep sitting in the Curia. Well, I'm going to teach the sheep honesty.'

Vespasian thought about giving an honest reply but decided against it. 'I'm sure you will be a great teacher.'

'You're right, old friend, I will be,' Caligula affirmed, turning his attention back to the dwarf column where the lead female dwarf had now, quite literally, mounted the top while her fellow climbers worked their hand-holds vigorously.

'Princeps, I have a favour to ask of you,' Vespasian said, hoping that the approaching climax – in many ways – of Caligula's favourite act would put him in the mood for granting requests.

'Vespasian, my good friend, name it.'

'I have some family business that needs to be taken care of in Egypt. Would you grant me permission to go?'

'And lose my companion for four or five months? What would I do without you? Get someone else to do it for you, but not a senator as it's still not safe; apparently the Phoenix has been reborn but hasn't yet flown east.'

'I have to go in person, and besides I couldn't go until my term as aedile has expired at the end of this year,' Vespasian pointed out, wondering what the Phoenix flying east had to do with senators travelling to Egypt in safety.

'Well, we shall see, perhaps I'll have tired of you by then and the Phoenix will have gone. Callistus!' Caligula's short and wiry steward, whom Vespasian recognised from his visit to Misenum, came scurrying in. 'Once my dwarves have finished, call for Clemens and get us some dirty tunics and hooded cloaks.' Caligula turned back to watch the inevitable, rather messy, finale. 'I want to go drinking and whoring in the city. We could get Magnus to show us some interesting places; I want to hear what the common people, the honest people, are saying about me.'

*

'It won't be the best you've ever drunk here, Magnus,' the portly tavern-keeper said, thumping down a full jug of wine onto the grimy, wine-stained table, 'but neither will it be the worst.'

'I'm sure it'll be up to your normal standard of gut-rotter, Balbus,' Magnus replied with a grin as he filled the chipped cups of his three companions.

'Who're yer mates? I don't think I've seen them before; not that I can really see their faces.'

'Associates from out of the city come to see the new Emperor.'

Balbus kissed his thumbnail. 'Jupiter hold his hands over our shining star, he's the new hope of Rome. I saw him today and he looked like a young god.'

'Perhaps he is,' Caligula suggested from beneath his hood.

'He may well be, Augustus was…is. Well, you're welcome, lads, but we prefer hoods to be down in here, if it's all the same to you.'

Vespasian and Clemens both pulled back their hoods but Caligula made no attempt to remove his; instead he pulled a gold aureus from his purse and handed it to Balbus. 'This should see us supplied with wine and women for a while.'

Balbus bit the coin; his eyes lit up as he realised that it was genuine. 'Anything you want, lads, you can even have me for that and I wouldn't care that I couldn't see your faces and the love in your eyes.'

The rumour of gold flew around the large, low-ceilinged tavern fogged with the fumes from a cooking fire behind the amphorae-lined bar; within moments all four of them had a plump, stale-sweat-fragranced whore sitting on their lap while others hovered close by hoping to be next in line should one of the lucky first-arrivals be rejected. All around the dimly lit room there were mutterings and dark looks from men on other tables who had been deprived of their female company as they gravitated across the wine-sticky flagstone floor towards the table with money.

'I'm not sure that flashing gold in here was a good thing, Gaius,' Magnus observed, struggling to take a sip of wine amid

233

the enthusiastic attentions of his new companion. They were all under strict instructions to use Caligula's first name.

Caligula adjusted his position to allow his partner access up his tunic. 'If you've got it, flaunt it, Magnus.'

'And you've certainly got it, my lovely,' the woman said, working her hand up his leg. 'And in more ways than one,' she added in surprise and admiration. 'Venus help me! Sisters have a feel of this one; I've never come across the like of it.'

Caligula sat revelling in the attention that his huge erection was receiving as the women took it in turns to stroke its almost one-foot length and grasp its impressive girth, simpering at its magnitude.

'That's worthy of Jupiter himself,' Vespasian's whore exclaimed as she took her turn, 'I can't even close my fingers around it.'

Vespasian took the opportunity to ease the woman off his lap and look around the room; many of the already angry customers were leaving their seats and gathering in a knot, looking with malicious intent towards their table. 'I'm not too sure that we're going to be very welcome here for much longer,' he muttered to Clemens next to him, nodding his head towards the menace.

Clemens looked around and then leant over to whisper in Caligula's ear while loosening in its scabbard the gladius concealed under his cloak. Brushing away a collection of groping female hands, Caligula stood up, keeping his hood still covering his head. 'Balbus,' he shouted, not bothering to adjust his hitched-up tunic, 'wine and food for everyone in the tavern.' He reached into his purse and pulled out another couple of gold coins. 'We will drink to the health of our new Emperor.'

A ragged cheer went up as a beaming Balbus took the coins and signalled to his slaves, who took amphorae from their holders behind the bar and began filling jugs of wine, which they placed, along with plates of bread and cooked pork, on the counter. All but a hard core of the threatening group made to help themselves, mollified, for the present, by the offer of free victuals and drink.

'Fill my cup, Magnus,' Caligula said, stroking the hair of a couple of the cluster of women now kneeling at his feet.

With his cup refilled, Caligula waded through the women before him and addressed the room. 'The son of Germanicus and descendant of the god Augustus has returned to Rome as emperor! Praise him!' Caligula downed his wine in one as cries of 'Caligula! Our shining star!' filled the room.

Vespasian stood and joined in the acclamation with an outward enthusiasm that concealed his inner anxiety: if Caligula remained beloved of the mob then he would be free to do whatever he pleased, and Vespasian knew only too well what pleased him.

'You see, my friend,' Caligula said, turning to him, his eyes, just visible under his hood, burning with pride, 'honest people love me.'

Caligula's gold had kept the wine flowing and Vespasian felt bleary. The tavern was now full to bursting as news of free drink filtered through the neighbourhood and scuffles had broken out as petty arguments, fuelled by excessive alcohol, ballooned into matters of great import. Knives had been drawn on a couple of occasions and bloodied victims had been thrown out into the street to fend for themselves as best they could.

Caligula had spent the time drinking steadily but that had not affected his prowess and he had satisfied numerous women as they took it in turns to ride up and down in his lap. His stamina had been impressive and Vespasian, who had allowed himself to be pleasured a couple of times, could but marvel at his ability to keep going.

Clemens had stayed alert, drinking little and refusing women, but Magnus had drunk and whored himself to a snoring heap, head slumped in a plate of cold pork with wine-stained saliva dribbling from the corner of his mouth and the contents of an overturned cup dripping into his lap.

'We should go,' Caligula announced as another whore pulled herself off him panting deeply, 'I'm tiring of this place.'

Relieved that the evening was finally over, Vespasian leant over the table and shook Magnus from his slumber.

'Are we off home, then?' Magnus asked sleepily, peeling off a slice of pork that had stuck to his cheek and taking a bite.

'No, I'm just tired of this place,' Caligula said, 'take me somewhere else.'

Magnus got wearily to his feet. 'Somewhere with a little more variety, if you take my meaning?'

'Variety? Yes, that's what I need.' Caligula pushed his way into the crowd.

'Hey lads, our goldmine's leaving,' an unpleasantly drunk, thuggish-looking man slurred, 'let's make sure he leaves us his money.' His two mates jumped at Caligula, grabbing his arms and knocking back his hood while the drunk went for his purse.

With a flash of burnished iron, Clemens whipped out his sword and forced it between the ribs of the assailant nearest to him. With a scream and a violent jerk the man let go of Caligula's arm and fell to the floor as Clemens pulled his weapon free in a slop of blood. Vespasian and Magnus both drew their knives from the sheaths in the smalls of their backs and pounced towards the other two men, upturning nearby tables with a crash of earthenware. Women screamed and knives flashed in the lamplight around the room as men immediately decided whether to protect their erstwhile benefactor or join the attempted robbery.

Vespasian slammed into the drunk, knocking him to the floor away from Caligula, but still grasping the purse, as Magnus, now suddenly fully awake, wrenched the hair of the third man and sliced his knife across his exposed throat. Blood sprayed over Caligula's face and cloak as Clemens put a protective arm around him, pulling him back towards the relative safety of a huddle of frightened women clustered around their table, while keeping his sword pointed at the free-for-all knife fight that had erupted in front of them.

Leaping towards the floored drunk, and narrowly missing a hurled earthenware jug spraying wine, Vespasian crunched a hard-sandalled foot between the man's legs; his body convulsed in a rapid ripple of sheer agony that sent his arms flying up and catapulting the purse across the chaotic room. Vespasian watched its trajectory towards the bar and tried to follow it but became entangled with Magnus grappling with a new opponent intent upon strangling him. All three crashed onto a table, which collapsed to the floor with Vespasian on top. Recovering first, Vespasian grabbed the man's ear, jerked his head up and pounded it down onto the flagstone, shattering his skull as the tavern door burst open and a new force swarmed in: the club-wielding Vigiles.

Made up mainly of ex-slaves, the night-watch had no cause to be overfond of the citizens of Rome and they set about breaking up the fight with a severity that eclipsed the violence they had come to halt. Without waiting to find out who was in the right or wrong they swept their clubs down indiscriminately onto heads, backs and outstretched arms, cracking bones, breaking teeth and splitting skin. Vespasian and Magnus just had time to pick themselves up off the floor and retreat to the far side of the room where Caligula, covered in blood and now laughing hysterically, was guarded by Clemens. They stood shoulder to shoulder in front of their Emperor and waited, weapons at the ready.

The Vigiles gradually subdued the remaining fights, with the loss of only one of their number, rounding up any miscreants still conscious and pushing them back across the room. Their optio, a stocky, bald man with forearms like mossy tree branches, suddenly noticed Vespasian and his comrades, through his crowd of prisoners, standing in the shadows.

'And you lot,' he growled, walking towards them, 'put down your weapons.' Then seeing Clemens' sword he stepped back. Knowing that the carrying of swords within the city was the prerogative of only the Urban Cohorts or the Praetorian Guard and then only when on duty, he made the reasonable assumption that this was a dangerous criminal whom he was faced with.

'I'd let us go if I were you, optio,' Clemens warned, keeping between Caligula and the Vigiles commander.

'Lads, on me,' he called to his men, 'these are going to have to go down hard.'

Corralling the disarmed prisoners towards the bar, the Vigiles lined up and faced Vespasian, Magnus and Clemens.

'You have served your Emperor well, optio,' Caligula said, pushing past Clemens.

'What would you know about that, you spindly rat?'

'Because *I* am your Emperor, and one more remark like that and you'll be serving me well in the arena.' Caligula stepped forward into the light and held his blood-stained head high. There was a brief silence in the room and then a communal gasp as most people recognised the man whom they had crowded into the city to see only that morning; even covered in blood he was unmistakeable.

'Princeps,' the optio spluttered, bowing his head, 'forgive me.'

'Our star!' someone shouted.

Others took up the shout and Caligula raised his arms and bathed for a while in their worship, and then pointed to his original attacker, still clutching his groin on the floor. 'That man's testicles seem to be troubling him,' he shouted over the din, 'relieve him of them, optio.'

The noise stopped as the optio looked down at the injured man and then back at Caligula and realised that he was in earnest. Fearing for his life, having insulted his Emperor, he had no choice. He drew his knife and bent down.

A shrill shriek announced the completion of the deed; Caligula smiled. 'Thank you, optio, I have forgiven you. You may release everyone else; they love me and will follow me as a flock follows its shepherd, trusting him to do them no harm.'

'Princeps, this is yours,' Balbus said, holding out the purse.

'Keep it, Balbus, but give some coins to the women.' Caligula moved towards the door, followed by Vespasian, Clemens and Magnus; the crowd parted for them.

'Thank you, Lord,' one of the whores cried out, 'we will remember your generosity and the pleasure you gave us; it was as if being satisfied by a god.'

'Satisfied by a god?' Caligula ruminated as they stepped out into the street. 'Perhaps they were; perhaps I am. After all, the shepherd rules over the sheep not because he's a superior sheep but because he is a superior being. It follows therefore that if I am the shepherd of the Roman flock sitting in the Senate House, it must be because I too am a superior being.'

Vespasian did not like the way Caligula's mind was working. 'That may be logical, Princeps, but remember that to live the shepherd regularly has to eat one of his sheep.'

The look on Caligula's face as he turned towards him made Vespasian instantly regret his line of argument.

'Exactly, my friend; the shepherd must remain fed and healthy for the good of his flock, so he chooses the sheep that will best satisfy his hunger.'

CHAPTER XV

VESPASIAN LOOKED AROUND the newly decorated atrium of Sabinus' rebuilt house as the last of the artisans collected up the tools of their trades. They had done a fine job, he reflected, with the limited amount of money, gleaned from his province, which his brother had been able to send back to Rome over the summer. Although it was not furbished to the most luxurious of standards he felt that Sabinus would have few complaints from Clementina when they eventually took up residence.

Vespasian had enjoyed overseeing the work; it had, along with his duties as the aedile responsible for Rome's streets, helped him to take his mind off the profligacy that had characterised the first seven months of Caligula's reign.

Anxious to secure the love of the mob, Caligula had not stinted them in his celebrations, nor had the Senate or priesthoods been ungenerous in their flattering support for their new Emperor, as Caligula had predicted. Over the first ninety days of his reign the temple altars flowed with the blood of sheep, bulls, fowl, horses and swine; one hundred and sixty thousand victims were publicly sacrificed to every god imaginable in thanks for the coming of the golden age. And to the common people of Rome it did indeed seem to be so; they feasted on the flesh of the sacrifices, they watched endless spectacles in the Circus Maximus and the other smaller arenas around the city and they had money to spend, Caligula having given them three gold aurei each – more than the annual wage for a legionary. To secure his position further he had paid another three aurei each to every legionary and auxiliary in the Empire as well as to the Vigiles; five apiece to the Urban Cohorts and ten apiece to the Praetorian Guard.

With all this ready money in circulation business had boomed as shopkeepers, tavern owners and merchants raked in the cash that their fellow citizens, anxious to emulate their beloved Emperor, spent freely under the misapprehension that the supply would never cease.

To neutralise the Senate's objections to this colossal outlay of coin he had recalled those of their number banished by the previous regime and had pardoned those still awaiting sentence, placing the House in his debt. He had then insulted them by refusing to accept the honours that they had voted for him in gratitude and ordered that they should never try and honour him again, thus demonstrating that he was not a creation of the Senate and did not rule by their favour.

To make the same point to what remained of his family he had freed Herod Agrippa, against the express wishes of Antonia, and had made him king of the Jewish tetrarchies of Batanaea and Trachonitius, east of the Jordan River; he had also given him a chain of solid gold to replace the one of iron with which he had been chained to his cell's wall.

To counter the effect of these attacks on the aristocracy he added to his popularity with the common people, milking the affection that they bore him, by personally bringing back the bones of his mother and two brothers from their island graves and interring them in the Mausoleum of Augustus in a ceremony so charged with emotion that no one in the vast crowd was left unmoved. Tears streamed down their faces as they watched their darling mourning, with sombre dignity, the family that had been so cruelly wrenched from him by the two people whom they hated most: Tiberius and Sejanus. The Senate had watched on, stony-faced, as he pulled this theatrical coup, knowing that, because of the guilt that they bore from their complicity with the murders of the imperial family, they had once again been side-lined. In a final insult to Antonia he had forbidden her to attend.

Not satisfied with the adulation he received from the people when he appeared at the circus or in the Forum, Caligula had taken to being carried around the city in an open litter throwing coinage left and right while displaying to the crowd, at their behest, his huge penis – rumour of which had quickly travelled around Rome after its first public display at Balbus' tavern.

Vespasian had been obliged to participate in many of the extravaganzas in his capacity as a middle-ranking Roman magistrate and friend of the Emperor and had been sickened by their extravagance. He had shared in a banquet for hundreds of senators, equites and their wives where each man had been given a new toga, each woman a new *palla*, and the gustatio had been of solid gold shaped as food, which the guests had been allowed to keep; he had watched with disgust – but had also taken part in – the fawning thanks that the guests had given their host. He had sat in the circus all day as four hundred bears and another four hundred assorted wild beasts were slaughtered in a spectacle that was, even by Rome's standards, excessive. Forced to endure it, thanks to Caligula's new policy of punishing severely anyone of importance who either left early or failed to turn up, Vespasian had watched pretending, with self-preserving sycophancy, to enjoy it, while the crowd cheered their benefactor who officiated over the blood-bath in the imperial enclosure surrounded by the priests of Augustus and being masturbated by his sisters and the most skilful courtesans in Rome.

Vespasian had had enough but there was nothing that he could do; he was trapped, as was everyone in Rome, and was obliged to share in this compulsory fun forced upon him by a seemingly deranged emperor supported by the blades of a loyal, well-rewarded Praetorian Guard.

A soft voice from behind him disturbed his grim thoughts. 'I thought that I'd find you here.'

He turned to see Caenis in the doorway; her eyes were red and rimmed with tears.

'Caenis, what's wrong?' he asked, walking over to her.

'My mistress sent me to find you, you must come at once.'

'Of course. What's happening?'

'She wants to say goodbye.'

'Goodbye? Where's she going?'

Caenis burst into tears and flung her arms around his neck sobbing. 'To meet the Ferryman.'

'I've had a succession of people, far more prestigious than you, Vespasian, trying to dissuade me,' Antonia said, 'so don't waste my time or yours; my mind is made up.'

'But why, domina?' Vespasian sat opposite Antonia, across her oaken desk in her private room. The lowering sun filtered through the bay window, a shaft hit her face and he could see lines of care and trouble etched around her eyes and mouth; for the first time she looked very old.

'Because I will not sit by and watch impotently while that fool of a grandson of mine bankrupts the Empire and throws away my family's hold over it. He ignores my advice and humiliates me in public; I was not even allowed to attend my other grandsons' interment. I have no control any more. The money is already starting to run out and if he's to keep buying the love of the mob then he'll have to find a new supply; the treason trials will start again and the rich and once-powerful will lose their estates so that the poor can be kept in bread and circuses. The Senate will tear itself apart as individuals denounce each other in an effort to stay alive, until what's left of it will realise that unless something changes they will all die; which is, of course, what Gaius wants. Within three or four years he will be assassinated, and what then? The Guard will choose its own emperor, but who?'

'Claudius or Tiberius Gemellus, perhaps.'

'Tiberius Gemellus will be dead before the year is out, Gaius will see to that, but that will be no loss; he has too much of his mother, Livilla, in him. And Claudius, well, who knows? I've left this house and as much of my estate to him as possible – the larger part I have left to Gaius to squander – perhaps the money will help Claudius if he is allowed to live, and that is part of the reason why I'm taking my own life. Claudius surprised everybody while he was Consul; he knew all the procedures, prayers and forms of words and very rarely stuttered over them or brought shame on the House; people are looking upon him in a new light. With me alive to support him, Gaius will see him as a threat and will most certainly have him killed, but with me dead there is a chance that he will carry on regarding him as an object of fun and worth keeping alive just for the amusement of it.

'My freedmen and -women will naturally transfer their allegiance to Claudius so Caenis will have a patron not a master, as I've freed her in my will.'

Vespasian's eyes widened, the moment for which he had longed for eleven years had finally arrived; yet it had come in such bleak circumstances.

'This is one reason why I have called you here, Vespasian; Caenis is like a daughter to me and I need to know that she will be safe, you must look after her for me.'

'Of course, domina, but how can I do that if she's living under Claudius' roof?'

'She won't be; Claudius isn't strong enough to resist Caligula if he should send the Guard to fetch her for him. If Caligula asks you about her, tell him that she has gone to Egypt with Felix to help him with my affairs there. I offered that she should do just that but she wanted to remain here, so I have bought her a house on the Quirinal very close to your uncle's; take her there tonight once I am gone. She will be safe enough if she stays inside; only you, Pallas and I know of it.'

'I will, domina, and thank you, you're most generous.'

Antonia smiled. 'It is a gift for Caenis, not for you, although I assume that you will benefit from it. For you I have something else, but first I have a request.'

'Anything you ask, domina.'

Antonia chuckled wryly, accentuating her care-lines. 'I would never say that again if I were you, Vespasian, you may find yourself unable to keep your word.'

Vespasian flushed.

The chuckle turned into a laugh. 'And letting your feelings play on your face like that is something that you need to start controlling. But no more advice, time is short.

'Gaius has kept his word to Macro and has promised him Egypt but not until next year, once he feels completely secure in Rome. This comes as no surprise as he still seems to be bedding Ennia as part of his busy sexual schedule. However, even though his new wife died in childbirth in January he's showing no sign of wanting to make Ennia his empress as he had promised. I believe that this is because he has become frightened of Macro; he's realised that just as Macro made him emperor he could easily take it away. You must exploit this fear; play on it anytime that you can. I have asked Clemens to do the same thing; he has always been loyal to Gaius and I think that Gaius may soon come to realise that he would be much safer with his friend Clemens as his Praetorian prefect rather than his potential rival Macro. If that could come about, then it would be just a question of convincing Clemens that Gaius is unfit to rule and the Guard should kill him.'

'You're asking me to help bring about your grandson's death?'

'Someone's got to before he goes completely mad and brings down Rome. When that comes to pass Claudius must be made emperor; I have charged Pallas with keeping him out of trouble and to make sure that he doesn't dabble in politics and continues playing the fool.'

'And if he's not successful, what then?'

'There will be another civil war.' Antonia pulled open a drawer and withdrew a sheathed sword, which she looked at fondly. 'This belonged to my father, Marcus Antonius. Just before he used it to commit suicide in Alexandria he wrote a letter to Augustus asking that he should return it to me so that I could pass it on to my future son. Augustus granted his erstwhile brother-in-law and friend's dying wish and brought it back to Rome for me. When Germanicus came of age I gave it to him and he used it to subdue the Germanic tribes and to push back the Parthians. After he too died his wife, Agrippina, wanted to pass it onto her eldest son, Nero Caesar. I refused her, saying that I would decide which of my grandsons most deserved it – it would be the one that I considered would make the best

245

Emperor. For a while I thought that I would give it to Gaius but then as his brothers were killed off I began to see his true nature, so I withheld it and I'm pleased that I did; he dishonours his great-grandfather's memory.

'In a short time I will use this sword to open my veins; when I am dead Caenis will bring it to you. It will be yours. Remember that it was borne by two of the greatest men of our age – use it well and perhaps you will live up to them.'

'Thank you, domina.'

'Now go and wait in the atrium for Caenis while she helps me to leave this world. Pallas will then show you both to her new house; take Magnus with you so that he knows where it is and after that it's up to you and him as to whether she lives in safety or in fear. Goodbye, Vespasian, and bear my father's sword in a manner worthy of him.'

Vespasian took one last look at the most powerful woman in Rome, in awe at the way that she could still try to order matters from even beyond the grave. Yet for all her political adroitness in life she had been unable to ensure that she went to that grave naturally. The power that she had sought for her family had been concentrated into the one person over whom she had no control: her grandson Caligula. This sudden departure from life – although, Vespasian reflected, it was no more sudden than any death – was her only chance to wrest that power back and place it into the hands of the son she had always despised: Claudius. The irony was bitter and Vespasian could tell from her saddened, green eyes that it was not lost on Antonia.

'Goodbye, domina, and thank you for the favour that you've shown me.' With a nod of his head he turned and left the room.

The day was fading and Vespasian had been waiting for more than an hour when Caenis, Pallas and Felix finally appeared. Tears rolled down their cheeks as they walked towards him through the atrium whose very air seemed heavy with grief; the whole household had come to a standstill as the mistress had bled to death in her bath.

'She's gone,' Caenis sobbed, offering Vespasian Marcus Antonius' sword with both hands. 'This is now yours, my love.'

Vespasian took the sword by its tightly bound red-leather hilt and drew it from its scabbard; the weight was perfect and the balance exact. A blue shimmer ran down the length of the burnished steeled-iron blade – engraved with its original owner's name – to the unadorned bronze, oval guard that bore the scars of long-ago parried strokes. The pommel too was of plain bronze and the scabbard was simple tan buck-leather glued onto the wooden case and strengthened by four evenly spaced bronze bands. Despite his grief at the knowledge that it had recently been used to open Antonia's wrists, Vespasian smiled; this was not a parade-ground soldier's weapon, this belonged to a fighting man and he understood why Antonia had used it to end her life.

He re-sheathed it with a soft rasp. 'How did she die?'

'Nobly,' Pallas replied, 'and without fear. She signed her will and Caenis' and Felix's documents of manumission and then dictated a couple of letters; she went to her bedroom and prepared herself and then got into the warm pool and ... and did it, without hesitation. She lay back with her eyes closed as she bled and then, before she grew too weak to speak, she cursed Caligula before all the gods and the spirits of her ancestors, calling on them to bring him down and to ease Rome's suffering.'

'If they would listen to anyone they would listen to her.' He looked at Caenis and lifted her chin; tears still glistened around her eyes. 'Stop crying now, Antonia Caenis, you are finally freed.'

Caenis smiled through her tears. 'Yes, I shall always bear her name to remember her by, she who was a mother to me.'

Vespasian pulled her close and kissed her perfumed hair. The sound of footsteps drew his eyes; they widened in surprise as Magnus walked into the room.

'What are you doing here?' he asked, and then realised that he could guess the answer. 'Oh, I see.'

'Yeah, well,' Magnus mumbled, looking bashful.

'We should go, Vespasian,' Pallas said, not wishing to dwell on the reason for Magnus' presence for the sake of his late mistress's dignity.

'Yes, we should,' Vespasian agreed, pleased also to change the subject. He turned to leave.

'Vespasian, before you go,' Felix said.

Vespasian looked back at Felix. 'Congratulations on your liberty, Marcus Antonius Felix.'

Felix smiled at being addressed by his new name. 'My thanks, Vespasian. My mistress has instructed me to go back to Egypt immediately to wind up her affairs there; it'll take me a year or so. She also told me that you were trying to get permission to visit; if you're successful and I can be of service please contact me. The Alabarch will always know where to find me.'

Vespasian nodded his thanks and, putting a protective arm around Caenis, walked towards the door.

Set in a quiet street just three hundred paces from Gaius' house, Caenis' new home was small and unobtrusive. Antonia had chosen well, Vespasian reflected as they approached the front door, Caenis would be safe from Caligula here.

'I shall leave you now,' Pallas said, pulling the bell chain, 'I have my mistress's funeral to attend to.'

Caenis kissed him on the cheek. 'Thank you, Pallas.'

'Most of your things are already here, the rest I'll have sent over tomorrow.'

'I'll come with you,' Magnus said with a grin, 'I imagine that I'll be in the way if I stay. I'll make arrangements to have one of my lads always watching the street, making sure no one unpleasant is snooping round if you take my meaning?'

The door opened as Magnus and Pallas walked off to reveal the largest Nubian Vespasian had ever seen. 'Antonia was evidently keen that your door should be well guarded,' he said, bending down and putting one arm under her knees and the other under her arms to lift her up. 'This is the nearest that we'll ever get to me being able to carry you over the threshold.'

Caenis giggled and, taking his face in her hands, kissed him long and passionately. The Nubian politely stepped back and, still kissing, Vespasian carried her into the vestibule and then through to the atrium. A clearing of the throat interrupted them. Vespasian looked up and immediately let go of Caenis' legs.

'Good evening, mistress,' a tall, elderly Egyptian said, bowing low. 'My name is Menes, I am your steward, and this,' he indicated to the fifteen slaves in a row behind him, 'is your household.'

Blushing furiously, Vespasian and Caenis stared at the line of slaves, then at each other and burst out laughing.

Vespasian watched the pillar of grey smoke begin to rise from the Campus Martius, just over a mile away, as he waited in the audience chamber of Augustus' House along with all the elected magistrates and many of the most senior senators. Caligula had already kept them waiting for more than an hour; on purpose, Vespasian guessed. Gaius shuffled uneasily beside him, trying not to show the vexation that he felt at the sight of the smoke. They had all received a summons, first thing that morning, to attend the Emperor at the third hour and they all knew that it was no coincidence that Antonia's funeral was due to begin at that time. In causing the most senior men in Rome to be absent from the ceremony Caligula had radically diminished the dignity of the occasion in a final insult to his grandmother; not even her son Claudius had been spared his spite.

The senators began to talk animatedly about any subject other than Antonia as they too saw, through the open windows looking out over the city, the sign that her funeral pyre had been lit. No one wished to be seen appearing displeased at their inability to add their weight to the mourning of the most powerful woman in Rome should their master be secretly watching and listening.

The red and black lacquered, panelled double doors at the far end of the room suddenly opened and all conversations stopped; Caligula entered flanked by Macro and a Praetorian tribune whom Vespasian did not recognise.

Theatrically feigning surprise, Caligula stopped in his tracks and looked past the gathering through one of the windows. 'There seems to be a fire on the Campus Martius,' he cried in mock alarm, 'has anyone called for the Vigiles to put it out?'

The senators rocked with sycophantic laughter led by Macro and the tribune.

Spotting Claudius among the group, bravely laughing with the rest, Caligula added insult to injury. 'Uncle, you're the fastest among us, run and alert the Vigiles at once and then report back to me once the fire is out.'

'At once, P-P-Princeps,' Claudius replied, breaking into a chaotic series of lurches that passed for running.

Caligula led the raucous laughter as his uncle shambled out of the room. 'It will have burned itself out by the time that cripple has even managed to stumble down the Palatine,' he shouted through his mirth.

The sycophancy increased and the laughter rose as if this were the funniest thing anyone had ever said. Caligula's face was puce and the veins in his neck and temples bulged; genuinely enjoying the joke, he kept laughing uncontrollably for what seemed like an age as the senators' attempts to keep pace with him grew more and more hollow. Eventually he tired, much to everyone's relief, and drew himself up.

'Gentlemen, I have an announcement to make concerning my beloved sisters.' He stopped and beamed at his audience, evidently relishing what he was going to say. His head twitched violently and he suddenly put his hands up to his temples. Macro went to support him as the gathering drew its collective breath.

'Get away from me,' Caligula snapped, regaining his composure and pushing Macro off. 'Now, where was I? Ah yes, my sisters. From now on they are to be included when an oath of loyalty is...' With a cry he collapsed to the floor, scrabbling at his head with his hands as if he were trying to pull something out of it.

The senators gasped; Macro immediately knelt down beside him. 'Chaerea, fetch the doctor,' he shouted at the Praetorian tribune after a brief look at his master. 'Get out, all of you, now!' he shouted.

The sight of the Emperor so physically compromised sent a shiver of fear through the senators and they fled.

'It looks as if the gods may have listened to Antonia,' Vespasian mumbled in Gaius' ear as they crushed through the door.

Whether or not the gods had acted upon Antonia's curse was debatable, but one thing was certain: they were the main beneficiaries of Caligula's illness as over the following days the people of Rome sacrificed victims in their tens of thousands for the return to health of the young Emperor. The poor did so out of genuine love, remembering the largesse that he had distributed among them and the lavish games that he had held for their entertainment. The senators and the equestrian order, however, did so out of the fear that all those who had not been seen making sacrifices and offering up prayers would be cruelly dealt with should Caligula recover; so they vied with each other to be the most generous with their offerings, sacrificing their finest bulls, race horses and rams, while the more rash vowed to fight as gladiators if the Emperor recovered. One eques, in a case of reckless sycophancy topping all others, even promised Jupiter to exchange his life for Caligula's.

Vespasian spent much of the time in the afternoons and evenings with Caenis, enjoying playing man and wife in the new privacy that they had together. In the mornings he attended the Senate, joining in the prayers and sacrifices and sharing with the rest of the House the same outward fervour that Caligula should recover and the same inner desire that he should die and this ghastly episode in Rome's history could be put behind them. After this daily ritual – no other business being possible through fear of it being construed as being insensible to the Emperor's wellbeing – the whole Senate, along with the equestrian order, then processed up to the Palatine, past crowds of sombre citizens, to present themselves at Augustus' House where they received the daily bulletin on the Emperor's health. Every day

251

the Praetorian tribune, Chaerea, delivered the same message in his unfortunately high and squeaky voice: no change, the Emperor remained drifting in and out of consciousness.

The city was at a standstill; the law courts, theatres and markets were all closed, business transactions suspended and festivals ignored. The only thing still running was the blood that flowed from Rome's many altars.

'This is getting ridiculous,' Vespasian muttered to Gaius as the Senate and the equites gathered outside the Curia for their daily trudge up the Palatine, for the thirtieth day in a row, in a steady, November drizzle. 'What's going to happen if he stays ill for another month? The city will start collapsing around us.'

'It's the same for everyone, dear boy, nothing's getting done. A lot of people are losing a lot of money but they would rather that than be seen as someone who made a profit while Caligula lay at death's door.'

'Well, I wish that it would open.'

'Don't say that too loudly,' Gaius hissed, 'especially around this group of unscrupulous sycophants.'

'Of which we are guilty members.'

'Hypocrisy, dear boy, can be a life-saving fault.'

Vespasian grunted.

'I thought I'd find you here,' Magnus called, easing his way through the crowd towards them wearing his citizen's plain white toga.

Vespasian smiled and gripped his friend's forearm. 'Are you joining us for our daily ritual?'

'Bollocks I am. There's a meeting of the Quirnal and Viminal Brotherhood leaders; we dress up smart to threaten each other. You lot and everyone else may have stopped working but our business carries on.'

'I'm pleased to hear it; extortion and protection should stop for no man, not even an emperor.'

'Now, sir, that ain't fair, we all have to make a living. By the way, aren't you the road aedile this year?'

'You know I am.'

Magnus pointed to his feet, covered in mud and ordure with pieces of rotting vegetation sticking to them. 'I call that a fucking disgrace; some parts of the city are ankle deep in shit – which makes you look stupid.'

Vespasian gestured helplessly. 'There's nothing I can do about it. My foremen won't supervise the public slaves cleaning the streets; they all claim to be too busy making sacrifices to Jupiter and Juno and praying for the Emperor.'

'Well, while they're about it perhaps they could sacrifice to the god of arseholes and pray for man and beast to stop shitting as well.'

'Shhh,' Gaius hissed with a pained expression on his face, putting a hand up to his mouth and moving away from treasonous talk.

Vespasian grinned. 'Have you come here just to give me advice on the religious practices of my staff?'

'No, it's a bit more serious than that,' Magnus said, looking around and lowering his voice. 'There was someone snooping around Caenis' house this morning for an hour or so, and then he buggered off. One of my lads watching the place followed him to the Aventine; he went into a nice new house on the same street as Sabinus.' Magnus raised his eyebrows.

'And?'

'And after making some enquiries he found out that it belongs to your good friend, Corvinus.'

Vespasian felt a chill crawl through his body. 'How did he find out about her?'

'Probably by having you followed, what does it matter? But being as I know that he ain't too keen on you and yours, I've doubled the guard in the street.'

'Thank you, Magnus.'

'I wouldn't worry too much; he just knows that you go there, he won't know who's inside. She should be safe enough if she doesn't go out.'

'She doesn't, except to visit my uncle a few score paces away.'

'If she wants to do that, I suggest that she sends a slave to my lads and they can escort her in a covered litter.'

'I'll tell her; thanks.'

'Yeah, well, it looks like you're all moving off; I'd best be going. I've got more lucrative ways to pass the time rather than worry about the sick, if you take my meaning?'

'What was that all about?' Gaius asked, rejoining Vespasian as they began to shuffle out of the Forum.

'Nothing, Uncle,' Vespasian mumbled, lost in his thoughts, 'Magnus has it covered.'

The procession of more than two thousand of the most prestigious men in Rome arrived in front of Augustus' House. Cassius Chaerea was already waiting under the portico to address them; the smile on his face was enough to tell Vespasian that death had indeed kept its door firmly closed to Caligula.

'There is at last good news,' Chaerea announced in his falsetto voice, 'one hour ago the Emperor made a miraculous recovery; I have just come from his room where he is sitting up in bed and eating. The crisis is over!'

A roar of cheers erupted from the rain-dampened crowd, carrying on until they were almost hoarse. The noise of the celebrations and the news of its cause filtered down from the Palatine and on throughout Rome, and by the time Chaerea was able to speak again the sound of joyous cheering echoed back up the hill from the city below.

'The Emperor thanks you all for your prayers and sacrifices and bids you to …' The doors behind him opened and the crowd gasped as Caligula walked out unsteadily but unaided. Unshaven for a month and palpably thinner with his eyes sunk even further in their sockets, he still looked ill and yet there was strength in the way that he held his head. He lifted his arms in the air to the raucous cries of 'Hail Caesar!' that greeted him.

Eventually he signalled for silence. 'It is not your fault,' he declaimed in a surprisingly loud voice, 'that you hail me only as your Caesar. You do not know what has happened to me in this past month.' He indicated to his emaciated body. 'This body, this weak human body, nearly died as I ravaged it with the agony of transformation. Had it died I would still be here but not as you see me now, because, my flock, I am not only your Emperor, I have now become your god. Worship me!'

At this stunning piece of news and outrageous order a few of the more quick-thinking senators immediately pulled folds of their togas over their heads, as if officiating at a religious ceremony. The rest of the gathering quickly followed their example and Caligula burst out laughing as he surveyed the crowd that was now swathed from head to toe in wool.

'You are truly my sheep; what a shearing we shall have. I believe one of you was good enough to offer his life to my brother Jupiter in return for mine; who was this noble sheep?'

'It was I, Princeps,' a voice oozing with pride came from behind Vespasian, who turned to see a well-built young eques smiling smugly at those around him, pleased to be the object of the Emperor's attention.

'What is your name, good sheep?'

'Publius Afranius Potitus, Princeps.'

'What are you doing here, Potitus? Don't keep Jupiter waiting; we gods expect promptness.'

Potitus' face fell as the hope of reward was replaced by the hideous realisation that Caligula was in earnest. He looked around at his companions for aid, but how could they countermand an order from their new god? They moved away, leaving him isolated in their midst. His shoulders sagged and he turned without a word.

'What a good sheep he was,' Caligula said, grinning approvingly as Potitus trudged away to his unnecessary death. 'Now that I'm back among you the business of the city shall resume and the Plebeian Games, which should have begun five days ago, will commence immediately; all those of you who swore to fight as gladiators in return for my health will get the chance to fulfil your oath in the arena tomorrow.'

*

'Save him, Caesar! Save him, Caesar!' the twenty-thousand-strong crowd filling the stone-built Statilius Taurus Amphitheatre on the Campus Martius chanted in unison. An all-pervading stench of urine filled the atmosphere from where people – for fear of losing their seat should they go outside – had relieved themselves where they sat, so that it trickled down to be soaked up by the tunic of the person sitting below them on the stepped-stone seating.

The victorious *retiarius*, the last man standing in what had been a six-man free-for-all, kept the points of his trident firmly pressed on the throat of his last defeated opponent, a *secutor* entangled in a net, and looked up at the Emperor. Vespasian glanced over at Caligula, sitting next to Drusilla, in the imperial box adjacent to the senators' seats, and wondered if he would grant the crowd's wish; he had on every other occasion during the long four days of combat, but they had always been demands for death.

Caligula removed his fingers from the anus of a youth kneeling between him and his sister and extended it forward, still clenched in the signal for mercy, tilting his head against his shoulder. The crowd's applause at their Emperor's clemency turned to jeers as his thumb suddenly jutted up in mimicry of an unsheathed sword: the sign for death.

The *summa rudis* – the referee – withdrew his long staff from across the retiarius's chest, who then pulled back to allow his opponent the dignity of a gladiator's death, kneeling on one knee before his vanquisher rather than lying like a wounded stag on the reddened arena sand.

The crowd's fury at their wish to spare a gladiator who had put up a brave fight escalated as the secutor, once free of the net, grasped his opponent's thigh in preparation for the killing stroke. The retiarius dropped the trident and unsheathed his long, thin knife and placed it, point down, on the secutor's throat just above his collar bone. With a nod of his head, completely encased in a smooth bronze rimless helmet with two small eye-holes in the face mask, the doomed man consented to the knife. As the two men tensed for the ritual killing the staff of the summa rudis abruptly slammed across the retiarius's chest, stopping him.

The crowd fell suddenly silent. All eyes turned to Caligula, who sat laughing hysterically, his thumb now pressed down on his clenched fingers representing a sheathed sword: the sign of mercy. 'I fooled you all!' he shouted through his mirth. 'Did you really think that I, I who have the wellbeing of all of you in my heart, wouldn't grant your wish? Of course I would.'

The crowd burst into laughter, enjoying the joke that their Emperor had played on them. The retiarius withdrew the knife and the secutor started to hyperventilate in relief.

Vespasian glanced again in Caligula's direction and saw his face suddenly change into a contorted mask of anger. He leapt to his feet and screamed for silence.

'But you jeered at me,' he shrieked, 'as if you didn't love me. Me! Your god and Emperor jeered at by you. How dare you! I wish you had one communal throat then I would slit it. You must be taught that from now on you will worship me and love me; I will have my statue placed in every temple to remind you of that, not only here in Rome but also around the Empire.' He paused and looked mournfully about him. 'I can give but I can also take away; I will no longer grant your wish.' He punched his clenched fist out with his thumb extended.

The crowd remained silent as the two gladiators took up the killing stance once more. The thrust of the knife down into the heart and the resulting spray of blood were not greeted with cheers and multiple ejaculations but, rather, a deflated sullenness. The retiarius saluted the imperial box and walked towards the gates leading down to the gladiators' cells with his trident and net raised in the air; no one acknowledged his victory.

Caligula beckoned Macro, seated behind him, to come closer. He whispered something in the prefect's ear while pointing to an area of the crowd. A brief argument ensued before Macro, visibly angry, left his seat and spoke to Chaerea who stood by the entrance to the imperial box. Caligula reinserted his fingers petulantly into the catamite and turned his attention back to the arena while Drusilla fondly stroked the lad's hair as if he were a pet. Chaerea left the box.

Down on the sand the carrion-man, dressed as Charon the Ferryman, bald-headed and robed in black, stalked around the dead checking for signs of life by pressing a red-hot poker to their genitals; once satisfied that a man was dead he removed his helmet and, with a heavy mallet cracked open his skull to release his spirit. This ritual complete, the bodies were dragged off for burial and the sand was raked and replaced in areas to get rid of the blood.

The crowd's mood began to lighten as they started to look forward to the next part of the spectacle, which had been advertised as four of the equites who had been rash enough to promise to fight in the arena on Caligula's return to health all pitched together in a fight to the death. A murmur of interest went around the amphitheatre as the gates opened and, instead of seeing four gladiators, the crowd heard the roar of beasts; a dozen hungry-looking lions tore into the arena goaded on by slaves waving flaming torches behind them. The gates closed leaving the lions alone on the sand. The crowd, knowing that lions would not fight each other and that their convict-victims or the bestiarii who would fight them were always in the arena first, began to wonder just who or what the lions were meant to kill.

The clatter of hobnailed sandals on the stone steps of two of the entrances to the seating area soon provided the answer. A half-century of sword-brandishing Praetorian Guardsmen stormed in, causing panic in the crowd nearby. Within a few heartbeats they had surrounded twenty spectators in the front row of the section to which Caligula had pointed. Behind them the crush of people desperate to escape the same fate that they guessed was in store for their hapless fellows caused many to be trampled underfoot amid a cacophony of screaming. The lions' roars tore over the screams as the first two of the victims were hurled, begging for their lives, into the arena. The men had not even hit the ground before great claws ripped at their flesh, knocking them sideways, spinning through the air as if they were dolls, towards open jaws with bared teeth that were soon stained with their blood.

258

The Praetorians made short work of throwing the rest of their prisoners to the lions; most were set upon immediately, throats torn out or limbs dismembered or disembowelled, but half a dozen or so managed to run from the carnage – except there was nowhere to hide. To Vespasian's amazement the sections of the crowd unaffected by the Praetorians' actions began to laugh and cheer as the escapees were pursued around the oval arena by lions more intent on the thrill of the chase than of feasting on the mangled carcasses. He turned again to look at Caligula, who sat with a grim smile of satisfaction on his face, working his fingers in and out of the catamite while masturbating vigorously. As the last of the victims was torn apart, the crowd roared their approval; they loved him again.

Vespasian sat through the rest of the day knowing that to try to leave, which used to annoy Caligula before his illness, could well prove fatal now that he seemed to have completely lost his sanity. Eventually the final life ebbed into the blood-soaked sand and Caligula stood to depart, accepting the adulation of the mob as he did so. Vespasian hurried out with the rest of the senators, none of them wanting to catch each other's eye for fear of having to pass comment on what they had witnessed.

He emerged into the street and turned to walk briskly home.

'There he is!' he heard Caligula shout from close by. 'Macro, have him brought to me.'

Vespasian turned to see Chaerea and two Praetorians pushing through the crowd; with a sickening feeling in his stomach he realised that they were heading towards him. To run would have been pointless, so he allowed the Guards to escort him to Caligula, who was almost in tears.

'I thought that you were my friend,' he sobbed, shaking his head as if he could not believe how the situation had changed. Drusilla held a consoling arm around him.

'I am, Princeps,' Vespasian replied, wondering just what he had done.

Caligula pointed to the ground. 'Then how do you explain this?'

Vespasian looked down; the street was covered with filth from where it had not been cleaned for the month-long duration of Caligula's illness.

'This is my city,' Caligula stated in a pitiful voice, 'and my friend is in charge of keeping the streets clean. Oh Drusilla, he's let me down.'

Drusilla wiped a tear from the corner of her brother's eye and licked it off her finger.

'I'm sorry, Princeps; it was just while you were …'

'Oh, it's my fault, is it?'

'No, no, it's completely mine.'

'You should have him prosecuted,' Macro said venomously, 'it's almost treason to be so negligent in one's duties.'

'Stop presuming to tell me what to do, prefect. Chaerea, have your men scoop up some of this filth and pile it into the aedile's toga.'

Vespasian stood still as handful after handful of the foul-smelling muck was slopped into the fold of his toga. 'I will have it remedied tomorrow, Princeps.'

'No, you will not, you're quite evidently not up to it, I'll find someone else to do it.' He glared at Vespasian and then suddenly smiled. 'Besides, my friend, I've got something for you to do for me.' His train of thought abruptly changed and he turned to Macro. 'Where was my cousin Gemellus today? Why wasn't he celebrating my transformation?'

'I've heard that he has a bad cough, Princeps.'

'A cough, eh? Or perhaps he just wishes that I wasn't here any more and doesn't want to see me in my glory. What do you think, Vespasian?'

'It must be a cough, no one would wish for your death.'

'Hmm, I suppose you're right. Nevertheless I think we should cure him of his cough, don't you?'

Vespasian did his best to hide his thoughts, mindful of Antonia's last piece of advice, knowing that to disagree could be fatal for him but to agree would be fatal for Gemellus. 'Perhaps it will go with time, Princeps.'

Caligula stared at Vespasian uncomprehendingly. 'Time? Time? No, time goes too slowly. Chaerea, go and cure my cousin of his cough; permanently.'

'Is that wise, Princeps?' Macro asked. 'Gemellus is very popular with the youth.'

'Then his funeral will be well attended,' Caligula snapped. 'That's the second time today that you've questioned me, Macro, don't let there be a third. Now get out of my sight.'

Macro opened his mouth to argue, then, thinking better of it, bowed his head and walked away.

'What are you still doing here, Chaerea?' Caligula shouted. 'Didn't I give you an order?'

Chaerea snapped a salute and, keeping his face neutral, turned and led his men off.

Caligula closed his eyes slowly, drew a luxurious breath and kissed Drusilla on the mouth. 'Isn't she beautiful, Vespasian? I will have a theatre built in the Forum so that I can display her properly. Would you like to be displayed, my sweet?'

'If it pleases you, dearest Gaius,' Drusilla simpered, tracing the outline of his lips with her finger.

Caligula looked lovingly at her and stroked her throat. 'Just think, Drusilla, I could have this pretty throat slit any time I want.'

Drusilla sighed with ecstasy. 'Any time you want, dearest Gaius.'

Caligula licked her throat and then put his arm around Vespasian's shoulder in a friendly fashion and began to walk him away, much to Vespasian's relief. 'I have a problem, my friend, it's like a persistent itch but if I scratch it I know that it'll get worse, but I must rid myself of it.'

'Surely you can do anything you want,' Vespasian replied, adjusting his arm to take the weight of the filth piled in his toga's fold.

'I can, but sometimes there might be a consequence that not even I can control.'

'What consequences?'

'I've tired of Macro's wife and I've tired of him, he's started to give me advice. Before my transformation he actually told me that it was not fitting for an emperor to laugh loudly at a joke in a play; it was Plautus, how can you not laugh at Plautus?'

'Impossible.'

'Precisely. And now today he questioned me; so he must go.'

'But the consequence would be upsetting the Guard.'

'Oh my friend, how well you understand me, that is the consequence; if only I could kill them all. What do you advise me to do?'

Vespasian thought for a few moments, wondering if giving Caligula advice would prove as fatal for him as it was going to be for Macro. 'If he's not the Praetorian prefect, then the Guard won't feel threatened.'

Caligula turned to him with a pained expression on his face as if he were dealing with a retarded child. 'But he *is* the Praetorian prefect, you idiot, and if I try and remove him it would have the same consequence.'

'You don't have to remove him, he's already asked to be removed and you, in your wisdom, have already granted it.'

'Have I? Oh good. When?'

'The moment the sailing season opens up again in the spring.'

Caligula frowned. 'Stop talking in riddles.'

'Princeps, you have very cleverly promised Macro the province of Egypt. The moment he sets foot on the ship in Ostia he will be prefect of Egypt, not prefect of the Praetorian Guard.'

Caligula beamed with understanding and slapped Vespasian on the shoulder. 'And I could have him killed then without fear of the consequence.'

'You could, but wouldn't it be better if you ordered him to commit suicide? That way there could be no possibility of anyone being accused of murder.'

'Oh, how fortunate I am to have a friend like you, Vespasian. You will tell me what the expression was like on his face after you've told him, won't you?'

CHAPTER XVI

T HE SMALL FLAME sputtered into life illuminating five bronze statuettes, standing on the *lararium*, representing Caenis' household gods; the reflected glow played on their polished forms giving them the ethereal quality of the deities they symbolised. Vespasian placed a fold of his toga over his head as Caenis set the oil lamp down onto the altar and took her place beside him; behind them stood the household slaves faintly lit by a small fire in the hearth next to the lararium – the only other light in the atrium.

Vespasian poured a wine libation onto the altar and sprinkled a handful of salt into the puddle before spreading his arms and turning his palms upwards. 'I call upon the *lares domestici* – or whatever name by which you would like to be called – to ensure that I and my household enjoy what we already have in good health, just as you have done for me before; and that you preserve us and this day safe from all dangers, if there are or shall be any on this day. If you grant a favourable outcome in the matter that we deem that we are speaking of and you preserve us in this present condition or better – and may you so do these things – then I vow that you shall have, in the name of this household, the tokens of our gratitude after the setting of the sun. Nothing more do I ask.'

Caenis then turned to the fire and completed the female part of the morning ritual by offering up a prayer to Vesta, goddess of the hearth, and throwing sweet-smelling incense into the flames. Vespasian watched her, as he had done every morning for the past six months, with an ache in his heart as she performed the duties of the wife that she could never be to him.

The morning prayers complete, the household slaves dispersed to their various duties as pale light seeped in through the windows looking out to the peristylium announcing the beginning of another cold, early April day.

Vespasian pulled the fold of his toga from his head and adjusted it around his shoulders. 'Our household gods will have another busy day ahead of them,' he observed with a wry smile. 'Caligula's due to inaugurate the theatre that he's had built in the Forum to display Drusilla to the mob and he wants me and a few others of his "friends" to be present; he said that he might want us to lend a hand. If the large bed with purple sheets in the middle of the stage is anything to go by, then I believe that it'll be more than just a hand we'll be having to lend.'

'Then don't go, my love.'

Vespasian looked at her with raised eyebrows. 'You know that he can't be refused, so don't make unhelpful suggestions.'

Caenis smiled sorrowfully. 'I'm sorry, I should know better; it's because he can't be refused that apart from a couple of visits to your uncle's house I've not set foot out of here since you carried me over the threshold.'

Vespasian looked deep into her sad eyes, beautifully set off by a necklace of clear, blue-glass cylindrical beads that shimmered softly around her throat in the pale light. He sympathised with her frustration at her virtual captivity, but, although Caligula believed her to be in Egypt and Magnus' brothers had not reported any more sightings of Corvinus' man or any other suspicious goings on, he still felt it best to keep her inside. He kissed her.

A loud knock at the door cut through the moment; the huge Nubian opened up and Aenor came nervously through the vestibule into the atrium and stood waiting to be spoken to.

'What does my uncle want, Aenor?'

'He has asked that you should come to his house at once, master,' the young German slave boy replied in his guttural accent.

'Did he give a reason?'

'He said to tell you that there was an important person waiting to see you there.'

'Who?'

Aenor scrunched up his face in an effort to remember the exact title that he had been told to pass on. 'The prefect of the Praetorian Guard.'

It was with great trepidation that Vespasian entered his uncle's house, passing through the cluster of clients, with their breath steaming in the cold, dawn air, waiting outside to greet their patron. He had allayed Caenis' fears that he was to be arrested with the logical argument that it would be beneath the prefect's dignitas to come in person to apprehend a junior senator. Nevertheless he felt a sense of foreboding as he stepped through the vestibule and into the atrium.

'Ah, there you are, dear boy,' Gaius boomed in a cheerful voice that betrayed no concern. He was sitting by the hearth with Clemens; both were munching on wrinkled winter apples. 'Have you breakfasted?'

'Yes, thank you, Uncle. Good morning, Clemens.'

'Good morning, Vespasian; the Emperor has sent me.'

Vespasian looked around the room, confused. 'Where's Macro?'

Gaius burst out laughing. 'What did I tell you, Clemens? He spends too much time in that nest of honey and delight; he hasn't heard.'

'Heard what?' Vespasian asked testily.

'I'm sorry, dear boy, that was my idea of a joke getting you here thinking that Macro was waiting. The Emperor formally relieved Macro of his position yesterday evening, and he's due to sail for Egypt today to take up his post as prefect there.'

Vespasian glanced at Clemens; a look of understanding spread across his face and he smiled. 'And you're the new prefect of the Guard?'

'One of them,' Clemens confirmed. 'However, the Emperor has decided to go back to Augustus' principle of having two prefects, so I share the position with Lucius Arruntius Stella.'

'It would appear that our Emperor is not as mad as he seems,' Gaius said, having got his mirth under control, 'he's appointed two prefects who hate each other. That should weaken the Guard, eh, Clemens?'

'It will certainly create two factions.'

'And make it twice as likely that a prefect will move against him,' Vespasian observed. 'Not that I would suspect you of disloyalty, Clemens – yet.'

Clemens looked worried. 'With Clementina due back in Rome with Sabinus this summer who knows what cause for disloyalty I may have if Caligula puts his mind to having her?'

'Then Sabinus should keep her safe out at Aquae Cutillae, as you do your wife at Pisaurum.'

'Not any more; Caligula ordered me to call her back and bring her to dinner at the palace. There was his new wife, Lolia Paulina, plus twelve other women present, all wives of his guests. He arrived dressed as Apollo and went round feeling each one and then chose two – not Julia, thankfully – and took them to bed while their husbands had to carry on eating as if nothing were happening. When he reappeared with them he started to compare and contrast with the unfortunate husbands the strengths and weaknesses in their wives' sexual performances. It was excruciating; the two women were obliged to recline there as if the conversation was the most natural thing in the world. Then he ordered Lolia to strip naked so that he could give everyone a practical demonstration of some of the finer points of his arguments.'

'I'd not heard about that,' Gaius said, looking horrified.

'You wouldn't have; it was last night at the banquet to celebrate Macro's new position, which was ironic in itself considering what Caligula has sent me here for.'

Vespasian groaned. 'Oh, I'd hoped that he'd forgotten about that.'

'If you mean about your offer to be the man who orders Macro to commit suicide as he gets on the ship today, then no he hasn't.'

'I didn't offer, I just suggested that if he wanted to get rid of Macro then that would be the best time, place and way to do it.'

'Well, however it came about that's what he wants you to do, and I've got to escort you with a turma of my cavalry to make sure that Macro obeys the order.'

'You do get yourself into some unpleasant situations, dear boy.'

'That's not a helpful observation, Uncle,' Vespasian replied tersely.

'No, but it's a pertinent one.'

'Have you got the warrant?' Vespasian asked Clemens, ignoring Gaius' remark.

'No; we're to go to his Drusilla theatre; he said he'd see us there, after the show, as he put it, which doesn't bode well.'

'No, it doesn't.' Vespasian got to his feet with a sigh. 'Well, if I've got to do this then I might as well do it properly; I've just got to fetch something from my room before we go, Clemens.'

Caligula's new theatre was not built on as grand a scale as he would have liked but this was for practical reasons; the semicircular structure filled the area between the Rostrum and the Temple of Saturn with its stage set hard against the steps of the Temple of Concordia, almost prohibiting access. However, it did hold over two thousand spectators who were thoroughly enjoying the show, much to the bemusement and disgust of Vespasian and the others of the senatorial order who had been forced to attend. In a humiliation of the Senate Caligula had dispensed with their reserved seating and they were forced to sit among the urban rabble. They had cheered as Caligula, dressed as Hercules in a golden lion-skin and brandishing a golden club, had slowly disrobed his sister. They had cheered louder as he had put her through a series of gymnastic poses, each designed to explicitly show off the female form. And then they had cheered even louder as he began to take her through a succession of sexual acts on the enormous, purple-sheeted bed, while she howled like a harpy.

'Bring me my gladiators,' Caligula shouted, pulling himself out of Drusilla, who knelt on the bed before him and then fell onto her belly, breathing deeply.

Vespasian was relieved to see four oiled, naked gladiators, an Ethiopian and three Celts, all at the peak of physical condition, striding onto the stage. He had been dreading a summons to join in the obscenity being acted out before him and now felt confident that his services would not be required.

'This is going to be worse than you think,' Clemens whispered in his ear as Drusilla turned her attention to the new arrivals clustered round her with an urgency and greed born out of uninhibited and shameless lust.

'How can it be worse?'

'You'll see. I've got archers stationed around the theatre to make sure that nothing happens to Caligula – he was concerned about letting one of the gladiators have a sword so close to him in the finale.'

Hardly able to believe his eyes, Vespasian watched in mounting horror as the siblings created a scene with three of the gladiators of such carnality that it made Caligula's behaviour in the circus with the catamite seem almost acceptable. The tangle of bodies began to writhe with escalating fervour, matched by the increasing clamour of the crowd, until reaching such a pinnacle of ecstasy that they were no longer aware of their surroundings. At this point a Praetorian walked onto the stage and handed a sword to the unoccupied fourth gladiator and then gave a signal towards the back of the theatre. Vespasian looked around and saw that archers were now standing at intervals behind the spectators; all had their bows drawn and were aiming at the newly armed man as he approached, from behind, the Ethiopian gladiator servicing Caligula. Sensing imminent blood the roar of the crowd, already deafening, swelled to ear-splitting proportions. Down on the stage, Caligula raised his fists to his shoulders and flapped his arms in imitation of a cockerel's wings and then slumped down onto his sister's back. Grasping Caligula's hips, the Ethiopian threw his head back and let out a roar, unheard over the din of the crowd, of satisfaction; it was the last sound he ever made. With a lightning flash the fourth gladiator swept his head from his shoulders, sending it spinning into the audience, and releasing a powerful jet of crimson blood, shooting from his torso, high up into the air to splatter down on Caligula and Drusilla. Once the blood had stopped raining down on them Caligula reached back and pushed the decapitated corpse out of him; it crumpled to the floor. The executioner raised his sword in a gladiator's salute to the crowd and was instantaneously struck by a dozen well-aimed arrows that hurled him back as if he had been yanked by an invisible rope. Seemingly oblivious of this development, Caligula and Drusilla were staring lovingly into each other's eyes as they rubbed blood over one another. The two surviving gladiators rose warily to their feet, looking anxiously at the archers who had reloaded and were now aiming at them.

'He was stupid,' Clemens shouted in Vespasian's ear, 'he had been warned to drop the sword as soon as he'd cut off the other man's head; if he'd listened he wouldn't be dead. The other two will be fine so long as they don't go near the sword.'

Vespasian could not think of anything to say and just stared dumbfounded between the Emperor and his sister smearing blood over their bodies and the crowd who had started to play catch with the decapitated gladiator's head. Where was the honour? What had happened to dignitas? Was this to be the tone of the new age, filth and degradation until the Phoenix returned in five hundred years? And yet this was the Rome that he had worked for in his support for Antonia; this was the Rome that she had unwittingly preserved while keeping her family in power. He had seen it in its infancy on Capreae in the court of Tiberius. He had seen the debauched Emperor's 'fishies' – dwarves and children copulating freely in the water – and had heard Caligula describe them as fun. He had witnessed Caligula's behaviour with his sisters and knew that incest was committed regularly; he had watched Caligula enjoy his troupe of dwarves and seen him service whore after whore in a public tavern. He had hoped that these were the heights of his excesses; but no, they had just been eclipsed. Vespasian feared then that the height had not yet been achieved.

Eventually the siblings came out of their private world; Caligula rose to his feet and signalled for silence. 'Who has the head?'

A young man dressed in a threadbare tunic and worn cloak held up the grisly item by an ear. 'I do, Caesar.'

'Then you win the game and one thousand aurei when you bring it to me.'

The young man's neighbours immediately set upon him, each desperate for such a sum that would raise them out of poverty for life. Caligula laughed and the fight quickly spread as more and more people tried to get close to the prize; he turned on his heel and offered his hand to his sister. Naked and red with blood, the two siblings walked from the stage, with heads held high, at a sedate pace as if they were a newlywed couple from an old and dignified patrician family making their way to the bridal feast. Behind them they left escalating chaos and death.

'We had better present ourselves to him now,' Clemens said, 'he was most insistent that we come and see him immediately after the…the…' He left the last word hanging and waved his hand vaguely towards the stage as if he could not find the right way to describe what they had just witnessed.

Vespasian understood his difficulty perfectly.

'Wasn't she wonderful?' Caligula enthused, licking blood from Drusilla's face as Vespasian and Clemens were ushered into his presence. They were standing in the centre of a pavilion of soft, purple fabric that let the sun's rays gently through. 'And was I not more potent than that mere demi-god Hercules?'

Looking at Caligula, Vespasian found it hard to find any similarities between the spindly legged Emperor and the immensely strong Hero. He tried to banish from his mind everything that he had seen and concentrated on keeping his face neutral. 'You outshone every one of the gods with your prowess, Princeps,' he lied blatantly in his most reverential voice, 'we mere mortals can only dream of stamina and vigour like you possess.'

'Yes,' Caligula agreed with a sympathetic look, 'your women must be very disappointed; it's no wonder that Caenis has spent so much time in Egypt. When's she due back?'

'I don't know, Princeps. I believe that you require a service of me?' Vespasian replied, anxious to change the subject.

Caligula cocked his head, looking momentarily confused; he ran a hand through his matted hair. 'A service? I always require service.' He snapped his fingers and Callistus brought forward a scroll that he handed, with much bowing, to his master. 'Macro and that slut wife of his, Ennia, are due to leave for Ostia at midday. I want you and Clemens to be at the port waiting for them to give them this; they should find it fairly self-explanatory.' He handed the scroll to Vespasian and looked at him thoughtfully for a few moments. 'I think that you should be a praetor next year; I like my friends to do well.'

'If you believe me to be worthy of it, thank you, Princeps,' Vespasian replied, hiding his unease at the thought of not being able to leave Rome for a whole year with Caligula out of control.

Caligula slapped him on the back and started to lead him from the pavilion. 'Of course you're worthy, your god and Emperor deems you so.'

A roar from the crowd gathered at the entrance greeted them as they emerged into the sun-lit Forum. Caligula – still naked, still sticky with gore – spread his arms and acknowledged them before taking Vespasian's hand and raising it. 'This man is about to do a great service for me and for Rome,' he called out. The crowd quietened to hear his words better. 'His name is Titus Flavius Vespasianus and despite being a senator he is favoured by me.'

Vespasian tensed his face into a strained smile and managed to hold himself with dignity as the crowd cheered.

'That's enough,' Caligula shouted; he turned to Vespasian as the noise died down and looked suddenly surprised. 'What are you still doing here? Go on, get on with it.'

'Yes, Princeps.'

'What about an afternoon's racing, Caesar?' a voice from the crowd called out as Vespasian and Clemens turned to leave.

'What an excellent idea,' Caligula replied enthusiastically. 'I shall summon the racing factions to the circus immediately, the racing will start in two hours and we shall see my new horse,

Incitatus, race for the first time, so make sure that you bet on the Greens in the first race.'

Vespasian looked at Clemens as they tried to battle their way through the horde of people surging across the Forum to get the best seats in the Circus Maximus. 'Now he's going to spend even more money on a day's racing because of a whim. After what we've seen today, Clemens, how's your loyalty?'

'Under strain,' Clemens admitted.

Gulls quarrelled with each other as they soared overhead on a warm breeze blowing in from the gently swelling sea; it thrummed stays and sheets and caused the timbers of the large assortment of bobbing trading ships, straining on their moorings at busy stone quays and wooden jetties, to groan and creak.

Vespasian and Clemens sat on a couple of barrels eating a meal of dried fruit and meat in the shade of a flapping awning. Neither spoke, both being busy with their own thoughts. A few paces away a tubby merchant inspected his newly arrived cargo of Egyptian enamelled-glass bowls and drinking vessels that had been recently offloaded from the large trader due to sail back to Egypt, with Macro aboard, later that day. Evidently unhappy about the state of some of his shipment, the merchant began a tirade of abuse at the ship's master that was met with a great deal of shrugging and waving of hands until the port aedile arrived to adjudicate. Just behind the arguing group the business of reprovisioning the vessel and loading the freight destined for Egypt carried on apace; a quick turnaround being vital to maximise the profits from the voyage. In the low-margin business of merchant shipping, time, as ever, was money and a prolonged stay in Ostia with its high port tax would not be something that the ship's owner would thank the master for upon his return to Alexandria.

'I'm amazed that anything made of glass can survive a voyage from Egypt, no matter how much straw it's packed in,' Clemens observed, breaking the long silence. Taking a generous swig at a goatskin of well-watered wine, he passed it to Vespasian.

'It does look to be very delicate,' Vespasian agreed, looking at the chipped ewer with a colourful depiction of Dionysus enamelled on its side that the merchant was showing the aedile as evidence of his case.

The arrival of the decurion of the Praetorian cavalry turma that had accompanied them to Ostia put an end to their idle chatter and their meal.

'Macro's carriage has just entered the town gates, prefect,' the young man reported with a salute.

'Thank you, decurion,' Clemens replied, getting to his feet. 'Have your men seal off this quay once it gets here.'

With another salute the decurion turned on his heels and made his way back to his turma, which was stationed out of sight behind the warehouses at the end of the quay.

Vespasian stood and adjusted his toga; the contents of the bag that he had retrieved from his room clinked in its fold as he withdrew Caligula's warrant. 'I hope Caligula isn't playing a nasty joke on us and this contains orders for Macro to execute the bearers,' he said with a grin.

Clemens scowled. 'That's not funny.'

'No, sorry,' Vespasian apologised, realising that it was exactly the sort of thing that Caligula would find hilarious.

Macro's carriage rumbled into view at the far end of the quay preceded not by lictors, as he was only of equestrian rank, but by ten fellow members of his order in recognition that one of the most powerful posts in the Empire was open only to them and not to the Senate. The equites cleared the way along the crowded quay forcing a few of the unfortunate dock slaves – some laden with goods – to overbalance into the fetid water. Cries of indignation from the owners of the lost merchandise were met with uncaring looks as the cortege cleaved its way to the waiting trader. Behind them the Praetorian turma appeared and sealed off their retreat.

Clemens smiled coldly and stepped forward as the carriage door opened and the bull-like frame of Quintus Naevius Cordus Sutorius Macro appeared followed by the voluptuous figure of his wife, Ennia.

'Clemens, how good of you to come and see me off,' Macro said upon seeing his successor. 'If, for any reason, you ever feel that you need a change of, how should I put it, commitment, then men like you would be welcomed by me in the East.' He proffered his forearm; Clemens did not take it.

'Going to the East wouldn't change my commitment to Rome; how could it?'

'Things change, Clemens, all things change,' Macro replied, still holding out his arm and staring meaningfully into Clemens' eyes.

'Indeed they do, prefect,' Vespasian agreed, appearing from behind the aedile's group who had now stopped their argument to listen to the conversation.

'You! What are you doing here?' Macro drawled.

Vespasian held out the warrant. 'I've come to give you an order from your Emperor and also to present you with a gift.'

Macro stared at it; uncertainty clouded his face; his eyes flicked up to Vespasian's. 'Why does the Emperor feel it necessary to give me new orders?'

'You'll have to read it for yourself, Macro.'

Macro took the scroll and, breaking the imperial seal, unrolled it; after a few moments his face paled. 'I see,' he said without looking up. 'And what if I refuse this order?'

'Then I will have a turma of my cavalry escort you back to Rome so that you can explain to the Emperor in person why you decided to disobey him,' Clemens said, pointing towards the waiting troopers.

Macro turned and saw that his escape was blocked. He gave a wry smile. 'It would seem that you have the better of me. I won't give you the pleasure of watching me humiliate myself by jumping into the water and swimming away; I will do as the Emperor commands.' He turned to his wife who waited a respectful distance away by the carriage. 'Ennia, your ex-lover has ordered us to take our lives.'

'That comes as no surprise to me, husband,' she said, walking forward to join Macro. 'I knew when he went back on his oath to me that he would also renege on his promise to you; you were never destined to see Egypt.'

Vespasian got his first close look at the woman whom Caligula had sworn to make his empress; she was indeed beautiful. Greek by birth, the daughter of Tiberius' astrologer, Thrasyllus, she had the fair skin and clear blue eyes of the more ancient part of her race; her blonde hair, partly covered by a saffron palla, was arranged Roman style: piled high on her head in intricate weaves and secured with jewelled pins. There was no distress on her face, just a world-weary resignation as she took her husband's hand.

'I have failed you, Quintus,' she said, 'I could not keep him ensnared in my bed for long enough, forgive me.'

'There is nothing to forgive, Ennia; you did all that a loyal wife could.'

'And you would have rewarded that loyalty with a betrayal.'

Macro looked shocked. 'You knew?'

'Of course I knew. You could never have achieved your ultimate ambition with me still alive; that was obvious.'

'Then why...?'

'Because I love you, Quintus, and I wanted to help. What crime has he charged us with?'

'You, with adultery with him; me, with pandering you to him.'

Ennia snorted. 'Is that all he could be bothered to come up with after everything that you've planned, adultery with him? What irony.'

Macro turned back to Vespasian. 'You said that you also have a gift for me, senator, but I'm struggling to see what would be of use with my life now over.'

Vespasian brought out a leather bag from the fold of his toga, opened it and pulled out two daggers. 'These are both yours, Macro. This one you left in my leg on the Aemilian Bridge twelve years ago and the other one you dropped in the Lady Antonia's house; you told me to keep it and promised to give me a third to make up the set. As you obviously are now unable to keep that promise I shall forgo completing the set and return them to you.'

He handed the daggers to Macro, who smiled with genuine amusement.

'It seems that my need is greater than yours; I appreciate the consideration, Vespasian, most thoughtful.' All trace of humour suddenly left his face and his eyes bored into Vespasian's. 'Let me tell you why you never received the third; it was for one reason alone: Caligula. He knew that I wanted you dead but, as a part of the deal in which I ensured that he became emperor and in return I became prefect of Egypt, I had to swear to keep you alive just because he likes you.'

'Why?'

'I asked him that and he told me that it goes back to the night that you rescued Caenis from Livilla. The two guards in the tunnel had been killed out of his view; but then, to get the key to release her, you had her start screaming to attract the attention of the guard on the stairs. As he came through the door you stabbed him in the throat; you were the first person whom Caligula ever saw kill a man outside of the arena and he's always respected you for that.'

Vespasian digested this for a few moments, playing the scene back in his mind. 'I was; but why is that so important to him?'

'Because nothing happened to you for doing so and he realised that one could kill with impunity; it was a joyful moment for him.'

Vespasian's eyes widened in horror, thinking of the blood that Caligula had caused to be spilled since. 'I started him on his path?'

Macro shook his head, slowly smiling without his eyes. 'He would have found it with or without you; it just means that you are the lucky one who will never suffer at his hands. I swore to him that I would forgo my vengeance and I kept that oath. Now he rewards me by throwing it back in my face and sending you, of all people, to order my death; I suppose that's his idea of a joke.'

'Perhaps it is, or perhaps I'm just here because this was my idea. I knew what you were planning to do in Egypt, the Lady Antonia had worked it out, and I assumed that even though she removed Poppaeus you would have found some other source of finance to help you become emperor of the East.'

'Poppaeus died naturally, everybody knows that.'

'No, Macro, he was murdered; I should know, I helped to do it.'

Macro looked at Vespasian appraisingly. 'You are more dangerous than I thought; perhaps I should have broken my oath and had you killed. But you're right, I did find another source of money but it's of no use now that my life is over.'

'If you want some privacy I suggest that you go to the master's cabin,' Vespasian said, bringing the conversation to a close.

'For that, at least, I thank you.' Macro handed one of the daggers to Ennia. 'Come, my dear, I have eternity to beg for your forgiveness.'

'There's nothing to forgive, Quintus,' Ennia replied, taking Macro's arm as they walked up the gangplank to their deaths.

Vespasian watched them go and then, after brushing off the master's vehement complaints that he had been deprived of two fare-paying passengers, he turned to Macro's escort of equites. 'Once they have carried out the Emperor's command take them for burial, but do it here immediately, not in Rome.'

'We had better check that they have indeed gone through with it,' Clemens said quietly as the equites nodded their sombre agreement.

'I suppose so,' Vespasian replied, feeling a strange lack of desire to see Macro's corpse. The way that Macro and Ennia had accepted their fate with a dignity worthy of any Roman had impressed him and, despite the fact that Macro would have revelled in Vespasian's death, he felt reluctant to intrude on that of his old enemy.

They made their way to the master's cabin at the stern of the ship and looked down through the hatchway. Below in the dim light Macro and Ennia lay slumped together on the floor, each with their left arm around the other and with their right hands still clutching the daggers that they had forced into each other's hearts.

'That was one of the few sensible decisions that Caligula has made,' Clemens observed, staring at the couple entwined in death.

'Yes,' Vespasian agreed, turning to go. 'We'd better be getting back to Rome to see what madness he has planned next.'

The madness, as it turned out, had a very practical function to Caligula's way of thinking. Feeling the need to commune on a daily basis with his brother Jupiter but not wishing always to be soiling himself by mixing with mere mortals, he decided to commission a huge wooden viaduct, five hundred paces long, which would connect his palace on the Palatine with the Temple of Jupiter on the Capitoline. This, he reasoned, would enable him to travel as a god should: high above the heads of the masses that he had come down to earth to rule.

The people watched in wonder over the following months as the monstrosity snaked its way between the two hills, scarring its skyline and disrupting trade and business as the resources of Rome were poured into the divine Emperor's latest whim. Oblivious to the inconvenience that he was causing, Caligula carried on his programme of compulsory fun for everyone. Every day there was either racing or gladiatorial shows, wild-beast hunts, plays or, of course, exhibitions of Drusilla, which were becoming more extravagant, not only in the amount of participants but also in their duration, inventiveness and abuse.

For his part, Vespasian had managed to keep a low profile since Macro's death. Holding no magistracy now in the city, he was able to remain uninvolved with the organisation of Caligula's extravaganzas other than attending them and feigning pleasure as he watched the treasury's already depleted coffers being swiftly cleared. His life revolved around Caenis and meetings of the Senate, which would slavishly agree to all Caligula's demands. He very rarely saw the Emperor in private and, apart from the occasional dinner at the palace, which he now dreaded as Caligula had taken to having criminals executed between courses for the amusement of his guests, he was able to live a quiet, unnoticed life.

On the morning of the viaduct's completion the whole city turned out to watch Caligula progress, with divine dignity dressed as Jupiter and brandishing a thunderbolt, along its length.

Vespasian watched with Gaius and the rest of the senators

from the Senate House steps as Caligula completed the journey and entered the most sacred temple in Rome to commune with his fellow god. After a short while he reappeared and announced to the vast crowd, via heralds, that Jupiter had conceded that he was now his equal.

'Furthermore,' the herald nearest the Senate House declaimed, reading Caligula's words from a scroll, 'I declare my sister, Drusilla, to be divine and I will show you proof of her divinity in the Forum Theatre.'

This announcement caused a near stampede as those in the mob closest to the theatre rushed to get the best seats.

'If I have to watch him tupping Drusilla again I think I'll go into voluntary exile,' Vespasian commented under his breath to Gaius.

'I think that we're excused today,' Gaius replied equally sotto voce. 'Caligula has another demand that he wants us to pass as soon as possible. Now he's finished his viaduct he's come up with a new way to waste money, so we'll have to forgo the pleasure of Drusilla's howls of ecstasy.'

'We'll probably still hear them from inside,' Vespasian observed, turning to enter the building.

'I'm sure you're right, dear boy,' Gaius replied. 'She has such stamina, hasn't she?'

Vespasian's fears were proved correct and the solemn opening prayers and taking of the auspices before the meeting could be declared open were conducted to the accompaniment of Drusilla's voice, rising to a crescendo of pleasure, as the Senior Consul, Marcus Aquila Iulianus, declared the day auspicious for the Senate to sit.

'The motion before the House today,' he announced once they were all seated, 'is to provide the finance for our divine Emperor to build two two-hundred-and-thirty-foot-long pleasure ships on Lake Nemorensis for him and his divine sister to relax in and to enable them to converse more easily with nymphs of the lake.'

This was greeted with sage nodding of heads and murmurs of agreement as if it were perfectly reasonable to want to have closer contact with water nymphs. As the debate proceeded with Drusilla's baying voice, punctuated by roars from the spectators, floating in from the theatre outside, Vespasian speculated that if just one of their number broke ranks and failed to keep a straight face, then the whole Senate would collapse to the floor in paroxysms of uncontrollable laughter. The image obliged Vespasian to suppress a snigger behind his hand and, as the Senior Consul listed the Emperor's requirements for the vessels – hot and cold running water, a suite of baths, marble floors and other ridiculous luxuries – he became increasingly concerned that he would be the first to drop the facade and give vent to his true feelings. He felt his uncle's hand rest on his shaking shoulder and managed to get himself back under control, wiping a tear from the corner of his eye.

Another shriller and even more prolonged screech caused the Senior Consul to pause as it transcended anything that could be construed as pleasure and entered the unmistakeable realms of agony. Abruptly it ceased, only to be replaced by a short gasp of horror from the audience; then silence.

A long, long silence.

All the senators turned their heads to look through the open doors towards the wooden theatre.

The silence endured; no one moved.

A wail of darkest grief, long and wavering, split the stillness, growing and growing until it filled the whole Forum. Every senator recognised the voice: Caligula's.

The crowd started to flood out of the theatre and away across the Forum, hurrying from their grieving, insane Emperor before he decided to wreak havoc on them in his despair. The senators left their stools and rushed for the door.

'I think Drusilla's stamina has just given out,' Gaius concluded as he and Vespasian squeezed through the crush and out into the sunlight.

'What do we do?' Vespasian asked. 'Go home and lay low until things calm down?'

'I think, dear boy, that anyone who is not seen to be sharing Caligula's grief would soon be a cause of grief for their own families. The best chance of surviving this is to go and face him, whatever the consequences.'

Vespasian drew a deep breath and followed Gaius and many of the senators who had reached the same conclusion down the steps and towards the theatre.

Caligula stood, now silent, in the middle of the stage holding Drusilla in his arms; blood dripped from her ruptured innards into a puddle that surrounded his feet. Lying dead around them were the bodies of the men who had had the misfortune to be involved in her fatal, last appearance. Clemens and half a dozen Praetorians stood to one side with bloodied swords.

The Senior Consul led the senators down through the deserted seating towards the stage. Caligula stared at them with uncomprehending eyes; Drusilla's head lolled from side to side over his left arm as he shook with grief.

'Where do I go for comfort and consolation?' Caligula suddenly shouted. 'Where? A child may turn to its mother, a wife may turn to her husband and a man may turn to his gods; but to whom does a god turn? Answer me that, you wise and learned men of the Senate.' He fell to his knees, splashing into the ever growing pool of blood, and broke down into sobs as he greedily kissed his dead sister's mouth and neck.

No one in the auditorium said a word as Caligula's ardour rose and he petted the corpse, murmuring into its unhearing ears. The shocked silence lengthened as he rolled the limp body over onto its knees. All knew he was capable of breaking any taboo – but this... this was abhorrent.

'I command you to live,' Caligula cried, driving himself into his lifeless sibling. 'Live!' Tears streamed down his face, creating flesh-coloured lines through the red stains left by his sister's blood, as he desperately attempted to pump life back into Drusilla's body. 'Live! Live! Live! Live!'

With a final, desolate wail enjoining his sister to return from the shades he climaxed and collapsed forward onto the floor to lie as motionless as her corpse.

No one moved as they stared at the Emperor, who showed no sign of breathing. Vespasian felt a thrill of hope, thinking that perhaps Caligula had committed one outrage too many and the gods had tired of his existence.

But that was not to be; with a sudden violent intake of breath Caligula seemingly came back from the dead, but alone. He got to his knees and looked around blankly at his audience. After a few moments his bloodshot, sunken eyes rested on Vespasian; he smiled wildly and slowly gestured to him to step forward.

With a sinking heart Vespasian approached the stage.

Caligula slithered forward and, putting his hand on the back of Vespasian's head, drew his face up close to his so that their foreheads touched. 'I have nothing to console me but my own greatness, my friend,' he hissed. 'Do you remember how I said I would build, Vespasian?'

'Yes, Princeps,' Vespasian replied, standing rigid with fear, 'you said you would build magnificently as you've already proved with your bridge.'

'Indeed, but that's just a trifling bridge. Now, in Drusilla's memory, I shall surpass the greatest achievement ever; I shall make the bridges that both Darius and Xerxes built from Asia to Europe seem like children's toys.'

'I'm sure that you could, but how?'

'I'm going to build a bridge worthy of a god. I will build one across the Bay of Neapolis, and then to show my fellow gods and all humanity that I'm the greatest leader that ever lived, I'm going to ride across it wearing the breastplate of the man I've surpassed: Alexander.'

'But that's in his mausoleum in Alexandria.'

Caligula grinned maniacally. 'Exactly, and you want to go there, so I give you my permission, on condition that you go to the mausoleum and take Alexander's breastplate from him. Bring it back to Rome for me.'

PART IIII

※ ※

ALEXANDRIA, JULY AD 38

CHAPTER XVII

'THAT HAS TO be the tallest building that I'll ever see,' Vespasian muttered under his breath as he looked up, his eyes wide with astonishment, at the lighthouse that soared above him to over four hundred feet into the sky. He calculated that if an *insula*, or apartment block, back in Rome had been that tall it would have almost fifty floors and then wondered what chance Caligula's proposed bridge had of outstripping it. He gripped the side-rail of the imperial trireme to steady himself as the ship was buffeted again by another large wave repelled by the huge mole that protected the Great Harbour of Alexandria. Fine spray flew on the salt-tanged breeze, dampening his toga and cooling his skin from the sun's intense heat. The stroke-master's piped beats slowed and the mainsail was furled; the voyage was nearing its end.

'That must be the biggest fucking thing in the whole fucking world,' Ziri said; his proficiency in Latin now matched that of his swearing. 'I'd say that it would look big even next to the biggest mountain in the middle of the fucking desert.'

'It must have taken some building,' Magnus commented beside him.

Vespasian nodded. 'Seventeen years. It was finished just over three hundred years ago. The first Ptolemy commissioned it and his son completed it. I suppose if you want to be remembered then that's the way to do it: build something magnificent.'

'Like Caligula's bridge?' Magnus asked with a smile.

'That'll just be remembered as a folly. I mean build something that's of practical use to the people, then they'll remember your name.'

'Who built the Circus Maximus?'

Vespasian frowned and thought for a moment. 'I don't know.'

'There you go, you see, it don't always work.'

Vespasian looked up again at the Pharos of Alexandria, which had been growing in size all day since, while more than fifty miles out to sea, they had first spotted its light – the rays of the sun during the day or a mighty fire at night, both reflected off a huge, polished bronze mirror. It was truly magnificent: set at the eastern tip of the long, thin Island of Pharos it was built on a base, ninety feet high and three hundred and fifty feet square, constructed of granite blocks fused together by molten lead to resist the impact of the sea. The tower itself had three different sections: the first was square and just over half of the whole tower's height, the next was octagonal, and the topmost part, in which were housed the mirror and fire, circular. The whole edifice was crowned with a giant statue of Poseidon and ornamented by four statues of Triton at each corner of the base. He could not imagine any building ever surpassing it.

'Stop gawping, Ziri, and go and pack up our stuff,' Magnus ordered after a few more moments of admiration. 'We'll be docking soon.'

'Yes, master.' The little Marmarides scuttled off towards their cabin in the stern of the ship.

Vespasian shouted after him: 'And don't forget—'

'No, I won't forget Sir's fucking box,' Ziri shouted back, cutting him off.

Vespasian looked at Magnus. 'Do I have to put up with that sort of cheek?'

Magnus shrugged. 'You don't have to, you could always ask me to keep him away from you, but then, seeing as you didn't bring a slave of your own, who would look after your needs?'

'I can see that it's high time that I invested in my own slaves,' Vespasian said. Hitherto he had always relied on his parents' or Gaius' slaves and it had never occurred to him to purchase his own; even when he had been in Cyrenaica he had been looked after by the official slaves in the Governor's Residence. 'The trouble is they're so expensive to buy and then feed.'

'Once you've cashed that bankers' draft with Thales you'll be able to afford plenty; until then stop moaning when I lend you mine for free.'

The ship slipped through the harbour mouth and all thoughts that Vespasian had about the hideous expense of slaves were put to one side. The Great Harbour of Alexandria was built on a scale that matched the Pharos: almost two miles across and a mile and a half deep. To his right was the Heptastadion, a huge mole, seven stadia or one thousand four hundred paces long and two hundred paces wide, that joined the Island of Pharos to the mainland; beyond this, in the commercial port that was almost as vast as the Great Harbour itself, Vespasian could see the massive hulks of the grain fleet docked next to large silos. To his left was the Diabathra, a dog-legged mole, equally as long, that ran from the harbour mouth to the Temple of Artemis next to the Royal Palace of the Ptolemys on the natural shoreline. Between these two mammoth man-made sea defences the waterfront was lined with buildings that rivalled in grandeur even those of Rome. At the waterfront's central point, on the tip of a small promontory, stood the colonnaded Timonium, built by Marcus Antonius after his defeat at Actium by Augustus. West of this, extending to the Heptastadion, were the jetties and quays of the military port. Here the massed triremes, quadremes and quinqueremes of the Alexandrian fleet bobbed at their moorings, looking clean and pristine after their recent winter refits. The sun glinted off their half-submerged bronze-plated rams and picked out the innumerable tiny figures toiling on their decks. Speckled around the three square miles of the harbour were a plethora of other, smaller craft, with bulging triangular sails and escorts of cawing seagulls, going about their daily routine, whether as lighters, ferries or fishermen, and adding to Vespasian's impression that he was entering the busiest and grandest port in the world.

Vespasian marvelled at the vision of the man who had caused all this to be built out of nothing: Alexander the Great, whose breastplate he had come to take back to Rome for the Emperor who thought he had surpassed him. Looking at this majestic city, just one of the many that Alexander had founded in the huge Empire that he had conquered, he realised the depths of Caligula's delusion: the greatest feat to be achieved by man had already been realised. No one would ever surpass Alexander – not even Julius Caesar or Augustus had come close to what he had accomplished in his short life. The best that anyone could hope for now was to be a pale shadow of the man whose legacy, or at least part of it, lay in front of Vespasian, bathing in the hot summer sun where, before Alexander's coming, there had been only a small fishing village perched on baking sands.

The trireme glided towards the dock; an order was bellowed and the larboard oars were shipped. The starboard oars backed water gently and with a soft thud and much shouting of sailors and dockers the ship's side came to rest against the thick wooden poles protecting the stone jetty. Lines were made fast, the foresail was furled and the gangplank lowered; the voyage was at an end.

Having confirmed with the *triarchus* the arrangement that the ship should wait for however long it took to complete the Emperor's business, Vespasian led Magnus and Ziri down the gangplank towards the port aedile waiting with sixteen legionaries and an optio of the Legio XXII Deiotariana on the jetty. The solid construction seemed to rock under Vespasian's feet after ten days at sea; he swayed slightly and felt Magnus' hand support his elbow.

'Easy, sir; we can't have a senator falling flat on his back in public like a vestal the moment she's completed her thirty-year vow.'

'Yes, thank you for reminding me, Magnus,' Vespasian replied testily, steadying himself for a few moments before handing his imperial warrant to the aedile. 'Senator Titus Flavius Vespasianus here on the Emperor's authority.'

The aedile read the document carefully then glanced up at the imperial banner fluttering on the masthead and raised his eyebrows. 'That seems to be in order, senator. It's four years since we've had a member of your order here; the previous Emperor banned you on the advice of his astrologer.' He paused for a wry chuckle. 'And arriving on one of the Emperor's personal ships no less; what can I do for you?'

'I wish to see the prefect immediately on imperial business.'

The aedile nodded and turned to the optio. 'Hortensius, escort the senator to the Royal Palace and then stay with him for the duration of his visit to provide him with any assistance that he needs.'

Vespasian muttered his thanks while suspecting that he had just been put under military guard.

'That is completely out of the question,' Prefect Aulus Avilius Flaccus informed Vespasian, having been apprised of Caligula's wishes. 'If the breastplate were to be removed, the whole of the city's Greek population, which is by far the largest section, would rise up in outrage. They worship Alexander and any sacrilege by us to his mausoleum would be seen as a declaration of war. Caligula's edict about putting his statue into all temples has already got the Jews up in arms, and I can't give the Jews a short, sharp shock and deal with the Greeks at the same time.' His firm-jawed, suntanned face set rigid and his dark eyes stared at Vespasian from underneath silvering brows, defying him to argue. Through the window behind him the expanse of the Great Harbour glistened in the late afternoon light. A gentle sea breeze blew in, cooling the chamber that Cleopatra, Julius Caesar and Marcus Antonius had all held audiences in.

'But it's Caligula's wish.'

'Then the little shit should wish for something else.'

Vespasian was taken aback by this open insult to the Emperor by one of his Governors. 'You can't talk about the Emperor in those terms, especially not in front of a senator.'

'And who's going to tell him? You? Well, go ahead, I don't give a fuck.'

Vespasian drew himself up. 'As a member of the Senate I outrank you, so I demand that you give me the breastplate.'

'You may be a senator and I only a mere equestrian but here in Egypt I rule, and I'm telling you that unless the Emperor wants Rome's grain supply cut off for the rest of the summer while I put down two rebellions, he can ride across his pathetic bridge wearing something else. And you can tell him I said so.'

'He'll have you replaced, brought back to Rome and executed.'

'He was replacing me, with Macro, but when he ordered him to kill himself he decided to reconfirm me in my appointment. I was hoping when I saw you that you were bringing my imperial mandate but that seems to have slipped the Emperor's mind; but no matter, I'm sure that it will arrive soon. But even if he does change his mind and decides to recall me I won't be going back to Rome. We may be a thousand miles away but I've still heard the stories. Caligula's mad, he even had his cousin executed for coughing; there's no way I'm going to set foot in Rome while he's emperor.'

'You can't stay here, surely?'

'Of course I wouldn't, the world is a big place and being prefect of Egypt is a very lucrative position; I have the money to go anywhere.'

Vespasian was about to contest the point but then thought better of it and decided to change the subject. 'I have some personal business to attend to that will take a few days and would appreciate being accommodated during that time.'

Flaccus smiled in a conciliatory manner. 'In that matter at least I can be of service, senator. I will have a suite of rooms placed at your disposal; you'll find it very spacious here. I hope that you will dine with me this evening; my wife and I have a few other guests.'

'Thank you, prefect, I'd be delighted,' Vespasian replied less than truthfully but disinclined to upset the man who seemed so secure in his province that he could defy an emperor.

'Is there anything else?'

'Yes, where can I find Thales the banker and also the Alabarch?'

Flaccus' face clouded over. 'Thales is in the Forum every day from dawn and the Alabarch lives next to the Jewish temple by the Canopic Gate, but why do you want to see him?'

Vespasian briefly explained about getting his father's late freedman Ataphanes' gold back to his family in Parthia.

'Well, you can trust him to do that, provided he gets his percentage,' Flaccus said. 'Dishonesty is the one charge I would never level against him; but he's a wily politician – don't allow him to use you for his own ends. The Jews have been making a lot of demands recently: full Alexandrian citizenship, the right to live outside the Jewish Quarter and the removal of the Emperor's statues from their temples to name a few; he'll get you involved if he can. Now, you'll have to excuse me as I have someone waiting to see me whom I hope will be a great help in dealing with those Jews.' Flaccus smiled coldly before walking Vespasian to the door. 'I shall see you at dinner, senator. If you wish to go out I've ordered your escort to accompany you everywhere. They will be waiting for you at the gate; it's the only way in or out of the palace.'

'We're just going to have to break in and steal it, then,' Magnus said as they sat, drinking chilled wine, on the terrace of Vespasian's second-floor suite watching the sun go down over the Great Harbour.

'We can't do that,' Vespasian replied appalled.

'Well, have you got any better ideas? How about going back to Caligula and saying that Flaccus wouldn't let you take it?'

'And whose neck's going to be right in front of him when I do, mine or the prefect's?'

'Exactly. So have you got any other ideas?'

Vespasian took a consoling sip of wine. 'No.'

'Then we're left with mine.'

Vespasian got up, walked to the marble balustrade and leant on it, deep in thought; Magnus joined him.

'If we're going to do that,' Vespasian said after a while, 'we'll have to make it look like nothing has happened, otherwise the whole Greek population will rise up.'

'You think that we should get a replica and do a swap?'

'Exactly; and we'll need to get in and out of the palace without anyone noticing.'

Magnus looked down at the fifty-foot drop to the water. 'That's the quickest way, straight down.'

'We'll need a boat.'

'Well, I wasn't planning on swimming.'

'Then we'll need to get past the guards, into the mausoleum and out again.'

'We'll do a recce.'

'With our escort?'

'Why not?'

'Flaccus will find out.'

'So? We're just seeing the sights, aren't we?'

'I suppose so.'

'What we will need is someone local who knows what the security arrangements are like inside the mausoleum at night and who can also provide the boat.'

Vespasian thought for a few moments. 'Felix?'

'Can we trust him?'

'What do you think?'

'Is there anyone else we could trust?'

'Antonia trusted him.'

Magnus paused and then nodded. 'We can trust him. How do we find him?'

'He said that the Alabarch always knows where he is.'

'So you'll ask him tomorrow?'

A knock at the door interrupted their planning. They looked into the suite and saw Ziri open it to a very attractive slave girl.

'Sir,' Ziri called out to them, 'she says that she's here to escort you to dinner.'

'Very well.' Vespasian looked at Magnus; he was eyeing the girl. 'What are you going to do?'

'Do you think that you could find your own way down to the triclinium?'

Vespasian raised his eyebrows. 'I'm sure I could.'

'Then I reckon that I'll be in all evening, if you take my meaning?'

After a few wrong turns Vespasian eventually found his way through the labyrinthine palace to a long, high and wide corridor, lined with statues; at its end there was a doorway from which emanated the sound of animated conversation. Following the voices, he passed by the statues admiring every one; they were life-like representations of each of the Ptolemaic dynasty, both male and female, starting with its founder, Alexander's general, Ptolemy Soter. Each of the men was dressed in original, full military uniform: helmets, muscled cuirasses, greaves and swords, all of great antiquity, had been buckled onto them. The women wore silken gowns, which fluttered slightly in the breeze, and their heads were adorned with lavish wigs. The stone limbs not covered by clothing had been painted in flesh tones and the faces were finished with realistic detail.

As he neared the end of the line he paused in front of the second to last, Cleopatra VII, and stared at the face that had beguiled first Julius Caesar and then Marcus Antonius. It was not classically beautiful, her nose was long and pronounced and her chin and mouth boyish, yet there was a sensuality in her appearance that he found very attractive; she had obviously been a striking woman.

'Still staring at women, quaestor? Or should I just say "senator"?'

Vespasian spun round to see a woman silhouetted in the doorway.

'At least that one isn't trying to get you to listen to her.'

'Flavia! What are you doing here?'

Flavia Domitilla walked forward into the light of the corridor. 'I've been here since I escaped from the riots in Cyrene. What about you?'

Vespasian gaped at her, she had not changed, and, judging by the blood rushing around his body, nor had his desire for her; she was still his idea of a proper woman. 'I'm here on the Emperor's

292

orders,' he managed to get out, feeling light-headed as he caught her scent, inflaming him even more.

Her eyes widened and her pupils dilated; she took another step towards him and smiled enticingly. 'Moving in high circles, are you? How fascinating; you must tell me about it at dinner.' She took his arm and led him through the door; he followed willingly, enjoying the soft touch of her hand on his skin.

'Ah, Flavia, you've found our senator, how very clever of you. Now we can eat.' A dumpy little round-faced, smiling woman, in her late forties, with a twinkle in her eye, bustled towards them. 'Senator Vespasian, I'm Laelia, the prefect's wife.'

Vespasian gently squeezed her proffered fingers. 'I'm pleased to make your acquaintance. I apologise if I'm late.'

'I sent a girl for you, did she not turn up? I'll have her whipped when I find her.'

'No, no, please don't. She did arrive but there was um...there were some matters that needed attending to in my suite so I left her there to deal with them and made my own way.'

'Well, no matter, you're here now. Seeing as Flavia found you she wins the prize of reclining next to you. The other women will be so envious.'

'She's just doing that to make sure her husband keeps his hands off me,' Flavia whispered in his ear as they followed Laelia towards the other five guests and Flaccus congregated around the low dining table.

Vespasian shivered involuntarily at the closeness of her mouth to his face, savouring the sweetness of her breath. 'Does he try that often?'

'Yes; sometimes I let him succeed.'

'Why? You could say no.'

'I've been here for over three years now, how else do you think I've survived without a man to provide for me?'

CHAPTER XVIII

VESPASIAN WAS WOKEN by a knock on his bedroom door.
Magnus stuck his head round the corner. 'I've ordered a chair to be…ah! I'll leave you to it.' He beat a hasty retreat.

Vespasian turned on his side and looked at Flavia; she opened her eyes.

'When he says "it" I assume he means me?' she said with a yawn.

'He could have meant the act itself.'

'That would be a preferable interpretation, but I'll only believe you if you prove it to be the correct one.'

Vespasian smiled and kissed her while running the tips of his fingers down over her breasts, across her flat belly before easing them in between her legs. Flavia moaned softly as she had done for most of the night as she had sucked on his mouth and his nipples and his penis between bouts of intense sexual activity; he had made love to her in a way that he had done to no other woman except Caenis.

Vespasian had decided to bed her the moment that he saw her again; and the feeling had seemed to become very mutual, especially once he had explained to her that he had found Capella and had brought him back out of the desert; he had not let her down. She had not seemed too distressed at the news of Capella's savage death and was genuinely surprised to learn that he had not been trading for camels. Vespasian did not, however, tell her what Capella had really been doing, and when she had pressed him on the subject he had just alluded to imperial business and it was better if she did not know; which, indeed, it was. Admiring his high connections, which she had evidently found irresistible, she had started to work her charms on him to the full, quite unnecessarily but much to Vespasian's enjoyment and the other guests' embarrassment. When the dinner broke up Flaccus appeared most aggrieved and a triumphant-looking Laelia did not even bother to ask Flavia if she wanted her litter called.

The orange glow of the newly risen sun filtered through the shutters and Vespasian was spent; he climbed off Flavia and sat on the edge of the bed. 'I should be going; I've got business to attend to.'

'What sort and how much?' Flavia asked, resting her head on her hand.

'Private and a lot.'

'I'll come with you.'

'No; you just be here when I get back.'

She sighed and lay back down on the pillow. 'I can't see that as being a problem.'

'Dinner was successful by the looks of it,' Magnus commented as Vespasian appeared from his bedroom.

'Very,' Vespasian replied while Ziri began to drape his toga around him.

'Well?'

'Well, we'll go to see the Alabarch first and then on to the Forum to Thales and then try and find Felix.'

'I know what we're going to do; I meant: well, who is she then?'

'You won't like it.'

Magnus thought for a moment and then slapped his palm on his forehead. 'Venus give you the strength to resist her: Flavia!'

'A small world, isn't it?'

'Too small; you're just about to cash a draft for a quarter of a million – she'll have that off you in no time.'

'Not if I marry her.'

'The last time you thought about that a whole load of people ended up dead. Why don't you just be content to have her as a bed-toy while you're here?'

'Because I'll be twenty-nine this year and I need to have sons; my parents write of hardly anything else in their letters.' Vespasian examined the folds of his toga draped over his left arm; he nodded with satisfaction. 'That's perfect, Ziri, you've finally mastered it.'

Magnus frowned. 'So you're going to take her back to Rome?'

'I'm not going to live here.'

'She might not want to come.'

'Oh, she'll come; it'll be the best offer she's had since she got here. Anyway, how was your evening?'

'Much the same as yours, but without the long-term commitment to a very expensive woman.'

'How come you both got a fuck last night and I didn't?' Ziri asked resentfully.

'Because, Ziri, you're a slave,' Magnus said, clipping him lightly around the ear, 'and besides, I haven't noticed any camels around the palace. Now stop moaning and go and get Sir's box.'

Optio Hortensius and his men were waiting for them at the palace gates, sitting in the shade of an outsized sedentary statue that reminded Vespasian of the image of Amun in the temple at Siwa but was, according to the Greek inscription, a representation in the Egyptian style of the first Ptolemy.

'You can guide us to the Alabarch's house near the Canopic Gate, optio,' Vespasian said, getting into the chair that Magnus had ordered, 'seeing as we're saddled with you.'

Hortensius saluted and his men fell in.

'You could make yourself useful and give us a guided tour as we go,' Magnus said with a grin.

Hortensius ignored the jibe.

'Don't antagonise him,' Vespasian muttered, as they passed through the palace gate and into the enclosed Royal Harbour, 'he may prove useful.'

'I can't remember the last time that anyone in the Twenty-second Deiotariana did anything useful; the legion hasn't seen proper action for ages.'

Clearing the Royal Harbour they entered the city itself and passed by the side of the old Macedonian barracks, two storeys high and now used for housing legionaries on duty within the city – the Roman military camp being situated outside the eastern walls. Turning left they walked along the length of its drab, two-hundred-pace, square-windowed facade, with their escort clearing the way through the crowd, and then turned right, into the Jewish Quarter.

Immediately there was a change of atmosphere; it was still busy but there was a sullenness in the air and, as they walked down the middle of the street, Vespasian noticed many a resentful glare at not only the legionaries but also at the thick, purple senatorial stripe on his toga. He kept his head held high and, disdaining to look either left or right, progressed with all the dignity befitting a Roman senator in a part of the Empire that belonged to the Senate and people of Rome.

As they got deeper into the quarter the people began to move aside less willingly and their escort were forced to draw their swords as a warning and occasionally push a more stubborn obstacle out of the way with their shields.

'Maybe it weren't such a bad thing to be given a guard,' Magnus said from behind his right shoulder, 'we don't seem to be too popular.'

They carried on for half a mile past rows of Greek-style houses – two-storeyed and built around an oblong central courtyard with a couple of small windows and a plain wooden door in the whitewashed facade – before turning east onto the Canopic Way. Nothing in Rome had prepared Vespasian for this sight: three and a half miles long and sixty paces wide, lined with temples and public buildings for all its length, it ran from the Canopic Gate in the eastern wall straight as an arrow's flight to the western wall and out into the Necropolis. Vespasian tried not to stare like some hill-farmer – which, he reflected, he was.

The going became easier as the width of the street and the more multicultural make-up of the pedestrians played their parts. Between the buildings to his left and right Vespasian noticed, out of the corners of his eyes, small areas shaped like the Circus Maximus with one open end, seating up to a hundred people, mainly Greek, listening to a speaker at the curved, far end. As they approached the fourth area the noise emanating from within was not what one would expect of a group of students listening to a philosophical debate.

Getting closer Vespasian could see that the audience was not only Greeks but Jews and native Egyptians as well. They were all involved in a fierce shouting match with scuffles breaking out and the two sides were not split by racial divides; a minority of Jews were taking issue with the majority of the audience – which included many of their race – who seemed to be supporting the main speaker, a short, balding man standing at the far end trying to make himself heard. Vespasian almost did an undignified double-take as he recognised the bow legs and imperious voice of the speaker shouting over the arguments: Gaius Julius Paulus.

'What the fuck's he doing here?' Magnus exclaimed as he too noticed Paulus.

'What he seems to do best, by the looks of it,' Vespasian replied. 'Causing fights and spreading discord.'

'Loathsome little shit!'

'This is the house of Alexander the Alabarch, senator,' Hortensius informed Vespasian as they approached a large house on the northern side of the street – the edge of the Jewish Quarter. It was Greek in style but built with a grandeur that fitted in with the Canopic Way's architecture. 'Me and my lads will wait for you out here, senator.'

'Thank you, optio,' Vespasian said, getting down from the chair and taking Ataphanes' box from Ziri. 'You and Ziri wait here too, Magnus; I'll be as quick as I can.'

'I still have some correspondence with that family, senator,' Alexander the Alabarch of the Alexandrian Jews assured Vespasian, 'and I can promise you that it'll be no problem getting this thing to them. There is a caravan leaving for Parthia at the next full moon in three days' time, its owner is a cousin of mine; you can trust him. May I see what's inside?'

Vespasian lifted the lid of Ataphanes' box, which stood on the desk between them. They were sitting in the cool of the Alabarch's study on the northern side of his house away from the threat of direct sunlight. The room was filled with many scrolls, labelled in Greek, Hebrew, Aramaic and Latin, giving it a musty smell reminiscent of a library storeroom. The only light came from two slatted windows in the wall opening out onto the central courtyard from whence came the sound of two young men reading aloud, at great speed, in unison.

'Your freedman was wealthy,' Alexander commented, fingering the gold coins and trinkets inside. 'How much is here?'

'I'm afraid that I don't know exactly.'

'Then I shall weigh it.' Alexander got up and retrieved a large set of scales from a wooden chest in the corner of the room. 'My fee, which will cover all expenses including those of my cousin's, will be eighteen per cent of the weight of the gold. I won't take into account the value of the workmanship; would that be agreeable to you?'

'Ten.'

'Sixteen.'

'Twelve.'

'Fifteen.'

'Eleven.'

Alexander smiled beneath his full, sand-coloured beard. 'You bargain strongly considering that it is not your money. Very well, twelve it is.'

'Done,' Vespasian said. Alexander started to weigh out the gold.

The Alabarch's appearance had surprised Vespasian; he had expected a wise-looking, old grey-beard with rheumy eyes, a dripping nose and, perhaps, a slight stoop. The reality had been far different: Alexander was a fit and powerful man in his late forties with alert, piercing blue eyes and long, almost blond hair with a beard to match. The only things about him that fitted in with Vespasian's stereotypical ideas of Jewishness were his clothes – very typical – and his pronounced nose – averagely so. He had the calmness about him of a man at ease with himself and his position in life and Vespasian could tell immediately that he was a man he could trust.

'Six minae, twenty-four drachmae and three obols,' Alexander said eventually.

'Which makes your percentage one obol short of seventy-five drachmae,' Vespasian said after a moment's thought, 'or, almost exactly, one Roman pound in gold.'

Alexander did some quick calculations on a wax tablet and raised his eyebrows. 'I can see that you would be a hard man to cheat.'

'Not that I believe you would try, Alexander.'

Alexander began to weigh out his share. 'I was brought up to be honest and truthful in all things, something that I hope I've passed on to my sons.' He indicated to the voices in the courtyard. 'That's them at their Torah studies, which, I'm afraid, they resent as much as I did at their age, but I insist upon them doing it because otherwise, when they come of age, how can they make an informed decision as to whether they believe in the religion or, like me, do not?'

'You're not a Jew?'

'Of course I'm a Jew racially, I'm just not a practising Jew. Why else do you think that I'm the Alabarch? With me Rome gets the best of both worlds: it has a Jew running the Jewish community here in Alexandria and collecting its taxes, which makes it acceptable to the Jews.'

'Even though you don't share their religion?'

Alexander chuckled. 'Oh, I do enough to be seen as a righteous man in their eyes. I recently paid for the nine gates of the Temple in Jerusalem to be gilded, so they have to accept me; but at the same time Rome has an Alabarch who isn't swayed by religious dogma. Rome can see me as being even-handed.'

'That's not the impression that Flaccus gave me,' Vespasian said, realising that he was talking out of turn. 'He said that you had been making too many demands recently.'

'There is an ongoing issue of Alexandrian citizenship and whether Jewish citizens are allowed to live outside the Jewish Quarter, not to mention the statues of the Emperor in the temples. But I've also been trying to mediate between the elders and the prefect on another matter: they want him to crack down on this new sect that they see as preaching heresy and consider it to be a Roman attack on their religion.'

'But that's ridiculous, there's nothing Roman about it at all.'

'The main preacher is a Roman citizen.'

Vespasian frowned. 'Paulus? Surely not; he's trying to eradicate it.'

'He was trying to eradicate what was known as The Way; four years ago he was here doing some very unpleasant things to anyone suspected of being a member of the sect.' Alexander indicated to the perfectly balanced scales.

Vespasian nodded his approval of the twelve per cent. 'Yes, I came across him in Cyrenaica; he was ruthless. I had him arrested and put on a ship back east.'

'A pity that you didn't have him killed.' Alexander tipped his gold into a bag and placed it in a drawer. 'Well, he claims to have had some sort of spiritual enlightenment since then while on his way to Damascus. He appeared out of the desert a couple of months ago, having lived there by himself for three years, and started preaching without permission. He claims that he has God's authority and it's not a Jewish matter at all; and in a way he's right. He's not preaching a reformed version of Judaism along the lines that the followers of The Way claimed that Yeshua bar Yosef preached to the Jews alone; he's preaching a completely new religion to Gentiles as well as Jews centred on our God but not the Torah. He claims that Yeshua bar Yosef is God's son who came to die for the sins of the world and redeem all mankind. Only through him, Paulus professes, can those who truly repent of their sins hope to live with God in the Kingdom of Heaven, which is not of this world, rather than wait for resurrection in an earthly paradise at the End of Days as most Jews believe. He also adds fear and urgency into his message by claiming that the End of Days, or the Day of Judgement, as he calls it, is close at hand. Paradoxically he blames the Jews for having this Yeshua crucified even though it is a Roman form of execution, and if he hadn't been executed Paulus wouldn't have anything to base his incoherent religion on. You can understand why the elders and my people are angry.'

'Yes, I felt it as I came through the Jewish Quarter. Why doesn't Flaccus do something about Paulus?'

'Ask him yourself,' Alexander replied, replacing Ataphanes' gold back in the box. 'I don't know, but I think that it's because he doesn't care; after all, what's another new religion to a Roman? You embrace them all.'

'And rightly so, if it doesn't involve having your foreskin cut off. But this one sounds different.'

Alexander closed the box. 'It is different and it's dangerous because it doesn't acknowledge any earthly authority; its appeal lies in the promise of salvation and reward in a world to come, not in the here and now. If it is allowed to take root, then the whole emphasis of our civilisation could change from a philo-sophical debate on how to live in the present, to a spiritual debate on how to prepare for a theoretical afterlife. I've been thinking about it and I wonder what would happen to science and learning if all that people worried about was the idea of an immortal soul.'

'I'm afraid that you've lost me there,' Vespasian replied as Alexander began to write out a receipt. 'However, I can see the danger of a religion that doesn't acknowledge the ultimate authority of the Emperor – whatever he may be like. But surely this is just a small sect created by one man?'

'But it will grow because Paulus aims his preaching at the poor and slaves who have nothing in this world to lose and everything to gain from his idea of salvation and spiritual riches in the next; it's very potent. Paulus is an extremely ambitious man who believes that his abilities have never been truly recognised and that all his life he's been denied his rightful place in society. He asked, demanded even, to marry the High Priest's daughter, just before he went to Damascus, and was refused; I think that he saw that as the final indignity and decided to find a way to power in his own right because it was shortly after that he disappeared. Now he's back and I believe that he has found a way to turn this world upside down with him finally at the top.'

'I'll speak to Flaccus and try to get him to arrest Paulus,' Vespasian said, before realising that Alexander had done exactly what Flaccus had predicted: got him involved.

Alexander smiled and handed him the receipt for Ataphanes' gold. 'Thank you, Vespasian, I would appreciate that; but he needs to do more than arrest him, he must execute him.'

Vespasian looked into the piercing blue eyes of the Alabarch and saw that he was in earnest. He was genuinely afraid of this new sect. 'Very well, I'll suggest that, Alexander,' Vespasian agreed, getting up and proffering his arm. 'I should go now; I've a busy day ahead. Would you be able to tell me where I can find the late Lady Antonia's steward, Felix?'

Alexander grasped his forearm across the desk. 'He's in the city at the moment; you'll find him at Antonia's house right next to the south side of the Gymnasium.'

Vespasian followed the Alabarch out into the courtyard; the reading stopped immediately and Alexander's two sons stood in the presence of their elders; they were both in their teens.

'Senator Vespasian, this is my eldest son, Tiberius,' Alexander said, gesturing to the taller of the boys who looked to Vespasian to be about seventeen, 'and his brother, Marcus.'

The boys bowed their heads.

'Your father keeps you hard at your studies,' Vespasian observed.

'He seems to find pleasure in our suffering,' Tiberius replied with a grin.

'Either that or he's trying to numb our minds with pointless repetition,' Marcus suggested; he was a couple of years younger than his brother.

Alexander smiled with pride at his sons. 'For that cheek you can learn an extra fifty lines. I shall test you at sundown.'

'You'll have to find us first,' Tiberius said, quickly ducking a playful clip around the ear from his father.

'Enough of this,' Alexander said laughing, 'back to your studies. I shall see you out, senator.'

Despite being carried, Vespasian was sweating profusely as they progressed west back along the Canopic Way; even though it was not yet midday the dry heat and the still air combined to make the conditions almost intolerable, especially when wearing a woollen toga. Unlike Cyrene, which was built upon a plateau overlooking the sea, Alexandria did not seem to benefit from a cooling breeze.

'How do you cope with this, Hortensius?' Magnus asked, sweltering even though he only had on a tunic. 'Your helmets and armour must be cooking you alive.'

'You get used to it, mate,' the optio replied in a friendly way, 'once you've been here for ten years or so.'

'You mean you just stop caring.'

'You're right, mate,' Hortensius concurred with a laugh, 'ain't he, lads?'

His men agreed good-naturedly. Vespasian could tell that Magnus had used the time waiting outside the Alabarch's house to fine effect and had got on good terms with their guards.

'Looks like Paulus has been moved on,' Vespasian commented to Magnus, seeing the arena where he had been preaching was now empty.

'Did you find out from the Alabarch what he's doing here?'

'I did, and you won't believe it—'

A series of shouts and the hard stamp of many running feet cut him off. A couple of Jews came pelting across the street, from south to north, followed by a howling mob of Greeks waving improvised clubs and hurling stones at their quarry.

With a sharp, curtailed cry the hindmost Jew was brought down with a direct hit to the back of his head; crashing forward on to the paved road he skidded along for a couple of paces tearing the skin off his face. His colleague ran on into the Jewish

Quarter as the chasing mob surrounded the stricken man, hitting and kicking him as he lay motionless on the ground.

'With me, lads,' Hortensius shouted, drawing his gladius, 'line abreast, two deep, shields up and use the flats of your swords.' He broke into a run with eight of his men on either side. Women in the street screamed and the men drew back, hurling abuse or encouragement depending on their race. Vespasian stepped out of his chair and, with Magnus and Ziri, followed slowly as the legionaries charged into the mob, who were so intent on beating their victim that they did not notice the threat until nine interlocked shields punched into them, cracking bones and hurling men to the ground. Burnished iron flashed in the sun as the legionaries brought the flats of their blades cracking down on the heads of the closest men still standing, felling them.

Those who could turned and ran, leaving the legionaries kicking and stamping on their fallen mates.

'That's enough, Hortensius,' Vespasian shouted, 'call your men off.'

It took a few moments for the legionaries to respond to their optio's orders but eventually, after a couple more arms were snapped and another skull cracked, they pulled back, leaving a half-dozen blood-stained bodies on the ground. A couple of them were shrieking in agony but the rest lay either unconscious or rolling around clutching shattered limbs and groaning with pain.

'Have a look at him,' Vespasian ordered Magnus, pointing to the blood-spattered Jew who lay motionless.

Magnus stepped over a couple of bodies and knelt down, turning the man over; one look at his glazed eyes told him all he needed to know. 'Dead,' he announced as men and women came rushing from the Jewish Quarter.

Hortensius formed his men up in a protective wall around the dead and the injured. 'Stay back!' he warned as the first of the Jews drew close.

'That's my brother,' a middle-aged man shouted, stepping forward from the crowd.

Vespasian recognised him as the Jew who had been running with the murdered man. 'Let him through, Hortensius,' he ordered, 'and get these injured men locked up; they should be tried by the prefect for murder.'

The legionaries parted, letting the man through to his stricken sibling; he knelt and, taking the lifeless head in his hands, wept.

'Why were they chasing you?' Vespasian asked.

'There's been a preacher of heresy in the city; he was here again this morning. My brother and I went to argue against him but he doesn't listen; he just insists that God loves all people whether they follow the Torah or not, and the way to God is through eating the body and drinking the blood of the man he claims was God's son, Yeshua. It's blasphemy.'

'Eating his body and drinking his blood? That's ridiculous; Yeshua's been dead for five years or so.'

'He says he turns bread and wine into his body and blood.'

Vespasian struggled to understand the concept. 'Do you mean literally?'

'I don't know; I can only assume so, why else would he say it? After the meeting was broken up the preacher told his followers that he would perform this ceremony; my brother and I followed them to find out what happens. They went to a house by the Lake Harbour, a few hundred paces away; we managed to climb onto the roof and look down through a crack in the tiles but before we saw anything we were spotted and had to run for our lives.'

'From the preacher's followers?'

'No, from ordinary Greeks; we Jews are not welcome anywhere in the city outside of our quarter at the moment. They chased us away but they've never done anything like this before.' He indicated to his battered brother's corpse and started to sob.

'Take his body for burial,' Vespasian said, sympathy colouring his words. 'Tell me, what is your name?'

'Nathanial,' the distraught man answered through his tears.

'I will ensure that his killers are brought to justice for this, you have the word of a Roman senator who owes your Alabarch a favour for a service he's just rendered me.'

'Thank you, senator,' he replied, lifting his brother with difficulty. He looked at Vespasian with bloodshot eyes. 'I don't think that my brother is going to be the last person killed in this city just for being Jewish.'

Vespasian turned to Hortensius who now had an escort of only eight legionaries, the others being busy dealing with the Jew's murderers. 'Let's get going, optio,' he ordered wearily, 'I've got much to do.'

'It ain't good when people start getting murdered just for being Jewish,' Magnus observed to Vespasian as they set off again.

'People get murdered just for having a weighty purse on them.'

'That ain't what I mean, sir. The way I see it is that if more of them get murdered for being Jewish then it won't be too long before they retaliate and people find themselves getting murdered just for being Greek or Egyptian or, the gods forbid, Roman.' He looked pointedly at the senatorial stripe on Vespasian's toga. 'If you take my meaning?'

Vespasian did indeed.

It was the fifth hour of the day by the time Vespasian and his depleted party reached the Forum, which was, like everything else he had seen in Alexandria, truly impressive. With a panoramic view over the Great Harbour it was set between the theatre, seating over thirty thousand, to its east and, to its west, the Caesareum, the palace, guarded by two needle-like obelisks, built by Cleopatra for her lover and named after him. Two hundred paces long and a hundred across and surrounded by a colonnade of immense proportions constructed of different coloured marbles, the Forum teemed with people of many races going about their business; it was the beating heart of a great city.

Thales proved easy to find as he turned out to be one of the most important and respected bankers in the city. Vespasian's senatorial toga enabled him to jump the queue but to the relief of the other disgruntled clients his business did not take long. He

307

left within a quarter of an hour with a receipt for his bankers' draft and a promise from the bald and immensely overweight Thales that upon his return the following morning there would be 237,500 denarii in cash, paid in gold for ease of transport back to Rome. Thales had made 12,500 denarii commission on the deal but Vespasian did not let that sour his mood as they made their way past the extensive Gymnasium complex and found the Alexandrian abode of his late benefactress.

Magnus pulled on the bell chain and almost instantly the door was opened by a dark-skinned, wavy-haired slave who looked very much like Ziri.

'Senator Titus Flavius Vespasianus here to see Marcus Antonius Felix,' Magnus announced.

They were immediately granted entry and were escorted through to an atrium with many fountains, not just in the impluvium but at intervals all around the room, cooling the atmosphere and filling the air with the constant but gentle sound of falling water.

'Senator Vespasian,' a voice said from the far end of the room, 'what a pleasure to see you; I had heard that you had arrived but did not expect to be honoured with a visit so soon into your stay.' Felix appeared from behind a statue of Poseidon – a small replica of the one crowning the Pharos but, nevertheless, twice life-sized; it gushed water from its open mouth.

'That is because you said to come if you could be of service, Felix,' Vespasian replied, walking towards his host, 'and, most certainly now, I do need your help.'

'I didn't say that it would be impossible,' Felix quietly reminded Vespasian and Magnus, 'I said it would be difficult but not impossible.'

'Well, it looks impossible to me,' Magnus muttered.

'But it has to be done,' Vespasian said flatly but wondering nonetheless how Felix thought that it could be achieved.

They were standing in the dim interior of the burial chamber in Alexander's Mausoleum at the heart of the Soma, the sacred enclosure where the bodies of his heirs in Egypt, the Ptolemys, rested. Before them, ten feet away, resting on a granite slab supported by two similar slabs on their sides, lay a sarcophagus of translucent sheets of crystal set in a latticed bronze framework. It shimmered orange and golden in the flickering light of three flaming sconces burning on its far side from low down, giving the impression that it glowed with a light generated internally. Cocooned tightly within it, Vespasian could see the silhouetted outline of the mummified body of the greatest conqueror known to the world: Alexander of Macedon.

Although the sarcophagus could be viewed by means of a shaft cut through the ceiling to the temple, thirty feet above, the chamber itself was not open to the public. However, the priests of Alexander's cult were happy to allow access to the body for visiting dignitaries, and as the first senator to visit Egypt for over four years Vespasian was admirably qualified and they had been honoured to grant his request. Only Ziri had been refused access because of his slave status and he now waited in the Temple of Alexander above them.

Despite the practical reason for his visit, Vespasian still felt overawed to see physical proof that Alexander had existed and was not just some hero conjured out of myth. He had felt close to the great man in Queen Tryphaena's palace in Thracia standing by the desk that Alexander had used and gazing at the same view that he had seen every morning when he had come to raise Thracian mercenaries for his conquest of the East; but that was as nothing compared to being in the same chamber as his preserved remains.

Vespasian walked forward to get a better view of the body and also to examine the sarcophagus to see how it might be opened.

'You may approach it, master, but it is forbidden to touch,' the priest standing behind them in the chamber's entrance warned.

Vespasian looked down through the crystal and found himself staring at a face that was at the same time both ancient and youthful. There were no lines on the smooth, brown skin, coloured by age not race, which stretched over the skull and jaw like the finest vellum; but neither was there substance to it, so the outline of the bone beneath was plainly visible giving the impression of great age. However, the mouth was closed with the thin lips pulled slightly up in a faint smile; the eyes, which had seen more wonders and riches than any others before or since, were shut as if sleeping. Long hair, still abundant and blond, covered the ears and lay perfectly dressed on the pillow framing the face with a soft outline of ochre; all this combined to give the effect that here was a young man resting peacefully. Vespasian drew his breath and looked closer; the only blemish was that the nostril on the shadowed side of the face had fallen away.

'The great Augustus did that by accident when he had the sarcophagus' lid removed so that he could touch Alexander,' the priest said, realising what Vespasian was examining.

'Was that the last time the lid was taken off?'

'No, Germanicus brought his sons here and also we take it off every year to replace the spices that surround and preserve Alexander.'

Vespasian walked around the sarcophagus looking at the seal between the top and bottom halves of the sarcophagus and saw that they were held together by nothing more than the weight of the lid. 'Do you think two men could lift that?' he whispered to Felix and Magnus who had joined him as he completed his circuit.

Magnus shrugged. 'If they can't they could certainly lift one end enough to get to the breastplate.'

Vespasian's eyes moved down to the object that Caligula had sent him to Egypt to steal; it was not what he had expected: gilded, inlaid and adorned with jewels. It was evidently the actual breastplate that he had worn in battle and not one made especially for his eternal rest. Just like Marcus Antonius' sword it was the choice of a fighting man: made of hardened leather moulded in the shape of the muscles it concealed. Its only decoration were two rearing horses of inlaid gold facing each other on the chest and bronze edgings around the neck, shoulders and waist to give it added strength.

'Can you memorise the inlays?' Vespasian murmured to Felix.

'There's no need to; almost every statue of Alexander in the city depicts him wearing this.'

'In which case our work here is done.' Vespasian straightened up and turned to the waiting priest. 'Thank you for allowing me the honour of gazing at the greatest man who ever lived,' he said with genuine feeling.

'I must stay for few moments to perform the short cleansing ritual that is prescribed every time we visit,' the priest said, acknowledging their thanks with an inclination of his head. He stepped aside to allow them to mount the two flights of stone steps leading back up to the temple.

Coming out of the dark staircase, past the armed guard in Macedonian uniform at its top, Vespasian's eyes took a short while to get used to the bright light; once they had done so he looked around the cavernous, circular chamber that he had only briefly glimpsed earlier as they had been ushered through its main doors and straight down to the tomb. It was dominated by a huge equestrian statue of Alexander, helmetless with his hair flowing behind him, mounted on Bucephalus and with a lance couched under his arm as if in mid-thrust. Next to it, rather incongruously, stood the now obligatory statue of Caligula.

In the absolute centre of the floor was a circular balustrade, waist high, surrounding the opening of the narrow shaft down which the public could gaze at Alexander's preserved corpse. Directly above this was a similar sized hole cut in the ceiling, fifty feet above.

'At noon on the tenth of June, the anniversary of Alexander's death according to the Roman calendar,' the priest informed Vespasian as he appeared at the top of the steps, his ritual complete, 'the sun is directly aligned to shine down onto his face. I'm afraid that you've missed that by a month.'

'That is a pity,' Vespasian said gazing up at the hole. 'What happens when it rains?'

'It rarely does here, but there is a hatch up there that we can close.'

Vespasian nodded thoughtfully. 'Thank you, you've been most accommodating.' As he turned to leave, his foot slipped and he would have stumbled had Magnus not caught his arm; he looked down at a smear of greenish slime on the floor.

'Please accept my apologies, senator,' the priest said hastily, 'I will have the slaves who clean the floor punished for their slackness.'

'What is it?'

'We keep geese in the temple at night as a security; should anyone overpower the guards outside and gain access their noise would raise the alarm. I'm afraid that is their residue.'

'You're right, the windows are out of the question; the best way in and out is through the roof, if the hatch is strong enough to attach a rope to,' Magnus agreed as they sat in some shade in the long and wide central courtyard of the Soma surrounded by the individual mausoleums of the Ptolemaic dynasty and with Alexander's temple at its northern end. At its centre stood an altar at which a priest waited to accept the offerings brought by the people of the city in the hope that their semi-divine dead rulers would intercede for them with the gods on matters close to their heart, be they financial, legal or personal.

'But first we've got to get into the Soma,' Vespasian pointed out, looking at the only gate through the high walls of the complex through which a group of Greeks walked leading a lamb.

'That should be fairly straightforward,' Felix assured them. 'The main gate is guarded but never closed so that the people have access to the altar day and night.'

'So we just pretend to be supplicants?'

'Exactly.'

'All right,' Magnus said sceptically, 'say that we do get in and manage to sneak off unnoticed to the temple, get up onto the roof and then down through that hole, how the fuck do we deal with the geese?' He indicated across to a small enclosure to the left of the temple in which were housed two dozen of the nocturnal guards.

Vespasian shrugged and looked at Felix.

'The problem of the geese I can solve,' Felix assured them, 'we just need to get a man on the inside the evening before we go in – Ziri could do that. The big dilemma is the replica breastplate.'

'What's so hard about that?' Vespasian asked. 'You said the pattern is easy to replicate.'

'It's not the pattern that worries me. You said that the switch must never be noticed, which would be fine if the priests were just looking at it through the crystal. The trouble is that once a year they take the lid off and would then see that the leather isn't old. No matter how much we try to age it it'll never match the original if they inspect it closely.'

'So we need to find a leather breastplate that's three hundred years old or so?' Vespasian questioned, raising his eyebrows.

'Exactly,' Felix replied, looking beaten.

'That won't be a problem; I saw more than a dozen of them last night.'

CHAPTER XVIIII

'THAT'S VERY GOOD, Felix, very good indeed,' Vespasian said, admiring the leather cuirass on the table in Felix's study.

'It looks old to me,' Magnus affirmed, nodding his head appreciatively.

'It's good enough,' Felix agreed, 'but it won't stand up to close scrutiny.'

'I can't imagine that anyone stops and takes a very close look at Ptolemy Soter's statue, and even if someone did it would be to examine it for the first time, in which case they wouldn't have seen the original and will accept this one as real.' Vespasian picked up the breastplate and examined the bronze edgings around the neck, shoulders and waist; they were not identical to Alexander's but looked exactly like the workmanship on the original that they would replace: that of the first Ptolemy. Vespasian had chosen Ptolemy Soter's breastplate because it was the plainest as compared to his descendants, whose armour became more and more ornate as their martial prowess diminished. As one of Alexander's generals he had emulated his leader's habit of wearing plain but functional Macedonian armour, so that there was no gaudy protuberance for a spear point to catch and gain purchase on to pierce the hardened leather. All that needed to be done to this breastplate was to replace the edgings and then inlay the rearing horses.

'What about Flaccus?' Magnus asked.

'He walks down that corridor every day and probably never even looks at the statues,' Vespasian replied, feeling the hardened leather of the cuirass and admiring how the craftsman had made it feel slightly supple, as if it were very old. 'And anyway, if he did notice that the breastplate had been swapped and then realise that I had done it and why, do you think that he would announce to the Greek population of this city that the Emperor of Rome, the man he represents, has had one of their most venerated artefacts stolen? Bollocks he would. He'd have an uprising on his hands before you could say "Caligula's mad".'

'He seems to have one on his hands already,' Magnus commented, 'which appears to be getting worse, judging by the smoke coming from various parts of the city this morning.'

'Yes, the civil unrest is escalating,' Felix agreed. 'Now that the Greeks see the Jewish demands for equal status as a threat to their dominant position, they're taking matters into their own hands; but that may work in our favour by acting as a diversion.'

In the ten days that they had been waiting for the breastplate to be made, interracial violence in the city had been on the increase. The Jews had retaliated for the man murdered on the Canopic Way, but when Flaccus had merely had his murderers flogged, not crucified, the Greeks had felt emboldened to escalate their violence and began burning Jewish houses that were not in the Jewish Quarter and attacking any Jew who ventured into another part of the city. For their part the Jews had started sending out sorties and attacking, sometimes killing, anyone not of their race. Flaccus had brought in more troops in an effort to keep the Jews confined to their quarter, but it had not been successful; the legionaries had become targets for both factions.

'So all we've got to do now is swap them over,' Magnus said. 'Who's going to do that?'

'I will, I'll do it late tonight,' Vespasian replied, fitting the breastplate to his chest. 'It should be simple enough; I'll wear this under a cloak, then swap it with the original from the statue and wear that as I go back to my suite. No one would dare stop and ask me, on the way there and back, what I'm doing and the corridor is in an area of the palace not used at night.'

Felix approved. 'Good. My craftsman reckons that it will take him five days to do the inlays and change the edgings so, assuming that I can get it to him tomorrow, we should aim for the night of six days hence.'

'How much will he charge this time?'

'Double; plus the value of the gold for the inlays, which he calculates to be about ten aurii.'

Vespasian did some quick mental arithmetic and blanched. 'Six hundred and fifty denarii! That's robbery.'

'He's not stupid; he knows exactly what he's making and wants to be paid for his discretion in the matter.'

Vespasian could not argue; the craftsman was entitled to a premium for not asking questions, and besides, since withdrawing the money from Thales, he had plenty stored in a large chest on the ship waiting to take them home. He was just not very good at parting with it, he reflected. 'Very well, I'll pick up the cash on the way back to the palace.'

'Thank you. So, gentlemen, I have enough rope and a boat and I've worked out how to get onto the roof of the temple without the guards outside seeing; that just leaves us with one outstanding problem: the geese.'

'I thought that you knew how to solve that.'

'I do; the only way to stop them from raising the alarm is to keep them occupied and the only way to do that is to feed them; so, as I said, we need Ziri already inside the temple to scatter grain for them before we come down the rope. The question is where can he hide? I went back there yesterday and there's nowhere within the temple itself; so that just leaves the burial chamber. Now, there is a small gap between the two uprights supporting the slab that the sarcophagus rests upon that a small man like Ziri could fit into but...'

'How do we get him past the guard who's at the top of the steps during the day,' Vespasian said, seeing the problem.

'We need a diversion,' Magnus suggested.

Felix nodded. 'Yes, but what? The priests know us so they'll be suspicious if we go in there and start fighting or arguing or whatever.'

'I could fall down pretending to be ill.'

316

'You could, but what kind of guard would leave his post for long enough for Ziri to slip behind him for the likes of you?'

'He's right, Magnus,' Vespasian said with a grin, 'a battered ex-boxer like you isn't going to elicit a great deal of concern no matter how much you writhe and wail; a beautiful woman on the other hand?'

'A diversion? You think of me as a mere diversion?'

'No, Flavia, I want you to be a diversion.'

'For you?'

'No, for somebody else.'

'You want me to whore myself to somebody else?'

Vespasian closed his eyes and took a deep breath; the conversation had not got off to the best of starts. 'Listen to me, will you? We...I need you to distract a guard for long enough to get Ziri past him.'

'What guard?'

'A guard in the Temple of Alexander.'

'Why?'

'So that he can get down to the burial chamber.'

Flavia looked at him suspiciously and sat up in the bed; sunlight filtering through the half-closed shutters dappled her fair skin and glistened on her ruffled, loose hair. 'What are you planning?'

Vespasian realised that he would have to be totally honest with her to stand any chance of getting her co-operation.

'Caligula wants you to act as his thief?' Flavia said once he had explained the situation. 'He really is mad.'

'Yes, but unfortunately he's also the Emperor.'

'And if you don't steal this thing for him?'

'He'll never forgive me; or worse.'

'Why don't you just take him the replica that you're having made?'

'I've thought about that but Caligula saw the real one close up when he visited Alexandria with his father; I daren't take the risk that there's a mark on it or something that we haven't seen and he can remember.'

'If there is then the priests will discover the fake.'

Vespasian shrugged. 'That's a risk I have to take; anyway we'll be back in Rome by then.'

'We?'

'If you want to come back with me, then yes, we.'

Flavia looked down at him and smiled. 'Does that mean that you want me to be your mistress or your wife?'

Vespasian swallowed, realising that for the second time in the conversation honesty would be best. 'I already have a mistress in Rome whom I will never give up.'

Flavia looked at him warily. 'Then what do you want from me?'

'I want sons, so I was thinking more of the second option.'

'And what if you get your mistress pregnant? Divorce me and marry her?'

'I could never do that, she's a freedwoman.'

'So she's no threat to my position, then?'

'No, Flavia.'

'What I want from you is security.'

'You will always be my wife and the mother of my children.'

Flavia fell on him and kissed him passionately. 'In that case I'd be happy to, Vespasian,' she said between kisses. 'I've been so worried recently.'

'About me leaving you here?'

'No; about me always being a mistress and never having the children that I pray for every day to Mother Isis.'

Vespasian's footsteps echoed in the grand stairwell as he made his way down from his suite to the ground floor of the Royal Palace. He had made no attempt to conceal his progress through the well-lit corridors of the upper storey; any slaves whom he had met in passing he had ignored as they bowed their respects to him. He paid no heed to the two legionaries on guard at the foot of the stairs who snapped to attention as he passed, choosing instead to act as if he had every right to be walking around the palace in the dead of night, which, indeed, he did. Acting with the confidence expected of his rank in society, he had reasoned, would be the best way to avoid any suspicion.

Turning left past the guards he walked down a wide corridor punctuated on either side by niches in which were housed the busts of previous prefects, set upon pedestals; the flickering glow of torches played on the features of the carved stone faces and reflected off the polished marble floor. Drifting in with the moonlight through a window at the far end of the corridor, over-looking the Royal Harbour below, came the shouts and cries of many voices and the unmistakeable rasping of oars being shipped as if a large vessel were in the process of docking. Turning right at the window, Vespasian glanced down to the palace's private port in the eastern corner of the Great Harbour, and glimpsed a trireme in the pale light being made fast to the quay as a small group of people waited at the top of the gang-plank to disembark. He briefly wondered why a ship should arrive in port in the middle of the night, and then realised that that was the advantage of the Pharos: its light could guide a ship into harbour at any time.

After a couple more turns, and meeting no one else, he arrived at the unlit corridor where the statues of the Ptolemys stood like a long line of silent sentinels, still and strangely forbidding in the gloom. Putting all ghostly thoughts to the back of his mind, he quickly pulled back Ptolemy Soter's heavy cloak and started working on unbuckling the breastplate, which proved to be a fiddly task owing to the lack of light and the stiffness of the buckles and leather straps. After an agonising few moments, while his heartbeat gradually quickened, the stiff leather straps finally came through the buckles and the plate was free; Vespasian placed it on the ground and removed the replica from under his cloak and began to attach it to the statue. As he secured the last strap a flicker of orange light glinted in the corner of his eye; he turned and, looking back up the corridor, saw a torch appear at the far end accompanied by the sharp sound of hard-ened leather soles striking marble. In the dim light he could make out three people, two men and a woman, walking directly towards him. He quickly slipped the statue's cloak around him, picked up the cuirass and stood pressing his body hard up against the stone Pharaoh and prayed that the approaching party would not notice in the dark that Ptolemy Soter had sprouted an extra pair of legs and a hunched back.

'I don't care how long the prefect has been in bed for,' a voice that Vespasian recognised but could not place said imperiously, 'you will tell him that I have just arrived from Rome and wish to convey to him, immediately, a message from our beloved Emperor.'

'I will knock on his door, master,' a servile, tremulous voice replied.

'You will do more than knock, you will get him up! I shall be waiting in the triclinium where I expect to be served wine and food for my wife and me while we await Flaccus. Now go and leave me your torch.'

As he heard the sound of a man scurrying back up the corridor, Vespasian put a name to the person walking, now not more than three paces away, past his hiding place: Herod Agrippa.

Once Herod and his wife had turned into the triclinum at the far end of the corridor, Vespasian peered cautiously from under the cloak; satisfied that no one else was coming towards him, he quickly left his hiding place and, holding the breastplate to his chest, began to retrace his steps.

The legionaries at the bottom of the staircase snapped to attention again as he passed; he mounted the stairs as quickly as decorum would allow and hurried towards his suite.

'What are you doing up, senator?' a voice called out as he approached his door.

Vespasian turned to see a bleary-eyed Flaccus peering down the corridor at him.

'I heard a ship docking and was curious as to who would be arriving at this time of night,' Vespasian lied, holding the breast-plate secure with an arm across his stomach.

Flaccus looked unconvinced. 'You could have just looked down from your veranda.'

'It doesn't overlook the Royal Harbour,' Vespasian replied, this time truthfully, 'so I went to find a window that did.'

'Was your curiosity satisfied?'

'Yes, I saw that it was Herod Agrippa so I came back to bed.'

'Back to the lovely Flavia, eh? Well, she'll just have to wait a while longer for your attentions. Herod wants to see me and, seeing as you're up, you can come along as a witness because I don't trust that oily oriental.'

'I've got no intention of staying here a day longer than I have to,' Herod declared, taking a sip of wine. 'I intend to pay my respects to the Alabarch tomorrow to return the money that he lent me, then make a couple of business arrangements before leaving the following day.'

'That may be your intention, Herod,' Flaccus replied, holding up the scroll with the imperial seal that Herod had just presented him with, 'but you can't just give me the Emperor's mandate confirming my position as prefect in private. It has to be done properly in front of the city council, the Jewish council of elders and delegations from the city councils of Memphis, Sais and Pelusium, as well as those smaller ones nearby, in order that everyone can see that I rule here with the Emperor's authority.'

'Then organise that for tomorrow.'

'Memphis is two days' travel by fast ship, so the earliest we can do it will be in five days' time.'

'I'll have left by then,' Herod said flatly.

'No, Herod, you'll still be here.'

Herod looked at Flaccus with an amused smile on his face; he turned to his wife, sitting next to him. 'The prefect seems to be getting above himself, Cypros, my dear.'

Vespasian had been watching the conversation seated next to Flaccus but had taken no part in it. Herod had been courteous to him in his greetings and Vespasian had felt much relieved when they grasped forearms by the fact that he had been able to slip into his room and discard the breastplate before descending with Flaccus.

Cypros raised her thin black eyebrows; jewellery dripped off her ears, neck and fingers. 'You are aware that the Emperor has made my husband a king, prefect?'

'Lady, I am a Roman, whether your husband is a king or not is neither here nor there to me; he will leave this province only when I give him permission to do so.'

Herod stood and helped his wife up. 'This has been a most interesting conversation, prefect, but you have failed to convince me. My wife is tired so we shall retire to bed. I assume that we can use the same suite that we had last time we were here.'

'I'm afraid that Senator Vespasian is occupying that.'

Herod looked at Vespasian, frowning. 'Your family makes a habit of inconveniencing me, does it not?' He turned and walked briskly out of the room.

'Arrogant shit!' Flaccus said once the footsteps had faded down the corridor.

'If you want a hold over him, I think that I know where to look,' Vespasian said.

'What do you mean?'

'I think that I can guess what the business arrangements are that he wants to make while he's here.'

'Go on then.'

'There is a price, naturally, for such information.'

'You are not having Alexander's breastplate.'

'I wasn't thinking of that. I want you to arrest the preacher, Paulus.'

'What, the bow-legged little preacher with half an ear missing? Why do you want me to do that?'

'I want you to try him for sedition and preferably execute him.'

Flaccus smiled archly. 'You mean the Alabarch wants me to do that. I warned you not to let him get you involved with his Jewish politics.'

'Paulus is a dangerous fanatic; I came across him in Cyrenaica when he was persecuting the cult that he has now supplanted. If he is preaching it with the same fervour as he tried to destroy the other one, then you may well have a big problem on your hands soon; he causes nothing but discord.'

'You're saying that the Alabarch's interests and mine are the same in this matter?'

'Yes, I believe they are.'

Flaccus thought for a moment. 'Very well then, I shall give the order tomorrow.'

'Thank you, prefect.'

'So, what is this hold that I could have over Herod Agrippa?'

'Grain. I would guess that the arrangements that he wishes to make are to get his illegal stockpile of grain shipped to his kingdom to buy the favour of his new subjects.'

'How do you know about this?'

'The Lady Antonia.'

Flaccus nodded. 'She knew about most things. Where is this grain?'

'I don't know exactly; somewhere in this province.'

'That's not very helpful. If I can't find it how can I impound it?'

'I'm sorry, that's all I know.'

'Who did he buy it off?'

'Claudius.'

'Did he, now? In that case I know someone who will be very helpful in finding it: Claudius' agent in Egypt, Thales.'

The morning had been very long and wearisome in the packed exercise arena at the heart of the Gymnasium complex. Every delegation had made an interminable speech of loyalty to the Emperor before going on to praise Flaccus for his just rule in the Emperor's name. Each delegation in turn tried to outdo the others with superlatives and rhetorical flourishes while studiously ignoring the cries of rioters and the hobnailed clatter of legionaries chasing miscreants through the streets of a city that teetered on the brink of anarchy. Even as they filled their lungs with air to spout their fawning tributes they could smell the acrid tang of smoke from the many burned-out Jewish homes and businesses.

Vespasian sat on the dais, facing the three-thousand-strong crowd, on Flaccus' right, as befitted his rank; Herod Agrippa sat stony-faced on Flaccus' left, still smarting from the humiliation of being forced, by someone he considered to be beneath him, to stay for the ceremony against his will.

Once Thales had been informed by Flaccus that his mandate from the Emperor had arrived and that he was likely to be the prefect of Egypt for at least another two years, the banker had become very accommodating and had provided the where-abouts of Herod's illegal grain stockpile without the least coercion. He had even, of his own free will, given Flaccus his copies of the bills of sale and certificates of ownership and offered him a large interest-free loan, which, after much insis-tence on Thales' part, the prefect had reluctantly but gratefully accepted. Thales had left the palace with a solemn undertaking that should anyone ever try to purchase grain illegally through him again, Flaccus would be the first to know about it; Flaccus had thanked him sincerely and had promised to consider repaying a small part of the loan each time Thales came to him with that sort of information. They had parted understanding one another perfectly.

Flaccus had then managed to reach an equally perfect under-standing with Herod: if he stayed for the ceremony, he could leave for his kingdom straight afterwards and, if he played his part well, could even take half of his grain with him; the other half he would naturally donate to Rome in grateful thanks for his new crown.

It was through gritted teeth, therefore, that Herod had deliv-ered his speech at the opening of the ceremony earlier that morning; firstly reading out Caligula's mandate confirming Flaccus' position and then following that with fulsome praise for the sagacity of the Emperor in making that decision. His tribute to Flaccus had not been as effusive as the delegations that followed him, but it was nevertheless adequate, in Vespasian's opinion, for him to keep one half of his grain. The part where he had expressed his sorrow at having to leave for his kingdom after such a short stay with his good friend Flaccus had forced Vespasian to suppress a violent giggling fit.

Eventually the delegations from the surrounding cities and towns had all finished extolling the virtues of the man who had the power of life and death over them and it was the turn of the representatives of the turbulent city of Alexandria to speak. It fell to the Jews to speak first, leaving to the more numerous Greeks the honour of speaking just before the prefect gave his reply.

Alexander the Alabarch stood up from the midst of a group of old men who were sweating profusely in the ever strengthening sun, dressed in their mantles and long robes.

'We the Jews of Alexandria,' he declaimed in Greek, 'also applaud our beloved Emperor for his wisdom in confirming our noble prefect in his position. We count ourselves fortunate that the Emperor Gaius has set such a man as Aulus Avilius Flaccus to rule over us as we know that we can count on his even-handedness in dealing with the great injustices that are at the moment being dealt to our people by the non-Jewish part of the population of this city.'

Flaccus' composure stiffened and there was a general stirring among the city delegations and the Alexandrian Greek mob in the audience behind them; this was not the sort of thing that custom and good manners decreed should form a part of a congratulatory speech.

'Although the ravages against Jewish property still continue and the murder and rapine of our people escalate daily, we have no doubt that the prefect will bring to justice those responsible and order compensation to the victims. We are also confident that he will give his word on this to King Herod Agrippa, the personal friend of the Emperor and the most exalted of Jews in the Empire.'

Indignant mutterings from the Greek mob began to escalate; Herod shifted uncomfortably in his chair, evidently unwilling to become involved in his co-religionists' struggle in this province.

'We must also thank Prefect Flaccus for his endeavour to track down and arrest the blasphemous preacher, Gaius Julius Paulus, in order to put an end to his disgusting heresy. Although he has so far been unsuccessful in finding Paulus, we feel sure that the prefect will redouble his efforts and very soon apprehend this divisive and dangerous man.'

This brought incensed cries of outrage from the audience; it was unthinkable that anyone should mention publicly that the prefect was unsuccessful in anything. Flaccus, however, remained seated with a faint smile on his face, looking outwardly relaxed, swathed in his toga, leaning with his right elbow on the arm of the chair and resting the other hand on the knee of his left leg extended before him; it would be beneath his dignitas to shout down the Alabarch.

There was a stirring at the entrance to the arena closest to Vespasian as Alexander continued. 'We would therefore promise to pledge our allegiance to him and will undertake to make sacrifices on his behalf to God once he has done these things.'

This was the final insult for the Greeks; Alexander had refused to recognise Flaccus' authority until he had met their demands, which would entail, among other things, that the Greeks would be liable to pay for the damage that they had caused.

Alexander's next words were drowned out by howls of protest that gradually turned into raucous laughter as the mob became aware of a strange procession making its way into the arena from the entrance nearest to Vespasian close to where Flavia and the other Roman women were seated. A filthy, toothless beggar was being carried, shoulder high, through the crowd wearing a purple cloak. On his head he wore a parody of a crown made of iron scraps attached to a leather headband and in his hand, in mimicry of a sceptre, he held a sponge fastened to the end of a stick, as used for personal hygiene in public latrines. The beggar cackled as his bodyguard of equally insalubrious vagrants pushed a path through the crowd crying, 'Make way for the King, so recently a beggar!'

'Hail the King!' the crowd roared repeatedly through their mirth.

Vespasian glanced over at Herod whose eyes bulged in outrage as his jaw locked solid in recognition that this farce was directed at him, the king who until only recently had been as penniless as a beggar as he languished in gaol. The destitute wretch being paraded around for Herod's humiliation had been plucked from the street and given royal attire and honours much as Caligula had plucked Herod from his confinement and made him a king almost overnight.

Herod got to his feet and, with as much dignity as he could summon, swept from the arena followed by the Alabarch and the Jewish elders to the mocking jeers of the Greek mob.

'I see what you mean, Vespasian,' Flaccus observed with a faint smile, indicating with his head to the entrance through which the travesty had come, 'he does sow discord very well.'

Vespasian looked round and saw, in the shadows of the archway, a short figure with half an ear missing, smiling maliciously; for a moment they locked gazes before Paulus turned and walked away on his bow legs.

CHAPTER XX

'I DON'T UNDERSTAND why Flaccus ain't doing a fucking thing about it,' Magnus announced, looking with disgust at the bodies of two Jewish women who had evidently been savagely raped before having their throats slit. A dead infant had been placed under the head of one corpse in mocking imitation of a pillow.

'Because at the moment the Greeks are doing his work for him by keeping the Jews confined to their quarter,' Vespasian replied, studiously ignoring the bodies and giving Flavia, travelling in another chair next to him, a concerned look; she had gone very pale despite Ziri's efforts with a large fan to keep her cool. She should not have too much trouble fainting in Alexander's temple, he reflected with morbid irony, especially if they should come across more corpses on the way there.

News of Herod's humiliation at the ceremony and his swift departure from Alexandria the previous day – forfeiting the other half of his grain – had spread through the city, and the Jews, taking this insult to be against everyone of their race, had rioted en masse and invaded the Greek Quarter. The Greeks had responded by driving their hated and outnumbered co-inhabitants back into their quarter and blockading it, thus confining the violence. They had, however, not been content with just bottling up the Jews and had pressed on into the quarter, pushing the Jews further and further back until almost their entire population was cramped into just a few streets along the coastal area to the east of the Royal Palace. And they were the lucky ones; those who had had the misfortune to be captured had been flayed, crucified and then burned alive on their crosses.

From the palace windows that morning, Vespasian had seen tens of thousands of women and children huddled on the beach, taking refuge, while their menfolk fought with whatever improvised weapons they had to hand to keep control of the areas that they still possessed; the rest of the quarter burned with such intensity that the fumes were strong even two miles away as he approached the Temple of Alexander. Although the violence was confined to the Jewish Quarter, Hortensius had requested, and been given, another sixteen men for his guard after Vespasian – having heard from Felix that the replica breastplate was ready – had disregarded all advice and insisted on venturing out on the pretext of showing Flavia Alexander's body.

'I still don't understand it,' Magnus said as a group of Greeks ran past them in the direction of the riot, yelling excitedly and taking a wide berth around Hortensius and his legionaries marching ahead of the chairs. 'If the riot's been confined, why allow the killing to go on?'

'Because the worse it gets the more grateful the Jews will be to Flaccus when he eventually stops it and they'll have to acquiesce to all his terms,' Flavia said weakly.

'Surely they'll just be very pissed off that he didn't act sooner?'

'They may well be,' Vespasian agreed, 'but Flaccus will just tell them that next time he might not act at all so they should shut up, stop making demands, be thankful that most of them are still alive and go back to how things were before. It's almost as if he engineered it.'

'Oh, but he did, I'm sure of it,' Flavia informed them.

'You mean he didn't prevent it rather than engineer it?'

'No, he caused it, I'm certain.'

'What makes you so sure?'

'I saw who organised the charade in the arena and I recognised him from the riots in Cyrenaica, he's a trouble-maker.'

'Paulus? I know, but that doesn't mean that Flaccus was using him; in fact, I had his word that he would try and arrest him.'

'And you believed him?'

'Why not? It was in return for some useful information about Herod and it was also in his interest to do so.'

'Then ask yourself this: if he had meant to arrest Paulus, then why didn't he do it yesterday in the Gymnasium? You saw him, I saw him, Flaccus saw him and yet he sent no one after him; Paulus didn't even run away, he walked.'

The realisation hit Vespasian like a sling-shot: she was right. 'Flaccus sat through Alexander's speech with a smile on his face because he knew what was coming next; he'd set it up. He knew what the result would be: the Jews would be provoked into a full-scale riot. So he's not going to stop the violence until the Jews almost beg him to, and then he can get them to agree to anything; just as he'd planned. And I gave him the means by telling him just how divisive Paulus was.'

Flavia raised her eyebrows. 'I wouldn't blame yourself, my dear, Flaccus already knew. You see, that wasn't the first time I'd seen Paulus in Alexandria. He was at the palace the evening I met you again; I saw him leave as I arrived.'

Recollecting that Flaccus had hurried off to a meeting after his first interview with him, Vespasian groaned. 'He's been using Paulus all along as another way to stir up discontent among the Jews; he never had any intention of arresting him. He's managed to get himself everything he wanted: an official ceremony where the people of the province witness the Emperor's emissary, Herod, hand over his mandate, at which he's so completely humiliated that he leaves without his grain – which Flaccus will now, no doubt, claim as his own – and leaving the Jews so incensed by the insult that they riot, stupidly putting themselves in a position that only Flaccus can rescue them from on condition that they agree to his terms.'

'He is a clever man,' Magnus commented appreciatively as they arrived at the Soma, 'but I reckon that you shouldn't dwell on it, sir; let's just do what we came here to do and get the fuck out of it and leave this shithole to rot.'

Vespasian sighed as Hortensius brought their bodyguard to a halt at the Soma's gates, resigning himself to the fact that any attempt at redressing the humiliation that he felt at being so played by Flaccus would have to wait for another time, and besides, he had the consolation of taking Flavia from him. He took her hand to help her down from her chair. 'Are you happy about the timing, my dear?'

'Perfectly, Vespasian.'

'Good. Hortensius, wait for us here, we won't be long; the lady wishes to see the great Alexander.'

The sun had now almost reached the horizon and Alexander's Temple was filled with a rich amber light giving it a feeling of restful peace, a far cry from the violence being meted out just a couple of miles away. Vespasian and Magnus watched from beneath the great equestrian statue as the priest led Flavia past the guard and down the steps to the burial chamber; Ziri waited close to its entrance as was expected of a slave attending his mistress. Vespasian had declined the priest's offer of a second visit to the chamber on the plausible grounds that Augustus had only visited it once, but in reality because it was vital that Flavia should appear at the top of the steps alone for the few moments that it took the priest to complete his cleansing ritual.

As Flavia's head disappeared below the floor level Vespasian turned to Magnus. 'You go and stand directly opposite the top of the steps. When Flavia comes back up she'll turn and walk towards me; as soon as you see the priest coming up, rub your nose and I'll give her the signal to faint.'

'Right you are, sir; let's hope that Ziri doesn't eat all the bread meant for the geese while he's waiting down there,' Magnus said with a wry smile and then walked around the temple to take up his position.

Vespasian glanced over at Ziri who nodded back and tapped the satchel slung over his shoulder. Satisfied that the little Marmarides was ready, Vespasian studied the full-bearded guard. He was dressed in the uniform of an *argyraspides*, the elite, veteran phalangites who had formed the backbone of Alexander's infantry: a crested, bronze Thracian-style helmet, a brown, hardened-leather cuirass over a plain white chiton, bronze greaves and a small, round, silver-plated shield – from which the unit took its name – emblazoned with the sixteen-pointed star of Macedon inlaid in bronze. He was armed with a short stabbing sword slung on a baldric over his right shoulder to hang on his left and, held upright, the fearsome sixteen-foot pike that, wielded two-handed, had swept away all armies before it, until it had come up against the Roman pilum. He and his four colleagues, two guarding the temple door and two at the Soma gate, were the only soldiers still allowed by Rome to wear the uniform in deference to Alexander. Vespasian prayed to Mars Victorious that this ceremonial guard would not show the same rigid discipline that had enabled his forebears to conquer the largest Empire ever seen and would leave his post to help a stricken lady.

After what seemed like an eternity, but was probably in reality less than half the time that Vespasian had spent in the burial chamber a few days earlier, Flavia reappeared. As she reached the top of the steps she paused next to the guard, and swayed slightly on her feet; giving out a little moan as if over-awed by what she had just seen, she put her hand on the guard's heavily muscled forearm to steady herself. He looked down at her, concerned. Vespasian smiled inwardly: she knew how to handle men, the touch had created a small bond between them. She smiled apologetically at the guard, patted his arm, turned towards Vespasian and began to walk slowly and unsteadily towards him. Vespasian kept his eyes on Magnus. After Flavia had gone four paces Magnus' hand came up to his nose. Vespasian looked at Flavia and nodded; with a weak cry she crumpled to the floor. The guard spun round and immediately dropped his pike with a clatter and leapt to aid the woman who had touched him so gently as the priest appeared at the top of the steps; he looked to see the cause of the commotion and hurried to help his erstwhile charge.

'Flavia!' Vespasian cried, running forward as the guard knelt down to lift her head from the cold marble floor.

'What happened?' the priest asked, looking anxiously over the guard's shoulder.

'I don't know,' Vespasian replied, concern written all over his face. He looked up to see Magnus approaching; Ziri had disappeared. 'Magnus, send Ziri to get the chairs ready.'

'He's already gone, sir.'

'Good, help me lift her.'

'It's all right,' Flavia whispered, fluttering open her eyes, 'I'll be fine in a moment, I was just a bit overcome, that's all.' She eased herself up with the guard's supportive arm around her shoulders.

'I've seen this happen before,' the priest said solemnly, 'people get overawed just looking down through the tunnel at Alexander's face.'

'Being so close to him in the chamber was completely overwhelming, especially for a woman,' Flavia said sweetly, 'I would advise you not to let women down there into the presence of such a powerful man.'

The priest nodded sagely. 'You might be right, lady; I shall form a committee of priests to review our policy on allowing women so close.'

'You are most kind,' Flavia said with sincerity, getting to her feet with the guard's help. 'I feel much better now; Alexander's latent vigour has washed right through me. Vespasian, shall we go? I have an urgent need to feel a man's arms around me.'

'We shall, Flavia,' Vespasian replied, hoping that would be the limit to her melodrama.

Flavia took his arm and looked at the guard with doe-eyes. 'Thank you, my strong Guard of Alexander.'

The man's mouth broke into a wide grin beneath his bush of a beard; Vespasian tugged Flavia forward with a fixed smile on his face. 'Come, my dear.'

'I shall pray to Alexander for your wellbeing,' the priest called after them as they passed through the doors.

Felix was waiting for them at the bottom of the steps eyeing the small enclosure filled with geese next to the temple; he had an empty sack over his shoulder. 'Is he in?' he asked once they were out of earshot of the exterior guards.

'Yes,' Vespasian replied. 'It was well done, if somewhat theatrical towards the end. We'll see you later, Felix.'

'Good. I'll be in the boat below your terrace at the fifth hour of the night; the breastplate will be with me. I shall now procure the final two items that we need.'

'That, my dear, was not theatre,' Flavia informed him as Felix disappeared off into the fading light towards the geese enclosure. 'That was done so that when those two men review the incident in their minds they will only see me. They won't notice the fact that Ziri could never have been given orders by Magnus and then got out of the doors from where he was standing in the time between me fainting and Magnus saying that he'd gone, after you had so foolishly drawn attention to his absence.'

'They would never notice that.'

'They certainly won't now, because I've made sure of it.'

Vespasian was not going to argue; she had shown spirit and they could not have achieved that part of the break-in without her. 'And I'm sure that they will treasure the memory. Now, my dear, when we get back you should get your maids to finish packing and get them on board the ship as, with luck, we will be sailing at first light.'

'I've already done that; I'm so excited about coming back to Rome with you.'

Vespasian looked at her and smiled. 'I'm looking forward to it too, my dear.'

The night sky was aglow with flames as they approached the palace complex; the cries and screams of conflict could be heard rising from the Jewish Quarter beyond.

'It seems to be getting worse,' Hortensius called back as a gang of Greeks dragged a screaming Jew towards them. 'I think that you should get out of the chairs and walk now, senator.'

'Very well,' Vespasian agreed, signalling his and Flavia's bearers to stop.

'Why must we walk?' Flavia asked Magnus as he helped her down.

'Because it will be easier to defend you if we're attacked. We can't have you getting hurt, can we?' His estimation of her had greatly increased after her performance earlier that evening.

As they pressed on for the last few hundred paces to the palace, passing anarchic groups running to and from the fighting, Vespasian was unsurprised to see the streets bare of legionaries; Flaccus was evidently playing brinkmanship with the lives of the Jews and he was determined to win and bring them to heel.

Finally approaching the gates the street became quieter, the mob being wary of the heavy guard of legionaries in full battle order posted outside.

Hortensius saluted their centurion. 'Optio Hortensius escorting Senator Titus Flavius Vespasianus.'

'Ah, senator,' the centurion said, 'there's a man here been waiting to see you this last half-hour, says his name is Nathanial – he swam along the coast from the Jewish Quarter.' He pulled a bruised and bleeding man forward. 'We didn't believe that he knew you at first,' he added by way of explanation for the man's looks.

'Senator, you must help,' the man said, stepping forward into the torchlight.

Vespasian peered at him and recognised the man whose brother had been murdered on the Canopic Way a few days before. 'What do you want, Nathanial?'

'You said that you would bring my brother's killers to justice because you owed a favour to the Alabarch. As you know, they were spared so you still need to repay that favour.'

'What of it?'

'The Alabarch and his sons are besieged in a temple not far from here; they have a few men with them but they can't last much longer. That preacher has allied his followers with the Greeks. The Alabarch sent me here, just before the building was completely surrounded, to ask for your help; will you come?'

Magnus raised his eyebrows and looked at Vespasian. 'Well?'

'Well, I owe him and I'd hate the thought of Paulus making his sport with him and his sons; we'll go. And besides, we may get the chance to finish off that odious little fanatic.'

'If we're going, you ain't going like that; a toga never kept Caesar alive in Pompey's Theatre.'

'You're right, we should get properly armed. Hortensius, wait here with this man and have your men sharpen their blades, we won't be long.'

Hortensius snapped a salute.

'You can't take legionaries into the Jewish Quarter, senator,' the centurion protested.

'Why not?'

'Because it would be going against orders; the prefect has forbidden it.'

'I'm sure he has, but has he forbidden senators from going in?'

The centurion looked nonplussed.

'I'm going, centurion, and if Hortensius and his men don't come with me then he will be breaking the prefect's direct order to him to accompany me everywhere I go in Alexandria.'

The sound of fighting grew nearer as Vespasian, now shielded and wearing his bronze cuirass, led Hortensius and his men at a quick jog through wafting smoke into the Jewish Quarter with Magnus and Nathanial at his side. Heat from the fires all around had already caused him to break out into a sweat and his scalp prickled beneath the felt liner under his plain legionary helmet. Marcus Antonius' sword slapped against his right thigh and tension flooded through his body as he contemplated using it in anger for the first time in the city where it had taken the life of its first master.

The presence of a unit of armed legionaries probing into what had hitherto been an authority-free zone caused the groups of pillaging Greeks in their path to drop the larger items of their spoils, looted from houses before they were torched, and run for the safety of side alleys. The occasional rock hurled at the soldiers as they passed clattered harmlessly off their shields but told of hostile intent.

'Two more blocks and then we turn left towards the sea,' Nathanial informed Vespasian through gritted teeth as he struggled for breath in the fume-filled air. 'The temple is at the end of that street.'

Mutilated corpses, body parts and debris were strewn around in an abundance that made the riot in Cyrene seem like a mere misunderstanding between neighbours: easily patched up and soon forgotten about.

'I don't know about you, sir, but I'm starting to think that just four *contuburnia* ain't really enough to take on the entire Greek population,' Magnus observed as another rock crashed into his shield. 'I'd like to hear a lot more hobnailed boots tramping behind me.'

'It's pointless worrying about it because it's all we have,' Vespasian replied testily. 'We just have to hope that Rome's authority will prevail and we can order their release.'

Magnus scoffed but said nothing.

They quickly reached the end of the second block and turned left into a wide avenue; Vespasian faltered. The street was littered with corpses, some smouldering, illuminated by fires in the houses on either side; the smell of burned flesh hung heavy in the air, which was filled with rasping wails of agony emanating from within the mass of a huge mob fifty paces ahead. Beyond them Vespasian could see a Jewish temple being consumed by fire.

Nathanial groaned. 'We're too late, they're flaying the prisoners alive.'

Vespasian brought his small unit to a halt. 'Hortensius, have the men form a solid square, facing out on each side.'

'We're not going to charge into that lot, are we?' Magnus asked disbelievingly, taking his place on Vespasian's right shoulder as the legionaries quickly formed up.

'Not if they know what's good for them. Draw gladii; advance at the walk!'

With some men walking backwards and some sideways like crabs, the small square eased forward keeping shields tight together, the razor-sharp blades of their swords protruding between them flashing orange in the fire's glow.

The screaming from within the mob kept up but gradually awareness of the Romans' presence filtered through, and by the time the square was twenty paces from them hundreds of faces were turned their way.

'Halt!' Vespasian ordered.

The square stopped with a stamp of hobnails on stone.

The clamour of the mob died down, leaving only the anguished cries of the tormented men within it.

'Who commands here?' Vespasian shouted.

There was a brief pause before a group of four men pushed their way forward.

'What do you want, Roman?' their leader asked, a tall muscular man with short black hair and a full beard; he held a club with a long nail punched through its thick end.

'I want to avoid having to kill any of you. What's your name?'

'Isodorus; but that is no secret, Flaccus already knows me.'

'And Flaccus has given you permission to kill and burn as you please?'

Isodorus smiled coldly. 'The prefect has made us no promises, but neither has he moved to stop us trying to rid this city of the canker within it that refuses to acknowledge great Caesar's divinity and yet wants equal status with us, his law-abiding subjects.'

'That is quite evident; but I am not Flaccus, nor am I under his authority. I was sent to this province by the Emperor and it's to the Emperor that I will report when I return to Rome. So you have two choices, Isodorus: come and kill me and see how many of your people we cut down with our swords before you over-come us with your sticks and eating-knives, or hand over the prisoners that you took from that temple before we come and get them.'

'You'd never make it.'

Vespasian hardened his eyes. 'Try me, Isodorus; we'll easily kill ten of your rabble for every legionary, that's over three hundred and you'll be the first.' He looked around the crowd. 'Which of you brave shopkeepers, tavern owners and thieves are willing to be one of the three hundred to die with Isodorus in order that you can keep your prisoners?' He pointed his sword at a fat, balding man with blood on his hands and tunic. 'You, perhaps?' The man slunk back into the crowd. 'What about you?' he shouted, pointing to the fat man's neighbour who also moved back. 'It seems like you have a problem, Isodorus, your brave townsfolk are keener to live than they are to hang onto your prisoners so that you can rip the skin off their bodies. Your decision, Isodorus; now!'

The Greek looked around at his ragtag mob of poorly armed townsfolk and, realising that they would not have the stomach to face the well-drilled blades of the legionaries, stepped aside.

'Very wise,' Vespasian sneered. 'Square! Forward at the walk.'

The legionaries moved on again at a slow deliberate pace so that those not walking forwards could keep formation, hunched behind their continuous wall of shields. The mob parted for them, pulling well back, out of reach of the blades bristling between every shield ready to kill or maim.

'I don't fancy our chances if they suddenly sprout a communal set of balls,' Magnus muttered as they neared the middle of the mob.

The cries of anguish from the prisoners within had subsided and there was an unnatural quiet broken only by the steady steps of the soldiers.

Suddenly a scene of disgusting carnage appeared before them: hanging naked from a sturdy wooden frame, suspended by the wrists so that their toes just reached the ground, were three men and a woman. Their heads slumped onto their chests, which heaved with the effort of breathing and the pain of their hideous wounds. They were in various stages of being flayed. The man nearest seemed to be the luckiest; just one strip of skin, a hand's breadth wide, had been stripped from his back to hang limply from his waist as if it were the end of a blood-soaked belt. The others had not been so fortunate; skin hung from their waists in abundance, flapping gently, like ghastly skirts, as their bodies writhed. In the middle of the frame staring with disbelieving eyes, first at the Romans and then back to the victims, was a group of male prisoners awaiting their turns under the knife; in their midst Vespasian saw Alexander squatting with his arm around his youngest son, Marcus.

'Surround this area!' Vespasian ordered.

The square dispersed as the legionaries formed a circle around the frame. The mob made no attempt to interfere and, in fact, shrank back from their erstwhile victims, looking on sullenly, as if the Romans' arrival had broken the spell of their hatred and they now felt shame at their actions.

'I did not think that Nathanial would get through,' Alexander said, urgently pointing to the least hurt man. 'Cut him down, quick.'

With one sweep of Vespasian's blade the man's bonds were cut and he slumped into Alexander's arms. 'Oh my son, my son,' Alexander wept, 'what have they done to you?' He sank to his knees, taking the man's head in his lap, and Vespasian saw that it was not a man but a youth: Tiberius, Alexander's eldest son; he was moaning quietly.

'He'll be all right, sir,' Magnus said, 'I've seen this before in Germania when we rescued some mates from the locals. Them that has just a bit torn off them, like him, will live.' He looked at the other two men and the woman, all mostly raw lumps of meat. 'The others, though, not a hope; we should finish them now and then get the fuck out of here.'

'Very well, but I will do it,' Alexander said. 'Marcus, help your brother.' He eased Tiberius' head into his brother's lap and stood. 'Give me your sword, Vespasian, my friend.'

'You must be quick,' Vespasian told him as he handed over the weapon.

Alexander nodded and approached the unconscious woman; the skin from her chest was missing and only one breast remained. He whispered into her unhearing ear before thrusting the blade through her yielding flesh up into her heart; a soft breath escaped her.

'Philo,' he said to an old grey-beard in his sixties, 'you and I will carry her.'

'We haven't got time to take the bodies with us,' Vespasian said.

Alexander glared at him. 'She was my wife, I will not leave her here; my brother and I will bear her.'

The two men were despatched with similar swiftness and their bodies taken up by the remaining prisoners.

'He was here, you know,' Alexander said as he returned the sword, 'it was him and his followers who urged the people into such cruelty.'

'Paulus? I know. But why? He's a Jew.'

'Not any more, he's not. He follows his own religion, remember, which hates us Jews.'

'Where is he?'

'He and his followers slipped away as you arrived.'

'Animals they were,' Philo spat, 'they whipped us with lashes like common Egyptian peasants from the fields; they didn't give us the dignity of the rod as befits our rank. The men wielding the lashes were the lowest class of Greek; it was a disgrace.'

Vespasian looked at him with a disbelieving frown and then turned to Hortensius. 'Optio, form a hollow square, two deep, facing forward; we march out of here like Romans, not scuttle out like this murderous rabble.'

Within moments the legionaries had formed up with Alexander and his compatriots in the middle. Nathanial helped Marcus with his brother who had now regained sufficient consciousness to realise that he was in great pain.

Vespasian gave the order to advance and they moved forward with swords drawn at a quick march.

'We'd better be getting a move on,' Magnus said as they turned right out of the avenue, 'Felix is going to be in position soon.'

'He'll have to wait,' Vespasian replied, 'I'll not be seen running away from an area that is theoretically under Roman law.'

Magnus shrugged and glanced over his shoulder. 'They don't seem to be following us, I suppose they've gone to find some other poor bastards to undress.'

'They may have, but some other bastard seems to have different ideas,' Vespasian muttered as, in the flickering flame-light, four hundred paces ahead, scores of shadowy figures started to pour out of side streets and form a deep line blocking the road. Judging by the flashes of reflections from their midst they were armed with more than clubs and knives.

'I'll venture that you could put a name to that particular bastard,' Magnus commented as he took in the threat.

Vespasian smiled grimly. 'I think I can, the odious, bow-legged little cunt.'

Fifty paces away from the opposing force, Vespasian brought the legionaries to a halt. Leaving the safety of the square he walked forward. 'In the name of the Emperor, let us through and none of you will be harmed,' he shouted so that all could hear.

'We acknowledge no one higher than God and his son our Lord Yeshua, our saviour, the Christus; in his name we demand that you hand over the leaders in this city of the race that put him to death,' a recognisable voice shouted back; Paulus stepped forward through a whiff of smoke.

'You are in no position to make demands, Paulus, get out of our way.'

The use of his name shocked the man and he peered forward.

'I'll remind you, Paulus: in Cyrene my knife should have slipped, it would have saved many lives.'

'You! Well, that is convenient; I shall have the pleasure of personal revenge as well as doing the Lord's work. Hand them over, Vespasian, or we'll come and get them; we'll surround your pitiful little band and tear you apart. Remember that this time you're not dealing with timid shopkeepers; these men are all armed and prepared to die doing God's work in the sure knowledge they will go straight to heaven because they have had their sins taken from them by Yeshua Christus.'

'I have no idea what you're ranting about, but if this heaven is a place where fanatics like you go then I want nothing to do with it.' Vespasian spun on his heel and yelled, 'Form a wedge!'

Vespasian took his place at the wedge's tip with Magnus behind his right shoulder and Hortensius on his left. The legionaries fanned out behind with the rescued Jews in their midst.

'He hasn't got any more pleasant since we last saw him, has he?' Magnus observed, testing his helmet strap. 'It'll be interesting to see if his men really will die for this god.'

'I've a nasty feeling that they'll all be vying to be the first,' Vespasian replied. Anger burned within him at the thought that Paulus had gulled his followers into thinking that they could throw away their lives and expect some sort of reward. Alexander had been right: it was a very dangerous and unworldly religion. 'Hortensius, are the men ready?'

'Yes, senator.'

'Advance!'

Vespasian led off the wedge at a jog heading directly for Paulus; he quickly retreated into the body of his followers, who shifted uneasily at the sight of a solid formation, now only twenty paces away, bearing down on them.

'He doesn't seem to be in too much of a hurry to get to his heaven,' Magnus puffed.

Vespasian's eyes narrowed behind his shield. He felt the perfect balance of the sword in his hand and desired one thing: to kill Paulus.

With ten paces to go Vespasian accelerated into a run; the legionaries behind him responded, keeping the formation solid. Paulus' followers stood, but not firmly, wavering as the V-shaped mass of shields and blades crashed towards them. With a sudden shriek a young man leapt forward and grabbed the top rim of Vespasian's shield with his left hand. Vespasian slammed the shield boss into his midriff and butted his helmet down onto the whitened knuckles, lacerating the skin and crunching the bones. A clinical jab from Hortensius sent the man down with a spurt of blood; but his example was enough and, as the wedge smashed into the faltering line, the sight of their comrade's blood galvanised Paulus' followers into reckless action. They hurled themselves with manic screeches and cries at the fast-moving wedge, cutting their swords haphazardly down onto shield rims and cracking their ribs on shield bosses punched towards them. The flanks of the line started to move round in an attempt to engulf the Romans.

Vespasian tore through the first and second ranks, holding his shield firm in front of him, the muscles in his left arm bulging with the effort. He worked his blade, as if it were an extension of his own arm, stabbing it forward into the soft belly of a middle-aged man, then, with a sharp twist, withdrawing it, bringing it back up in an arc of blood to parry, with a spray of sparks, a cut from his right while slamming his hobnails onto his victim's kneecap, shattering the joint. Breathing heavily he kicked the screaming man aside, as Magnus severed the arm of the assailant to his right, and pressed on into the third rank; behind him the ever broadening wedge forced their opponents back in an increasingly tightening scrum. Swords flashed from between the shields into this press of unprotected human flesh on both sides of the formation, slitting open bellies with a welter of slimy, grey offal and the noisome stench of internal gases and waste.

As the rearmost legionaries hit the disordered and shaken line with a communal, grunting exhalation of breath, Vespasian forced his arms forward then out and exploded through the third rank; his shield boss slammed into the ribs of a man to his left and his sword pommel cracked into the mouth of the last man between him and the palace. The man's front teeth splintered, his jaw dislocated and he crumpled back screaming, his face contorted with pain in the glow of a burning house; the back of his head struck the paved road and a violent shudder ran down through the length of his body; his cry ceased. With the mechanical reaction of years of drill a legionary forced his sword tip into the stricken man's throat as he straddled him.

They were through.

Vespasian slowed his pace to allow the men behind him to keep in contact as the thickest end of the wedge punched and cut its way through the tangle of bodies, some dead, some alive, with a desperate urgency to avoid being taken in the rear by the two flanks now swirling in towards them. Their task became easier as screams of the maimed and the broken took the fight out of Paulus' followers closest to the bloodshed and they began to back off, pushing into one another in their desire to keep their bodies whole. The line split and the wedge emerged intact, painted with blood. Vespasian carried on at a jog for another fifty paces before glancing over his shoulder. Seeing that they were not being followed, he brought them to a halt. The legionaries gasped for breath after the intense exertion in what had been less than a hundred or so heartbeats but had felt like ten times that amount.

'Hortensius, have the men form a column,' Vespasian ordered. He looked back to see a score or more of bodies littering the ground where the wedge had cut a swathe through the line; the cries of the wounded still rang out and the survivors stood looking forlornly at their stricken fellows. In among the carnage a diminutive bow-legged figure moved about, comforting the injured; he was completely unharmed.

Vespasian spat, then turned and ordered the column forward towards the palace complex just five hundred paces away.

At the gates to the Royal Harbour Vespasian halted the column and turned to Hortensius. 'Optio, have two contuburnia escort these Jews to my ship in the harbour; they should be safe enough there until morning.'

Hortensius looked unsure. 'But senator…'

'Just do it! I'll be responsible to the prefect.'

Hortensius ran back down the column.

A few moments later Alexander and his compatriots came past with their escort.

'I owe you my life, Vespasian,' the Alabarch said, 'and those of my sons and brother; I will never forget that.'

'I'm sorry that we came too late for your wife,' Vespasian replied, looking at the bloody corpse draped between Alexander and Philo. 'Go quickly now, these men will take you to my ship, I'll meet you there in the morning.'

'We need to bury our dead,' Philo insisted.

'No, you need to be safe and you need to get Tiberius' wound seen to.'

'But our law says—'

'Come, brother, forget about your precious law,' Alexander interrupted, 'if we follow that now then we'll have more bodies to bury. We'll see you in the morning, Vespasian.' He led the Jews off bearing their grisly burdens.

'We'd better get a move on, sir,' Magnus reminded Vespasian.

'Yes, you're right,' Vespasian sighed, feeling immensely fatigued. He led the remainder of the column through the gates and into the Royal Harbour; its quays were empty except for the occasional scuttling rat in the torchlight.

They had almost reached the far end when the gates to the palace swung open and Flaccus appeared in full uniform surrounded by the legate and tribunes of the XXII Deiotariana.

'Just what the fuck have you been up to, senator?' he bellowed, his face almost purple with rage.

'What you should have been doing yourself instead of conspiring with religious maniacs: saving the lives of decent people.'

'And how many Roman lives did that cost?'

'None; now get out of my way.' He pushed past the prefect, almost throwing him off-balance.

'You're confined to your suite, senator, until I decide what to do about you,' Flaccus shouted after him. 'All the guards will have orders not to let you out.'

'Shit!' Magnus spat. 'Where does that leave us trying to get to the ship in the morning?'

'We'll have to take our bags with us tonight and go straight from the mausoleum.'

'What about Flavia?'

'Flavia's in for a shock.'

CHAPTER XXI

'JUST ANOTHER TEN feet,' Vespasian called softly up to the struggling figure of Flavia suspended on the end of a rope. Forty feet above her Magnus could be seen in silhouette on the terrace slowly lowering her down. Vespasian checked his balance as he fought to remain upright while the boat bobbed on the mild swell of the Great Harbour; Felix laboured with a single oar to keep it in a fixed position hard up against the palace's sea wall.

After another few anxious moments Vespasian grabbed her ankles. 'Got you; now stop kicking or we'll all be in the sea.'

Flavia went limp as she was lowered the last few feet. 'That, Vespasian, was the most undignified way to leave the Palace of the Ptolemies,' she informed him as he undid the knot around her waist, 'and painful.'

'But necessary,' he reminded her, giving the freed rope a tug. 'Now sit down and stop complaining.'

Flavia shook her head with a wry smile and went to sit in the bow next to their large travel-sacks as Magnus, with his sack slung over his back, slithered, with surprising agility, down the rope.

He landed in the small boat and looked back up at the rope. 'That's going to be a giveaway when Flaccus finds it.'

'Flaccus won't think that we've done anything more than escape from his custody.'

'And he'll find that annoying enough,' Magnus mused, unslinging his sack and stowing it next to Vespasian's.

'Are we all set,' Felix asked, 'or are there any more surprises?'

Vespasian sat down by Flavia. 'No, Felix, once we've dropped Flavia off at the ship it'll be everything as planned.'

Felix snorted and pushed against the wall with his oar. As the boat came round he deftly hauled up the triangular sail and took his place at the steering-oar; with a light snap, the soft breeze filled the sail and drove the boat forward over the moon-dappled water.

Magnus tried not to touch Flavia's behind as he and Vespasian helped her up the ladder onto the stern of the ship but the task was impossible without doing so. 'Sorry, sir,' he muttered as he placed his right hand under her firm left buttock.

'Help yourself.' Vespasian grinned, his hand already wedged under the right cheek. With a co-ordinated shove they propelled Flavia, with a squeal, up the ladder and into the arms of the triarchus and Alexander. Her two maids came to her rescue, clucking in concern.

'Be ready to sail in a couple of hours,' Vespasian told the triarchus as he clambered aboard with his sack.

'It'll still be night then, senator; I won't be able to get the port aedile to stamp our exit warrant,' the triachus replied as Magnus appeared with the last two sacks.

'Exactly, so do it quietly.'

The triarchus shrugged and gave orders to wake the crew, who were sleeping, wrapped in blankets, on the deck.

'You will all have to come with us, Alexander,' Vespasian said as he helped Felix up; over his shoulder was a bulging leather bag and in his hand a small cage containing two geese.

'We can't desert our people. We must stay and get back to them.'

'That's your decision. We'll be back in a couple of hours; use that time to work out how you're going to do that with three dead bodies and a wounded man.'

'Where are you going?'

Vespasian smiled and, patting Alexander on the shoulder, moved off without a word.

Apart from the occasional sailor asleep in a drunken stupor where he had fallen, the docks were deserted. By the light of the quarter-moon, Vespasian, Magnus and Felix moved swiftly along the empty quays and climbed the steps up to the promenade, coming out next to the Caesareum. Vespasian paused as they passed one of the obelisks guarding the building; the crescent moon seemed to be balanced perfectly on its point as if it were a part of the monument. Wondering if it could be construed as an omen of any sort, he hurried after his companions as they flitted through the deep shadows of the colonnade surrounding the building.

'We should walk from here,' Felix said as they descended some steps onto a wide thoroughfare, 'we don't want to attract undue attention.'

Although most of the city's population had sensibly decided to stay behind locked doors after dark, there was no curfew being enforced and there were a few people abroad. They slowed down to a brisk walk, crossing the thoroughfare into another street heading south. The night sky to the east still glowed with the fires burning in the ransacked Jewish Quarter, but there was no sign of the violence spreading and they pressed on for another quarter of a mile unnoticed until they came to the gate of the Soma.

The two Macedonian guards stood with their pikes crossed barring the entrance.

'We've come to make an offering,' Felix explained, lifting the geese in their cage.

'It's a busy night for the priest,' one of the guards commented as they stepped aside. 'You come to put a curse on the Jews too?'

'Something like that,' Felix replied with a grin as they passed through the archway.

Swathed in the thin light of the crescent moon the courtyard felt even larger than it had by day; the fire on the altar at its centre, silhouetting a cluster of people gathered round making their offerings, seemed far off.

While still in the shadow of the wall, Felix nipped away to the right; Vespasian and Magnus followed. Keeping close to the wall they made their way north towards the Temple of Alexander, skirting around the mausoleums of various

Ptolemys. Without mishap they arrived in the shadow of the mausoleum closest to the temple, just thirty paces away; between the two buildings was open, moonlit ground. The two night-time guards could be just seen at the top of the steps in the gloom under the portico.

'Look around for some stones,' Felix whispered, setting down the goose cage, 'half a dozen should be fine.'

'What for?' Vespasian asked, feeling the ground and immediately finding a couple of small pebbles.

'To encourage the geese forward.' Felix took a goose out of the cage and handed it to Magnus before retrieving the other one, holding it firm under his arm. 'On the count of three, Magnus, hurl your goose as far as you can towards the temple and then when they land, Vespasian, throw your stones at them to move them forward.'

'Won't they fly off?' Vespasian asked, finding the last few stones that he needed.

'They've had their wings clipped; they can't fly more than a few paces. All right; one, two, three.'

Felix and Magnus hurled their geese towards the temple; the birds flapped their wings and flew as best they could, hissing in outrage, until they landed heavily just short of the steps. With a couple of well-aimed shots Vespasian got them waddling forward, honking loudly. From within the building the geese could be heard taking up their fellows' cries. The guards looked at each other and exchanged a few words before one handed the other his pike and started slowly to descend the steps. The geese eyed him suspiciously; as he got to within three paces of them they extended their necks, flapped their useless wings at him and hissed threateningly. He pounced and, much to his mate's amusement, began chasing one of the honking birds in a series of twists and curves until eventually capturing it as it tried but failed to mount the steps. Gathering the goose in both arms he jogged, laughing, back up to his mate, who pulled a key from a cord around his neck and turned to the door.

'Now!' Felix whispered.

As the two guards busied themselves with opening the door and shoving the goose inside, much to the honking consternation of its fellows already within, Felix led Vespasian and Magnus at a sprint across the open ground to the temple, getting around the side wall out of view of the guards as they closed the door.

'How did you know that they would try and catch the geese?' Vespasian asked as they made their way along to where the temple abutted the Soma's surrounding wall.

'I stole them from the geese enclosure this evening,' Felix replied, stopping by a wooden ladder attached to the wall. 'The guards would have known that they were two geese short so when they saw them they assumed, rightly as it happens, that they were the missing two. Up we go.'

At the top of the ladder they stepped over a low parapet onto the flat roof and crept towards the hole in the centre.

'This should be fine,' Felix said with relief, testing the solid iron hinges with which the hatch was attached to the roof. 'I didn't fancy having to hold the rope all by myself.' He rummaged in his bag and pulled out a coil of hemp rope with a lead weight tied to one end and began to knot the other around the hinge. 'Now we wait.'

'What for?' Vespasian asked, looking down through the hole. As he did a pale light faintly illuminated the chamber and he could make out the shapes of geese waddling around the floor; a cacophony of honking erupted as the second goose was thrown into their midst. The light went out; the door had closed.

'That.' Felix began to let down the rope.

Far below, the dim glow of the sconces in the burial chamber showed the position of the viewing passage; after a couple of nervous attempts Felix managed to get the lead weight into its entrance and continued feeding out the rope, swinging it slightly so that the weight clattered lightly against the stone sides of the passage.

'That's to alert Ziri that it's on its way down,' Felix explained. 'We don't want it cracking the crystal, do we?'

A few moments later he felt a couple of tugs on the rope. 'Good, he knows we're here.'

Vespasian peered down into the gloom and eventually was able to make out a shadowy figure at the top of the steps leading to the burial chamber, seemingly waving its arms around; there was a slight increase in the honking and the patter of many feet.

'Down you go, gentlemen,' Felix said, giving Magnus his leather bag. 'The breastplate is in here; be as quick as you can. The geese won't want to eat all night.'

'I'll go first, sir,' Magnus offered, 'I'm the heaviest.' He took hold of the rope and lowered himself through the hole.

Vespasian watched him descend; as he reached the balustrade around the viewing passage he swung slightly and managed to land on the temple floor. There was a slight increase in goose activity as he landed in their midst but the bread and grain seemed to be doing a good job at distracting them from their guard duty.

Felix helped Vespasian into position on the rope. 'They're unsettled at the moment so the guards won't worry about a bit of honking; just make sure that you don't tread on one.'

'Thanks for the advice, Felix,' Vespasian replied as he let himself down into the gloom.

Following Magnus' example, Vespasian swung gently over the balustrade and landed lightly next to it, eliciting a smattering of honks from the geese close by before they settled back down to their surprise midnight feast. Stepping carefully around the dim grey forms pecking at the ground, he came to the steps, swiftly descended and joined Magnus and Ziri down in the burial chamber.

With no light source other than the flaming sconces, Alexander's body seemed even more ethereal in its crystal cocoon than it had when they viewed it with daylight seeping down the shaft.

'Ziri, get the rope and untie the lead weight,' Vespasian ordered as he and Magnus got either side of the coffin. 'We lift it just enough to get the rope under, all right?'

Magnus nodded and, easing their fingers under the lip of the lid at the level of Alexander's chest, they braced themselves.

'Ready, Ziri?'

'Yes, sir,' the little Marmarides replied standing at the head end.

'Go.'

With a huge effort they prised the lid from the base lifting it at an angle; a waft of the preserving spices and incense filled the chamber. Ziri quickly fed the rope through and they lowered the heavy crystal back down with relief.

'Minerva's slack tits, that's heavy!' Magnus exclaimed, rubbing his fingers together. 'Here, Ziri, give me that rope.' He took the loose end and tied it in a secure knot back on itself around the lid. 'All right, Ziri, you and I help support this while Sir does his bit.' He gave the rope a tug and the slack was taken out of it as above them on the roof Felix began to pull.

Very gently the lid rose until Vespasian could see the mummified face undistorted by the crystal; in the soft flame-light it looked more weather-beaten than preserved but the dry skin lacked the sheen associated with living flesh and Vespasian felt an illogical relief: he would not be disturbing the great man from a deep sleep, he was quite patently dead.

The lid was now raised high enough to be able to get at the breastplate; Magnus and Ziri stood with legs braced taking some of the weight from the rope.

Vespasian leant in and, feeling the buckles on either side, started to work on them to find that they were not done up: the cuirass had been simply laid on the body's chest. 'That makes matters simpler,' he muttered, placing his fingers in each of the arm holes and lifting the plate tentatively. It came free. Holding it with his left hand he moved his right hand down to gently lift Alexander's arms, which were folded across his body at the waist. The touch of the dried skin thrilled him as he raised the arms a thumb's breadth and slid the breastplate out.

He held it up in the faint light to examine it and sucked in his breath. 'Shit!'

'What is it?' Magnus asked nervously.

'There's a stain here,' Vespasian replied, pointing to an area just below the left pectoral.

'Blood?'

'Could well be.'

Removing the replica from the bag, he laid the two breast-plates side by side on the floor and then, taking his knife from its sheath, slit the tip of his thumb. The blood oozed out and Vespasian carefully rubbed his thumb on the replica, creating what he hoped would be a tolerable imitation of the stain. Once satisfied he buffed the stain with his tunic, drying it and then, picking up the replica, began the process of replacing it.

It fitted perfectly.

'Let's get out of here,' Magnus said, giving two tugs on the taut rope.

Very slowly the lid lowered. Vespasian looked at his handi-work; in this light it was impossible to tell the difference, then something caught his eye. 'Shit! Stop.'

Magnus and Ziri took the weight of the crystal lid; the rope went slack for a moment and then tautened, taking the strain.

'What's the matter?' Magnus hissed.

'I've left blood on the neck-edging,' Vespasian replied, leaning forward and wiping away a spot of blood that must have dripped from his thumb.

Magnus gave another couple of tugs on the rope and the lid lowered until it was a hand's breadth above the base when Magnus and Ziri halted it; Vespasian quickly undid the knot and slipped the rope out before they lowered it the last short distance. With a slight grate it came to rest.

'That was surprisingly easy,' Vespasian commented, putting the breastplate into the leather bag.

'We ain't out yet,' Magnus said, heading for the steps. 'Come on, Ziri, and watch out for them geese.'

A short bout of honking greeted them as they reached the temple level but it was half-hearted as most of the geese seemed to be intent upon settling down for a nap while they digested their bread and grain.

Ziri clambered up the rope first, scaling the fifty feet in surpris-ingly quick time; Vespasian followed, though not quite so nimbly.

'Did it go all right?' Felix asked as he helped Vespasian out of the hole.

'Fine,' Vespasian replied, looking at Ziri who was urinating prodigiously.

'Fuck me, I needed that,' Ziri said with evident relief, 'hours I've been waiting.'

'No wonder you climbed the rope so fast.' Vespasian grinned. 'So, Felix, back the way we came?'

'No, you three go straight over the Soma wall from here, then I'll throw the rope down to you and make my way back down the ladder; if I get caught in the Soma's grounds all I'll have on me is an empty bird cage.'

Once Magnus was up, Felix undid the rope and, keeping low, they moved to the rear of the temple roof. Felix wrapped the rope around him and threw it down over the Soma wall. Ziri and Magnus quickly descended into the street below.

Vespasian clasped Felix's forearm. 'Thank you; come and see me when you're back in Rome, Felix, I'm in your debt.'

A loud disturbance at the Soma gate prevented a reply. They looked back; a unit of legionaries was running towards the temple led by a centurion with a flaming torch; next to him ran a priest.

'Cybele's flabby arse!' Vespasian exclaimed. 'Flaccus must have guessed.'

'Go, quick, I'll be fine, they'll go straight to the temple.'

Hitching the leather bag over his shoulder, Vespasian slipped over the parapet as Felix braced himself against it taking the weight of the rope.

Burning his hands, Vespasian slid down and landed with a jolt in the street below; the rope quickly followed.

'What's the panic?' Magnus asked, collecting the rope.

'Just run!'

Taking the steps three at a time Vespasian hurtled down to the docks followed by Magnus and Ziri. Ahead he could see the ship; its furled sail had been hoisted ready for departure. Sprinting along the stone quay he hurdled a coil of rope and a drunken sailor before turning sharply left onto the jetty to which his ship was moored. Although there had been no sign of pursuit during their dash across the city he was desperate to sail as soon as possible for fear that their theft of the breastplate had been discovered.

'Triarchus,' he shouted, running up the gangplank, 'we sail immediately!'

'You seem to be in quite a hurry,' a familiar voice said as he jumped down onto the deck. 'Now, why would that be, I wonder?'

Vespasian turned and saw Flaccus leaning against the mast. The rescued Jews and Flavia were huddled behind him guarded by two soldiers.

'When I found your rope dangling from the terrace I thought that you'd just decided to run,' Flaccus said, walking forward as Magnus and Ziri ran aboard. 'So I rushed down here only to find that you'd given orders to prepare for sea and would be back in an hour or so. Been doing a little late-night burglary before whisking the lovely Flavia and your new Jewish friends back to Rome, have you? What's in that bag?'

'Nothing that concerns you, Flaccus.'

'Oh, but it does concern me. If you've done what I expressly forbade you to do then it concerns me deeply, so I would be much obliged if you would open it.'

'Prefect, I would remind you that this is an imperial ship.' Vespasian pointed at the imperial banner on the masthead. 'It is therefore under the direct command of the Emperor himself, you have no jurisdiction here. Whatever may be in this bag is the property of the Emperor.'

Flaccus gave a half-smile and tilted his head. 'That may be so, but no matter, I've sent one of Alexander's priests to go and check his tomb; if he finds a certain item missing then we might review where my jurisdiction ends.'

'You can review it all you like but it would be unwise to interfere with Caligula's property.' Vespasian handed the bag to Ziri. 'Take that to the cabin, Ziri.'

'It wouldn't be Caligula's property if Caligula's thief hadn't stolen it, but we shall find out soon enough – I can see our priest approaching.'

Vespasian turned and saw the priest running along the quay with his legionary escort.

'He can come on board, but the soldiers stay on the jetty.' Vespasian put his hand on his sword hilt. He felt Magnus take a pace closer to him.

'Very well,' Flaccus agreed, walking to the top of the gang-plank, 'I have no need for military muscle, yet. Centurion, keep your men there, but have them ready to board if I shout. Send the priest up.'

The priest who had escorted them down to the chamber made his way onto the deck.

'Well?' Flaccus asked him.

'I don't understand it,' the priest said, shaking his head. 'Someone has been in there; they must have got in through the roof, the soldiers found a puddle of fresh urine up there. There was grain and some bread scattered on the temple floor that they must have used to keep the geese quiet. The guards said that they had seen and heard nothing except that a couple of the geese that had escaped turned up and they caught them and put them back inside.'

'Yes, but what about the breastplate?' Flaccus pressed.

'That's what I don't understand; it was still there. I had the soldiers lift the lid off and I examined it; it was the real breast-plate, I can swear to it, there is a stain on the left-hand side. Nothing else was missing but someone must have taken the lid off earlier.'

'What makes you so sure?'

'Because there was a drop of fresh blood on the neck of Alexander's tunic, it was still moist.'

Flaccus glared at Vespasian. 'Just what have you done, senator?'

Vespasian shrugged. 'Quite evidently nothing, prefect; now, if you'll excuse me, I need to get back to Rome. Triarchus, we sail as soon as the prefect and his men have disembarked.'

'Fine, you can go but I'm taking those Jews.'

'If you do then my report to the Emperor will be even more damning than it already is, and believe me, Flaccus, no matter how much money you have he will have you found and hideously despatched. He's mad, don't you know?'

Flaccus looked at Vespasian, uncertainty in his eyes, and then, spitting at his feet, stormed off the ship.

'If you know what's good for you,' Vespasian shouted after him, 'then you should pull the Greeks off the Jews and get the Emperor's city back under control.' He walked over to the two soldiers left guarding the Jews. 'You two, off!'

'What a terrible man,' Philo commented as the legionaries left. 'I shall write such a diatribe about him that his name will be blackened forever.'

'Try not to make it too rhetorically flowery like the rest of your works, brother,' Alexander said with a sad smile. 'Just the facts.'

Philo snorted.

'We shall have to bury your dead at sea,' Vespasian said as the gangplank was hauled up and the mooring cables dropped.

'That won't be necessary,' Alexander replied, 'we've decided to go back.'

'How? We're sailing.'

'In that boat that you came in; once we've left the harbour we can sail back to the beach bordering the Jewish Quarter.'

'Flaccus will kill you if he finds you.'

'No, he won't, he'll be needing me to broker a peace. If my people see that I do not ask for revenge for my murdered wife then they may be able to forgo their demands for retribution.'

'And Flaccus gets what he wants?'

'Maybe; but we cannot afford to fight any more, we would be exterminated. However, we will never forgive Flaccus. Once we have peace my brother will lead a delegation to the Emperor to complain about his treatment of our people.'

'And Paulus?'

'Our only condition will be that Flaccus at least expels him but preferably executes him, then we will be prepared to go back to how things were before. We've realised that we are not strong enough in the city to make demands, we should be content even if that means being second-class citizens and having a mad emperor's statue in our temples.'

Guided by the blazing light of the Pharos the ship glided out of the harbour under sail and oars as the first glow of dawn broke in the eastern sky.

Once clear of the mole it heaved to for the Jews to disembark into the boat. The flayed corpses were lowered in and the survivors quickly followed.

'Thank you, Vespasian,' Tiberius said as he prepared to go over the side. His torso was heavily bandaged and blood stained his back. 'I owe you more than my life, I owe you my hide too. I will always be in your debt.'

'One day I will call it in,' Vespasian said, helping him over the side.

Alexander was last to go. 'We overheard your conversations with Flaccus and then with the priest; tell me, did you get the breastplate?'

Vespasian slapped him on the shoulder. 'Alexander, my friend, let me put it this way: if you had to choose between giving the man who has the power of life and death over you what he asked for or a replica of the thing, which would you choose?'

Alexander nodded. 'It makes me feel better to know that the Greeks have lost something precious to them, even if they aren't aware of it.'

Vespasian looked over Alexander's shoulder at the scores of fires still burning in the Jewish Quarter and shook his head at the wanton destruction. 'For my part, Alexander, I'd rather it stayed here with them. Now that I've got it, I'm loath to take it back to Caligula. Who knows what new madness possessing it will push him to?'

PART V

❦ ❦

Rome and the Bay of Neapolis, August AD 38

CHAPTER XXII

THE DOCKS AT Ostia were strangely quiet; gone was the frenetic bustle of activity, to be replaced by a languid indolence that was not at all in keeping with a busy port at the height of the sailing season. Apart from a couple of gangs of dockworkers unloading two small traders, the quays were almost empty with only the occasional food vendor or whore attempting to sell their wares to sporadic, uninterested passers-by. Even the seagulls seemed to have lost motivation, and instead of cawing overhead or diving for scraps they sat in long lines on the warehouse roofs looking down balefully at the inactivity below that brought with it, for them as well as the citizens of Rome, a shortage of food.

'Do you think that the plague could have broken out again?' Magnus asked as the trireme came to rest alongside one of the many deserted jetties.

'They wouldn't have let us dock if it had,' the triarchus informed him as the gangplank was lowered.

'We'll soon find out what's happening,' Vespasian said, watching the anxious-looking port aedile walking briskly towards them accompanied by a scurrying clerk.

'Is the senator Titus Flavius Vespasianus aboard?' the aedile called out as he mounted the gangway.

'Yes, I am.'

'Thank the gods, senator, I am so pleased to see you; now perhaps we can get this madness over with and get back to normal.'

'What are you talking about?'

'The Emperor's bridge, of course. Trade has come to a standstill and the people are getting hungry; he's requisitioned every ship that's arrived in the waters around Italia and sent them down to the Bay of Neapolis. There're thousands of them down there all chained together and he won't let them leave until he's ridden across them and he won't ride across them until he's got whatever you're bringing for him. I hope for everyone's sake, especially yours, that you have it because he's getting very impatient. He sends messengers two or three times a day to see if you've arrived.'

'Well, I do have it.' Vespasian lifted the leather bag in confirmation.

'It's as well for you that you do; I've orders to have you sent to Rome in chains if you come back empty-handed. As it is, you're to ride to the Emperor immediately; I have a fast horse waiting for you.'

'I'm accompanying a lady.'

'She'll have to follow behind in a carriage – I'll organise one. And triarchus, as soon as those two merchantmen are offloaded you're to sail with them down to the bay to become an integral part of that fucking bridge.' With that he gave a harassed look, shook his head disbelievingly and quickly disembarked.

'What was that, my dear?' Flavia asked, appearing from the cabin.

'I'm to present myself to the Emperor at once. Magnus and Ziri will accompany you back to my uncle's house. With luck I'll already be there when you arrive.'

'I don't think that it will have anything to do with luck,' Magnus observed darkly. 'It'll be more to do with an insane man's whim, if you take my meaning?'

Vespasian scowled at Magnus and then briskly walked down the gangway.

'He refused to let you have it?' Caligula was outraged and shook his trident threateningly at Vespasian. Behind him a long line of Rome's urban poor shuffled incongruously through the grand atrium of Augustus' House watched over by Praetorian Guards. 'Why didn't you just take it?'

'I did, Divine God of the Sea,' Vespasian replied, using the form of address that Clemens had recommended on account of the Emperor's recently stated ambition of usurping Neptune's place in the Roman pantheon. 'But I had to break into the mausoleum, steal it and replace it with a replica without it being noticed.'

'Ooh, that sounds like fun.' Caligula emerged, with some difficulty, from the impluvium and struggled to walk in the tight skirt of scaly fish skin that adorned his lower body. 'Was it a jolly caper?'

'It had its moments.'

'I should have come too; I could do with some distraction from all the demands made upon me, both by gods and men.'

'I'm sure that it would have gone much more smoothly had you been with us, Divine God of the Sea.'

'What?' Caligula looked momentarily confused and then glanced down at his dripping fish-skirt. 'Oh yes, of course, it must be confusing for you; I'm no longer in the water so I'm back to being the Divine Gaius. Now show me the breastplate.'

Vespasian reached into his bag.

'Clemens!' Caligula screamed, suddenly forcing the points of his trident hard against Vespasian's chest, piercing his toga.

Vespasian froze as Clemens came pushing through the ragged queue that had come to an abrupt halt at the Emperor's scream.

'Is he trying to kill me?' Caligula blurted out, glaring at Vespasian with his dark-rimmed sunken eyes. A stain of blood surrounded each trident point.

'No, Divine Gaius,' Clemens assured him as he took the bag, 'I checked it for weapons myself; it only contains the breastplate.'

'Show me!'

Clemens slowly put his hand into the bag; Caligula jerked his trident from Vespasian's chest to Clemens' throat. Keeping his chin high and looking down the trident's shaft at his Emperor, Clemens gradually pulled out the breastplate.

'You're right.' Caligula breathed deeply. 'It's just the breastplate; hold this.' He handed the trident to Clemens, oblivious to the fact that he had just given him the means to murder him, and took the breastplate. He rubbed a hand over it and looked up at Vespasian, smiling wildly. 'That's it, my friend, you haven't tried to cheat me, this really is it, I remember the stain. I remember asking my father why the priests hadn't been crucified for allowing something to soil Alexander.' He held it to his chest. 'How do I look?'

'Like the great Alexander, only more divine,' Vespasian replied solemnly, thinking that he looked like a man draped in fish skin wearing a breastplate that did not fit him.

'Excellent! You will dine with me and my friends tonight. Your brother has finally come back from his province so he'll be here – as will my horse.'

Vespasian wondered if he had heard correctly. 'I look forward to seeing them both, Divine Gaius.'

'Yes, Incitatus will be particularly pleased to see you, he's so looking forward to pulling me across my bridge in a chariot; we can do that now.' He looked with genuine pleasure at the breastplate. 'I must show this to my sisters, if they're not too busy servicing the poor.' He turned and, forced to take ridiculously small steps, waddled off.

Vespasian wiped the sweat from his brow. 'Servicing the poor?'

'I'm afraid so,' Clemens replied, examining the trident and considering what to do with it. 'Since Drusilla died he's become increasingly suspicious of everyone, especially his other two sisters, so he's decided to punish them for whatever he imagines that they've been plotting by making them fuck every receiver of the grain dole in Rome. In his twisted mind he also thinks that it compensates the people for the shortages caused by his bridge. They've been at it for three days now and were up to over two thousand at the last count.'

'That'll kill them like it did Drusilla.'

'More than likely, but then he's going to kill us all so what difference does it make? It's got to the stage now that I just don't care; I stay loyal to him to protect my family for as long as I can.'

Clemens looked at Vespasian with tired eyes. 'I don't know how much longer I can stomach it. I'll see you at dinner.' Handing the trident to Vespasian, Clemens walked back over to the queue to continue his distasteful task of supervising the mass rape of two of Germanicus' children.

Vespasian looked at the trident and then at the blood stains on his toga as the urban poor continued to shuffle past. He threw the trident back into the impluvium in disgust and, contemplating the options open to him and his family, turned and made his way, with a heavy heart, towards his uncle's house.

'Don't even think about it, dear boy,' Gaius warned Vespasian, helping himself to another honey and almond cake, 'it would be suicide.'

'Not if we succeed, Uncle,' Vespasian argued.

A cooling breeze blew through Gaius' shaded courtyard garden providing some relief from the mid-afternoon heat. The fish pond heaved with lampreys enjoying their daytime feed.

'Even if you could kill Caligula and manage to avoid being cut down by his extremely loyal German Bodyguards, you would be dead within two days.'

Vespasian threw another fish fillet into the pond. 'Why?'

'The next Emperor would see to it, of course. Granted, he would be very grateful to you for leaving the position vacant for him to fill but then he'd have to have you executed because it wouldn't do for people to see that someone outside the imperial family can assassinate an emperor, however depraved, and live. It would be an invitation for anyone with a grievance to murder him, surely you can see that? And don't go giving me any naïve nonsense about restoring the Republic – the Praetorian Guard would never stand for that; the Emperor is their reason to exist.'

'But something must be done, Uncle, before it's too late.'

'It's already too late. There are too many people with vested interests in Caligula staying emperor. Only when he completely runs out of money and can't pay them any more will they begin to look elsewhere; but I doubt that'll ever happen because when his treasury is empty he'll just start taking money from the rich.'

'So what do you recommend?'

'Two things: firstly, do not deposit that gold that you've brought back with you in a bank, because Caligula will hear of it. Keep it hidden here so that when he does start culling the wealthy you won't be a target. Secondly, humour him, praise him, support him, worship him, laugh at his jokes, do whatever it takes to stay alive and wait for someone else to be foolish enough to try and kill an emperor.'

'But what if everyone reasons the same way as you? He could remain emperor for years.'

'Caligula's bound to offend someone in such a way that their sense of honour will overrule their judgement, and then we just have to pray that they're successful.'

'Yes,' Vespasian agreed gloomily, flicking another fillet into the pond and watching the feeding frenzy. 'Just imagine what Caligula's retribution would be like on the guilty and innocent alike if a plot against him failed.'

'All the more reason to stay in his favour, dear boy. Take Livius Geminius, for example: he swore an oath that at Drusilla's funeral he saw her spirit ascending into the heavens to commune with the gods. Complete rubbish, of course, but he was handsomely rewarded for it.'

The tinkling of the door bell floating through from the atrium interrupted them.

'Ah, that'll be Magnus and Ziri,' Vespasian said, getting up. 'They've, er... they've brought Flavia with them.'

Gaius looked at him quizzically. 'Flavia? Is she some relation of yours, a cousin or something?'

'She must be distantly related; but anyway, I intend to marry her.'

Gaius looked suitably pleased. 'It's about time you took that step, dear boy.'

'Exactly; and with my father's business keeping him away in Aventicum I need you to negotiate the marriage terms.'

'I'd be delighted. What's her father's name and where does he live?'

'North of Rome in Ferentium. Flavia's travelling there tomorrow so she could take your letter to him; apparently you know him, his name is Marcus Flavius Liberalis.'

Gaius frowned. 'I do know him, he was one of the clerks when I was a quaestor in Africa; he was having trouble proving he was a full citizen and not just the possessor of Latin Rights.'

Vespasian shrugged. 'He's certainly a full citizen now; he's done well enough for himself to have been enrolled into the equestrian order recently.'

'But what about Flavia? She was born before he sorted out his legal status – I remember her as a child.'

'She claims full citizenship; I wouldn't be marrying her otherwise.'

'It would be as well to check, dear boy, you don't want your offspring to have legal problems.'

'Vespasian, my dear,' Flavia said, walking with breathtaking elegance into the garden as if she owned it, 'this must be your uncle. Won't you please reintroduce us?'

'There's no need, Flavia,' Gaius said, gently squeezing the fingers of her proffered right hand, 'even though it was twenty years ago I remember you perfectly as a little girl of six or so. Did you stay in Africa long?'

'My father left five years ago, but I stayed on; I was attached, shall we say.'

'Indeed. Your father was having some trouble with his citizenship status while I was there, as I recall.'

Flavia looked blank. 'If he was, he never told me about it.'

'No, why should he have? You were only a child; besides it must be all right now, Vespasian tells me that he's become an equestrian.'

'Yes, and I hope that he will settle a large dowry on me so that Vespasian and I can enjoy the finer things in life.'

'I'm sure he will and I'm equally sure that Vespasian will enjoy spending it on luxurious frivolities.' Gaius raised a surreptitious, plucked eyebrow at his nephew.

Vespasian thought it best not to express his opinion on the subject and contemplated the fertile ground for many a marital disagreement in the future.

Flavia indicated that the men should be seated. 'Shall we sit down and call for some wine?'

'By all means,' Gaius agreed, visibly surprised by Flavia's virtual assumption of the role of hostess in his domain.

Vespasian helped Flavia to a chair. 'I'm afraid that I must leave you, I have to dine with the Emperor.'

Flavia's eyes widened with delight. 'How exciting; should I come, do you think?'

'It would be best to stay here, Flavia,' Gaius assured her, 'the Emperor's liable to take fearful liberties with his female guests. You won't have that problem with me, I can promise you that.'

Vespasian leant down and kissed her on the cheek. 'I don't know when I'll be back so don't wait up for me. Where's Magnus?'

'Oh, I left him and Ziri to help my maids put my bags into my room.'

'And he didn't object?'

'Why should he? I asked him so nicely.'

Vespasian raised his eyebrows and turned to go to find Magnus, wondering whether his friend had been right about Flavia.

'All I'm saying, sir,' Magnus concluded as they reached the summit of the Palatine, 'is that just because Flavia's come back with you to Rome that's not a reason for you to have to go through with the marriage. You'd be mad to – she'll make your life a misery. Granted she showed good spirit in Alexandria, and yes, she would have formidable sons, but you should have seen her at the port once you'd gone; just because you'd been summoned by the Emperor she started ordering everyone around and shouting at people who weren't even slaves. She's using you, which is fair enough, but what are you going to get in return, eh? You can't even bear the thought of buying and feeding just one slave; how are you going to feel when she demands that you purchase a whole household? You're going to find yourself having blazing rows about how many hairdressers she has because a woman like that is going to want more than two, as sure as a new recruit wants to go home to his mother.'

'Two?'

'More than two.'

Vespasian grimaced, acknowledging that Magnus had a point. He had realised that Flavia was going to be expensive but had only thought in terms of dresses and jewellery and not all the things that accompanied them. One of them – and he felt sure that it would not be her – would have to change if the marriage were to work. But then, he reflected, what other woman would be happy to become his wife knowing that he would have a life-long mistress? And if he were to find another, would she get his blood racing in the way that Flavia did by his just thinking of her? She was making a sacrifice, Caenis was making a sacrifice, there-fore, he reasoned, he could bear to buy a few slaves for the sake of some sort of harmony in his domestic arrangements.

'No, my mind's made up, Magnus, I will marry her and try to accommodate her wishes; after all, what's the worst that could happen?'

'She could spend all your money and you could be expelled from the Senate,' Magnus informed him as they reached Augustus' House. 'Anyway, I'll leave you here, sir, I sent Ziri straight over to the crossroads, so the brothers know I'm back; they should have a decent party prepared for me when I get there. I'll be willing to bet that it'll be a fuck sight more civilised than what you're going to get in there.'

'That may well be true,' Vespasian said softly, looking at a steady stream of senators arriving with nervous-looking wives and wondering whether Magnus might be right on both counts.

Watching his friend disappear back down the hill he had a moment of self-doubt but then, shaking his head and dismissing it, he turned to follow the senators in. As he did so a familiar voice drawled in his ear. 'I hear that you've been lowering your-self to petty theft now.'

'Piss off, Sabinus,' Vespasian said, spinning around to face his brother.

'That seems to be your standard greeting to me these days, brother.'

'If you started by thanking me for sending your things on to you in Bithynia and supervising the completion of your house then you might have got something more cordial.'

'Fair enough; thank you.'

'Where's Clementina? I hope you're not bringing her here.'

'Not a chance. Caligula seems to have forgotten about her, he hasn't mentioned her once since I got back. I've left her at Aquae Cutillae.'

'She should be safe enough there.'

'Let's hope so. Come on, we should go in and see which poor sod the Emperor's going to publicly cuckold tonight.'

'So how do you know about me stealing the breastplate?' Vespasian asked as they began walking towards the palace doors. 'I only got back today and I gave it straight to Caligula.'

'Pallas.'

'Pallas? How did he find out?'

'Oh, he knows everything now that he lives here in the palace. Caligula ordered Claudius to move in so that he could humiliate him on a daily basis; Pallas is part of his household now so he came too.'

'And Narcissus?' Vespasian asked, thinking about the gold in his uncle's house.

'Yes, and Narcissus,' Sabinus confirmed, looking sideways at his brother. 'Did I detect a note of concern in your voice?'

'I'd just rather not see him at the moment, that's all.'

'Well, you won't this evening, he's down at the Bay of Neapolis. Caligula put Claudius in charge of getting all the ships for his bridge but then demanded that he stay in Rome so that he could carry on humiliating him; Claudius handed over the practicalities to Narcissus.'

Vespasian was shocked. 'A freedman with the power to commandeer ships! That's outrageous.'

Sabinus grinned. 'Just imagine how Corbulo feels about it; he's got to work with him. He's been charged with building the road across the bridge and getting running water to it.'

'Running water on a bridge?'

'Oh, it's not just a bridge going from one end to the other; it's got peninsulas attached to it with accommodation furnished in the manner that Caligula feels is suitable for a god: triclinia in which two hundred people could easily recline, atriums with fountains, even a couple of bath houses.'

'All that in two months!' Vespasian exclaimed as they entered the atrium with its ragged queue of urban poor.

'The industry of Rome has worked on nothing else, I'm told.' Sabinus leant closer to Vespasian and whispered in his ear. 'It's a phenomenal waste of money but I'm really looking forward to seeing it.'

'You're going to travel down there just to have a look?'

'You will as well; Caligula's ordered every senator to escort him down to the bay and witness his triumph.'

The gardens to the rear of Augustus' House were stepped on two levels, clinging to the edge of the Palatine and overlooking the arched facade of the Circus Maximus. Along the low balustrade of the upper level, dining tables had been arranged in such a way that all those reclining at them would have a good view down to the second level where two stages had been set. Although it was still at least three hours until the late, summer dusk, torches, in tall brass holders, burned beside each stage and all around the gardens' perimeter as well as at intervals among the tables. Brightly coloured linen canopies littered the lawn of the upper garden under which the Emperor's dinner guests stood or sat drinking chilled wine and talking in the animated manner of people ill at ease but trying to conceal it.

Vespasian and Sabinus stood at the top of the steps leading down from the house and admired the beauty of the scene before them: the colour, the elegance, the soft evening light.

'It would be a pleasure to be here if one knew for certain that one would leave alive, would it not, gentlemen?' a voice behind them commented quietly.

The brothers turned, both smiling at the truth of the statement.

'Pallas,' Vespasian said with genuine pleasure, 'how are you? Sabinus tells me that you live here now.'

Pallas looked grave. 'I think that you've answered your own question, Vespasian: I live here.'

'It's as bad as that, is it?'

Pallas pointed down into the garden to where some guests were laughing with evidently feigned hilarity at a man in their midst. He stood with his hands outstretched, except he had no hands, just cauterised blackened stumps; his hands were tied to a piece of rope and hung around his neck along with a sign.

'The sign says: "I stole from the Emperor",' Pallas informed them.

'And did he?' Sabinus asked.

'A small strip of decorative silver had fallen off a couch and he was taking it to the steward to be mended when Caligula saw him with it; life here has become very arbitrary.'

'Life has always been arbitrary.'

'Granted, but generally within the parameters of the law; our new god seems to have forgotten about the law. My patron, Claudius, however, loves the law; think about that, gentlemen.' Pallas patted them both on the shoulder and walked away.

'Don't get involved,' Vespasian warned Sabinus as they descended the steps.

'I've no intention of doing so,' Sabinus replied, taking two cups of wine from a slave and handing one to his brother, 'I intend to stay alive. However, it's comforting to know that we have a good friend close to the only obvious heir to the Purple.'

A fanfare of *bucinae* blared over the garden and all conversation stopped as everyone looked with sycophantic longing towards the main doors of the house at the top of the steps. A horse trotted out and looked around in a semi-curious equine fashion. From behind it came a shout of 'Hail Incitatus'.

The dinner guests responded immediately. 'Hail Incitatus! Hail Incitatus!'

Having never paid homage to a horse before, Vespasian found it a struggle to keep a straight face as he joined in with an enthusiasm fired more by the absurdity of the situation rather than any great respect for the beast being lauded.

The chant quickly turned into 'Hail Divine Caesar!' as Caligula, flanked by Clemens and Chaerea, appeared next to his favourite subject, dressed soberly – Vespasian thought, considering some of the costumes that he had seen him wearing – in a purple toga edged in gold and crowned with a golden laurel wreath.

'This evening,' Caligula declaimed, 'we are here to honour not only me but also my good friend, my trusted ally, my comrade, the man who brought the breastplate of Alexander back from Egypt to me: Titus Flavius Vespasianus. Tomorrow at noon we can begin our progress down to the Bay of Neapolis where I shall ride in triumph across my greatest creation. Come forward, Vespasian, and receive my thanks – you shall be a praetor next year.'

Vespasian walked slowly back up the steps to a beaming Caligula, who held his arms open to him. As he reached the penultimate step he was enfolded in a purple embrace and kissed on each cheek to the applause of the people below.

'Only a man like this,' Caligula declared, turning Vespasian around to face the audience and putting a hand on each shoulder, 'could I trust to go to Egypt, the source of so much of Rome's wealth. No senator has visited it for four years, not since Tiberius' astrologer, Thrasyllus, warned him of the imminent return of the Phoenix, heralding a great change and made a prophecy about it. Did you see the Phoenix while you were in Alexandria, Vespasian?'

'No, Divine Gaius,' Vespasian replied truthfully.

Caligula looked triumphant. 'Of course not, because it has flown. Last year, three years after its rebirth, it was seen leaving

Egypt flying east; Thrasyllus' prophecy was not fulfilled. You are blessed, my sheep, because the change heralded by the Phoenix is that Rome is ruled by an immortal god; I will rule for another five hundred years until the Phoenix is sighted again. Until then I open Egypt back up to any member of the Senate who has good reason to travel there.'

This was greeted with a loud cheer from the many senators who had dealings with the Emperor's private province.

'And now we shall eat; Vespasian shall have the great honour of reclining on my right.' He moved past Vespasian and began to descend the steps.

'Divine Gaius,' Chaerea said in his high-pitched voice, following him down, 'what is the watchword for the night?'

Caligula stopped and laughed. 'I love his sweet voice!' He turned and put his middle finger to Chaerea's lips, parting them slightly and then wiggling them provocatively. 'Such a sweet voice deserves a sweet watchword, does it not?'

Sycophantic cries of agreement compounded the Praetorian tribune's humiliation.

'In which case the watchword is Venus; the sweetest of gods for the sweetest of men.'

Caligula turned and skipped daintily down the steps to the raucous laughter of his guests. Vespasian saw the anger burning in Chaerea's eyes but otherwise his face remained impassive. Clemens' hand went to his sword hilt as he watched his junior colleague control himself. Finally Chaerea saluted and matched stiffly away.

Magnus would not have lost his bet, Vespasian reflected as he tried to swallow a mouthful of perch while watching yet another beheading on one of the stages below. In a strange juxtaposition the other stage contained a group of dancers performing to the soft melody of two flutes.

'Something for everyone,' Caligula enthused, feeding an apple to Incitatus whose head nuzzled between him and Vespasian. 'Art or death, take your pick and enjoy.'

'P-p-personally I'll t-t-take death, Divine and Supreme G-G-Gaius,' Claudius stammered, watching the blood spurt from the severed neck with relish; his arousal was plain for all to see and the pretty, fair-skinned girl reclining next to him had edged as far away from him as good manners would allow. 'I could never understand the p-p-point of dancing.'

'That's because there's no point in you dancing, cripple,' Caligula observed, 'your legs would buckle underneath you.' He fell about laughing far more uproariously than the observation deserved; his dinner companions had no option but to join in.

'Your d-divine insight is faultless,' Claudius said through his own laughter.

'So let's prove the point; go and dance with them, Uncle.'

Claudius' slack-lipped mouth fell open and his bloodshot eyes flicked around the table appealing for help; it was not forthcoming, not even from his pretty companion, who looked away with a faint smile of regret edging her moist, pale lips.

'Go!' Caligula hissed with quiet menace; malice played in his eyes.

Realising that he had no choice but to humiliate himself in front of the whole company, Claudius got to his unsteady feet and lurched off down the steps to the lower garden.

'This will be highly amusing,' Caligula affirmed. 'I've made him run, skip, jump and crawl but I've never made him dance.' He turned to Claudius' attractive companion. 'Can you make him fuck, Messalina, or are you putting that horror off until your wedding night?'

Messalina joined in the communal laughter but the mirth did not reach her cold, dark eyes, which Vespasian felt glare at him as he pretended to wipe a tear from his eye.

Claudius shambled onto the stage and began a series of jerky jigs and pirouettes, waving his arms in an ungainly manner while the confused dancers carried on their graceful routine around him. On the stage next to them four chained lions began to devour the corpse of the decapitated criminal. Behind them the sun sank below the Circus Maximus.

'Look at him,' Caligula said through his mirth, 'if we didn't happen to have a god in the family he could have become emperor. If that had been the case, then I think that Thrasyllus' prophecy would have been fulfilled.'

'What was his prophecy, Divine Gaius?' Sabinus enquired as down below Claudius collapsed into an undignified heap to the amusement of all present.

'He prophesied that if a member of the senatorial order witnessed the Phoenix while it was within the boundaries of the Kingdom of Egypt he would go on to be the founder of the next dynasty of emperors.'

Vespasian almost choked on his wine. 'So if a senator saw it flying over Judaea, for example,' he asked innocently, 'it wouldn't count?'

'He was very specific; it had to be within Egypt itself, that's why we refused permission for senators to travel there for so long.'

Vespasian nodded thoughtfully, missing Sabinus' questioning look.

Caligula leant back to stroke Incitatus and then turned to Clemens. 'Incitatus says he's tired and wishes to sleep; like me he's excited about tomorrow. Clear all the residents out of the houses within a quarter of a mile of his stables and post guards to make sure that no one makes any noise; I want him well rested for the journey.'

'A sensible precaution, Divine Gaius,' Clemens said without a hint of irony, getting to his feet.

Caligula followed him. 'If you'll excuse me, I'll see Incitatus out; he'll be greatly offended if I didn't.' He kissed the horse on the lips. 'Isn't he beautiful? Perhaps I should make him a consul; he would be a fine colleague for me next year, much more suitable than the horse-faced idiot I've already chosen.' With another fond kiss he led his special guest off.

'What was it about the Phoenix prophecy that made you ask that question?' Sabinus asked once Caligula was out of earshot.

Vespasian looked at his brother with an amused grin. 'According to that old charlatan, Thrasyllus, I've narrowly missed being the founder of the next imperial dynasty.'

'You said that you didn't see the Phoenix.'

'I didn't in Alexandria but almost four years ago in Cyrenaica I did; I witnessed its rebirth. But Cyrenaica's not Egypt so the prophecy can't apply to me.'

'It used to be a part of the Egyptian Empire, I remember someone telling me that in Judaea.'

'A province of Egypt, not a part of the kingdom itself. Even so, I was in Siwa, which is an oasis out on its own in the middle of nowhere.'

Sabinus looked at Vespasian intently. 'When Alexander conquered Egypt he went to the Oracle of Amun in Siwa, it was a part of the kingdom then. It's only us who have put it in Cyrenaica for administrative reasons; historically, it has always been a part of Egypt.'

Vespasian's eyes opened wide and then he shook his head and waved his hand dismissively. 'No, no. I was taken to the Oracle of Amun after I saw the Phoenix. The Oracle spoke to me and it didn't tell me that I was going to start an imperial dynasty; it didn't tell me anything really, it just said that I had come too soon and that next time I should bring a gift to match the sword that Alexander had left there.'

'What sort of gift?'

'That's what I asked, but it's for you to decide.'

'Me? Why me?'

'Because, Sabinus, the Oracle said that a brother will understand and, whether we like it or not, we will always be brothers.'

Caligula's growing excitement at the prospect of setting off on the progress to the Bay of Neapolis caused him to curtail the dinner shortly after dark, announcing that he wished to spend the rest of the night settling his feud with Neptune so that he would not send a storm to destroy his bridge. The guests departed with obvious relief at being able to leave with their lives, limbs and virtues intact.

Vespasian left Sabinus to make his own way home to the Aventine and, despite the lateness of the hour, set off to make a call that he was dreading but knew he could not put off.

Apart from a couple of crossroads brothers on watch at the corner, Caenis' street was empty. Vespasian nodded his regards to the lads and walked purposefully to her door.

The huge Nubian answered his knock within moments and he was quickly and silently admitted.

'I knew you'd come,' Caenis said gently as he walked into the dimly lit atrium, 'I've been waiting up for you.' She walked over to him and, looping her arms around his neck, kissed him on the lips.

Vespasian closed his eyes and responded in full, drinking in her intoxicating scent and caressing the curve of her back with his hands. 'How did you know I was back in Rome?' he asked as they finally broke off.

She looked up at him with moist eyes and a smile. 'Occasionally, as you know, to relieve the boredom I go to your uncle's house; I went there this evening.'

Vespasian sucked in his breath. 'So you've...'

'Met Flavia? Yes, my love, I have. She's very beautiful.'

Vespasian swallowed and wondered how that might have gone. 'I wanted to tell you about her first.'

'That's why I knew you'd come tonight. But you don't need to tell me about her, she's done that already and in great detail; if you wish to marry her you do so with my blessing.'

'You will always be first and foremost, my love.'

'I know that, that's why I'm happy to let you go; it's my own private victory over her. I may be second in line when it comes to receiving your attention and can never bear your children, but I will always be first when it comes to your love and I'll settle for that.'

He held her shoulders and looked down at her, smiling, and then kissed her gently on the forehead. 'Should I stay?'

'I'd never forgive you if you didn't.'

379

CHAPTER XXIII

A SHORT CHORUS of bucinae echoed around the Forum Romanum, followed by the mass barking of centurions bringing five cohorts of the Praetorian Guard to simultaneous attention with a single crack of hobnails on stone. Along the crowd-lined Via Sacra trotted two alae of Praetorian cavalry, keeping pace with the star of the spectacle, Caligula, fifty feet above them and a hundred paces to their left, as he traversed his bridge from the Palatine to the Capitoline Hill riding Incitatus and dressed as Vulcan: a single-shouldered tunic, a pileus and brandishing a smith's hammer in one hand and a large clamshell in the other. Behind him followed ten naked women painted gold, representing the slave girls whom Vulcan had forged out of the precious metal to serve him.

All around the vicinity of the Forum bonfires burned into which people threw live fish or small animals – rats, mice, puppies and kittens – as a sacrifice to the god of fire in the hope that he would spare the city from burning during the hot, dry summer. In their capacity as the city's fire fighters the Vigiles kept a close eye on every bonfire.

From the steps of the Curia, Vespasian and the rest of the Senate watched Caligula progress onto the Capitoline, dismount and then descend the Gemonian Stairs past the Temple of Concordia and stop before the Volcanal, the sacred precinct to Vulcan, and one of the oldest shrines in Rome. Here, before the altar, shaded by a cypress tree, there waited a red calf and a red boar ready to be sacrificed to the god whose festival it was that day.

'Having made his peace with Neptune I suppose that our Emperor is now ensuring that Vulcan doesn't burn the city down in his absence,' Vespasian observed as the sacrificial knife flashed in Caligula's hand despatching the calf.

'Or send fire out from his smithy under Vesuvius to burn his bridge,' Sabinus muttered.

'Wrong mountain, dear boy,' Gaius corrected him as the boar collapsed spurting blood. 'Vulcan lives under Etna in Sicilia. Anyway, he only does that every time his wife, Venus, is unfaithful to him, so if we wanted to avoid an eruption in Sicilia perhaps it's her that we should be sacrificing to, in order to ensure her good behaviour.'

Vespasian grinned at his uncle and brother. 'I should certainly offer a sacrifice of thanks to her after Flavia's behaviour this morning.'

'You should indeed,' Gaius agreed.

Sabinus looked confused. 'Who's Flavia?'

'She, dear boy, is the woman whom your brother intends to marry. The same woman who, when Vespasian turned up soon after dawn, having spent the night with Caenis, gave him a kiss and asked if he'd had a pleasant evening before calmly finishing her breakfast and then, having packed, left for her father's house, with my letter opening the marriage negotiations, and with no more than a warning to your younger brother that he should ensure that he has something left for their wedding night next month.'

Sabinus stared in disbelief at Vespasian who shrugged innocently. 'She must be a very stupid woman if she didn't realise that he'd spent the night with someone else.'

'Oh, she knew all right; in fact, she even met Caenis yesterday evening and explained to her the rules.'

Vespasian was alarmed. 'The rules, Uncle?'

'Yes, dear boy, the rules.'

'What are the rules?'

'The rules are simple: Flavia has first call on you if she is entertaining, wanting a holiday, needing to discipline children, wishing to take a walk around the city or trying to get pregnant. At any other time Caenis is welcome to have you but not for more than four nights in a row, going down to three once the first child is two and more in need of a regular paternal figure, and then two once it is seven.'

Sabinus guffawed, much to the outrage of the senators nearby; he quickly controlled his face into one more befitting a religious ceremony. 'It sounds like they've parcelled him up very neatly.'

'Oh, they both knew very well what they wanted. They were icily polite to each other, complementing one another's hair and trinkets and suchlike, but they came to a peaceful understanding despite their obvious mutual loathing; it was a wonder to behold and confirmed to me the wisdom of my lifestyle.'

Vespasian was indignant. 'And you let them negotiate about me as if I were a gladiator that they'd both taken a fancy to.'

'I didn't let them do anything, dear boy,' Gaius replied, shrugging his shoulders, 'it's nothing to do with me; I just observed. You're the one who's insisting on having a complicated domestic arrangement. I just hope that you don't have to pay too high a price for it, both emotionally and financially.'

A roar from the crowds brought their attention back to the day's proceedings; the auspices having evidently been declared favourable, Caligula had mounted a quadriga, with Incitatus now installed in his place on the left of the team, and was leaving the Forum followed by the cavalry alae. Cohort by cohort, the Praetorians began to march out after them to the cheers of the crowds.

'I think that their enthusiasm is less for the spectacle and more for the fact that once Caligula's driven over his bridge the ships can be used to bring some much needed food to their bellies,' Gaius observed as they and the rest of the Senate began to follow. 'Let's hope that we can get this sorry affair over with quickly.'

Two miles outside the Porta Capena, in a field alongside the Via Appia, the senators' carriages waited with their wives already installed and being fussed over by slaves in the ever growing heat. The chaos of reuniting over five hundred men with their vehicles lasted for more than an hour and was not helped by Caligula riding his chariot, followed by a turma of grinning Praetorian troopers, up and down the rows of carriages and lashing out with his whip in an effort to speed up the process. Many a mule team bolted, dragging their burdens, with their screaming passengers, over the rough ground to an inevitably calamitous conclusion.

'I'm over here, sirs,' Magnus' voice eventually shouted over the din.

Vespasian, Sabinus and Gaius followed the voice and were relieved to see Magnus in the driving seat of a covered carriage drawn by four sturdy-looking mules; next to him sat Aenor and another young German slave boy. A horse each for Vespasian and Sabinus were tethered to the carriage's rear.

'Magnus, gods be praised,' Gaius shouted back, breaking into a fast waddle, as the two slave boys dismounted to see to their master's needs. 'I didn't think we'd ever find you in this madness.'

As they reached the safety of their carriage Caligula appeared in his chariot, lashing at a group of elderly and bewildered senators running alongside him. 'Why do the old always slow down the young?' he bellowed at them, giving the rearmost of his quarry a furious beating on the back, sending him tumbling to the ground with a scream to disappear beneath the hoofs of the following turma. 'Useless old shit,' he called out with a grin as he caught sight of Vespasian and Sabinus and brought his chariot to a skilful halt, letting the rest of the senators run on. 'His family have probably only been in the Senate for a generation or two; no breeding, you see, dulls the memory. He probably couldn't even remember where his arsehole was; it's no wonder that he was having such trouble finding his carriage.'

'I'm sure that you're right, Divine Gaius,' Vespasian agreed, not wishing to point out that he too was only a second-generation senator.

Caligula beamed at him. 'At least you all managed to be ready on time; you'll join me at the front of the procession as we near the bay. I'm looking forward to seeing the wonder on your faces

383

when you first see my bridge.' His eyes opened even wider with pleasure. 'And you Sabinus, I'm especially looking forward to seeing yours; I've got a lovely surprise for you.' With a crack of his whip over his teams' withers he accelerated away with the turma following, leaving the crumpled and bloody body of the old senator for his family to reclaim.

Gaius shook with suppressed fury. 'This is going too far; riding down senators and leaving them in the dirt as if they were fleeing savages rather than men who have served Rome all their lives. It's an outrage!'

'Uncle,' Vespasian said, putting a calming hand on his shoulder, 'remember your own good advice to me.'

Gaius took a breath and got himself back under control. 'You're right, dear boy: stay alive and don't let your sense of honour overrule your judgement. Let it be someone else that he pushes over the edge; with behaviour like that it won't take long.'

'At least with behaviour like that you can see it coming,' Magnus pointed out. 'You know what to expect, and can accept it before it even happens; it makes it easier to control yourself. It's when things take you by surprise that you lose your judgement.' He stared darkly at Sabinus who was looking pleased with himself, having been singled out for favour so conspicuously by the Emperor. 'And if there's one thing I wouldn't like it would be Caligula preparing a surprise for me, if you take my meaning?'

The procession south along the Via Appia, however, was far from surprising: it was long, hot and very uncomfortable. Caligula had impetuously decided to start out the day after Vespasian had brought him the breastplate. There had been no time to consider the complex logistical problems of moving so many people through a region already suffering from the privations caused by Caligula's impounding of every ship entering Italian waters. By the fifth day the Praetorian Guardsmen's marching rations had run out and any food that the senatorial party had brought along was either finished or had gone off in the baking heat of high summer.

By the sixth day the progress had not even reached the halfway point due to Caligula taking a sudden interest in the civic doings of every town they passed. He would halt the mile-long column as his litter passed through the Forum, and from beneath the shade of his swan-down canopy dispense justice – as he saw it – and decree new civic laws while his quartermasters stripped the community bare not only of their new harvest but also of their livestock and winter stores. The column would then move on an hour or so later, leaving a handful of decapitated, crucified or maimed criminals, new laws concerning the sacrifice of peacocks or suchlike to their emperor deity, and a community unable to feed itself for the coming months, but in possession of an imperial promissory note for such an eye-watering amount of money that the civic fathers knew it would never be honoured.

In the evenings Caligula would order the Praetorians to build a full marching camp with ditch and palisade as if they were on campaign in hostile territory – which indeed, after his activities during the day and the felling of trees for miles around, they generally were. Unless they were one of the few to have had the foresight to bring their own tent, the senators and their wives were obliged to sleep in their sweltering carriages parked tightly together in one corner of the camp with no hope of any seclusion. The one consolation of this arrangement for the women was being able to take advantage of the limited privacy of the latrines built especially for them. Their husbands, who had generally all served under the eagles, had, like any soldier, no problems relieving themselves in the open during a rest halt. For the women, however, this was an ignominy too hideous to bear, and consequently their pained expressions and very short tempers by the end of each day were the product of more than just being jolted around in their carriages for the past few hours.

Vespasian and his companions tried to remain unobtrusive, anxious to have as little to do with Caligula's entertainments as possible. Those senators who suffered the misfortune of being summoned to his huge pavilion in the evenings inevitably came back with tales of mutilation, sodomy and rape, as well as other excesses that they and their mostly hysterical wives refused to – or were simply unable to – find words for.

Their success in avoiding Caligula's notice and invitations, perversely, gave rise to another worry: why had he not invited them? The Emperor counted Vespasian and Sabinus among his closest friends and, by the time they were just one day away from their destination, not to have been asked to share one of his lavish dinners, however distasteful the entertainment, had started to play on Sabinus' mind.

'I wouldn't worry about it, dear boy,' Gaius boomed from the relative comfort of his cushion-infested carriage, 'he seemed pleased enough with you the last time you saw him outside Rome.'

'But that's just it, Uncle,' Sabinus replied, riding alongside. 'He knows that we're here, he's under the unfortunate misapprehension that we're his friends and yet he's ignored us for fifteen days now; what have we done to offend him?'

'You'll get a summons to join him for the final day later this evening, as he promised.'

'But why has he waited this long?'

'Perhaps he doesn't want to ruin the surprise that he has waiting for you,' Vespasian ventured, enjoying a gust of cooling wind blowing in off the calm Tyrrhenian Sea just a hundred paces to their right.

'Very funny, you little shit.'

'I thought so,' Magnus agreed.

Sabinus scowled at him and then turned back to his brother. 'The point is: I would rather have the dubious security of knowing that I'm in Caligula's favour rather than worrying that I've done something to displease him and live in fear of being executed at any moment.'

Vespasian grinned. 'At least that might get me a dinner invitation.'

'What do you mean?'

'Clemens told me that a couple of months ago Caligula ordered a father to attend his son's execution; the father naturally

386

tried to get out of it by claiming ill-health so he sent a litter for him. Afterwards he invited the poor man to dinner and spent the evening trying to cheer him up by telling jokes. Perhaps he'll extend the same courtesy to a brother.'

'If he does, I'm sure that you'd have no problems laughing at his jokes having watched my blood flow.'

A long rumble of Praetorian cornu signalled the end of the penultimate day's march, the column halted and the business of making camp commenced. As the Flavian party waited in the shade of their carriage a horseman made his way down the crowded road towards them. In just a tunic and wearing the wide-brimmed floppy sunhat that the cavalry auxiliaries had favoured in Cyrenaica he was evidently not a Praetorian. As he passed he glanced in the brothers' direction and suddenly pulled his horse around.

'Sabinus, the Emperor sent me to find you,' the rider announced, taking off his hat. 'He wishes for you and your party to present yourselves to him in the morning.'

Vespasian stared at the rider in shocked recognition.

'Thank you, Corvinus,' Sabinus replied, stepping forward to grasp the proffered forearm. 'We'll be there at dawn. I haven't seen you on the progress, where have you been hiding?'

'I've only just caught up with it; I had some business to attend to.'

Sabinus turned and indicated to Vespasian. 'Do you know my brother, Titus Flavius Vespasianus?'

Corvinus' eyes narrowed fractionally. 'Oh yes, we've met. Until tomorrow, then.' He turned his horse and sped away.

Vespasian looked at his brother in apprehension. 'How do you know him?'

'Corvinus? We live on the same street on the Aventine and have often found ourselves walking home together from the Senate since I got back. We've become quite friendly in a short time. But I'm surprised that he's never mentioned knowing you; he's asked about the family and I mentioned your name.'

'What else have you told him?'

'Oh, nothing that I wouldn't mention to any senator who makes a polite enquiry: where we come from, who our parents are, who my wife's family are; that sort of thing.'

'Did you tell him about Caenis?'

'I don't think so; why?'

'He has no cause to like me; in fact, he's threatened me.'

'Why would that be, dear boy?' Gaius asked, looking concernedly in Corvinus' direction.

'He was a cavalry prefect while I was in Cyrenaica, I made a couple of decisions that he didn't like – and perhaps he was right. Do you know him?'

'Marcus Valerius Messala Corvinus? Of course I know of him. It would seem that you've made yourself an enemy who has the potential to be rather influential. Provided his future brother-in-law manages to stay alive, his sister could well end up as empress.'

'How could—' Vespasian stopped suddenly and sucked in his breath as he remembered a pair of dark eyes glaring at him as he laughed at one of Caligula's jokes.

Gaius nodded gravely. 'Yes, dear boy, his sister is Claudius' future wife: Valeria Messalina.'

It was with a certain amount of trepidation that the brothers approached Caligula's pavilion the following morning in the pale dawn. All around them the business of dismantling the camp was progressing apace and smoke and steam from freshly doused cooking fires swirled on the warm sea breeze.

Caligula's close entourage were already gathering to greet him and stood around the entrance murmuring in small groups.

The brothers dismounted and handed their horses to a couple of slaves; from over by the pavilion entrance they saw a familiar face detaching himself from a group consisting of Claudius, Asiaticus, Pallas and, much to Vespasian's unease, Narcissus.

'I wondered if I would see you two here,' Corbulo said, walking over to them.

'Corbulo, you're well, I trust,' Vespasian replied, grasping his forearm.

'As well as can be expected for a man who has had to build a three-and-a-half mile-extension of the Via Appia over more than two thousand ships in less than two months.' He gripped Sabinus' arm. 'That's the last time that I make a speech in the Senate complaining about the state of the roads.'

Vespasian had to suppress a grin. 'Is that why he gave you the task?'

Corbulo's long, aristocratic face looked downcast. 'Yes, he said if I didn't like the roads as they were then I could build him a nice new one. Now my family will be associated with the biggest waste of money ever, and to compound our dishonour my whore of a half-sister has been disgracing herself by cavorting in public with the Emperor at any and every opportunity; she's even got herself pregnant by him, or at least she claims it's by him.'

'We hadn't heard,' Sabinus said sympathetically. 'I'm sorry for your shame.'

'Well, you've both been away and I'd rather that you heard it from me. Anyway, she's been down here for the last few days. Caligula sent her to me to ensure that she rests during the pregnancy because if it goes its full term he plans to marry her. Although judging by the tired looks of the turma of Praetorian cavalry that escorted her here I don't think that she had much rest on the way down.'

'So is the road ready?' Vespasian asked, anxious to change the subject before the grin managed to overcome his self-control.

'Of course it's ready,' Corbulo snapped, 'I'm a Domitius, we complete our tasks, however ludicrous.'

'Yes of course, that's why the Emperor chose you.'

'I can't say that it was made any easier by being forced to work with that jumped-up freedman, Narcissus. The man's intolerably addicted to power; he even tried to give me an order once, can you imagine it?'

'I'm sure Caligula will reward you well for your pains.'

Corbulo puffed up with pride. 'He's nominating me as his colleague in the consulship next year; that will go some way to restoring the family's honour.'

Vespasian thought it best not to tell Corbulo that Caligula was also thinking of nominating his horse. 'He's nominated me a praetor.'

Corbulo looked down his highborn nose at Vespasian. 'It's most unusual for a New Man to be given that honour in the first year that he's eligible for it. What have you done to deserve that?'

'Oh, the same sort of ludicrous things as you; just obeying Caligula's will.'

The crowd around the pavilion suddenly went silent as Clemens appeared from within. 'Senators and People of Rome,' he called out, 'I give you your Emperor, the Divine Gaius, Lord of land and sea.'

'Hail Divine Gaius, Lord of land and sea!' the crowd began to obediently chant.

After a few choruses the pavilion flaps opened and Caligula appeared wearing Alexander's breastplate over which a cloak-like *chlamys* of purple silk, pinned on the right shoulder, fluttered in the breeze; his head was adorned with a crown of oak leaves and he held a gilded sword and a shield of the argyraspides with the sixteen-pointed star of Macedon inlaid upon it. At the sight of him the intensity of the chant grew for he did indeed look like a young god.

Caligula raised his sword and shield to the heavens and held his head back soaking up the laudatory chant. 'Today,' he called out eventually, 'I complete my greatest achievement so far. I will ride my chariot across the water in fellowship with my brother Neptune; our feud is at an end!'

Despite being uncertain as to the nature of the feud the crowd cheered in relief.

'Once this day is completed we will return to Rome to prepare for a year of conquest to start next spring. To show the world that I am the true Lord of land and sea I will lead our armies into Germania and exorcise the shame that still sullies Roman honour by retrieving the one remaining lost eagle from the Teutoburg Forest disaster: that of the Seventeenth Legion. When that is done we shall proceed north to the edge of the known world and, in concert with my brother Neptune, I will lead our armies across the sea and conquer, for me and for Rome, Britannia.'

Even Vespasian found himself getting carried away by the magnitude of the idea along with the rest of the crowd: here at last was an enterprise that would not be a vast exercise in squandering money, it would be for the greater glory and profit of Rome. Perhaps, just perhaps, the young Emperor had found a way to satisfy at the same time his desire for the grandiose statement – no matter what the cost in lives and coin – and his subjects' desire for conquest and renown.

'Follow me, my friends,' Caligula shouted, 'follow me to the bridge and we shall ride across to the victory and the glory that awaits us on the other side.'

For the first time in many years Vespasian followed Caligula willingly.

CHAPTER XXIIII

VESPASIAN COULD NOT contain a gasp of surprise as the head of the column, led by Caligula in his quadriga, crested the western slope of Mount Nuova at the most northerly point of the Bay of Neapolis.

Caligula turned in his chariot and shouted triumphantly at the sea of faces, all with the same expression of astonishment written upon them. 'What did I tell you, my friends? Is it not truly amazing, the work of a god?'

It was undeniably truly amazing. Below them, stretching from Baiae, just north of the humped Promontory of Misenum, right across to Puteoli, three and a half miles away across the glittering azure water, stretched a double line of ships, chained together side by side, undulating gently on the calm swell of the sea. Across them had been laid a road, straight as the Via Appia, but wider, much wider. However, the bridge was not just a straight line; at intervals along its length single lines of ships curved out like tentacles to end up in peninsulas of round clusters of vessels that had been completely covered over to form solid platforms upon which stood, unbelievably, buildings. Beyond it the Portus Julius, home of the western fleet, stood empty.

Cracking his whip over his team's withers and shouting a prayer to his own Genius, Caligula accelerated away down the hill; sparks from his iron-shod wheels grating against the stone road flew up behind him. Fired with enthusiasm at the sight of such a magnificent creation, Vespasian and the rest of the younger senators on horseback sped after him, whooping and shouting like juveniles and vying with each other to be the first onto the bridge after their Emperor. The Praetorian cavalry followed close behind them, leaving the infantry and the wagons to make the half-mile journey at their own slow speed.

With Caligula just ahead, Vespasian clattered down the main street of the small fishing port of Baiae with a wide grin on his face. As it opened out onto the harbour the bridge stood ahead of him, fading into the distance. Its true scale only became apparent close to: the road that Corbulo had engineered across it was over thirty paces wide. It was not constructed just out of planks of wood nailed haphazardly over each vessel; it had been laid as if on land because, indeed, it was on land. The deck of each ship had been filled with earth, from the mast to the stern, to the height of the rail. To compensate for the weight, great boulders had been placed in each bow, levelling the vessels, which had been chained together, hull to hull, in two lines. Then, with all the steering oars removed, the lines had been attached stern to stern. The small gaps between the ships had been boarded over with thick planks secured with foot-long nails driven through the decks. The earth had then been pounded down, levelling it to make one three-and-a-half-mile-long smooth, unbroken surface. But as if this were not extraordinary enough, it had been paved with foot-square stones laid a thumb's breadth apart so that they would not concertina with the undulation on the ships.

Caligula drove his quadriga straight onto his creation and brought it to a halt next to a collection of thirty or so chariots of strange appearance, pulled by pairs of short, sturdy-looking ponies with shaggy coats.

He turned to address his followers. 'These are replicas of the chariots used by the British tribes, but the ponies are properly trained chariot-ponies imported from Britannia itself. Come, my friends, take a chariot and ride it across the water. When the rumour that we can not only drive their chariots but also ride them over the sea reaches the ears of the savages of Britannia they will fall before me and beg for mercy from your god. Come, my friends, come!'

Vespasian leapt off his horse and joined the headlong rush to get to a chariot, there being more willing drivers than vehicles.

Grabbing a set of reins from one of the Celtic-looking slaves in charge of each chariot, he clambered aboard the nearest one. It was a simple design: a rectangular wooden base set on iron-rimmed wheels, two feet in diameter, with a semicircular wicker frame on either side and left open at the front and rear. The ponies were attached to the up-curved central pole by a yoke and controlled by reins running from their bits.

'Can you drive one of these things?' Sabinus called, grinning wildly as he leapt onto the chariot next to him.

'There's only one way to find out,' Vespasian shouted back, flicking the reins as the slave jumped in behind him.

'Kneel, master,' the slave said as the chariot moved forward, 'like this. That way the reins are not high.'

Vespasian glanced back to see his companion kneeling low on one knee and immediately copied his position so that the reins flowed along the ponies' backs. He pulled slightly to the right and the little beasts responded, edging the chariot out into the centre of the road. All around, the other drivers were getting the same lesson from their instructors with varying degrees of success.

Once all the chariots were occupied and in position behind him, Caligula waited no longer and, with his gilded sword raised in the air, set off at a walk towards Puteoli, shimmering in the morning sun and crowned by dun-brown hills climbing up behind it. Those senators who had been unable or unwilling to get a chariot followed on horseback along with the near thousand-strong contingent of Praetorian cavalry. Just under a half-mile further back up the hill the dark mass of the Praetorian infantry, followed by hundreds of carriages, could be seen approaching Baiae.

Vespasian pulled his chariot closer to that of Corbulo. 'How did you do this, Corbulo? It feels so stable.'

Corbulo glanced over with an expression that looked remark-ably close to enjoyment on his normally rigid face. 'A lot of slaves; I commandeered every healthy male slave within fifty miles. There are more than a few fat merchants who've had to go without their massages or a decent fish stew for the last two months.' He snorted a few times in what Vespasian assumed was a valiant attempt at a laugh.

As they passed the first of the peninsulas, a third of the way across, Caligula increased the pace to a trot. The extra speed meant that Vespasian was more aware of the gentle roll of the bridge as he moved from ship to ship more rapidly and their slight difference in pitch registered quicker. To his right the curve of the causeway leading to the peninsula made a harbour in which were moored leisure boats, too small to be of use in the bridge, but plentiful enough to provide everyone with some aquatic amusement later on.

Behind them the carriages rolled onto the bridge followed by the infantry.

Just over the halfway point, marked by a causeway extending out on either side, Caligula cracked his team into a canter. The exhilaration among the charioteers began to grow as, looking left and right over the wicker sides of their vehicles, they were too low to see the bows of the ships supporting them and could only see water; apart from the masts flicking by they had the sensation that they really were riding over a vast expanse of sea.

A quarter of a mile from the end of the bridge Caligula let his horses loose into an outright gallop; the hardy Celtic ponies followed suit and behind them the cavalry thundered on. The pounding of thousands of hoofs echoed strangely through the hollow hulls of the ships below, amplifying the sound fivefold into a deafening drumming, drowning out the cries and hollers of the charioteers and troopers. Oblivious to all else but the sensation of great speed, the tumult in his ears and the wind in his face blowing his cares from his mind, Vespasian followed Caligula blindly, screaming at the top of his voice.

As the bridge came to an end Caligula did not stop.

On he went; on towards the mass of citizens of Puteoli who had turned out to watch the extravaganza. Brandishing his gilded sword he swept his team into the unbelieving crowd, skittling over and trampling under hoof those too slow to move out of his way. An instant later, unable to pull up short because of the cavalry pressing them from behind, the rest of the chariots hit the fragile wall of unprotected flesh and bone. Screams and wails rent the air, louder even than the drumming of the hoofs still pounding the bridge behind, as the momentum of the stocky ponies, with the weight of their burdens behind them, drove ragged gashes through the throng that only moments earlier had been in a holiday mood.

Vespasian looked in horror as his team ploughed into a family, sending a howling infant flying up into the air as its parents and elder siblings, with shrill curtailed screeches, disappeared beneath his ponies' hoofs, to reveal another set of faces, petrified with fear, taking their last look at a bewildering world. On either side of him, Sabinus and Corbulo were causing equal carnage, while behind them, the cavalry, also unable to stop suddenly due to the weight of numbers to their rear, fanned out left and right and hurtled into parts of the crowd as yet untouched but trying desperately to escape.

In among the pandemonium of broken limbs and cracked skulls, Vespasian managed to bring his terrified team to a halt; his incredulous slave ran along the pole and jumped down between the necks of the rearing beasts, grabbing their bits and pulling their heads down, stilling them. All along the line a gradual loss of momentum telegraphed itself back through the main body of cavalry still on the bridge and the column slowly came to a halt. The pressure eased on the crowd who were able to stampede towards the bottlenecked streets leading away from the harbour, trampling the weakest underfoot with the abandon of those who just want to live at any cost.

From amidst the tangle of crushed and broken bodies Caligula emerged on foot, leading his team and laughing hysterically. The wheels of his chariot bumped over the dead and the injured, of whom he took no notice. 'Back to the bridge, my friends; we shall offer a sacrifice to my brother Neptune in thanks for the smooth sea without which this glorious victory would not have been possible.'

Vespasian and Sabinus looked at each other, horror stamped on their faces and shame burning in their hearts. Horror at what they had taken part in and its consequences and shame at being gulled into believing, at first, that it was a magnificent and exciting feat, a prelude to greater things to come, and taking part in it with such fervour.

There was nothing to be said as their slaves, still shaking their heads in disbelief at what they had witnessed, turned their teams, which remained wide-eyed with fright, away from the long pile of mangled bodies and remounted the chariots. All around them on the quayside and back along the bridge the Praetorian cavalry were trying to regroup from the chaotic aftermath of the charge and form into the regimented lines that they so prided themselves on.

Caligula, however, was not interested in military precision; as soon as the Celtic chariots were turned behind him he leapt onto his quadriga and whipped his team forward into the disorganised Praetorians, who had no option but to part and make way for their Emperor. Those still on the quay had little trouble doing so but as Caligula mounted the bridge, pressing his team ever forward, the cavalry struggled to make room for him in the closer confines of the relatively narrow road. Not wishing to be the trooper who delayed the Emperor, each man in his path pulled his mount forcefully to one side, pushing the horse next to him to produce a domino effect that sent whinnying horses and their riders tumbling or jumping off the side of the road and onto the decks of the ships, thankfully, only four feet below. Vespasian and the other charioteers followed Caligula through the shambles until he burst through the rearmost ranks and onto a clear road where he whipped his team into a canter and headed off, straight towards the carriages and infantry.

Vespasian's ponies were blown as they reached the central point of the bridge where the causeway to the largest peninsula curled off to the south. Caligula had arrived there well before them but at the same time as the carriages, judging by the overturned vehicles still attached to screeching horses both on the road and to the decks on either side. He had abandoned his quadriga and, having unhitched Incitatus, he and his favoured horse were now leading the senators and their wives on foot along the curved, one-vessel-wide causeway at the end of which stood what looked to be a temple, complete with columns and steps on every side. In the harbour formed by the causeway and around the temple platform scores more small boats were moored, but unlike those in the first harbour these were manned and their furled sails were raised or their oars were already set in their rowlocks.

Vespasian, Sabinus and the rest of the charioteers hurriedly dismounted and ran to catch up.

'Ah, dear boys, I was waiting for you,' Gaius called out from beneath a parasol held by Aenor; the other boy was doing his best work with a fan to keep his master cool in the growing heat. 'How was it? It looked spectacular from the other end.'

'It was murder, pure murder!' Vespasian spat, gratefully taking a water-skin from Magnus. He took a deep draught and passed it to Sabinus, wiping his mouth with the back of his hand. 'And now we're to give thanks to Neptune for allowing Caligula to slaughter half the population of Puteoli.'

'He only slaughtered half?' Magnus questioned. 'He must be losing his touch.'

Vespasian scowled at his friend and stalked off down the causeway.

Flanked by eight of his German Bodyguards and Incitatus, Caligula stood in front of the temple, his arms covered in the blood of a bullock. 'Fearful of my power, my brother Neptune has gratefully accepted the sacrifice so as not to cause me offence,' he announced to the massed ranks of senators and their wives crowded onto the temple peninsula. The temple itself, Vespasian had noticed, was not a proper building but constructed of canvas cleverly painted as marble, with tree trunks, likewise coloured, as columns. 'Seeing as he is so evidently terrified of me, we have nothing to fear from him, so before the victory feast we shall all take to the sea. To the boats, my sheep, to the boats!'

Leading his bodyguard he strode to the edge of the platform and jumped down into an eight-oared, flat-bottomed boat of a sleek design; his Germans got in after him and manned the oars.

'I suppose a little boating before dinner could be convivial,' Gaius commented as Vespasian, Sabinus and Magnus helped him down into a small sailing skiff crewed by a foul-smelling, weather-beaten old man and his grandson. He made himself comfortable in the bow with Aenor with his parasol and the other boy with his fan in close attendance. The brothers and Magnus settled amidships, while the grandson pushed off and the old man unfurled the triangular leather sail; the boat slipped slowly on the light breeze out into the bay.

As they embarked in various craft, the mood among the senators and their wives, who had not witnessed the slaughter at Puteoli, was jolly as most took Gaius' view that some pre-dinner boating would indeed be convivial. Before long over a hundred small vessels, under either oars or sail, were bobbing around on the smooth water between the temple and the bridge upon which the Praetorian infantry and cavalry had formed up in long, dark lines. Those who had been unable to find a berth or thought that their constitutions were not up to braving Neptune's element, strolled along the causeway, admiring the pretty scene and waving to friends who had been luckier or braver than themselves.

Caligula's boat skitted around, turning left and then right, while he stood in the stern holding the steering oar, whooping madly. As he passed close to the Flavian party, Vespasian noticed him cock his head and look quizzical as if he suddenly did not know where he was. He sat down and looked at his German rowers. 'Ramming speed!' he ordered with a shrill shout. The lead oarsman responded immediately and his rhythm was taken up by his heavily muscled fellows. The boat accelerated forward towards a cluster of slow-moving sailing boats.

Unaware of the threat coming towards them the vessels did nothing to alter course. Within moments Caligula's boat was upon them and its solid wooden prow cracked broadside into the hull of the nearest, overturning the flat-bottomed boat with remarkable ease, spilling its occupants into the sea. Caligula's boat carried on at speed as with two hands he adjusted his steering oar so that it smashed into the next small craft with the same effect. On he went for another two successful rams as panic spread around him. Suddenly he turned the boat and aimed it back the way he had come.

Passing by his floundering and spluttering victims he took his steering oar from its housing and, two-handed, cracked it down onto their heads, laughing maniacally, as the unfortunates, both male and female, sank unconscious below the surface. 'My brother Neptune deserves some dinner guests too, give him my regards,' he shouted after them as his boat ploughed on, still at ramming speed, directly towards the Flavians' small craft.

For a shocked moment they watched it approach and then all turned to the old man who, judging by the terror in his eyes, had seen it too. With no chance to manoeuvre quickly out of the way due to the light wind the old man sat paralysed, staring at the oncoming threat. It was pointless shouting at him to do something, there was nothing that he could have done; instead they grabbed on to anything solid and prepared for impact.

It came moments later with a shuddering jolt.

Vespasian hit the water as the boat rolled over. He had the presence of mind to dive deeper so as to avoid the thrashing of Caligula's oar. He counted to thirty before considering it safe and then kicked for the surface. He and Sabinus appeared at almost the same time and quickly looked about. Magnus suddenly bobbed up.

'Where's Gaius?' Vespasian shouted.

All three of them looked around in panic; from behind the capsized boat the old man and his grandson appeared, both swimming strongly. Gaius was not in sight; Vespasian dived. Although neither a strong nor natural swimmer, desperation lent force and co-ordination to his limbs and he swiftly descended, passing the body of Aenor with blood seeping from an oar-wound to his head. The water was clear and he soon saw the bulk of his uncle struggling weakly, his eyes bulging with the pressure of holding his breath, but being dragged down by the weight of his toga. He kicked out for him; Sabinus and Magnus both followed. Grabbing Gaius' arm he began to haul him up, while Magnus and Sabinus struggled to undrape his toga. As the garment finally came free, Vespasian felt the drag lessen, but at that moment Gaius gave him a look of agony and copious bubbles of air escaped from his nose and mouth; he convulsed as his lungs filled with water.

Between the three of them they managed to propel Gaius to the surface; as they drew explosive breaths Gaius remained still, his lips pale and his eyes closed.

'Get him ashore quick,' Vespasian yelled at his companions.

The old man and his grandson came to their aid and with their strong strokes they dragged Gaius the twenty paces or so to the causeway as fast as they could.

There were many willing hands to help lift the heavy body out of the water as behind them Caligula continued to terrorise the pleasure craft.

Once Gaius had been hauled onto the road, Vespasian turned him onto his stomach letting his head loll down over the edge; water seeped from his mouth. 'Magnus, remember what you said when we were dealing with Poppaeus? You have to wait a while before you get the water out of their lungs because they can come back to life.'

Magnus' face lit up. 'You're right, sir,' he said, getting astride Gaius' waist and placing his hands on the back of his ribcage.

Vespasian and Sabinus knelt on either side.

'Ready?' Magnus said. 'Now!' Six hands squeezed the chest in unison. 'Now!' Then again. 'Now!' And again.

For half a dozen pumps they carried on until a gush of water erupted from Gaius' mouth; after another couple of pumps came a second, greater, spurt followed by a choking gasp. A single pump more resulted in a lesser expulsion but the ensuing rasping breath caused Gaius' eyes to open. With a massive spasm he heaved out the contents of his sea-water-filled stomach and then took a series of congested gasps as the last of the water sprayed from his lungs. Magnus gave him a couple more pumps and then got off him.

After a few moments Gaius was able to breathe quickly and shallowly but with difficulty. He looked back up at Vespasian uncomprehendingly. 'I drowned, I remember.'

'Well, you're alive again now, Uncle. Perhaps Neptune was worried about how much of his dinner he would have to share with you.'

A look of dismay spread over Gaius' face. 'My boys?'

Vespasian shook his head slowly then looked out towards the harbour to where, just next to their capsized boat, two small bodies floated, face down, in the sea.

Whether Caligula tired of providing dinner guests for his brother god or whether he became concerned that if he provided many more his victory feast would be sparsely attended was uncertain, but soon after Gaius' recovery he came ashore and ordered everyone to repair to the huge triclinium erected on a peninsula to the north of the bridge.

He was in a cheerful mood as he and Incitatus walked down the causeway, playfully pushing back into the water the occasional senator trying to clamber out of a boat; but, flanked as he was by his Germans, no one dared touch him. The brooding presence of the Praetorian Guard, still formed up on the bridge, doubly ensured his safety. The Emperor was the only reason they existed, so the rank and file owed him absolute loyalty and any attempt to assassinate him in such an exposed area would be met with swift and calamitous vengeance: the Senate would be completely annihilated. And they knew it; as did Caligula.

In recognition of this fact, Caligula delivered a long speech of congratulations to his loyal troops on their stunning victory over the town of Puteoli and promised them a bounty of a year's wages when they returned safely to Rome. There was no question of them not ensuring his safety after that.

By mid-afternoon Caligula was leading the Senate down the isthmus to the victory feast. Vespasian and Sabinus walked close behind him with Gaius, still weak from his ordeal and grief but not daring to leave, limping along, supported by Magnus.

'Ah, Sabinus,' Caligula called back, pausing to wait for the Flavians to catch up. 'I think that the time for your surprise is upon us.'

Sabinus kept his face rigid. 'You honour me, Divine Gaius.'

'I know. But I need men I can trust for my year of conquest; I can't do everything myself, you know.'

'If you say so, Divine Gaius.'

'I do. I will need the Ninth Hispana for my expedition to Germania next year so I'm getting rid of the timid imbecile who's currently commanding and appointing you as its legate; you served with it as a tribune, I believe.'

Sabinus looked at his Emperor with a mixture of astonishment and gratitude.

Caligula burst into cold laughter. 'The relief of being honoured and not abused; I knew that I'd enjoy the look on your face after days of apprehension.'

'I never doubted you, Divine Gaius. How can I repay you?'

Caligula slapped a hand on Sabinus' shoulder as they approached the high wooden doors of the triclinium. 'I didn't know that until yesterday. Now I believe a way will present itself; perhaps sooner than you think.'

Chaerea was waiting to report to Caligula as the doors were swung open by a couple of slaves.

'The watchword, Chaerea,' Caligula said, pushing him aside, 'is "Eunuch".'

Vespasian saw the same hatred burn in the Praetorian tribune's eyes as he passed into the interior but that was soon forgotten as he gazed around and suddenly realised that, although the day had been chaotic and haphazard, run according to Caligula's whim, this part had been timed to absolute perfection. The chamber was as vast as it was magnificent; constructed in the same fashion as the temple with painted wooden columns supporting the roof, it had a feeling of space and airiness. At its far end were doors leading to further rooms; in front of these, a group of musicians plucked on lyres and blew soaring notes on pipes. All around its marble floor, scores of tables surrounded by couches were set at regular intervals; but what made it so breathtaking was that cut into the ceiling above each table were small square holes, so positioned that only at this exact time of day would the sun shine down and perfectly hit each table, illuminating only them and not the couches that surrounded them.

'Perfect!' Caligula cried to Callistus who stood, next to Narcissus, with his head bowed just inside the door. 'Callistus, you've done well; I'm minded to reward you with your freedom.'

Callistus raised his head; his face showed no sign of gratitude at his impending manumission. 'As you wish, Divine master.'

'Everything is as I wish.' Caligula turned to Narcissus. 'I wish you to see to the comfort of our principal guests, the rest can just recline where they like.'

'Of course, Divine Gaius,' the Greek crooned as Caligula brushed past him towards a group of ladies, one holding a baby, waiting by the table of honour at the far end of the room to greet him. They were escorted by Clemens, Claudius and, of all people, Corvinus.

Narcissus caught Vespasian by the arm as he passed and whispered in his ear. 'Congratulations on acquiring your new wealth. I haven't told the Emperor yet; we'll keep it just between the two of us for now, shall we?' He patted him on the shoulder and went off to supervise the senators flooding in through the doors.

'What did that oily freedman want?' Sabinus asked, still visibly glowing with pride at his promotion, as they followed Caligula across the floor.

'Nothing much; just a veiled threat implying that my life is in his hands should Caligula start running out of money.'

'A distinct possibility should we have another day like this, dear boy,' Gaius said weakly.

Vespasian looked at the golden platters piled high with exquisite delicacies that slaves had begun to set on the tables as the senators and their wives began to take their places. 'Someone has to stop this.'

Gaius slumped down on a couch. 'I have to admit that if I felt stronger I would do it myself.'

'Don't worry, sir,' Magnus assured him, 'that feeling will soon pass and your self-preservatory instincts will take over again.'

'I do hope you're right, Magnus; somehow I don't think that I'm nimble enough to wield the assassin's blade.'

'Chaerea is,' Vespasian observed, 'and with a few more insults like that from Caligula he'll be ready to. The question is: where will Clemens stand?' He looked over at the pasty face of the Praetorian prefect and was shocked by the look of devastation on it; next to him Corvinus stood smiling smugly as Caligula approached the group.

'Agrippina and Julia Livilla,' Caligula enthused, greeting his sisters with a kiss apiece, 'I hope that you have learnt your lessons.'

The two women looked none the worse for their recent ordeal.

'Yes, dear brother,' Agrippina replied; her sister just nodded. 'We are all yours again.'

'Good, my sweet,' Caligula said, patting the shock of ginger hair sprouting from the head of the baby she held. 'How is young Lucius Domitius?'

'He's strong and wilful.'

'He'll need to be strong if I'm forced to banish you to that barren rock where our mother lived out her last days.' He gently lifted her chin and kissed her mouth. 'Please don't make me do that.' Without waiting for a reply he turned to the woman next to her. 'Messalina, your brother, Corvinus, has done me a great service. I look forward to welcoming you into my family next month – even if it is to marry this buffoon.' He looked contemptuously at Claudius, who bowed his head, mumbling his thanks at being noticed.

Messalina smiled, her dark eyes flicked quickly over to Vespasian and held his for an instant while her brother,

Corvinus, looked triumphantly at him. Clemens appeared to be struggling to control himself. All around the room the couches were filling up.

Caligula moved on to the fourth and final woman; she was older than the other three and not at all attractive, having the same long face and nose of her half-brother Corbulo.

'Caesonia Milonia,' Caligula said, putting his hand on her stomach, 'how goes your pregnancy?'

'I carry the child of a god, Divine Gaius, and it thrives.'

'Of course; but nevertheless I will rest you for now and take my pleasure elsewhere; but first we shall eat.'

Caligula chewed on a swan leg and waved a dismissive hand at the hundreds of senators reclining at the many tables around the room. 'Look at them all,' he confided disdainfully to Vespasian and Sabinus on the couch next to him. 'They all hate me now after what I've been doing to them in the last couple of years; but what would they give to be here where you are, next to your Emperor?'

'You honour us with your favour,' Vespasian acknowledged, looking at the food on the table in front of him with little appetite.

'I do; and each one of those sheep is spitting jealous that they aren't receiving the same treatment. No matter what I do to them they still feign love for me.'

'It's not a feigned love, they don't hate you.'

Caligula looked at Vespasian in amusement. 'Don't lie to me, my friend. What do you think I've been doing since I became emperor? Ruling justly?'

Vespasian studied Caligula's face for a moment and was surprised to see his eyes clear and lucid. 'You have done some great things and next year you will do greater deeds,' he replied cautiously, trying to put the massacre that day out of his mind.

'I have; but the greatest thing that I've achieved is to hold a mirror up to the Senate so that they can see themselves for what they really are: sycophants and flatterers who know no other way to live. All those years of treason trials when they denounced one another in the hope of gaining favour with Augustus, Tiberius or Sejanus and in the knowledge that if they brought a successful prosecution they would gain the estate of their victim has left them morally bankrupt. It also cost me most of my family and I'm honour bound to avenge them.'

Vespasian and Sabinus looked at each other, both startled that Caligula was confiding in them in a way that had a hint of truth in it.

'These humiliations have been all about revenge?' Sabinus asked.

Caligula smiled coldly. 'Naturally. You see, Vespasian, your brother is not dissembling now; you should try it. Do you think I'm mad?'

The answer stuck in Vespasian's throat; either way he would condemn himself.

'Answer! And answer truthfully. Do you think that I'm mad?'

'Yes, I do, Divine Gaius.'

Caligula burst out laughing but the humour did not reach his eyes. 'My friend, well done, you are the first person who has told me the truth even though you fear for your life. Of course you think I'm mad, who wouldn't? And perhaps I am or perhaps I just have no desire for self-control. However, by each seemingly mad act I humiliate the Senate even more; I want to see how low they will stoop and yet still try to flatter me in the hope of favour. As I lay sick, each day they came to my door having offered prayers and sacrifices for my recovery and I knew that they only wanted news of my death. So I decided to make them crawl, make them do what no Roman has ever done: worship a living god. And look at them, they do. But I'm no god; they know that I'm not, and, furthermore, they also know that I know that they know it, and yet we all now maintain the pretence. Even you pretend to my face that I'm a god, don't you?'

Vespasian swallowed. 'Yes, Divine Gaius.'

'Of course you do, you have to preserve yourself. I'm the most powerful man in the world and what is power if you don't flaunt it? People worship those who hold it out of a desire to be shown favour. It's deliciously amusing. Do you remember that idiot who offered his life in exchange for mine? He expected reward for such sycophancy but I took him at his word. But then I rewarded with a million sesterces the liar who swore that he saw Drusilla's spirit rise into the heavens to commune with the gods, so now they don't know what to do. Sheep! I'll push them and push them because I can and it pleases and amuses me to do so.'

Vespasian frowned. 'But one day you'll push someone too far.'

'Will I? I don't think so. If someone did manage to kill me, which would be very difficult, they would themselves die. Who here would do that and lose all his property, thereby making his family destitute? Would you?'

Neither Vespasian nor Sabinus answered.

Caligula sneered and got up. 'You see, you wouldn't, would you? You're both as bad as the rest of them; and I'll prove it to you.' He walked over to Corvinus who stood by one of the doors; Clemens was next to him still looking devastated. Music continued to rise from the players nearby. 'Corvinus, if you please?'

'A pleasure, Divine Gaius,' Corvinus said, opening the door and disappearing through it; there was a brief cry before he emerged leading a naked woman roughly by the arm.

'Clementina!' Sabinus shouted, leaping up from his couch.

Vespasian slammed a restraining arm across his brother's chest as he tried to go forward. 'No!' he hissed. 'Caligula's right, you'll die and your property would be forfeit; Clementina and the children would be destitute.'

'Doesn't that look delicious,' Caligula said slowly and with palpable relish. 'Corvinus took it upon himself to fetch her from wherever you'd hidden her, Sabinus, without me even asking him to. Wasn't that kind of him, Clemens?'

Clemens closed his eyes and breathed deeply, shaking with suppressed fury. Behind the ugly scene the pipes and lyres blended their notes in delicate harmony.

Vespasian held onto Sabinus who still struggled and was now heaving with sobs.

Caligula grabbed Clementina's wrist. 'Your husband was only now wondering how he could thank me; how fortunate he is to have found a way so quickly.' He gave the brothers a malicious, questioning look. 'Sheep?'

Time seemed to slow; sound became muffled and indistinct as Vespasian suppressed his horror. With his feelings wiped from his face, he held Caligula's gaze for a moment and knew then that the Emperor had been wrong: he would be killed and his death would be soon; how could it not be so?

But who would stand in his place?

Vespasian turned and stared, his face still impassive, at Claudius, the only direct adult heir of the Julio-Claudian line, twitching and drooling in lust at the sight of Clementina's body while unconciously cupping Messalina's breast. He saw Messalina and her brother, Corvinus, both staring at Clemens and then share a brief, satisfied look of ambition. Vespasian understood what Corvinus had knowingly set in motion when he had seized Clementina, the sister of the prefect of the Praetorian Guard, and brought her here for his master to defile – Corvinus knew that Messalina could ultimately benefit, for what choice as emperor was there other than her future husband?

Vespasian looked past Messalina to Caligula's sister, Agrippina, who was staring with loathing at her while holding her carrot-topped infant – another male heir but far too young. His eyes moved on to Caesonia Milonia, swelling with Caligula's seed, looking haughtily down her long nose at the other two women, and he knew that the fruit of her belly could not be allowed to survive the Emperor's death. It would be Claudius, he thought, certain now. He looked back at the malformed man whose erection protruded shamelessly from under his tunic. This would be the best that Caesar's line could offer. For how long could that be tolerated?

The wavering note of a pipe pierced his consciousness and from that germ the song of the Phoenix filled the silence within his head. Thrasyllus' prophecy came unbidden behind it and, as his gaze lingered on the heirs of Caesar, Vespasian knew for an instant the question that would one day take him back to the Temple of Amun at Siwa. It disappeared as quickly as it had come as sound flooded back into his ears and time ground back up to its unrelenting pace.

Clementina looked first at her husband and then her brother, her eyes pleading, but they could do nothing as the arbitrator of life and death dragged her out of the dining room.

The door closed; Clementina screamed; Clemens walked over to the brothers and whispered into Sabinus' ear: 'Not here, not now, but at a time and place of my choosing, together.'

Sabinus gave the faintest of nods as tears streamed down his face and, for the first time in his life, Vespasian feared for his brother: the man whose sense of honour would be strong enough to overrule his judgement.

And then he began to fear for himself; he knew that when Sabinus next returned to Rome it would be with death in his heart and he, Vespasian, would be forced to make the choice between turning his back on the sacred bonds of blood or aiding his brother in assassinating an emperor.

AUTHOR'S NOTE

This historical fiction is based on the writings of Tacitus, Suetonius, Cassius Dio, Josephus and Philo.

The events surrounding the crucifixion of Yeshua are, to say the least, opaque. To my mind motivations and timelines seem to be very confused; no doubt due to ancient writers trying to construct a story piecemeal to suit the agenda of the newly conceived Pauline Christianity. My version of the story is set down with no claims to scholarship; it is purely constructed to have Sabinus witness the birth of a man-made religion that will become an important strand of the story as the series progresses.

I am grateful to A. N. Wilson in his *Paul: The Mind of the Apostle* for his suggestion of Paulus' full name and for his intriguing idea that he may have been the Temple guard who had his ear chopped off by Peter and also that he may well have witnessed the crucifixion itself.

There is no evidence that Paulus went to Creta and Cyrenaica in his persecution of Yeshua's followers. Vespasian was quaestor there in AD 34 or soon after if we follow the dating in Barbara Levick's excellent biography *Vespasian*. I chose AD 34 because that was the year, according to Tacitus, that the Phoenix was again reborn – Cassius Dio puts it in AD 36. Tacitus clearly believes in the Phoenix and spends more than half a page describing it.

Silphium was dying out at this time and that would have put quite a strain on the Cyrenaican economy. Nero was said to have been presented with the last plant in existence twenty years later.

I have probably done the Marmaridae a disservice by portraying them as ruthless slavers, for which I apologise.

The Oracle of Amun was in Siwa and Alexander did travel there and was spoken to; he never revealed what he had been told.

Caligula did have a long affair with Macro's wife, Ennia, and did swear to make her his empress and Macro prefect of Egypt before ordering their suicide for adultery and pandering. Vespasian's part in the suicide is, of course, fiction.

Poppaeus died a natural death in AD 35 and Tacitus wrote of him that he was up to the task and no more. There is nothing to suggest that he had anything to do with Pomponius' suicide the year before; that seems to have been Tiberius' doing.

The Parthian mission did come to Rome at this time and Tiberius backed the claim of Phraates, sparking off two years of Roman intervention in the East under the generalship of Lucius Vitellius, the Governor of Syria. It is my fiction to have Herod Agrippa involved in it, as indeed it was having him in Jerusalem at the time of the crucifixion and also conspiring with Macro and Poppaeus to grab the eastern provinces.

Sabinus being the aedile in charge of grain is also my invention but he would have achieved that rank at about this time. Tiberius did give a lot of money towards rebuilding the Aventine after a fire in the last months of his reign. Tacitus records that Macro did smother him and Cassius Dio says that Caligula had the Senate overturn his will on the grounds of insanity, which was self-evident because he had named a mere boy as his co-heir.

We get a pleasing clue as to how Vespasian survived Caligula's reign from Suetonius: he records that Vespasian stood up in the Senate and made a speech thanking the Emperor for inviting him to dinner the previous evening, showing us that he was considered a friend by Caligula and also he realised that abject sycophancy was, indeed, a life-saving fault.

As to Caligula's excesses: they were many and varied if we are to believe the historians and I have no reason not to, although I am happy to accept that they may have exaggerated. All of the acts that he commits in the book are reported or alluded to by either Suetonius or Cassius Dio – Tacitus' account being unfortunately lost. I have only exaggerated two points: firstly the extent of his public sex with Drusilla; I can find no record of his building a theatre for these shows, but it has been suggested by some of the more imaginative modern writers on the subject and I liked the idea so I borrowed it. If someone could show me where it is historically documented, I would be only too pleased to learn that it was true! Secondly: Caligula forcing his two other sisters to have sex with the urban poor in the palace is also from similar sources; I included this because it seemed like a good way to combine both his turning the palace into a brothel and also his prostituting his sisters to his friends, both of which are in Suetonius.

Caligula's illness is mysterious and there have been several theories as to what it was. What is for certain is that he was never the same after. I have shamelessly borrowed Robert Graves' idea that he thought himself metamorphosed into a god after his recovery, because it was such fun. My thanks to the shade of one of the greatest writers of historical fiction.

Vespasian was the aedile responsible for Rome's streets during Caligula's reign. Suetonius makes much out of Caligula, disgusted at the state of the streets, ordering filth to be piled into Vespasian's toga fold; he claims that it was a sign that Rome would one day fall into Vespasian's lap. Personally I think that it was a sign that Vespasian did not really care for the job.

Valerius Catullus claimed to have worn himself out buggering Caligula, not Clemens; but it was a nice detail that I wanted to get in.

Antonia was driven to suicide by Caligula's behaviour and more than likely freed Caenis in her will, as she would have been thirty by then.

Vespasian's part in fetching Alexander's breastplate from Alexandria is again my fiction; however, someone had to go and get it, so why not our man? It also puts him in Alexandria for the Jewish riots of AD 38. The riots and Herod Agrippa's humiliation I based on Josephus' and Philo's accounts as well as the excellent *Alexandrian Riots of 38 CE and the Persecution of the Jews* by Sandra Gambetti. Paulus being there at the time is my fiction, but if he did live for three years in the desert after his

Damascene conversion, he would have been reappearing in about AD 38, though probably not in Alexandria.

My favourite comment on the riots comes from Philo, brother of the Alabarch, Alexander, whose main cause for outrage was not so much the killing but the fact that high-status Jews were whipped like common Egyptian peasants in the fields, rather than given the rod as befitted their rank; and then, to compound it all, those whipping them were Greeks of the very lowest class. Disgraceful!

Vespasian must have met Flavia Domitilla during the time span of the book. She was the mistress of Statilius Capella from Sabratha and the daughter of Flavius Liberalis, a quaestor's clerk who became an equestrian.

Caligula's bridge over the Bay of Naples must have been a wonderful sight; it did, however, cause a massive food shortage in Italy. The events described are all taken from historical sources; I have only changed it in that it all happens on one day rather than two. Corbulo probably had nothing to do with the building of the road across it, but he did complain about the state of the roads in the Senate and was made road-czar by Caligula for his trouble – perhaps as a joke?

Caligula's rape of Clementina at the end is fictional but very much in character.

My thanks again to my agent, Ian Drury at Sheil Land Associates, and also to Gaia Banks and Virginia Ascione for their hard work on my behalf in the foreign rights department.

Thanks to Sara O'Keefe and Toby Mundy at Corvus/Atlantic for believing in the Vespasian series and continuing to publish it.

Once again it has been a pleasure to work with my editor, Richenda Todd, who has, as always, made the book much better than I could have done by myself.

And finally, thank you, Anja, for listening to my day's work every evening.

Vespasian's story continues in Germania and Britannia in *Rome's Fallen Eagle.*